New Casebooks

POETRY

NOVELS AND PROSE

(continued overleaf)

GEORGE ORWELL Edited by Bryan Loughrey
SHELLEY: *Frankenstein* Edited by Fred Botting
STOKER: *Dracula* Edited by Glennis Byron
WOOLF: *Mrs Dalloway* and *To the Lighthouse* Edited by Su Reid

DRAMA

BECKETT: *Waiting for Godot* and *Endgame* Edited by Steven Connor
APHRA BEHN Edited by Janet Todd
MARLOWE Edited by Avraham Oz
REVENGE TRAGEDY Edited by Stevie Simkin
SHAKESPEARE: *Antony and Cleopatra* Edited by Johm Drakakis
SHAKESPEARE: *Hamlet* Edited by Martin Coyle
SHAKESPEARE: *Julius Caesar* Edited by Richard Wilson
SHAKESPEARE: *King Lear* Edited by Kiernan Ryan
SHAKESPEARE: *Macbeth* Edited by Alan Sinfield
SHAKESPEARE: *The Merchant of Venice* Edited by Martin Coyle
SHAKESPEARE: *A Midsummer Night's Dream* Edited by Richard Dutton
SHAKESPEARE: *Much Ado About Nothing* and *The Taming of the
Shrew* Edited by Marion Wynne-Davies
SHAKESPEARE: *Othello* Edited by Lena Cowen Orlin
SHAKESPEARE: *Romeo and Juliet* Edited by R. S. White
SHAKESPEARE: *The Tempest* Edited by R. S. White
SHAKESPEARE: *Twelfth Night* Edited by R. S. White
SHAKESPEARE ON FILM Edited by Robert Shaughnessy
SHAKESPEARE IN PERFORMANCE Edited by Robert Shaughnessy
SHAKESPEARE'S HISTORY PLAYS Edited by Graham Holderness
SHAKESPEARE'S ROMANCES Edited by Alison Thorne
SHAKESPEARE'S TRAGEDIES Edited by Susan Zimmerman
JOHN WEBSTER: *The Duchess of Malfi* Edited by Dympna Callaghan

GENERAL THEMES

FEMINIST THEATRE AND THEORY Edited by Helene Keyssar
POSTCOLONIAL LITERATURES Edited by Michael Parker and Roger
Starkey

New Casebooks Series
Series Standing Order
ISBN 0–333–71702–3 hardcover
ISBN 0–333–69345–0 paperback
(*outside North America only*)

You can receive future titles in this series as they are published by placing a standing order. Please contact your bookseller or, in case of difficulty, write to us at the address below with your name and address, the title of the series and the ISBN quoted above.

Customer Services Department, Macmillan Distribution Ltd,
Houndmills, Basingstoke, Hampshire RG21 6XS, England

New Casebooks

THE RAINBOW and WOMEN IN LOVE

D. H. LAWRENCE

EDITED BY GARY DAY AND LIBBY DI NIRO
WITH THE ASSISTANCE OF JOY DYE

First published 2004 by
PALGRAVE MACMILLAN
Houndmills, Basingstoke, Hampshire RG21 6XS and
175 Fifth Avenue, New York, N. Y. 10010
Companies and representatives throughout the world

PALGRAVE MACMILLAN is the global academic imprint of the Palgrave
Macmillan division of St. Martin's Press, LLC and of Palgrave Macmillan Ltd.
Macmillan® is a registered trademark in the United States, United Kingdom
and other countries. Palgrave is a registered trademark in the European
Union and other countries.

ISBN 0–333–73665–6 hardback
ISBN 0–333–73666–4 paperback

This book is printed on paper suitable for recycling and made from fully
managed and sustained forest sources.

A catalogue record for this book is available from the British Library.

Library of Congress Cataloging-in-Publication Data
The Rainbow and Women in love : D.H. Lawrence / edited by Gary Day and
Libby Di Niro ; with the assistance of Joy Dye.
      p. cm. – (New casebooks)
   Includes bibliographical references and index.
      ISBN 0–333–73665–6 (cloth)
      1. Lawrence, D. H. (David Herbert), 1885–1930. Rainbow. 2. Lawrence,
D. H. (David Herbert), 1885–1930. Women in love. I. Day, Gary, 1956–
II. Di Niro, Libby, 1959– III. Dye, Joy, 1972– IV. New casebooks (Palgrave
Macmillan (Firm))

PR6023.A93R3355 2003
823'.912–dc21

                                                      2003055265

10   9   8   7   6   5   4   3   2   1
13 12 11 10 09 08 07 06 05 04

Printed in China

For readers of Lawrence everywhere
but especially Charlotte, Clara, Paul and Wesley.

Contents

Acknowledgements

A big thank you to Anna Sandeman and Sonya Barker at Palgrave Macmillan for patience, persistence and good humour. And thank you to Martin Coyle and John Peck, the general editors, for their continued faith in the project, their encyclopaedic knowledge and their eagle-eyed editing. Finally, thank you to Lynda Peachey for last minute and much appreciated assistance.

The editors and publishers wish to thank the following for permission to use copyright material:

Robert Burden, for 'The Discursive Formations of History in D. H. Lawrence's The Rainbow', Anglia: Zeitschrift für Englische Philogie, 115:31 (1997), 323–51, by permission of Max Niemeyer Verlag GmbH; Gerald Doherty, for 'The Metaphorical Imperative: From Trope to Narrative in The Rainbow', South Central Review, 6:1 (1989), 46–61, by permission of the author; and for 'Death and the Rhetoric of Representation in D. H. Lawrence's Women in Love', Mosaic: A Journal for the Interdisciplinary Study of Literature, 27:1 (1994), 55–72, by permission of Mosaic; Roger Ebbatson, for 'The Rainbow and the Language of Origins', Worcester Papers in English, 1 (1997), 3–13, by permission of Worcester Papers in English; Elizabeth M. Fox, for 'Closure and Foreclosure in The Rainbow', D. H. Lawrence Review, 27:2–3 (1997–98), 197–215, by permission of D. H. Lawrence Review; Earl Ingersoll, for 'Staging the Gaze in D. H. Lawrence's Women in Love', Studies in the Novel, 26:3 (1994), 268–80. Copyright © 1994 by the University of North Texas, by permission of Studies in the Novel; James F. Knapp, for 'The Discourse of Knowledge: Historical Change in Women in Love' from Literary Modernism and the Transformation of Work by James F. Knapp (1988), pp. 59–73, by permission of Northwestern University Press;

Liang-ya Liou, for 'The Problematics of Sexual Liberation: D. H. Lawrence's *The Rainbow* and *Women in Love*', *Studies in Language and Literature*, 7 (1996), 57–87, by permission of the author; Jorgette Mauzerall, for 'Strange Bedfellows: D. H. Lawrence and Feminist Psychoanalytic Theory in *The Rainbow*' from *Approaches to Teaching the Works of D. H. Lawrence*, ed. Elizabeth M. Sargent and Garry Watson (2001), pp. 89–98, by permission of the Modern Language Association of America; David Parker, for 'Into the Ideological Unknown: *Women in Love*', *Critical Review*, 30 (1990), 3–24, by permission of the author.

Every effort has been made to trace the copyright holders but if any have been inadvertently overlooked the publishers will be pleased to make the necessary arrangement at the first opportunity.

General Editors' Preface

The purpose of this series of New Casebooks is to reveal some of the ways in which contemporary criticism has changed our understanding of commonly studied texts and writers and, indeed, of the nature of criticism itself. Central to the series is a concern with modern critical theory and its effect on current approaches to the study of literature. Each New Casebook editor has been asked to select a sequence of essays which will introduce the reader to the new critical approaches to the text or texts being discussed in the volume and also illuminate the rich interchange between critical theory and critical practice that characterises so much current writing about literature.

In this focus on modern critical thinking and practice New Casebooks aim not only to inform but also to stimulate, with volumes seeking to reflect both the controversy and the excitement of current criticism. Because much of this criticism is difficult and often employs an unfamiliar critical language, editors have been asked to give the reader as much help as they feel is appropriate, but without simplifying the essays or the issues they raise. Again, editors have been asked to supply a list of further reading which will enable readers to follow up issues raised by the essays in the volume.

The project of New Casebooks, then, is to bring together in an illuminating way those critics who best illustrate the ways in which contemporary criticism has established new methods of analysing texts and who have reinvigorated the important debate about how we 'read' literature. The hope is, of course, that New Casebooks will not only open up this debate to a wider audience, but will also encourage students to extend their own ideas, and think afresh about their responses to the texts they are studying.

John Peck and Martin Coyle
University of Wales, Cardiff

Introduction: Lawrence and Criticism

GARY DAY

This introduction is divided into eight sections. The first asks what is meant by criticism; the answer is that that depends on your view of art and indeed society. In this section Lawrence's ideas about the novel and society are examined and related to *The Rainbow* and *Women in Love*. Generally speaking, critics have tended to focus on two aspects of Lawrence's work: his symbolism and his depiction of the relations between men and women. The second section discusses the nature of Lawrence's symbolism, the shifting meanings of his symbols and the novels' scepticism towards those symbols. The third and fourth sections show how relationships are either a struggle for power or else an achieved harmony with a greater life force. Both Lawrence's symbolism and his representation of relationships are discussed in connection with the nature of the modern world. The fifth section considers Lawrence's view of art as it appears in *Women in Love* and links it to his view of relationships and also, albeit briefly, to modernist art.

The sixth section examines feminist responses to Lawrence and so returns to the nature of criticism, as does the seventh section, which discusses the poststructuralist reaction to his work. While a great deal of feminist criticism was hostile to Lawrence, post-structuralist criticism largely ignored him since his views on nature and being belonged to what it claimed was a discredited tradition of western metaphysics. In both cases, Lawrence was overlooked because his work did not conform to an existing agenda. This raises the question of whether criticism should use works to validate its own concerns or to be responsive to what a work has to offer.

The final section of this introduction discusses the order and significance of the essays which appear in this volume. With one exception, they are examples of different forms of poststructuralist criticism which do engage with Lawrence. The exception is David Parker's essay (10), the final essay in the volume, which represents a possible new development as the poststructuralist era begins to come to a close. Throughout, the concern of this collection, and of this introduction, is to emphasise the challenge that Lawrence still offers us today.

The nature of criticism

For Ursula, one of the central characters in *The Rainbow*, the 'most tedious' aspect of school is 'the close study of English literature'.[1] It is a view that Lawrence would seem to share, famously declaring that 'we judge a work of art by its effect on our sincere and vital emotion and nothing else'.[2] Where one person may be profoundly moved by a poem, novel or play, another may regard it with complete indifference. Anna, for example, does not consider it of 'the slightest importance' that she fails to learn 30 lines of *As You Like It*, while Ursula gains 'a poignant sense of acquisition and enrichment and enlarge[ment]' from the same play (*R*, pp. 95, 310). It is not hard to see that this view of criticism does not take us very far. How can we talk meaningfully about literature if the sole criterion of its worth is whether or not we *like* it, whether or not it appeals to our emotions? And, in any case, what does Lawrence mean by 'sincere and vital emotion'? How, if we feel them, can emotions be insincere and in what sense can they be non-vital? Although these are legitimate questions, we can approach the problem in another way and ask why Lawrence felt it necessary to emphasise the role of emotions in our response to art. What was it about the period in which he was writing that made him give them such a prominent place?

The Rainbow and *Women in Love*, originally conceived as one novel called first *The Sisters* and then *The Wedding Ring*, suggest that the emotions are foregrounded because they are denied expression in modern society. The process, as Ursula discovers, starts in school where the 'first great task was to reduce sixty children to one state of mind or being', a necessary preparation for the world of work where each person is interchangeable with every other. 'One man or another,' says Ursula's Uncle Tom, 'it doesn't matter very much. They're all colliers' (R, pp. 355, 323). Gerald, in *Women in Love*, puts the same idea more brutally: 'The sufferings and feelings of individuals did not matter in the least. What mattered was the pure instrumentality of the individual. As of a man, as of a knife: does it cut well? Nothing else mattered.'[3] Skrebensky is the ideal citizen of this society with his belief that the individual is of no importance 'except as he represented the Whole', defined as the 'social fabric, the nation, the modern humanity' (WL, p. 304).[4] In this world people seem to have no substance, which partly explains Birkin's otherwise dismissive statement 'they don't exist, they aren't there' (WL, p. 24). We find a similar sentiment in Lawrence's essay 'Why The Novel Matters' where he writes: '[s]o much of a man walks about dead and a carcase in the street and house, today: so much of women is merely dead.'[5] The role of novel in this situation is to 'help you not to be dead man in life'.[6] To that end it reminds us that life is flux and that we ourselves are constantly changing. The novel sets itself against whatever is defined, fixed, rigid and solid, what Lawrence calls 'the ugly imperialism of the absolute'.[7] It loosens, dissolves and liberates, it gives all things full play, 'for out of the full play of all things emerges the only thing that is anything, the wholeness of a man, the wholeness of a woman, man alive, and live woman'.[8]

Lawrence's conception of art, then, is a consequence of his conception of society, though he does not understand that term in any structured sense since he maintains that the individual is wholly determined yet, paradoxically, at the same time free to develop as he or she chooses. Graham Holderness voices a similar reservation about Lawrence's stance. Lawrence, he writes, recognises that the central feature of capitalism is 'the contradiction between human relationships and an inhuman and economic social system, but only as a static metaphysical opposition, not as an active contradiction, a developing process, a living relationship between people.'[9] Lawrence's failure to grasp the dynamic complexity of society is evident in his characters' large and sometimes disturbing generalisations. Ursula detests money because it confers a false equality on people: 'I hate it, that anybody is my equal who has the same amount of money as I have. I *know* I am better than all of them. I hate them. They are not my equals. I hate equality on a money basis. It is the equality of dirt' (*R*, p. 427). Birkin's declaration that 'democracy is an absolute lie' would seem to lend weight to those who regard Lawrence as an authoritarian,[10] but in fact his objection is to the way democracy seems to deny the differences between people. While he wants 'every man to have his share in the world's goods', Birkin's principal contention is that '[o]ne man isn't any better than another, not because they are equal, but because they are intrinsically *other*, that there is no term of comparison' (*WL*, pp. 106–7). It is in the difference between people that Lawrence locates their special quality of being alive, and he regards it as the job of the novel to counteract all those collectivist ideologies from nationalism to the common good which would make everyone the same.

Symbols in *The Rainbow* and *Women in Love*

One difficulty with Lawrence's work is that he uses metaphors of nature to describe mechanisms of society, which means that his writing on these matters, though undoubtedly powerful, is more condemnatory than comprehensive. The symbolic weight of flowers, water, the moon and darkness in both *The Rainbow* and *Women in Love*, mystifies the experience of the industrial revolution and the First World War (1914–18), the effects of which Lawrence attempts to deal with in both novels. Another difficulty is the opposition he sets up between personal and social relationships. Ursula's frustration that she cannot get beyond Skrebensky's 'habitual actions and decisions', that she cannot reach his 'vulnerable, variable quick' (*R*, p. 410) hints at Lawrence's belief in the fundamental nature of the relation between men and women. It is a relation so profound, so deeply implicated in the life force itself that it can only be expressed on a cosmic scale. 'What I want,' Birkin announces to Ursula, 'is a strange conjunction with you an equilibrium, a pure balance of two single beings as the stars balance each other' (*WL*, p. 152). His imagery shows how far his idea of the relationship between men and women transcends the conventional expressions of love. Birkin wants to move beyond that state altogether, to deliver himself 'without reserves or defences' into the unknown, a plane where 'one is outside the pale of all that is accepted, and nothing known applies' (ibid., pp. 150–1). It is this experience which will move humanity forward to the next stage of its development, a creative utterance of sensation, emotion, truth and beauty that will newly align it with what Birkin variously refers to as the 'unseen hosts' and the 'incomprehensible' (ibid., pp. 58, 133). Later, however, he revises this opinion, claiming that 'a permanent relation between a man and a woman isn't the last word, [there] is the additional relationship between man and man – additional to marriage' (ibid., p. 366).

Why, in *The Rainbow* and *Women in Love*, does Lawrence rely so heavily on symbolism and set so much store by the relation of men and women? We can partly understand the role he gives to images such as the moon by placing him in the context of the modernist preoccupation with symbolism. Like T. S. Eliot in *The Waste Land*, or James Joyce in *Ulysses*, Lawrence searches for a mode of writing that can restore to wholeness the fractured condition of modernity. Eliot uses the myth of the Fisher King to redeem the urban wasteland, while Joyce invokes the myth of Ulysses to render significant a day in the life of Leopold Bloom. Lawrence looks to nature rather than myth because he wants to reconnect humans, not merely to a cultural past, but to the cosmos, once again establishing that 'sense of being at one with the great universe continuum of space-time-life'[11] which he feels modern life has lost. We can see this most clearly in *The Rainbow*. At first Tom feels like a 'broken arch' in his relationship with Lydia, but later they meet to 'span the heavens' (*R*, pp. 63, 91). The image of the arch recurs in the description of the cathedral 'where the thrust from earth met the thrust from earth and the arch was locked on the keystone of ecstasy' (ibid., p. 188). Finally, this arch becomes the rainbow, a symbol of 'the earth's new architecture', the old world giving way to the 'living fabric of Truth' (ibid., p. 459).[12]

Although we can visualise the image clearly, its meanings are more complex. Indeed, there is even a question as to how far we should trust symbols as a form of truth. At a very simple level, it appears that the arch changes from a piece of Christian architecture to a natural phenomenon, suggesting the replacement of a religious outlook by a more instinctive one. However, this change is not quite so straightforward as it seems, for Lawrence questions how far we can trust symbols as a form of truth and this self-reflexive quality places *The Rainbow* and *Women in Love* if not firmly, at least recognisably, in the modernist tradition, as do the discussions about the nature of art found mainly in *Women in Love*.[13] Anna may reject the symbol of the lamb as Christ, proclaiming that she likes lambs 'too much to treat them as if they had to mean something', but Ursula also scoffs at the idea of the daisy as being a symbol of democracy (*R*, p. 150 and *WL*, p. 135). Both are examples of humans 'painting the universe with their own image' (*WL*, p. 274), whereas Lawrence is gripped by the non-human, as indeed were a number of his modernist contemporaries, for example the Futurist Filippo Marinetti and the founder of scientific management, Frederick Winslow Taylor.[14]

Despite their difference, both religious and natural symbols embody a desire to transcend the routines of social existence so that the individual becomes meaningful in relation to a greater whole. As Ursula puts it, '[s]elf was a oneness with the infinite' (*R*, p. 409). This desire is primarily associated with women and is present early in *The Rainbow* where the Brangwen females look to 'the far-off world of cities and governments and the active scope of man where secrets were made known and desires fulfilled' (ibid., p. 11). It is, initially, a social desire and, as such, can be related to the demands of the suffragettes in the novel – Winifred Inger, Maggie Schofield and Dorothy Russell – but through Ursula's disillusion with 'the man's world', it is gradually transformed into a 'yearning for something unknown' (ibid., p. 443). During the course of *The Rainbow* there is a growing realisation that self-fulfilment is ultimately incompatible with social reform. The turn to the self is accompanied by a change in the meaning of the arch and its associated images of doors and rainbows. By the time we reach Anna and Will's relationship, in the middle section of the novel, the arch has ceased to comprehend couples within the larger life force, and instead signifies the distance between them. Far from reaching out and meeting Will in a relationship of mutual support, Anna 'was a door and threshold, she herself' (ibid., p. 182). As in this case, characters either become symbols or else the symbol stands for a desire that cannot be fulfilled in their relations with others; in either instance, the symbol no longer designates a whole. The changing meaning of the moon in *The Rainbow* illustrates this very clearly. Gathering in the sheaves under 'a large gold moon', Anna and Will move to and fro in a tidal rhythm that portends their imminent union; later, however, as 'a dazzling, terrifying glare of white light', the moon presides over the disintegration of Ursula and Skrebensky's relationship (*R*, pp. 113, 443). It is also a symbol of Ursula's longing for the unknown, something which the conventional Skrebensky cannot satisfy, and she 'plung[es]into it', leaving him behind, 'a shadow ever dissolving' (ibid., p. 444). The

symbol's decline from an expression of cosmic unity to a cry of ago-
nised yearning reaches its nadir in the final pages of the novel.
Ursula's vision of the rainbow as a sign of renewal is nothing more
than her own desire projected onto 'the sordid people' whom she believes will 'quiver to life in their spirit' (ibid., pp. 458–9).[15] The
changing meaning of Lawrence's symbols and his scepticism towards
them should put paid to the view that Lawrence uses them in a sim-
plistic way.

Relationships in *The Rainbow* and *Women in Love*

The changes in the meanings of the symbol are connected with a
new emphasis on the self understood not as a fixed entity but as a
potential to be developed. It is precisely the split between the
religious symbol and everyday reality, between 'the Sunday world'
and the 'week-day world', that conditions Ursula's sense of herself,
forcing her to accept the 'numbing responsibility of living an
undiscovered life' (*R*, p. 263). She is driven by the question of 'How
to become oneself, how to know the question and answer of
oneself, when one was merely an unfixed something nothing?'
(ibid., p. 264). And part of that answer means finding some connection between a transcendent realm and her ordinary sphere of activity. It is in *Women in Love* that Lawrence attempts to bring these
two worlds together in the relationship between men and women.
The self is realised or, to use one of Lawrence's most frequent
images, it unfolds like a flower, though only through its relation
with the other.[16] There are two basic forms of this relation: one
based on power, represented by Gerald and Gudrun, the other
based on balance, represented by Birkin and Ursula.

Both Gerald and Gudrun exercise power over animals. The
episode where Gerald compels his Arab mare to endure the clank of
passing railway trucks is paralleled by Gudrun's strange dance
before the cattle (*WL*, pp. 114, 172).[17] In both cases, though not to
the same degree, we can see human will triumphing over animal
instinct which, along with 'angels', is part of that darkness
Lawrence believes we ignore at our peril (*R*, p. 406). Gerald and
Gudrun, in short, deny something of themselves and are thus
incomplete; Birkin, for example, is irritated by Gerald's 'fatal
halfness' (ibid. p. 214). To compensate for this lack in herself,
Gudrun 'must always demand the other to be aware of her'

(*WL*, p. 170), but it is a demand that remains unsatisfied because both she and Gerald are distanced from their society. Having accidentally killed his brother as a child, Gerald is 'set apart like Cain', and Gudrun, too, always feels as if she is 'outside of life, an onlooker' (ibid., pp. 177, 170). This position seems to call for struggle with others, even for their elimination. The class dimension of this should not be ignored. When a group of colliers' wives comment on Gudrun's stockings, her reaction is 'violent and murderous. She would have liked them all to be annihilated' (ibid., p. 11). As a boy, Gerald 'longed to go with the soldiers to shoot [the striking miners]', and, as a man, he applies the new principles of scientific management to the colliery, so that the miners 'were reduced to mere mechanical instruments' (ibid., pp. 233, 238).

On the surface, the attitude of Gerald and Gudrun towards the 'lower orders' is very different from that of Ursula who, in *The Rainbow*, gives her necklace to the bargeman's baby (*R*, p. 292) and, in *Women in Love*, gives the chair she and Birkin have just bought to a young working-class couple (*WL*, p. 372). Both gestures are perhaps redolent of the paternalism that dies with Thomas Critch. However, Ursula's perception of the young man as 'hardly a man at all' matches Gerald's view of his workforce as miners rather than men, while her climbing aboard the barge demonstrates the right of the middle class to inspect the domestic interiors of the working class as much as to monitor their performance in the production of coal. Although class divisions seem distinct, a consistent pattern of imagery occasionally makes them more problematic. The young man, for example, is compared to a 'rat', which associates him with the Italian countess at Breadalby, with Gerald and with Loerke (ibid., pp. 372, 103, 186, 445). The rat, though, is not necessarily a negative image because it is associated with the rejection of the ideal that is necessary for a new direction in human development and so the image links with the larger themes of the novel, transporting it beyond its immediate contexts.

The key point, however, is that the relation of domination and subordination which characterises the presentation of class is also an intrinsic feature of Gerald and Gudrun's relationship. It begins, after all, with her striking him across the face and ends with him nearly strangling her (ibid., pp. 175, 490). The episode with the rabbit (ibid., pp. 249–51) shows that there is a perverse kinship between them born of their need to dominate, but that need is also what destroys their relationship. They comply with and confront one another simultaneously. This dual feature is clearly brought out when Gerald comes to visit Gudrun the night his father dies: 'she knew there was something fatal in the situation, and she must accept it. Yet she must challenge him' (ibid., p. 356). The trip to the Continent and the meeting with Loerke aggravates this unstable condition and causes that explosion of violence in the snow before Gerald pushes onward to his inevitable death.

The relationship between Birkin and Ursula appears to contrast strongly with that of Gerald and Gudrun. Instead of two wills striving for supremacy we have 'two single beings' in equilibrium, 'constellated together like two stars' (WL, p. 207). Later, as Birkin puts it, there is the 'wonder of existing not as oneself but in a consummation of my being and of her being in a new one, a new paradisal unit regained from the duality' (ibid., p. 385). The couple progress from balancing each other to fusing in a new creation but, in the end, Birkin does not find this as fulfilling as he had hoped, telling Ursula that in order to be 'complete, really happy', he needs 'eternal union with a man too' (ibid., p. 499). Although the relationship between Birkin and Ursula seems to be less fraught than that between Gerald and Gudrun, it is not ultimately more satisfactory, and the novel closes with their disagreeing with each other, which underlines the conflict that has, in fact, always been an element of their relationship. Birkin insists that Ursula acknowledge his male superiority, an assertion, incidentally, that Lawrence comically deflates by having him draw a parallel between his own situation and that of Mino, the cat, who cuffs a little female stray 'to bring her into a pure stable equilibrium, a transcendent and abiding rapport with the single male' (WL, p. 154). Ursula fiercely resists Birkin's arguments, wanting him to love her and saying that all the rest is 'far-fetched' (ibid., p. 157). Later Birkin wants Ursula to 'surrender her spirit', and she immediately rounds on him, accusing him of just wanting her 'to be there, to serve you' (ibid., p. 259). The climax comes in the 'Excurse' chapter (23) where Ursula furiously denounces Birkin for what she sees as his double standards, wanting her for sex and Hermione for spiritual sustenance. After that Ursula seems, at times, a mere echo of Birkin, telling Gudrun that 'one has a sort of other self that belongs to another planet', that she believes in 'something inhuman of which love is only a little part' and that 'we must fulfil [what] comes out of the unknown to us' (ibid., p. 455). But she rouses herself at the end when Birkin tells her that he needs something more than the male–female relation.

Birkin's desire to bond with a man as well as a woman can be seen either as a failure to achieve a new state or as an indication of the inherent dynamism of human relations. His use of biblical imagery signifies not so much a failure to transcend the normal relations of men and women as a regression to the very problem to which personal relations were intended as a solution. Ursula, it will be remembered, became conscious of an unbridgeable gap between the sacred and the secular world, and looks to male–female relations to make everyday life more rich in meaning. A rhetoric of nature is used to endow these relations with a symbolic value but there is also a heavy dependence on biblical idioms, something that was particularly marked in *The First Women in Love*.[18] Birkin refers to Ursula as Eve, she looks upon him as 'one of the sons of God' and herself as 'one of the daughters of men', and they hear a snatch of a hymn as they come to the inn for tea, reconciled after their worst quarrel (*WL*, pp. 155, 323–4). In short, and this makes the point perhaps too strongly, a redundant rhetoric is called upon to reveal a new condition of being. That condition of being, furthermore, has a faintly incestuous character. Ursula's relationship with Birkin gets underway when she sees him 'sawing and hammering away', an activity which associates him with her father (ibid., p. 127), and Birkin feels 'born out of the cramp of the womb' once he and Ursula have established themselves. And if, as a metaphor, incest betrays a desire to return to the source of life, then what are we to make of Ursula's thrill at 'the strange mystery of Birkin's life motion, there at the back of the thighs, down the flanks' (ibid., p. 325)?

Ursula seems to intuit a new source of life, one that is normally associated with waste and decay. The love between her and Birkin seems to overturn established perceptions as it reaches for new forms of expression. In this it contrasts with the relationship between Gerald and Gudrun which is characterised by a struggle for dominance that reflects class relations. However, as we have seen, the relationship between Ursula and Birkin is not entirely free of conflict, but their arguments are to do with the condition of new relationships rather than who should be dominant in the old ones.

Relationships and modernity

The desire to articulate a new kind of relationship between men and women, one that connects with a beyond, is hampered by a discarded rhetoric and haunted by an intimate, if not incestuous, connection with the known. A potentially more positive approach to the relation between Birkin and Ursula is to stress its dynamic character. As we have seen, the relationship undergoes a series of changes and the final dialogue, where nothing is resolved, emphasises its open-ended character. And yet these very qualities are symptomatic of modernity itself: restless, provisional and future-orientated. Hence Birkin and Ursula do not so much react against the age as become its representatives. In tune with the spirit of Gerald's scientific management, which stands for the mechanical principle against which the novel is in revolt, the couple spurn the past. Birkin regards it as 'a snare and a delusion', while Ursula 'want[s] a new birth without any recollections or blemish of a past life' (*WL*, pp. 99, 425). Earlier we asked why Lawrence was so committed to refashioning the relation between men and women. One answer is that it has to carry that numinous quality formerly borne by religion, but a second, closely related answer is that the love between men and women combats the fragmentation of modernity. The drama of the couple, their needs, desires and expectations, and the problem of coping with each other's difference, is a way of negotiating the upheavals and dislocations of the industrial revolution and the First World War. Like Jane Austen, Lawrence rarely refers, in these novels, to the major events of his time but they nevertheless shape the narrative, if only indirectly. In *The Rainbow* the turbulent history of nineteenth-century Britain, the disruption of communities, insurrections and attacks on the social hierarchy is projected onto Poland, while in his 1919 Foreword to *Women in Love* Lawrence said he wished 'the time to remain unfixed, so that the bitterness of the war may be taken for granted in the characters'.[19] It is, however, through his intense preoccupation with the male–female relation that Lawrence most clearly addresses the experience of the modern world. Specifically, his explorations of how relationships fail and the ways in which they might succeed reflect wider anxieties about the dissolution of traditional social bonds and the constitution of new ones. Lawrence's presentation of the concept of the couple at once allows it to register the disturbances of modernity and to become the means of dealing with its discontents.

In particular, the male–female axis offers an alternative mode of being to the material and mechanistic character of mass society.

Birkin, speaking to Gerald, compares people to 'insects scurrying in filth, so that your collier can have a pianoforte in his parlour and you can have a butler and a motor-car in your up-to-date house', and he is contemptuous of those who 'live for the sake of the reflection in human opinion'(*WL*, p. 54). Ursula recoils from '[a]nother shameful, barren school week, mere routine and mechanical activity', while Gudrun shudders at the 'hideous, boring repetition of vulgar actions, vulgar phrases [and] vulgar postures' (ibid., pp. 199, 482). The human beings of this society cling to the past 'till they become infested with little worms and dry-rot' (ibid., p. 130),[20] and they are deformed to the extent that one or other of their faculties is developed at the expense of the others. The self therefore needs to be brought into some sort of equilibrium; it is, says Birkin in *The First Women in Love*, 'a balancing point within the flux'.[21] Men and women learn to balance themselves and to enter the next phase of human development by radically rethinking their relationships and replacing a 'horrible merging' with 'the pure duality of polarisation' (ibid., p. 207), an image that recalls the two halves of a broken arch that we encountered in *The Rainbow*. Neither image is, however, ultimately satisfactory since Birkin needs to love a man as well as a woman; a triangle would thus be a more appropriate trope since this captures and transcends the idea of the mere couple.

Lawrence nudges his characters towards the unknown where they connect with a beyond that restores their capacity not just to be creative but also to be a channel through which the greater reality can flow. The emphasis throughout is on change and growth. The self is a 'curious assembly of incongruous parts' whose 'yea of today is oddly different from [its] yea of yesterday', and it is because the man and woman are never the same that they defy each other's 'inertia'.[22] That, at least, is the theory, but as we noted above, the relationship between Birkin and Ursula is not so different from the surrounding world as they like to imagine. For example, 'the pure duality of polarisation' is a mechanistic image oddly out of place in Lawrence's organic pantheon. It is also a rather static image and thus exists in some tension with the otherwise dynamic character of the relationship. Furthermore, the impersonality of the image, like that of stars balancing one another, may serve Lawrence's purpose of shedding old ideas about personality and relationships, but it also underwrites a growing state bureaucracy and a philosophy of scientific management that sees humans as machines. Ironically, Lawrence's elevation of the couple establishes a romantic principle that, in the form of popular literature, becomes an institutionalised form of escapism rather than the means of transcendence that he had hoped it would be.

Lawrence's view of art in *The Rainbow*, *Women in Love*

The relationships between Gerald and Gudrun and Birkin and Ursula find their counterpart in views about art. Gudrun's sculptures are always of 'small things' and this reflects her habit of watching people 'with objective curiosity', seeing 'each one as a complete figure a finished creation' (*WL*, pp. 38, 12). In contrast to the hard outline of Gudrun's sculptures we have those of Rodin and Michael Angelo who 'leave a piece of raw rock unfinished to [their] figure' (ibid., p. 71). Birkin applies this directly to life, telling Ursula that 'you must leave your surroundings sketchy, unfinished, so that you are never contained, never confined, never dominated from the outside' (ibid.). Loerke has quite the opposite view, taking to an extreme the modernist doctrine of the supremacy of form over content by claiming that there is absolutely 'no connection' between 'art' and the 'everyday world' (ibid., p. 447). Loerke's statuette of a young girl sitting on a horse invites comparisons with Gerald astride his Arab mare. In the earlier episode we have an example of a man imposing his will on his horse, but Loerke depicts the rather cowed figure of a girl sitting sideways on 'a massive, magnificent stallion, rigid with pent up power' (ibid., p. 446). Do we see in the one triumph of will over instinct and in the other the triumph of instinct over will?

Despite the symmetry of such antitheses, the two are not so easily comparable. Gerald's struggle with his horse is, within the terms of the novel, a 'real' event, whereas the girl on the horse is merely a statuette and as such is better discussed in relation to the carved figure of the negro woman in labour (*WL*, p. 80). Both are female, but one represents sensuality whereas the other is barely a physical presence. At the same time both are connected with birth. The African woman is in labour while the young girl is 'a mere bud', a metaphor that loosely associates her with Ursula who is consistently described in terms of a seed slowly coming to fruition: 'her life was like a shoot that is growing steadily, but which has not yet come above ground' (ibid., pp. 445, 51). The two kinds of birth also perhaps relate to what Birkin calls 'the river of darkness' and 'the river of light' (ibid., p. 177). Both are types of creation, the river of darkness producing 'sensuous perfection' that links it with the African carving which is 'so sensual as to be final, supreme' (ibid., pp. 80, 177). Although she is presented as a 'bud', it is hard to see the pubescent girl as corresponding to the river of light, Birkin's metaphor for 'a new cycle of creation' (ibid., p. 178). She is, after all, a '*mere* bud' and she has been subdued by Loerke, who beat her 'harder than I have ever beat anything in my life' (ibid., p. 450), in much the same way that Gerald had subdued his mare. Her forced pose, the rigidity of the horse and the fact that Loerke has no use for models once they have passed eighteen, all suggest that the statuette is an image of life held in check, its flow dammed up.

The point to note is that comparisons ultimately break down, and this is a variation of Birkin's view, quoted earlier, that because everyone is intrinsically other, they are radically incommensurable.[23] The problem with comparing two things is that difference may be sacrificed to likeness or one of the terms of comparison may be privileged over another. What Birkin proposes instead, as we have seen, is a 'pure balance of two single beings' where neither is subordinated to the other and where difference is a governing principle of the relation. Here it becomes hard to follow exactly what Lawrence means but, given that he is endeavouring to transcend the conventional co-ordinates of social life, this is perhaps to be expected and, furthermore, he is pointedly challenging his readers to question the basis of their own existence rather than stipulating how they should live. The question Birkin asks Gerald 'What do you live for?' (*WL*, p. 55), is the question Lawrence asks of us. It is not just a question of knowing what you live for, it is a question of feeling it too. In fact it is only by being in touch with your feelings that you can know the answer. The emphasis on emotional understanding is what separates Lawrence from his modernist contemporaries. Eliot, for example, famously declared that poetry was 'an escape from emotion'.[24] Birkin is impatient with the denizens of Bohemian London because they want to know things intellectually, while he wants to know them viscerally. Hermione demands to know why Birkin is copying a drawing of Chinese geese: 'She must know. It was a dreadful tyranny, an obsession in her' (ibid., p. 91). His reply, that it enables him to 'know what centres they live from – what they perceive and feel' (ibid.), is an identification with otherness rather than using it as means of self-reflection. Birkin accuses

Hermione of having nothing beyond her 'fixed will', what he calls her 'mirror', and mirrors stretch along the wall at the Pompadour café (ibid., pp. 41, 63), reflecting what is. In place of this endless reproduction of the same Birkin proposes a 'lapse into unknowingness'. ' "You've got to learn not-to be," he tells Ursula and Hermione, "before you can come into being" ' (ibid., p. 43).

The conceptions of art in *Women in Love* reflect and refract ideas about relationships. The attempt to limit relationships corresponds largely to formalist views of art, while the attempt to discover new ways that men and women can be together corresponds to a largely visceral form of art. This rather summary statement, however, should not blind us to the complexities of either art or relationships that we have noted in this section.

Lawrence and feminism

Lawrence's views about art and relationships bring us to the critical reception of his work. How have critics responded to what Lawrence has had to say about these and other matters in *The Rainbow* and *Women in Love*? The short answer is very little. Rather than attend to the complexities of his writing many critics prefer to condemn it as sexist, reactionary and therefore irrelevant.

It is partly impatience with Lawrence's portentous symbolism and his preoccupation with relationships that accounts for the fact that a number of critics have either ignored him or been downright hostile. The early history of Lawrence criticism can be summarised very quickly.[25] Both T. S. Eliot and John Middleton Murry took a biographical approach to his work, with Eliot finding fault with Lawrence's spiritual pride, emotional sickness and self-deception, while Murry took issue, among other things, with Lawrence's apparent hatred of women. It was F. R. Leavis who, more than anyone else, installed Lawrence in the English canon, praising his capacity for life and his openness to new forms of living in contrast to the spiritually impoverished routines of industrial society.[26] Lawrence's place in the canon was also helped by change in British society in the 1950s and 1960s. His rise from miner's son to literary genius seemed an early example of the working-class talent that flowered in the middle years of the century and this, together with the Lady Chatterley trial (1962), seemed to place Lawrence at the heart of the social and particularly the sexual revolution.

Kate Millet's *Sexual Politics* (1977) altered this view, arguing that Lawrence was not so much the 'priest of love' as the apologist for 'phallic consciousness',[27] his views of love effectively mystifying 'masculine ascendancy' by being presented through symbolism and a 'feminine consciousness'.[28] Although Millet's critique was valuable in revealing Lawrence's patriarchal bias, her analysis was too dependent on *Sons and Lovers* (1913) and *Lady Chatterley's Lover* (1928) for it to hold good about Lawrence's work as a whole. Dorrit Einersen complains that not only does Millet sometimes misquote Lawrence but also that she 'always quotes [him] out of context', while Chris Baldick accuses her of being 'relentless in presenting Lawrence as the pontiff of a murderous phallic cult'.[29] Millet's tendentious reading, a product of the militant feminism of the late 1960s, takes too little account of the complexity of Lawrence's representations of women and none at all of their class position, something that concerns Hugh Stevens, who argues that 'a consideration of class in relation to gender frustrates the central binary in Millet's writing which argues that the politics of sexuality equates masculinity with power and femininity with passivity'.[30] Harry T. Moore, one of Lawrence's biographers, notes that 'he would sometimes ask the women he knew to write down what they had felt or possibly would feel in certain situations: in this way various women provided him with some of his sources'.[31] No wonder some reviewers thought Lawrence's first novel, *The White Peacock* (1912), was written by a woman.

If Millet is to be believed, then Lawrence was simply a man who wanted to oppress women. In fact he was sympathetic to the demands of the suffragettes and many of his female friends – Jessie Chambers and Alice Dax in Nottingham and Helen Corke and Louie Burrow in London – were active in the campaign. After the war, however, he began to believe that women were simply taking on male roles rather than developing themselves as women and this made him set his face against reform.[32] But, as Janet Barron argues, we should not judge Lawrence too harshly for sharing the patriarchal attitudes of his time; so, too, did many women writers.[33] Anaïs Nin was an early supporter of Lawrence, declaring that he understood a woman's point of view, a claim enthusiastically endorsed some 40 years later by Carol Dix, who found much to identify with in Ursula.[34] Sheila MacLeod is more reserved in her comments, observing that while Lawrence often shows 'uncannily intuitive insight into his female characters', this is frequently 'wiped out by a wave of apparent misogyny'.[35] The chief contradiction in his presentation of women, she continues, is that while he is prepared to allow them to be strong and independent, he does not permit them to cope successfully with those qualities. Lawrence's treatment of Gudrun, for example, her final state of futility, is his revenge on the modern independent woman. More recently, Marianna Torgovnick praises Lawrence for his treatment of sexuality, 'his willingness to *narrate* [it] rather than simply evade it or reduce it to a series of mechanical, repeatable or quantifiable actions'.[36] And if this seems too conventional a compliment in a critical climate that favours the intensities of desire, then we can point to how Lawrence reverses, particularly in *Women in Love*, the male gaze. That is to say, he empowers women to look at men in the way that men have traditionally looked at women and hence can be read as a challenge to patriarchy.[37] We have already mentioned how Ursula is thrilled with Birkin's body, and Gudrun, too, is similarly enamoured of Gerald's 'firmly moulded contours' (*WL*, p. 183). Why see, as Millet does, such moments as the privileging of masculinity? Why not use them to develop what Barron thinks is missing from feminist criticism generally, 'an adequate vocabulary for comment on female erotica'?[38]

Lawrence's treatment of women goes through a number of phases. Prior to the First World War, he is largely sympathetic to them and asks them to collaborate on his writings. After the war, he begins to see them as a threat and wants to assign them subordinate roles. In the final phase, represented by *Lady Chatterley's Lover*, Lawrence extols and exalts the phallus, and the bulk of adverse feminist criticism is a reaction to this aspect of his writing. Indeed, Millet's attack on Lawrence was probably more responsible than any other for the decline in his reputation. It was hard to justify the study of a writer who seemed so hostile to women, especially at a time when feminists were challenging how women were portrayed in patriarchal society. More important for first-wave feminists than studying dead, white, male writers whose work had, in any case, contributed to the ideological oppression of women, was the recovery of women's history and women's writing. Lawrence, with his apparent belief in a male and female essence and his dictatorial attitude – women should not cut their hair as combing it keeps them quiet[39] – had nothing to offer those who wanted to improve the position of women in society.

Feminist criticism is, of course, very different from the kind of criticism advocated by Lawrence. Instead of considering how works impact on our 'vital emotions', the feminist critic aims to show how texts represent women, how those representations articulate with the portrayal of women in patriarchy generally, and how those representations may be challenged. In other words, literature is read strategically rather than as a good in itself. And yet, feminist criticism was morally conservative. The objection to Lawrence's phallocentricism is an uncanny repetition of those early condemnations of his work where *The Rainbow* was condemned by one male reviewer for its 'monstrous wilderness of phallicism'.[40] One criticism is more political, the other is more moral, but both are uncomfortable with Lawrence's treatment of sexuality and its implications for the social relations of men and women. Both fail to recognise that Lawrence was trying, in his own way, to resist the atrophying of the sensuous and affective life in capitalism. That his answers may not have been acceptable does not invalidate his analysis. To read strategically should mean, where possible, enlisting those aspects of a writer's work that are useful for your particular cause. But this raises ethical questions, not just of appropriating the work rather than appreciating it as an autonomous creation, but more importantly, of the values that allow the work to be appropriated in the first place. The study of literature is, in part, a coming to terms with what is involved in making a valuation and merely to make a work serve a larger project is to opt out of that process. The work, that is to say, is always in danger of being prejudged by the values of criticism whereas it may be more useful for the critic to enter into a dialogue with the values of the work.

Lawrence and poststructuralism

What feminism began, poststructuralism finished, with the result that even now Lawrence is 'an increasingly disregarded and often despised writer'.[41] I use the term 'poststructuralism' to refer to a wide variety of writing, from psychoanalysis to deconstruction, that takes its cue from Ferdinand de Saussure's claim that language does not so much refer to the world as provide us with the concepts that organise our understanding of it.[42] The idea that language constructs reality rather than corresponds to it has a bearing on the idea of literary value and hence on the canon. Instead of being seen as an intrinsic property of works, value is viewed as being projected onto them by groups who have a vested interest in creating a hierarchy of texts that validate their view of the world. Feminist criticism had already challenged Lawrence's place in the canon and, with the advent of poststructuralism, the canon itself came under attack. If there is no such thing as literary value on which the idea of the canon depends, then we cannot say that one text is 'better' than another and so Leavis's claim for Lawrence as a 'great' writer, a 'genius', looks distinctly shaky.

Central to poststructuralism is the idea that language is not a nomenclature but a system of signs that signify by their difference from one another. What is more, if the meaning of a word depends on its relationship with other words, which in turn get their meaning from yet more words, then it is hard to see where meaning ever comes to rest. The poststructuralist emphasis on the indeterminacy of meaning causes it to be suspicious of claims to artistic unity and it is especially sceptical of terms like 'organic' which imply, when applied to art, some sort of natural, self-regulating whole that could not have been organised in any other way. As one of the chief aims of the poststructuralist project is to show that there is no necessary connection between words and world, it is severely critical of those views of language which appear to suggest the contrary. For, if language is a true reflection of the world, then it can never be a tool for changing it. The notion of the organic work of art underwrites this conservative view of language because it promotes the idea of a natural link between signs and society. Moreover, it is a short step from seeing a natural connection between words and world to conceiving of a natural order of society that, precisely because it is *natural*, should not be tampered with.[43]

It should be clear from this why poststructuralists would have little interest in Lawrence. His determinedly organic vocabulary is redolent of everything poststructuralists oppose: nature, unity and fixity. Moreover, his attempt to embody male and female essence in language is at odds with the poststructuralist claim that the sign cannot express presence precisely because it is a mark of its absence. The sign is a substitute for the thing and so, to adapt Wittgenstein, that which is not there is that of which we must speak.[44] Similarly, Lawrence's belief in a deep connection between humans and the larger creative universe belonged to a philosophy of being which was at odds with a politics of identity. Finally, there was his flirtation with fascism. How could anyone with such leanings have anything to offer a criticism whose aim was to empower people? And yet the very qualities that poststructuralists celebrate – difference, heterogeneity and plurality – are to be found in Lawrence's work. He attacks modern society precisely because its structures try to make everyone the same, and his declaration that 'there is always excess'[45] chimes nicely with the current view that meaning is always multiple. His view that any work of art 'must contain the essential criticism on the morality to which it adheres'[46] suggests that novels are not unified wholes, while his claim that 'all vital truth contains the memory of that which is not true'[47] shows an awareness of the double nature of all communication that forms the theme of Lacanian psychoanalysis and Derridean deconstruction.

More specifically, David Lodge has drawn attention to the parallels between Lawrence and Mikhail Bakhtin in their respective views of the novel. Bakhtin distinguished between the monologic novel, where the author controlled the characters and directed them to the desired conclusion, and the dialogic or polyphonic novel, where the author retreated into the background and let the characters have their say without drawing matters to a close. Lodge argues that Bakhtin's description of Dostoevsky's *Crime and Punishment* applies to *Women in Love*:

> Everything in this novel – the fates of the people, their experience and ideas – is pushed to its boundaries, everything is prepared, as it were, to pass over into its opposite, everything is taken to extremes, to its uttermost limit. There is nothing in the novel that could become stabilised, nothing that could relax within itself, enter the ordinary flow of biographical time and develop in it, everything requires change and rebirth. Everything is shown in a moment of unfinalised transition.[48]

Lodge also finds Bakhtin's description of the carnivalesque relevant to Lawrence's fiction. Briefly, Bakhtin uses the term carnivalesque to refer to forms of licensed behaviour on set dates during the church's calendar year which celebrate the flesh and mock and temporarily overturn established hierarchies. There is an affinity, Lodge claims, between Bakhtin's view that carnival behaviour was suppressed in the era of bourgeois capitalism and Lawrence's view that instinctual life had been repressed by the same social forces.[49]

M. Elizabeth Sargeant and Garry Watson also believe that Lawrence's theory of the novel is 'uncannily close to Bakhtin's', citing particularly his essay 'Why the Novel Matters' as significant.[50] Their argument is that Lawrence belongs to a tradition of thinking about otherness that goes from Martin Buber to Emmanuel Levinas. Lawrence's claim that 'we must learn to think in terms of difference and otherness'[51] would certainly not be out of place in today's critical climate, especially given that the point of such learning was to be changed by the experience. Indeed, Lawrence sounds positively postcolonial when he declares that 'the old white psyche has to be gradually broken down before anything else can come to pass'.[52] He does not, however, restrict his understanding of otherness to human beings. 'The business of art,' he writes, 'is to reveal the relation between man and his circumambient universe ... me and another person, me and other people, me and a nation, me and a race of men, me and the animals, me and the trees or flowers, me and the earth, me and the skies and suns and stars, me and the moon ...'[53] The determination to find a living relationship with nature allies Lawrence's writing, particularly works such as *Birds, Beasts and Flowers* (1923) and *St Mawr* (1925), with the emerging tradition of eco-criticism. Lawrence can also be seen as a forerunner of cultural studies since he rarely confines himself to literary matters even when writing about them, calling on painting, politics, history, science and sexual relations to bolster his observations. There are, in other words, a number of ways of allying Lawrence with current critical concerns, but if we were simply to assimilate him to them, we would lose much of his power to confront and challenge us.

The present collection

For the reasons outlined briefly above, Lawrence has not received a great deal of attention from feminist or, more generally, poststructuralist critics. In fact much of the commentary on his work remains very traditional. Nevertheless, as the contributors to this volume show, it is possible to read Lawrence in the light of the 'linguistic turn' of the late 1970s. I have given a very schematic account of that development but these essays focus in detail on different aspects of it. As the essays are each followed by a short summary all that remains is to explain how they fit into my brief history of criticism. For the sake of convenience, the essays on each novel follow the same pattern; that is, there are essays on language, psychoanalysis, and then history. Although feminist criticism is an integral part of particularly the psychoanalytic essays, there is one long, free-standing essay by Liang-ya Liou (essay 9) which covers both novels from a number of different feminist perspectives. The volume concludes with an essay by David Parker which points to one possible direction for future Lawrence criticism.

As for how the essays fit into my brief history of criticism, Gerald Doherty's close reading of the tropes of both *The Rainbow* and *Women in Love* (essays 2 and 6), reflects an interest less in what is said than in how it is said and this was increasingly characteristic of criticism after the late 1970s, particularly under the influence of Jacques Derrida. Similarly, Roger Ebbatson (essay 1) shows how, in *The Rainbow*, Lawrence's concern with the divisions wrought by language parallels the concerns of number of other writers from Walter Benjamin to Julia Kristeva. Robert Burden and James F. Knapp (essays 5 and 8) are also interested in Lawrence's language, but their approach is more historical than linguistic. Burden provides a Foucauldian reading of *The Rainbow*, identifying a number of different discourses – colonialism, evolution, sexology and electromagnetism – and using them to show that the novel is not, as Leavis maintained, an account of English history, or, as Frank Kermode claimed, history as apocalypse. Meanwhile, Knapp in his reading of *Women in Love*, relates Lawrence's famed opposition between organic and mechanical living to the effects of management revolution of the early part of the century before questioning whether these two discourses are in fact as separate as Lawrence maintains.

Jacques Lacan was an important figure in poststructuralism and his influence is strongly marked in Elizabeth Fox's essay on *The Rainbow* (essay 4), which argues that Lacan's theory of psychosis is a useful way of understanding the novel's final vision. Earl Ingersoll relies more on Freud for his reading of *Women in Love* (essay 7), but his remarks about how looking is a means of objectifying the other resonate with Lacanian ideas about the gaze. Jorgette Mauzerall offers a feminist recuperation of Lawrence in her reading of the barn scene in *The Rainbow* (essay 3), claiming that the depiction of Tom in a nurturing role with Anna as they feed the animals shows that Lawrence had a less rigid view of men and women than has often been assumed. Liang-ya Liou (essay 9) is more critical of Lawrence's depiction of women in the two novels, arguing that while he may respect the demands of female sexuality,

he only does this within the context of a monogamous and heterosexual relationship. Furthermore, she continues, Lawrence uses the
promise of a fulfilled female sexuality to woo women away from
politics. However, she does concede, towards the end of her long
piece, that the text itself seems to deconstruct some of the oppositions it sets up between normal and deviant sexuality.

In a recent review of Lawrence's critical and cultural legacy
Chris Baldick suggests some of the likely developments that
Lawrence studies may take in the future. He calls for 'a more fully
historicised Lawrence',[54] and Burden and Knapp would seem to
point the way forward here. Baldick also suggests that we need a
substantial analysis of Lawrence's 'alarmingly uneven prose
style',[55] and Doherty's essays can be seen as a first step in this un-
dertaking. One thing which Baldick does not mention is ethical
criticism. Of course, by its very nature all criticism is ethical, and
even the decision to discuss one work rather than another implies
a choice, but the grounds of this choice are not always made explicit: values are often assumed rather than argued. David Parker's
essay, which closes this volume, is one example of ethical criticism.
Taking issue with the claim that only political[56] forms of reading
are able to uncover the binary oppositions in texts, he argues,
through his analysis of *Women in Love*, that works of art perform
this operation on themselves, citing Lawrence's remark that 'the
degree to which the system of morality, or the metaphysic, of any
work of art is submitted to criticism within the work of art makes
the lasting value and satisfaction of that work'. Parker believes
that the ethical reader does not impose his or her reading on a
work, while the ethical poem, play or novel is one that explores
ethical positions without embracing them. This chimes with
Lawrence's own position: 'If the novelist puts his thumb in the
pan, for love, for tenderness, sweetness, peace, then he commits an
immoral act: he prevents the possibility of pure relationship, a
pure relatedness, the only thing that matters.'[57] Part of what
Lawrence meant by this was that no one element in a novel should
be allowed to dominate over all the others; ethics is a matter of
bringing things into relation. 'The novel,' he wrote, 'is a perfect
medium for revealing to us the changing rainbow of our living relationships.'[58] Hence, when Lawrence says that we should judge a
work of art by its effect on our emotions, he wasn't talking about
whether it made us behave well or badly but rather how it adjusts
our relationships to the 'living universe' about us, how it brings us

into a new balance with 'the things we move with and amongst and against'.[59] If the idea of balance seems inherently conservative, then it should be stressed that Lawrence believed this relation changed from day to day; what really interested him, he said, was the question 'what next?'[60] And, as the critical revolution of the last 30 years begins to slow down, that seems an appropriate question on which to end.

Notes

1. D. H. Lawrence, *The Rainbow*, ed. Mark Kinkead-Weekes and with an introduction and notes by Anne Fernihough (Harmondsworth, 1995), p. 310. The novel was originally published in 1915. Hereafter it is referred to as *R*, with all page references given in the text.

2. D. H. Lawrence, 'John Galsworthy', in *Study of Thomas Hardy and Other Essays*, ed. Bruce Steele (Cambridge, 1985) p. 209.

3. D. H. Lawrence, *Women in Love* (Oxford, 1998), p. 230. The novel was originally published 1920 by Thomas Secker in America and then published in England 1921 by Martin Secker. Hereafter it is referred to as *WL*, with all page references given in the text.

4. In this connection, see W. H. Auden's poem 'The Unknown Citizen', in *Collected Shorter Poems 1927–1939* (London, 1966), pp. 146–7.

5. Lawrence, 'Why the Novel Matters', in *Study of Thomas Hardy*, pp. 197–8.

6. Ibid., p. 197.

7. Ibid., p. 196.

8. Ibid., p. 198.

9. Graham Holderness, *D. H. Lawrence: History, Ideology and Fiction* (Dublin, 1982), p. 37.

10. See, for example, John Strachey, *Literature and Dialectical Materialism* (London, 1956). For an account of Lawrence's politics, see Rick Rylance, 'Lawrence's Politics', in Keith Brown (ed.), *Rethinking Lawrence* (Buckingham, 1990), pp. 163–80.

11. Lawrence, 'John Galsworthy', p. 211.

12. For a discussion of the significance of architecture in *The Rainbow*, see Tony Pinkney, *Lawrence and Modernism* (Iowa, 1990), pp. 68–86.

13. For an account of Lawrence's relationship with modernism, see Michael Bell, 'Lawrence and Modernism', in Anne Fernihough (ed.),

The Cambridge Companion to D. H. Lawrence (Cambridge, 2001), pp. 179–96, and Pinkney, *Lawrence and Modernism*.

14. Both Marinetti and Taylor saw humans principally in terms of machines. See *Marinetti: Selected Writings*, trans. R. W. Flint (London, 1972) and Frederick Winslow Taylor, *The Principles of Scientific Management* (New York, 1911 & 1964).

15. 'We are such egotistic fools. We see only the symbol as a subjective expression: as an expression of ourselves ... [when] it is necessary to grasp the whole.' Lawrence, cited in Harry T. Moore, *The Priest of Love* (Harmondsworth, 1974), p. 271. Ursula is certainly trying to see the whole but it is a matter of debate as to how far her vision is subjective or objective. I have suggested that it is the former.

16. It was also an image Lawrence used about himself. The war and the banning of *The Rainbow* made him finally decide to leave England. 'My life is ended here. I must go as a seed that falls into new ground.' Cited in Moore, *The Priest*, p. 307.

17. Dancing occurs in both novels. In *The Rainbow* the pregnant Anna dances 'to the unseen Creator' (p. 170) and in *Women in Love* Ursula, Gudrun and the contessa dance a performance of the widowed Naomi, and her widowed daughters-in-law Ruth and Orpah (p. 93 and see Book of Ruth 1). The first dance is an expression of joy at creation, the other an expression of grief at loss. Another difference between the two dances is that Anna's dance is spontaneous whereas Ursula's, Gudrun's and the contessa's is 'in the style of the Russian ballet of Pavlova and Nijinsky' (p. 93). Dancing in *The Rainbow* is therefore more instinctive and immediate whereas in *Women in Love* it is more imitative and deliberate: Gudrun's dance before the cattle is the most dramatic instance of keeping instinct at bay. These differences illustrate *Women in Love's* closer proximity to the modernist tradition of formalism, though it certainly does not endorse it. Finally, we should not overlook the fact that Anna's dance is also, in part, an expression of loneliness: 'Where there was no-one to exult with then one danced before the Unknown' (p. 169). In other words, dance in both novels contains, to a lesser or greater degree, an element of sadness.

18. For an account of the relation between the two novels, see John Worthen's and Lindeth Vasey's Introduction to *The First Women in Love* (Cambridge, 2002).

19. Quoted by Hugh Stevens, 'Sex and the Nation: "The Prussian Officer" and *Women in Love'*, in Fernihough (ed.), *Companion*, pp. 49–65 (p. 58).

20. Stevens, 'Sex', interprets this image in terms of Lawrence's ambivalent attitude to homosexual intercourse. See also Stevens, 'Love and

Hate in D. H. Lawrence', in *Men and Masculinities*, 4: 4 (2002), 334–45.

21. Lawrence, *The First Women in Love*, p. 27. This remark is omitted from the 1920 version of the novel, which saw a number of other changes as well.

22. Lawrence, 'Why the Novel Matters', p. 196.

23. On this point, see Maria Di Battista who writes that to combat 'the se-ductiveness of analogical language', Lawrence aimed 'to radicalise metaphor and all other terms of comparison by eliminating the mediating middle term in the vital transfer of meaning from the depths to the surfaces. He wants his language to destroy or incapacitate that part of the verbal consciousness, best represented in the mind of Gudrun, which habitually employs language to encircle, complete, and define the real.' See '*Women in Love*: D. H. Lawrence's Judgement Book', in Peter Balbert and Philip L. Marcus (eds), *D. H. Lawrence: A Centenary Consideration* (Ithaca & London, 1985), pp. 67–90 (pp. 78–80).

24. T. S. Eliot, 'Tradition and the Individual Talent', in *Selected Essays* (London, 1976), p. 21.

25. For a useful overview of Lawrence criticism, see Chris Baldick, 'Lawrence's critical and cultural legacy' in Anne Fernihough (ed.), *Companion*, pp. 253–69.

26. See F. R. Leavis, *Thoughts, Words and Creativity: Art and Thought in Lawrence* (London, 1976).

27. 'I shall always be a priest of love'. Lawrence used this description of himself in a letter to a friend, Mrs Hopkins, in 1912 (see Moore, *The Priest*, p. 200). Moore claims that Lawrence's 'career and doctrine are caught up in that phrase'.

28. Kate Millet, *Sexual Politics* (London, 1977), p. 335.

29. Dorrit Einersen, 'Feminist Criticism of D. H. Lawrence', *Proceedings of The Nordic Conference For English 5* (1992), pp. 364–75 (p. 367), and Baldick, 'Critical legacy', p. 264.

30. Stevens, 'Love and Hate in D. H. Lawrence', p. 335.

31. Moore, *The Priest*, p. 74.

32. For an account of Lawrence's involvement with the suffragettes, see Hilary Simpson, *D. H. Lawrence and Feminism* (London, 1982). See also Anne Smith (ed.), *Lawrence and Women* (London, 1978), and Carol Siegel, *Lawrence Among the Women: Wavering Boundaries in Women's Literary Traditions* (Charlottesville and London, 1991).

33. Janet Barron, 'Equality Puzzle: Lawrence and Feminism', in Brown (ed.), *Rethinking*, pp. 12–22 (p. 17).

34. Anaïs Nin, *D. H. Lawrence: An Unprofessional Study* (Chicago, [1932] 1964), and Carol Dix, *Lawrence and Women* (London, 1980).

35. Sheila MacLeod, *Lawrence's Men and Women* (London, 1985), p. 76.

36. Marianna Torgovnick, 'Narrating sexuality: *The Rainbow*', in Fernihough (ed.), *Companion*, pp. 33–48 (p. 36).

37. It can also be seen as an instance of Lawrence's homoeroticism; see Stevens, 'Love and Hate'.

38. Barron, 'Equality Puzzle', p. 21.

39. Ibid., p. 15.

40. Robert Lynd in *The Daily News*, cited in Moore, *The Priest*, p. 306.

41. Jonathan Dollimore, *Sexual Dissidence: Augustine to Wilde, Freud to Foucault* (Oxford, 1991), p. 268.

42. There are numerous introductions to poststructuralism or 'theory', but the most accessible is Peter Barry, *Beginning Theory* [2nd edition] (Manchester, 2001).

43. A more nuanced understanding of the organic can be found in Anne Fernihough's study of Lawrence where she maintains that 'the organic has many faces [and] if one points towards something politically ominous, the other points to something more positive'. See Anne Fernihough, *D. H. Lawrence: Aesthetics and Ideology* (Oxford, 1993), p. 9.

44. 'Whereof one cannot speak, thereof one must be silent.' Ludwig Wittgenstein, *Tractatus Logio-Philosophicus* [trans. C. K. Ogden] (London & New York, 1990), p. 189.

45. *Study of Thomas Hardy*, p. 31.

46. Ibid., p. 89.

47. D. H. Lawrence, *The Letters of D. H. Lawrence: Volume 2 1913–16*, ed. George Zytaruk and James Boulton (Cambridge, 1981), p. 247.

48. Bakhtin, cited in David Lodge, 'Lawrence, Dostoevsky, Bakhtin', in Brown (ed.), *Rethinking*, pp. 92–108 (p. 96).

49. Ibid., p. 108.

50. M. Elizabeth Sargent and Garry Watson, 'D. H. Lawrence and the Dialogical Principle: The Strange Reality of Otherness', in *College English*, 63: 4 (2001), 409–36 (p. 410).

51. D. H. Lawrence, *The Symbolic Meaning: The Uncollected Version of Studies in Classical American Literature* (New York, 1964), p. 17.

52. D. H. Lawrence, *Studies in Classic American Literature* (Harmondsworth, 1977), p. 70.

53. D. H. Lawrence, 'Morality and the Novel', in *Study of Thomas Hardy*, pp. 171–6 (pp. 171–2).

54. Baldick, 'Critical legacy', p. 267.

55. Ibid.

56. Of course, all readings are political too.

57. Lawrence, 'Morality and the Novel', p. 173.

58. Ibid. p. 175

59. Lawrence, 'Art and Morality', in *Study of Thomas Hardy*, p. 167.

60. Lawrence 'The Future of the Novel', in *Study of Thomas Hardy*, p. 154.

1

The Rainbow and the Language of Origins

ROGER EBBATSON

The challenging opening pages of *The Rainbow* seem to demand a radical reading, founded in theories about the nature and origin of language, which they have scarcely received. The early generations of Brangwens are described as working upon the horizontal land below Ilkeston; when each man looks up, he sees the church tower in the distance 'standing above him and beyond'. Although they are 'thriftless', the narrator observes, these men are conscious of a connection beyond that of money:

> They felt the rush of the sap in spring, they knew the wave which cannot halt, but every year throws forward the seed to begetting, and, falling back, leaves the young-born on the earth. They knew the intercourse between heaven and earth, sunshine drawn into the breast and bowels, the rain sucked up in the daytime, nakedness that comes under the wind in autumn, showing the birds' nests no longer worth hiding. Their life and interrelations were such; feeling the pulse and body of the soil, that opened to their furrow for the grain, and became smooth and supple after their ploughing, and clung to their feet with a weight that pulled like desire, lying hard and unresponsive when the crops were to be shorn away.
>
> (p. 42)

This passional life is enough for the men, 'their faces always turned to the heat of the blood, staring into the sun, dazed with looking towards the source of generation, unable to turn round' (p. 43). The Brangwen women, in contradistinction, look out 'from the

heated, blind intercourse of farm-life, to the *spoken world* beyond'
(p. 42, italics added), seeking another sphere:

> But the woman wanted another form of life than this, something that
> was not blood-intimacy ... She stood to see the far-off world of cities
> and governments and the active scope of man, the magic land to her,
> where secrets were made known and desires fulfilled. She faced
> outwards to where men moved dominant and creative, having turned
> their back on the pulsing heat of creation, and with this behind them,
> were set out to discover what was beyond, to enlarge their own scope
> and range and freedom; whereas the Brangwen men faced inwards to
> the teeming life of creation, which poured unresolved into their veins.
>
> (p. 43)

This enlargement of scope is represented in the novel by the vicar
at Cossethay, one 'who spoke the *other, magic language*' (p. 43,
italics added), a language which eludes the speech rhythms and
silences of the 'slow, full-built' Brangwen males. The authority
which the cleric wields over the women 'raised him above the
common men' into a more 'vivid circle of life' accessible only
through 'education, this higher form of being' (p. 44). This quest
for a 'higher form' is the dominant motif of the novel: as John
Worthen notes in his introduction, the Brangwens of this opening
section 'are less inhabitants of the English eighteenth or
nineteenth century, than human beings at an early stage of development' (p. 18). The question of development is linked incontro-
vertibly with language.

In these mystical pages Lawrence confronts a crucial issue of
modern thought, the question of human entry into history. The
Brangwens, trapped contentedly upon their 'horizontal land'
(p. 41), exemplify Nietzsche's description, in 'The Use and Misuse
of History', of the 'unhistorical animal' confined within a horizon
which is almost a point, but in a sense happy'.[1] The ability to
encounter life in a nonhistorical mode, Nietzsche argued, was the
foundation for the works of humanity. Such a Nietzschean foundation, with its division into pre- and post-lapsarian worlds, is of
course as mythical as the opening of Lawrence's novel, but it was a
myth with potent attractions for European thought. In the
Grundrisse, for example, Marx had argued for the aboriginal existence of man within the communal group. Human beings, he
posited, 'become individuals only through the process of history'.
The originary appearance of man is as 'a *species-being, clan being,*

herd animal', and the emergence out of 'species being' is at the prompting of economic imperative:

> Exchange itself is the chief means of this individuation. It makes the herd-like existence superfluous and dissolves it. Soon the matter [has] turned in such a way that as an individual he relates himself only to himself, while the means with which he posits himself as individual have become the making of his generality and commonness.[2]

In this state of 'generality', what stands opposite to man, Marx suggests, 'has now become the true community, which he tries to make a meal of, and which makes a meal of him'.[3] *The Rainbow* explores the consequences of this diagnosis in its depiction of the 'harsh and ugly disillusion' which possesses Ursula at the training college. Academic life and the world of learning to which her female forebears aspired now stands exposed as a 'second-hand dealer's shop', 'a little side-show to the factories of the town'. College is 'a sham store, a sham warehouse, with a single motive of material gain, and no productivity' (p. 485).

The dislocation inherent in a belief in human emergence from a 'herd-like' instinctual life into individual being, dramatised in *The Rainbow*, lies at the heart of a seminal modernist debate about language between Walter Benjamin and T. W. Adorno. In his essay 'On Language as Such and on the Language of Men', Benjamin meditates on the opening chapters of the Book of Genesis, emphasising the value of an Ur-state prior to linguistic differentiation. Emergence out of plenitude involves stress and suffering: 'how much more melancholy to be named not from the one blessed, paradisiac language of names, but from the hundred languages of man'.[4] In primordial fullness, language and nature coincide. 'God's creation is completed', Benjamin suggests, 'when things receive their names from man, from whom in name language alone speaks.'[5] The 'paradisiac state' of this beginning represents a fullness of being because it 'knew only one language'. Benjamin here imagines a life like that of the early Brangwens, complete in and for itself:

> The paradisiac language of man must have been one of perfect knowledge; whereas later all knowledge is again infinitely differentiated in the multiplicity of language, was indeed forced to differentiate itself on a lower level as creation in name.[6]

Linguistic difference leads to 'the decay of the blissful, Adamite language-mind' because, in stepping outside 'the purer language of name, man makes language a means (that is, a knowledge inappropriate to him), and therefore also ... a *mere* sign'. The fall from grace consequent on slippage between sign and referent results in that 'plurality of languages' and 'linguistic confusion' which typifies the babel of the modern world.[7] Benjamin's position is clear: in the prelapsarian unity with nature, with its concordance of word and object, the life of mankind 'in pure language-mind' was 'blissful'. But with the Fall, humanity 'abandoned immediacy in the communication of the concrete name', descending into 'the abyss of prattle' engendered by employing the word as means.[8] Just so does Lawrence both delineate Ursula plunging into the sordid world of Brinsley Street School, and seek through the composition of *The Rainbow* to resurrect the form of the novel from the Barthesian 'prattling texts' of Edwardian realism. Benjamin's writing has aptly been characterised as 'marked by a painful straining toward a psychic wholeness or unity of experience which the historical situation threatens to shatter at every turn',[9] and it is the mythical sense of primal oneness that Adorno was to critique in his essay, 'Subject and Object'. Contemplating the notion of the Marxian clan-being, Adorno writes that 'it probably was only in association, by rudimentary social toil' that human beings could originally survive. The principle of individuation would thus be secondary, 'a hypothetical kind of biological division of labour'.[10] But the undifferentiatedness towards which Lawrence and Benjamin gesture is 'romantic', 'a wishful projection at times, but today no more than a lie'.[11] The dialectical quality in Adorno's thought, which insists upon the falsifying tendency inherent in all theories of the world, leads him to insist upon that fragmentation of modern society which Ursula discovers for herself:

> The more individuals are really degraded to functions of the social totality as it becomes more systematised, the more will man pure and simple, man as a principle with the attributes of creativity and absolute domination, be consoled by exaltation of his mind.[12]

Lawrence had embodied this insight into his portrayal of the totalised industrial system of the mining town of Wiggiston, presided over by Uncle Tom Brangwen and, later, Winifred Inger, the systematised mentality which marks Skrebensky's militarism, and in contradistinction, Ursula's exultant vision of the rainbow in the closing pages. At this moment of visionary closure, the writing seeks, through evocation of one of the paradigmatic moments of modernist 'exaltation',[13] to cancel or subvert the implications of its own diagnosis of the ills of an industrialised society:

> And the rainbow stood on the earth. She knew that the sordid people who crept hard-scaled and separate on the face of the world's corruption were living still, that the rainbow was arched in their blood and would quiver to life in their spirit, that they would cast off their horny covering of disintegration, that new, clean, naked bodies would issue to a new germination, to a new growth, rising to the light and the wind and the clean rain of heaven. She saw in the rainbow the earth's new architecture, the old, brittle corruption of houses and factories swept away, the world built up in a living fabric of Truth, fitting to the over-arching heaven.
>
> (p. 548)

The contradictory power of *The Rainbow* may be said to find its imaginative source in the theoretical impasse articulated by Marxist cultural theory. Benjamin and Adorno, for all their differences, share a sense of the dialectic involved in the recognition of an interiority both blocked and insisted upon, valued and dismissed, by alienation from industrialism and materiality. This sense of alienation is enacted in the structure of *The Rainbow*, in the movement from primal community, through the lives of the two central couples, to the isolated figure of Ursula, standing at 'the advance-post of our time to blaze a path into the future', as the (possibly Lawrentian) publisher's blurb put it in the hastily suppressed first edition.

In Lacanian psychoanalytic theory, as is well known, the arbitrary system of classification known as language becomes our reality when we enter it as children. We are socialised, not into a world of objects, but into a 'symbolic order', words which are signs made of a 'presence made of absence' as Lacan puts it[14] – the world of words creates the world of things. The Brangwen women of the opening pages evolve towards education and culture through the acquisition of an elaborated language code.[15] They reject the primal linguistic undifferentiatedness of the Marsh; it is 'this education, this higher form of being, that the mother wished to give to her children' (p. 44). What Lacan designates the 'real' (the primordial stuff of nature) is structured through the giving of meaning, but this process entails division within the self. The individual subject is produced through language in conformity to the symbolic order. Once language is entered, the man or woman can never re-attain the unity of the Imaginary, because his/her difference is constituted symbolically through difference. One cannot collapse the sign and the referent, except in the realm of the Imaginary, from which language bans the subject. The Lacanian child, a mass of instinctive drives, is thus analogous to the early Brangwen males who are located in the Imaginary of a maternal plenitude. The boldly conceived project of *The Rainbow* is to dramatise ways in which language works to enable individualisation out of this primal state, and to examine the costs of that enablement. In the Hardy study written concurrently with the novel, Lawrence appears intriguingly to be offering a commentary on his fictional opening gambit:

> Life starts crude and unspecified, a great Mass. And it proceeds to evolve out of that mass ever more distinct and definite particular forms, an ever-multiplying number of separate species and orders.[16]

This draws upon the evolutionary terminology of Herbert Spencer's *First Principles* (1862), a text which Lawrence knew well, and of which *The Rainbow* offers a kind of fictional elaboration. But the Hardy essay then goes to refer to a process akin to the Lacanian mirror-stage:

> With his consciousness [man] can perceive and know that which is not himself. The further he goes, the more extended his consciousness, the more he realises the things that are not himself.[17]

The rite of passage involved in entering into the symbolic order is foreshadowed when Lawrence muses upon how 'the Uttered Word can come into us and give us the impetus to our second birth'.[18] The uttered comes into being through recognition of the Lacanian Other which lies on the horizon beyond the subject, but this mastery is bought at a price – in linguistic terms, the texture of *The Rainbow* embodies the Kristevan unsettlement wrought through the dialectical play between an instinctive maternal poetic language and a more functional prose. The realist project is subjected to uncontainable eruptions of the 'semiotic' in Lawrence's text – not only in this opening sequence, but also for instance in the pregnant Anna's naked dance before the mirror, in Will's ecstatic response to

Lincoln Cathedral, in the sheaf-gathering scene and elsewhere. Whilst in *The Rainbow* it is the female who is the agent of change, in the Hardy essay woman is characterised as 'the unutterable which man must for ever continue to try to utter'. The male, representing the 'Will-to-Motion', exists 'in doing'; the female, the 'Will-to-Inertia', exists 'in being':[19]

> The woman grows downwards, like a root, towards the centre and the darkness and the origin. The man grows upwards, like the stalk, towards discovery and light and utterance.[20]

Prior to splitting, the subject is a mesh of inner and outer, a state to some extent mirrored in the Brangwen males' quasi-sexual union with nature or in Will's experience in the cathedral. Towards the end of his life, in the Galsworthy essay of 1928, Lawrence uncannily anticipates these Lacanian ideas:

> It seems to me that when the human being becomes too much divided between his subjective and objective consciousness, at last something splits in him and he becomes a social being. When he becomes too much aware of objective reality, and of his own isolation in the face of a universe of objective reality, the core of his identity splits, his nucleus collapses, his innocence or his naïvete perishes, and becomes only a subjective-objective reality, a divided thing hinged together but not strictly individual.[21]

Before a man suffers the fall, Lawrence goes on, 'he innocently feels himself altogether within the great continuum of the universe'. He is not 'divided or cut off', possessing 'the sense of being at one with the great universe-continuum of space-time-life'.[22] What is sacrificed by entry into the symbolic order is powerfully expressed in the novel by Dr Frankstone's exposition of scientific materialism, Skrebensky's patriotism, or the mechanistic corruption of Uncle Tom Brangwen. If the unconscious is structured like a language, it is a potent language which lurks beneath the smooth discourse of realism to erupt with shattering effect, as in the climactic encounter with the horses.

Finally, Lawrence's opening pages might also be productively reinflected in relation to Jacques Derrida's meditation in *Of Grammatology* upon Rousseau's essay on the origin of languages. Rousseau argued that speech is natural, and that writing ensued as a parasitic growth. Derrida, as is well known, insists upon the priority of writing and the illusory nature of myths of origin. Under the ideology of presence, writing came to be defined as a condition of social inauthenticity. Society takes its origins, Derrida suggests, from the 'displacing of the relationship with the mother, with nature, with being as the fundamental signified'.[23] The quest for the originary moment, in Derridean thought, is continuously undermined by the duplicity of language. The '*birth of society* is therefore not a passage, it is a point, a pure, fictive and unstable, ungraspable limit'.[24] The principle of substitution, of supplementarity, is the undeclared originary principle. In describing the awakening of a small agrarian community, Lawrence would, like Rousseau, illustrate the workings of a 'classical ideology according to which writing takes the status of a tragic fatality come to prey upon natural innocence; interrupting the golden age of the present and full speech'. Writing, in this tradition, signifies 'the very process of the dispersal of peoples unified as bodies and the beginning of their enslavement'.[25] Rousseau, like Lawrence, perceives origin as 'the inaugural decadence', since the downward spiral into history has always already begun: Ursula's closing vision of the rainbow here, Birkin's insistence upon blood-consciousness in *Women in Love*, or the sanctuary of the gamekeeper's cottage in *Lady Chatterley's Lover* are all symptomatic of the Lawrentian urge to escape the effects of that spiralling movement. Yet whilst history is 'degenerative in direction', as in *The Rainbow* it is also 'progressive and compensatory in effect'.[26] The binary opposition which enables us to think the emergence from non-language is that between need and passion. Language, in Rousseau's essay, 'springs forth when passionate desire exceeds physical need, when imagination *is awakened*',[27] as it is in the Brangwen women. What the Lawrentian text nominates the 'other, magic language' of education and culture is decisive, as Derrida maintains:

> There is no social institution before language, it is not one cultural element among others, it is the element of institutions in general, it includes and constructs the entire social structure. Since nothing precedes it in society, its cause can only be pre-cultural or natural.[28]

The warm ambience of the Brangwen men is characterised by the Rousseauesque archaeological moment, a first moment of the sign without speech – Derrida's moment of 'the immediate sign'. Emerging out of this Ur-world of gestural immediacy, it is speech which has engendered the Derridean endless movement of signification: because supplementarity is of the essence of language, speech is perceived as already carrying in itself death and absence. Thus Rousseau desiderates what Derrida terms the 'dream of a mute society, of a society before the origin of languages, that is to say, strictly speaking, a society before society'. With reference to this 'society of mute writing', the advent of speech 'resembles a catastrophe, an unpredictable misfortune'.[29] This romantic intimation of cultural catastrophe may be closely allied to the Lawrentian blood-consciousness which was to be prescribed as a panacea for the ills of a hyper-conscious civilisation.

The mystical opening pages of *The Rainbow* were some of the last to be composed, early in 1915. In his study of the tortuous generation of the novel out of Lawrence's earlier projects, 'The Wedding Ring' and 'The Sisters', Charles Ross observes that this section was

> ... the last altogether unforeseen section to be created. Lawrence finally saw the overarching structure of the Brangwens moving gradually, generation by generation, into history; and he shored up the structure with a late but vital cornerstone.[30]

F. R. Leavis's insistence upon the essentially English quality of this text has recently been modified, notably by Tony Pinkney's proposal that the novel, whilst refracting some key ideas and images of the Ruskin–Morris tradition, embodies a distinctively modernist consciousness. In the course of his analysis, Pinkney specifically identifies *The Rainbow* with the North-European modernism of German Expressionist painting and architecture exemplified by the *Die Brucke* group and by Walter Gropius's *Bauhaus* manifesto.[31] This is a suggestive and fertile context, which may be supplemented by reference to the Franco-German modernist debate about language and origins briefly outlined here. As Lawrence wrote in his essay 'Education of the People' (1918), 'the whole sum of the mental content of mankind is never, and never can be more than a mere tithe of all the vast surging primal consciousness, the affective consciousness of mankind'.[32] Elsewhere, he would speak of a 'strange surging, some welling-up of unknown powers' in the 'souls' of 'men in Europe': All that real history can do is to note with wonder and reverence the tides which have surged out from the innermost heart of man, watch the incalculable flood and ebb of such tides.[33]

The Rainbow tellingly dramatises the dialectical to-and-fro between a humanity wedded to mental content and progress but riven by that 'surging primal consciousness' which is internalised in successive generations of the Brangwen family.

From *Worcester Papers in English*, No.1 (1997), 3–13.

Notes

[Roger Ebbatson's short essay looks at the main theme of *The Rainbow*, the passage from communal to individual life, through the lens of a number of thinkers. The quest for individuality is inseparable from the development of language whose ultimate effects are to create a rift between body and mind and a barrier between self and other, a truly ironic view of what is supposed to be *the* instrument of communication. Ebbatson shows how Lawrence's account of the development of language matches that of Walter Benjamin and Jacques Lacan, for both of whom entry into language represents a fall from the fullness of being. Theodor Adorno and Jacques Derrida are invoked to question the idea of original state of plenitude while Julia Kristeva's notion of the semiotic is used to illuminate those moments in the novel, such as Anna's dance when she is pregnant, which seem to challenge the constraints of language. Ebbatson concludes by questioning F. R. Leavis's account of the novel as an essentially English text, citing Tony Pinkney's argument that it embraces elements of German expressionism.

Ebbatson's essay is a useful guide to how poststructuralist theories of language can be applied to literary texts but the similarities he finds between these theories and Lawrence's novel prompt the question of what new understanding they bring to it. All references to *The Rainbow* are to the Penguin edition of the novel, edited by J. Worthen (Harmondsworth, 1981) and are given in parentheses in the text. Eds]

1. Friedrich Nietzsche, *On the Advantage and Disadvantage of History for Life*, tr. D. Preuss (Indianapolis, 1973), p. 11.

2. Karl Marx, *Grundrisse*, tr. M. Nicolaus (Harmondsworth, 1973), p. 496.

3. Ibid., p. 496.

4. Walter Benjamin, *One-Way Street and Other Writings*, tr. E. Jephcott & K. Shorter (London, 1985), pp. 121–2.

5. Ibid., p. 111.

6. Ibid., p. 119.

7. Ibid., pp. 119–20.

8. Ibid., pp. 121, 120.

9. Fredric Jameson, *Marxism and Form* (Princeton, NJ, 1974), p. 61.

10. T. W. Adorno, 'Subject and Object', in *The Essential Frankfurt School Reader*, ed. A. Arato and E. Gebhardt (Oxford, 1978), pp. 510–11.

11. Ibid., p. 511.

12. Ibid., p. 499.

13. Other such moments include Stephen Dedalus's encounter with the girl in Joyce's *Portrait* (1915), the final horse-riding scene in Forster's *Passage to India* (1924), Hans Castorp's vision in the Alps in Mann's *The Magic Mountain* (1924), and Lily Briscoe's completion of the painting in Woolf's *To the Lighthouse* (1927). The Lawrentian image of the 'new, clean, naked bodies' emerging into a revitalised fallen world is echoed in Stanley Spencer's Cookham paintings.

14. Jacques Lacan, *Ecrits*, tr. A. Sheridan (London, 1977), p. 65.

15. On Lawrence's engagement with the literature of evolution see my essay, '"Sparks Beneath the Wheel": Lawrence and Evolutionary Thought', in *D. H. Lawrence: New Studies*, ed. C. Heywood (London, 1987).

16. D. H. Lawrence, *Study of Thomas Hardy and Other Essays*, ed. B. Steele (Cambridge, 1985), p. 42.

17. Ibid., p. 42.

18. Ibid., p. 44.

19. Ibid., p. 94.

20. Ibid., p. 127.

21. D. H. Lawrence, 'John Galsworthy', in *D. H. Lawrence: Selected Critical Writings*, ed. M. Herbert (Oxford, 1998), p. 212.

22. Ibid.

23. Jacques Derrida, *Of Grammatology*, tr. G. Spivak (Baltimore, MD, 1976), p. 266.

24. Ibid., p. 267.

25. Ibid., pp. 168, 170.

26. Ibid., p. 202.

27. Ibid., p. 217.

28. Ibid., p. 219.

29. Ibid., pp. 240–1.

30. Charles L. Ross, *The Composition of The Rainbow and Women in Love* (Charlottesville, VA, 1979), p. 31.

31. Tony Pinkney, *D. H. Lawrence* (Hemel Hempstead, 1990).

32. D. H. Lawrence, *Phoenix*, ed. E. D. McDonald (London, 1961), p. 629.

33. D. H. Lawrence, *Movements in European History* (1921) (Oxford, 1971), pp. xxvii, xxviii.

2

The Metaphorical Imperative: From Trope to Narrative in *The Rainbow*

GERALD DOHERTY

The plot of D. H. Lawrence's *The Rainbow* has never been an object of much fascination since commentators have generally assumed that Lawrence's dispensing with plots was a major mark of his modernity. In so far as classic realist plots traded on 'the vulgarities of a plausible concatenation' – Samuel Beckett's phrase – then such an assumption is entirely justified. Marking the contrast with *Middlemarch*, where, as he puts it, the mechanics of the Raffles affair soak 'up so much authentic, thematic interest', Frank Kermode rightly concludes that 'Lawrence abandoned plot'.[1] He rejected the types of plot which the Barthesian proairetic and hermeneutic codes activate – those based on cause and effect, action and consequence (proairetic), and those which identify enigmas, build up suspense through exploitation of false leads or trails, which delay the denouement (hermeneutic). He refused to invent stories which in Kermode's phrase '*explain* how one thing leads to another'.[2]

Drawing on what he terms a 'classic distinction', Barthes identifies these explanatory plots in which the narrative units are distributed along a horizontal axis with the figure of metonymy. Such plots organise details, clear up mysteries, and further the action in obedience to the logic of sequence in precisely the manner that Lawrence refused to accept. Barthes distinguishes these

41

metonymic type plots from those which synthesise narrative units along a vertical axis: these he identifies with the figure of metaphor.[3] Based on the paradigm of resemblance, such plots locate recurrences, integrate motifs and actions, identify similarities between elements which appear to be different, and intensify mysteries instead of clearing them up. It is with plots of this kind that we shall be preoccupied here.

David Lodge once noted that Lawrence is essentially a 'metaphorical' novelist, whose writings, in Lodge's fine phrase, 'feed metaphorically upon his own metonymies'. Each successive phrase, though apparently forwarded by contiguity, unfolds 'the deeper significance of the same facts', and in so doing, accretes a 'vague metaphorical meaning'.[4] In effect, what one critic identifies as Lawrence's three 'representative techniques' – 'patterns of recurrence, exposition by scenes, and repetitive style'[5] – all carry strong metaphorical implications. In the first, patterns of event or of action are repeated, as in metaphor, on the basis of the similarities which bind them together; in the second, symmetries of theme or of thought through which each scene develops correspond to the modes of analogy or interrelationship through which metaphor generates meanings; the third is metaphorical in exactly the way that Lodge has identified: through lexical, syntactical and rhythmical repetition, fresh metaphorical meanings slowly accrete.[6]

If Lawrence's 'representative techniques' – those relating to pattern, structure and style – all turn on metaphor, could the same be said of the plots he employs? Does he – unwittingly – use plots of a metaphorical kind as opposed to those metonymic-type plots which he abandoned? What *are* these 'deep' plot structures through which the internal operations of metaphor are projected as external action-events? Do the characters in such plots behave like Greimesian actants, obedient to the regularities which these occulted structures dictate? Do they embody the kind of relationships which theorists of rhetoric uncover between the metaphorical term(s) and the sentence in which it is embedded? In the Lawrentian texts, are plots of suspense and surprise – those of metonymy – superseded by plots of predestination and prophecy, those to which the similarities and symmetries through which metaphor functions give rise?[7] That such specific plot-types do exist, and that they shape and determine the patterns of recurrence within the three-generational structure of *The Rainbow* the present essay will attempt to demonstrate.

I

The perception that trope and narrative co-implicate each other is not, of course, new. It is implicit in Nietzsche's celebrated pronouncement – 'What then is truth? A mobile army of metaphors, metonymies, anthropomorphisms: in short, a sum of human relations which became poetically and rhetorically intensified, metamorphosed, adorned, and after long usage, seem ... fixed, canonic and binding truths'[8] – which derives the varieties of human relations upon which narrative thrives from the predetermined operation of tropes. Narratologists too have explored the connection: Seymour Chatman, for example, lists a number of formalists who have 'noted the resemblance of plot structures to rhetorical tropes'; and Tzvetan Todorov, formulating a conception of Shklovsky's, speaks of 'certain narrative figures which are projections of rhetorical figures'.[9] Hayden White in turn has extrapolated both a theory of history and historical narratives from a traditional tetradic tropology.[10] At another level, the connection itself may be used to deconstruct the truth-claims of the discourse in question as knots undermine plots: Paul de Man, for example, reading Locke, Condillac and Kant, raises the possibility that 'temporal articulations, such as narratives or histories, are a correlative of rhetoric and not the reverse'; and Jacques Derrida shows how metaphor generates 'secret narrative(s)' of its own detours and errancies, which threaten the return to proper meaning and reference.[11] Other critics have uncovered the operations of such secret narrative agents in specific texts.[12]

In an interesting article, Patricia Parker has elaborated a typology of plots – of 'transference, transport, transgression, alienation, impropriety, identity' – projected by metaphor as a structuring principle.[13] Each major theory of metaphor from the Aristotelian one onwards not only engenders specific plot types but also projects character types whose interactions correlate with the exchanges between terms which each specific theory comports. It is precisely in terms of such correlations that we shall explore the sequence of plot types as they unfold in *The Rainbow*. In so doing, we shall show that the metonymic plot structures which Lawrence abandoned are replaced surreptitiously by more occulted structures generated by the agents and operations of metaphor.

The first major plot type has its matrix in Aristotelian substitution theory, the tradition of classical rhetoric, which dominated

European thinking about metaphor down to the late eighteenth century. Aristotle's definition – 'metaphor consists in giving the thing a name that belongs to something else' – posits the intrusion of an unusual or anomalous term into an established linguistic order. Here the notions of transfer and disruption are associated together; the metaphorical term violates the norms of the context into which it intrudes. Thus it is doubly alien, since it is a present but borrowed word, and the substitute for an absent one, filling a lexical gap or lacuna. In so doing, it behaves transgressively, unsettling the conventional exchanges through which language orders its meanings; it disturbs 'a whole network by means of an aberrant attribution'.[14] However, in so far as it gives 'appropriate names to new things, new ideas, or new experiences',[15] it is assimilated into the context in which it first appeared as an alien.

As Parker has noted, this double movement of substitution and transfer generates 'a number of plots, narratives, or theatrical "scenes" ', plots which involve the intrusion of an alien character, a 'foreigner', into the matrix of a regulated society whose norms s(he) unsettles (Parker, for example, locates Heathcliff in exactly this context).[16] The stranger carries all the disturbing force of the metaphorical term to disrupt the old literal order in which s(he) is newly embedded. S(he) is perceived by the insiders as the kind of outsider who is at once charismatic and dangerous. Since, however, s(he) fills a gap which no native could fill, s(he) is usually integrated through those fresh unions or contracts which s(he) initiates. Deviance ends up in congruence, as the foreigner is domesticated through a love-affair or through marriage.

Classic authors from Defoe to Dickens have improvised countless variations upon this plot type.[17] In *The Rainbow*, the narrative of each generation is triggered by the intrusion of an alien character into a traditional pastoral setting whose mores s(he) disrupts and unsettles. S(he) comports all the potential of the metaphorical term to revitalise old senses enfeebled through usage, and to remobilise old relationships which had become set in their ways. Through the repercussive effects s(he) produces, s(he) transforms the life of at least one of the members of the host society in which s(he) has now gained acceptance. In their early scenes of encounter and recognition, the couples in *The Rainbow* – Lydia and Tom, Anna and Will, Ursula and Skrebensky – act out the kind of transfers and exchanges which this classical conception of metaphor comports.

It is out of the limitations of this classical theory as it expended itself in endless taxonomic refinement that the second major theory of metaphor emerged. It has its roots in the Coleridgean valorisation of the imagination as the faculty which connects, blends and unites, an activity coterminous with the metaphorical process itself; the imagination functions as metaphor, or, as one commentator puts it, [18] 'Coleridge conceives of metaphor as Imagination in action'.[18] Here the notion of metaphor as substitution and deviation is replaced by that of the interaction between two (or more) semantic domains, between 'a logical subject and a predicate', to form a new contextual whole.[19] Deviant denomination is overtaken by deviant predication. Developed by I. A. Richards, this 'interaction' theory was refined by Max Black, Monroe C. Beardsley, Nelson Goodman, and by Paul Ricoeur.[20]

Two movements deserve attention. First a *blocking* effect highlights that resistance to change of the literal term, which Goodman's definition encapsulates; 'a metaphor is an affair between a predicate with a past and an object that yields while protesting.'[21] Then as the denotations of the literal term give way and collapse, the 'primary reference founders'.[22] This yielding in turn precipitates a semantic withdrawal, a *retreat* into the 'inner space of language', a reconstituted site where a 'change of distance between meanings' occurs.[23] Here the tension between 'identity and difference in the interplay of resemblance'[24] is maximised, as the gap between semantic domains is progressively narrowed. In this space, the radical interpenetrations of anagogic metaphor are activated, as A *becomes* B, and as 'everything is potentially identical with everything else'.[25] In this rhetorical symbiosis the meanings of *both* terms are transformed.

Projected as plot, these two effects – blocking and retreat – correlate with two specific phases in the interaction between the couples once the initial scenes of recognition are played out. The blocking effect is externalised in the interplay of advance and retirement, giving and withholding, the stage of suspense which precedes the retreat which these movements precipitate; the transformation sought by both partners is deferred and delayed. In the Lawrentian universe, as Kermode has noted, the struggle between partners is proper; things often go wrong before they go right.[26] With the entry into the space of retreat, conventional space time coordinates are suspended, as reverie supersedes action. This is the 'bower of bliss' to which the lovers break through, the scene of erotic entrancement, and the vertiginous site at which fresh senses proliferate and overwhelm the protagonists. As in the rhetorical exchange between subject and predicate, the couple interpenetrate one another as separate identities fuse or (as in Lawrence) an identity in difference is disclosed. This is the plot of discovery, revelation and transfiguration.

Romantic poetry abounds in such charmed plots, those poetic green spaces, where, as in Keats's *Ode to Psyche*, the enraptured lovers lie 'couched side by side'. They occupy an ever-increasing middle-space in the late nineteenth- and early twentieth-century novel – the 'Red Deeps' in Eliot's *The Mill on the Floss*, the secluded courtship scenes which form the centre-pieces in Hardy's pastoral novels, reaching their apogee in the seven love-encounters in *Lady Chatterley's Lover*, which usurp the greater space of the text. In *The Rainbow* they occupy the middle-space of the narrative of each generation, where the lovers retire from the workaday world, and the Lawrentian 'two in one' is, at least temporarily, accomplished (in their failure to achieve it as state, Ursula and Skrebensky confirm it as type).

But, as Parker notes, such plots are neither final nor completely fulfilling;[27] they contain the seed of the fallen, the taint of an Edenic transgression which necessitates a return to the world. The dangers of solipsistic withdrawal, of narcissistic self contemplation, are never quite overcome. It is precisely this threat which motivates the retreat *from* the bower – in rhetorical terms, from the world of sense opened up in the bower to the world of reference where the 'truths' of this sense are grounded and put to the test. It is around the transition from inner to outer, from private to public, from the world full of sense to one full of events that the third plot of metaphor crystallises. No longer an 'innocent', transparent space, this world of the work is penetrated by 'the inescapably paradoxical character surrounding a metaphorical concept of truth'.[28] Here the law of 'stereoscopic vision' predominates, as the tension between the 'is' and the 'is not', the same and the other, is exacerbated. Put differently, literal senses are not simply abolished, but submit to while resisting the metaphorical affirmation which they tend to subvert. Further narrative, in turn, is incited to account for and to recount the difference.[29]

Projected as narrative, this plot type turns on a return to the world by the lovers, but to a world bereft of its 'innocent' contours, charged with all the tensional character surrounding a metaphorical affirmation of 'truth'. Deprived of its simple transparency, the world now vacillates between the contradictory attributes – the is/is not – of the copula. In *The Rainbow*, these range from the benign oscillation between identity/difference, intimacy/remoteness through which Tom and Lydia encounter their world to the extremes of order/anarchy, truth/illusion, attraction/repulsion through which Ursula encounters hers. For each successive generation, the relapse from the 'two in one' of the space of retreat becomes increasingly problematic. With the eclipse of the old literal order of meanings, the new order is marked by ambivalence, by equivocal discriminations in a world which has lost its stability. Each couple acts out – with progressive exacerbation – the unresolved tension between subject and predicate, between literal and figurative sense, in the metaphorical contract. In this progress (to employ Ricoeurian terms) the 'incision' of the literal 'is not' comes increasingly to prevail over the 'vehemence' of the metaphorical 'is'.[30]

The remainder of the present essay will track each of these three major plot structures as they unfold in the narrative of each generation. It will show that while *The Rainbow* dispenses with the cruder mechanics of purely functional plots, it submits to the more occulted imperatives of the emplotments of metaphor. Such emplotments in effect determine the *fate* of the couples – their initial choice of each other, the rhythms of their subsequent encounters and conflicts, as well as the interplay of acceptance/rejection as they gravitate towards those destinations which are also their destinies.

II

Jacques Derrida once designated the sun as the originary or proper name in the Aristotelian rhetorical system, as 'the nonmetaphorical prime mover of metaphor, the father of all figures' towards and around which 'everything turns'.[31] It is exactly in this sense that Marsh Farm is initially represented as the heliotropic site par excellence, the site from which the Brangwen men immemorially not only 'star(e) into the sun', but also draw it 'into the breast and bowels' (pp. 42–3).[32] They are caught up in a fluid system of analogical relations, in which one element flows into another, and where everything is potentially identical with everything else, 'at one with the oneness of the flesh and the world', as Kermode puts it.[33] In this solar economy, without constraint or obstacle,

everything turns around and turns towards 'the source of generation' (p. 43) in a circumambulatory movement about a fixed node
of reference. It is left to the women to disrupt this synchronic state,
to break out of this settled enclosure which 'emasculates' narrative,
reducing its pace to a minimum; they strain towards those centres
of action – the world of 'cities and Governments' (p. 43) – source of
those counter-narratives which will propel the plot into motion.

It is precisely with the intrusion of an alien lady from a 'far-off'
country, an 'emissary of the disinherited',[34] into the settled context
of Cossethay that plot one is inaugurated. Like the metaphorical
term whose agent she is, Lydia first appears as a stranger without
credentials or antecedents – she has neither a father nor a husband
from whom a 'proper' name may be derived. Instead she has only a
mysterious past, one which makes her 'doubly alien' in the context
of the society into which she intrudes. As 'the foreign woman with
a foreign air about her', she imports into Cossethay an intimation
of the world of the beyond towards which the Brangwen women
aspire; she exudes the sense of belonging 'to somewhere else', of
being 'strange, from far off, yet so intimate' (p. 67), the bearer
of disturbing new connotations within the regulated relations of
Cossethay. Indeed just as metaphor violates the norms of conventional exchange, so too Lydia transgresses the mores of Cossethay
when she unexpectedly knocks on Tom's door to buy butter for the
vicar who always gets it from elsewhere (pp. 69–73).

Tom in turn is inscribed as the established literal term, tightly
circumscribed and contextured, yet aware of a lack which only a
stranger can fill. In rhetorical terms, he anticipates the transgression of metaphor which will revitalise old senses grown stale
through constriction and custom. When Lydia *does* arrive, his
greatest source of satisfaction is that she is a 'foreigner' (p. 67).
Until the revelation of that 'secret power', however, that 'invisible
connection' which will 'transfigure' them both, he remains 'frag-
mentary, something incomplete and subject' (pp. 74–5). The proposal scene enacts exactly such a tumultuous 'trespass', the
penetration of a circumscribed subject by the proliferation of
metaphorical attributes which almost obliterates him; in her 'gathering force and passion', she was 'thundering at him till he could
bear no more' (pp. 81–4). As agent of metaphor, it is she who initiates the movement of transfiguration which he at once fears and
desires. In this scene the dynamics of blocking and retreat around
which plot two revolves are inaugurated.

The blocking effect is highlighted in Tom's sustained 'self-thwarting', his resistance to Lydia's mobile transports and transfers, as she unfolds 'new as a flower that unsheathes itself and stands always ready', before it withdraws and slowly folds up once again (pp. 92–3). As Tom's resistance collapses, the final breakthrough is accomplished: 'he let go his hold on himself, he relinquished himself'. It is this which precipitates their entry into that 'inner space', inscribed in the figure, as they 'throw open the doors to each other', and pass into the 'further space' disclosed through this opening (pp. 132–3). In this space of 'transfiguration', Lydia's 'otherness' – the alien attributes of the metaphorical term – are absorbed and domesticated. Domestication is the trope around which the description is organised; the couple take possession of the house – their 'bower of bliss' – which their union produces and within which they feel enclosed and protected: 'When at last they had joined hands, the house was finished, and the Lord took up his abode' (p. 134).

The return to the world (plot three) is briefly enacted as those paradoxes which the space of retreat opened up are explored. In this world of the work, in this new order of reference, the 'deep structures of reality' are revealed to those 'who *dwell* in it for a while'.[35] In our text, these 'deep structures' are framed by the newly constructed figure (the house) which grounds and delimits them. Here the law of 'stereoscopic vision' typical of plot three is at its most benign. The Brangwen pair are at once free yet constrained, near yet remote, wholly absorbed in, without the need to think of, each other, both locating the destination towards which they are moving as the domestic site which they already inhabit (p. 134). Such paradoxes are all benevolent forms of traditional ontotheological discourse, which succeeding generations will sharpen into figures of irreconcilable division and difference.

III

The description of Anna's childhood (pp. 135–44) enacts her intensive contextualisation, her assimilation to the habitual rhythms of Marsh Farm, her gradual translation from initial 'changeling' (p. 69) into a literal native. Resistant to change from without, she becomes 'easy at home' on the farm (p. 138). In this manner she resumes the same rhetorical role as her father, that of the literal term firmly embedded in context, yet anticipating the intrusion of an alien element from without to revitalise and transform her. She too wants 'to get away' (p. 142), to transgress the bounds of the home which appears as a restrictive enclosure. With the arrival of Will, the strange, unpredictable outsider, plot one of the second generation is inaugurated.

From the start, Will is inscribed as a 'curious' and 'mysterious animal', an underground creature, dark and nocturnal (pp. 144–5), bearer of all the disruptive force of the metaphorical predicate (as subject term, Anna by contrast is associated with daylight and the known world of the farm). As such, Will possesses the same alien aura, an 'air of beyondness',[36] the same charismatic power to infiltrate and unsettle which Lydia possessed for Tom. His voice, for example, has that uncanny vibrancy 'which transport[s]her into his feeling'. His talk too exudes that strange remote reality which carried everything before it, 'and through which the bounds of her experience were transgressed' (pp. 151–2). Just as for the first generation, Lydia appeared as a rule-breaker, an unwitting violator of local exchange rules, so too Will violates long-established custom in Cossethay by singing too loudly in church, thereby reducing Anna to helpless confusion and laughter (pp. 148–9).

With the celebrated sheaf-gathering scene, plot two is initiated. In this elaborate space of suspense, of meeting and parting, exposure and veiling, giving and withholding, intimacy and distance, a calculated play of delay and deferral is staged. Here the blocking effect is inscribed in terms of the dialectic of advance and retreat which prevents the couple from coming together ('As he came, she drew away, as he drew away, she came. Were they never to meet?'). Through a subtle stitching and restitching of traces, the moonlit field is transformed from an initial stasis, the site of collapsed and immobile figures, where the sheaves lie like 'bodies prostrate in shadowy bulk', into a highly mobile textual space. As Will and Anna thread 'backwards and forwards like a shuttle across the strip of cleared stubble, weaving the long line of riding shocks', a dense textual space is created in which the couple locate their still centre. As this intricate dance of signifiers comes to an end, the space of retreat is disclosed. In this erotic plot the lovers at last encounter each other as Will 'overcome[s]', Anna with his kisses (p. 162). This decomposition of familiar reality, through which the quotidian world is eclipsed, reaches its apogee in the honeymoon scene. In this paradise, 'complete and beyond the touch of time or change', rhetorical and ontological force coincide.

Derrida once identified the two central modes through which metaphysic's 'infinite mastery' over the limits of being is ensured: in the mode of *envelopment,* the whole – the still centre – is stabilised as each lesser circle is enclosed in a greater one which contains and completes it: in the *hierarchical* mode, each particular part is subordinated to a general order or structure which determines its state or its status.[37] Around these two modes the ontological dimension of the relationship between Will and Anna is organised. In the timeless, ahistorical space which the lovers briefly inhabit, the concept of total envelopment has its base in the immobility and certitude which such a concept comports: 'Here at the centre the great wheel was motionless, centred upon itself. Here was a poised, unflawed stillness that was beyond time, because it remained the same, inexhaustible, unchanging, unexhausted.' Through the hierarchical mode, the range of vertiginous joys, the gradations of ecstasy, are delineated: 'Then gradually they were passed away from the supreme centre, down the circles of praise and joy and gladness, further and further out ...' (p. 185). Yet, of course, this centre itself is illusory, self-destructing at the moment its contours are mapped, and 'real', chronological time – the strokes of the church bell – breaks in and dismantles its structures. In this retreat or withdrawal, the senses opened up in the 'bower' encounter the harsh world of the work to which the lovers return. The law of 'stereoscopic vision' – typical of plot three – becomes the new law of relationship.

Instead of the lovers achieving a fluid exchange of identities, the 'two in one' of the Lawrentian union, Will retains his status as the failed metaphorical term which lacks essential connection, while Anna retains hers as the literal term which resists transformation; in the text's own characterisation, they remain 'opposites, not complements' (p. 210). Anna clings to her familiar, separate self, while Will, though embracing the 'unknown' connotations of the metaphorical term, is unable to circumscribe them or articulate them in a way which makes sense to Anna. Recognising the rhetorical dimension, one critic pin-points their dilemma: Anna is defined by a 'literal approach', and Will by a symbolic one, while both refuse to see their 'complementary connection'.[38] In this struggle for supremacy, literal and figurative senses subvert and destroy one another. Two central scenes allegorise this rhetorical tension.

In the first, Will reads the 'yellow figure of the lamb' in the stained-glass church window as pure metaphorical affirmation; he was 'in correspondence with the creature', investing it with the power to transfigure both him and his surroundings. By contrast, Anna reads the lamb-figure literally, refusing to recognise it as 'more than it appeared': 'Whatever it means, it's a *lamb*' (pp. 200–2). In this clash of interpretative modes, metaphor functions as one hermeneutic type among others, one which – as Will's defensive posture underscores – needs special justification in the face of the incisive literal thrust which would 'emasculate' and undo it.

The changing of water into wine at the wedding feast at Cana provides the context for the second collision. For Anna, 'historical fact' precludes the possibility of such radical transmogrifications: how could, she implies, a transparent, literal term become an opaque, indeterminate one (wine)? Compelled by the logic of the literal, Will at first doubts the possibility of such a type of transfer: could water 'depart from its being and at hap-hazard take on another being?' In the end, he chooses to live 'as if the water *had* turned into wine' (pp. 212–14), in the mode of the split vision or the 'consciously false' to which he makes an 'experimental assent'.[39]

Like a trope that is dormant or dead, Will submits to Anna: 'The lion lay down with the lamb in him' (p. 233). In effect, Anna's naked dance in which she 'annuls' Will celebrates the triumph of literal sense. It exhibits what Derrida calls the 'proper nudity' of the literal term, the unadorned truth as 'presence without veil', without tropological disguise or concealment.[40] Her pregnancy, she implies, is a literal fact, requiring no figurative addition to augment or authenticate it (pp. 224–6).

Indeed the text's most eloquent celebration of metaphorical syntheses – those 'consummations' and 'ecstasies' which Lincoln cathedral induces in Will – is staged at precisely the point at which such infinitist aspirations are dismantled, taken apart from within. Will's 'transports', his drive towards an absolute fusion, are destructed, reduced by those 'wicked' faces in stone, the sly little gargoyles who jeer 'their mockery of the Absolute'.[41] At one level, they represent the literal 'is not', the excluded domain – the many things that had been 'left out of the great concept of the church' – yet which inhabit the space that rejects them. At another, they generate a subtle incitement to narrative, those simple, sequential plots of domestic division and difference which Anna invents ('nice man'/'shrewish woman') and which the great gothic arches negate.

This space of maximum metaphorical force is undermined by a literal difference, which reduces the 'absolute, containing all heaven and earth' to a 'shapely heap of dead matter' (pp. 244–7). As Will later comes to perceive them, gothic arches assert only 'the broken desire of mankind' (p. 280).

IV

From the start, Ursula is identified as a powerful metaphorical force, interested both in transforming herself and inducing transformation in others. Even as a girl, she rejects the literal Jesus of the revivalist groups – he was 'just a man' – in favour of the remote, luminous figure whom she invents, 'the non-literal application of the scriptures', as the text puts it (pp. 319–22). In so doing, she resumes the same rhetorical role as her father, with the resurrection into life – the reconstruction of revitalised senses upon the ruins of the old literal ones – as her master-trope (p. 326). With the intrusion of the foreign Skrebensky into the claustrophobic enclosure of Cossethay, plot one of the third generation is inaugurated.

Like Lydia, he too has a mysterious past, an unknown, unaccountable one, since, as an orphan, he found his real home in the army. Like Lydia and Will before him, he carries 'a strong sense of the outer world ... of distances and large masses of humanity' (pp. 335, 338), which fascinates Ursula. Crucially, however, and unlike the other two strangers, Skrebensky bears none of the affirmative force of the metaphorical predicate. From the start, he represents an immutable literal term, isolated, 'self-contained, self-supporting', 'fatally established' beyond change or question; he is thus a non-entity who did 'not ask to be rendered before he could exist, before he could have a relationship with another person' (p. 337). As Daleski puts it, 'he has no real identity'.[42] Skrebensky will suffer the rhetorical fate – catachresis – of an entity which has no sign of its own. As his engagements with Ursula show, he is a character without a proper or distinctive sign. As a consequence, the 'bower of bliss' to which they retire is transformed into a theatre of cruelty.

Before they retire there, however, the blocking effect is inscribed as they challenge each other in a prolonged and competitive kissing 'game', before Ursula puts forward 'her maximum self' and overcomes Skrebensky (pp. 348–9). As the latter gives way, this 'collapse' of the literal term precipitates their entry into the space of retreat. In effect Ursula's first significant love encounter with Skrebensky enacts the violent inscription of her sign on a space that is fundamentally empty. Instead of intimate interpenetrations and transports, plot two is the *mise en scène* of a destructive catachresis.

Traditionally catachresis has been defined as 'the violent, forced, abusive inscription of a sign, the imposition of a sign upon a meaning which did not yet have its own proper sign in language'[43] – the intrusion of a sign to fill a lexical gap or lacuna. In so doing, it violates the rules of semantic exchange upon which the conventional transfers of metaphor are based. No longer predicated on the basis of a shared resemblance or likeness, this 'abuse of language'[44] dismembers the figures and texture of language. Such a dismemberment is staged when – at the end of the moonlit dance – Skrebensky wraps his dark cloak about Ursula and leads her away (p. 365).

In this space of retreat, corrosive metaphors – ones designed to obliterate rather than augment their referents – appear for the first time in the text. Ursula's hands are transformed into cutting machines – 'like metal blades of destruction ... to lay hold of him and tear him and make him into nothing' – and her psyche into the kind of chemical acid – 'fierce, corrosive, seething' – which infiltrates and 'annihilates' him (pp. 366, 368). These metaphors narrate the plot of their own destructive attributes, as they first incise and then obliterate the entity to which they refer. Just as catachresis incises its sign on a space that is void, so too Ursula's hands 'triumphantly' inscribe her desire for destruction, the mark of her abusive will, upon a site which has no meaning of its own. Skrebensky is disclosed as a 'nothingness'; there was 'no core to him' (pp. 368, 369). From this point on, he is, so to speak, a marked man, ripe for final annihilation.

But the violence of catachresis may, through familiarity, repetition and usage, decline into the state of non-tensional metaphor: it becomes a cliché or idiom.[45] Exactly such a decline is enacted in the lovers' relationship when, on Skrebensky's return from abroad, they both enter the space of 'darkness', where all tension between them dissolves. Troped variously as 'darkness cleaving to darkness', or as the 'one fecund nucleus of fluid darkness' which binds them together, or as 'the dark fields of immortality' which both briefly attain, the undifferentiated medium of darkness embraces them both (pp. 497, 502). This represents at once the plot of collapsed metaphor, which lacks sufficient tension to revitalise meaning, *and* of a rhetorical incest, the encounter of two separate subjects within the homogeneous confines of identity. If in the plot of catachresis, one figure takes over a space which is sufficient for two, *this* plot fuses two figures into a space sufficient for one. It turns on a near-incestuous coupling, the ceaseless return of the same which precludes variation or difference. It is precisely this sense of invariance which compels Ursula to break out of her claustrophobic confinement – 'she must be gone' (p. 507) – and seek release in the novelty and strangeness of places – London, Rouen, Oxford, the Downs, London. Instead of that enlargement of sense and sensation which such detours should comport, this circular journey revolves on a further return of the same: they feel 'the first sense of the death towards which they were wandering' (p. 507). When they do separate out, Skrebensky re-emerges as a cipher without content, an empty semantic space upon which Ursula can impose her own mark. The scene is set for their final cataclysmic encounter.

Like the moonlit scenario, this too is constituted as a violent, catachrestic enactment. First, Ursula 'clinche[s] hold' on Skrebensky, 'tightening' her grip on him, as if he were already unconscious – a blank entity – awaiting the surgical knife. Then, with her 'beaked, harpy's kiss' – that cuts and castrates – she incises her absolute sign on him. If, as she later perceives it (p. 546), she created Skrebensky out of nothing, this death-mark returns him to the state from which he began. He gives way 'as if dead', feeling as if 'the knife were being pushed into his already dead body' (pp. 531–2).[46]

Out of this catachrestic extremity, plot three emerges as the antithetical play between opposites – creation/destruction, stability/anarchy, reality/illusion – Ursula's 'stereoscopic vision' which vacillates between old forms and new structures, discarded and projected meanings, enclosure and freedom. With Skrebensky's departure for India, however, the dynamics of the trope/narrative connection alter significantly. From this point to the end, metaphor no longer projects plots of specifically *human* relationships – those interactions between characters around which our three plot structures have crystallised – but of a primordial and eschatological type. In the two final scenarios – involving the horses and rainbow configurations – a new order of plotting emerges, through which those equivocations and paradoxes which articulated the human dimension are subjugated to an annunciatory and revelatory force. The full 'vehemence' of the metaphorical 'is' – its self-authenticating and affirmatory power – is asserted over against the literal 'is not' which would infiltrate and subvert it. As a consequence, familiar literal elements (such as horses and rainbows) are recharged with significance, becoming portentous, strange and uncanny. In this process, metaphor 'triumphs' absolutely. It does so in two distinct modes; in the first (the episode of the horses) it meta-figures its own secret operations as knot is transformed into plot; in the second (the rainbow configuration), it delivers a message, a plot of predestination, the prophecy of a brave new world to come.

The horses first make their appearance as a 'powerfully, heavy knot' in the text – the metaphorical knot out of which the plot of Ursula's nightmarish encounter unravels. Three times this knot of horses unloosens, radiating out in concentric circles which have Ursula as their nucleus, before they contract and enclose her again. Here the hidden movement of metaphorical predication is mimed, as senses proliferate centrifugally, releasing fresh connotations, before they close up again, condensing to form new knots of meaning. In this process, the intimate knot/plot connection is dramatised. Each 'swerve' of the trope, so to speak, generates fresh twists in the narrative. In unpicking knots, the reader constructs the plot of Ursula's ordeal, the 'turns' and returns of its crises, as tensions mount and subside (pp. 540–2).

The twin-arcs of the rainbow in turn span the arch of the sky. As such it is paradigmatic of those 'vertical' plots which synthesise and unite (in contrast to those 'horizontal' plots which distribute their units along a sequential axis). It announces a mystery, a transcendental enigma, just at the point – as the text moves towards its close – at which functional plots are busy clearing mysteries up. This master-plot for the future casts its long shadow over events in the text – the flood at Marsh Farm, for example – which precede it; it draws different temporal perspectives together. Through this new world, 'built up in a living fabric of Truth', the narrative of eschatological renovation, of a past revivified in a radiant future, is unfolded. In this realignment of origins and ends, structure and meaning, form and content, traditional sequential plots are transvalued. The mastery of metaphor – its power to predict and predetermine – is asserted (p. 548).

And yet this mastery is itself illusory, based, as it is, on a simple strategic consideration – the rainbow's privileged location at the text's point of closure. It turns on a sleight by means of which contending interpretations within the same text are excluded. The narrator retains sovereign hermeneutic control; he alone determines what the rainbow means, as he unveils the plot tied up in the knot. In splendid isolation, the rainbow overarches those plots of human relationships – fragile, vulnerable, always subject to deterioration – which have been the special concern of this essay. Because of its strategic location, it remains free from subversive interpretations which, in transmitting the message, subtly diminish its force. Yet inevitably subversive readings soon circulate, emerging of necessity from outside the text. One of the most compelling of these comes paradoxically from the narrator himself. Perhaps nowhere is the possibility of the absolute 'Truth' which the rainbow announces subjected to such sustained and strenuous scrutiny as in the sister volume *Women in Love*.

From *South Central Review*, 6 : 1 (Spring 1989), 46–61.

Notes

[Gerald Doherty starts his essay by distinguishing between two kinds of plot, one which involves the solving of mystery and the other which is the fulfilment of a prophecy. The former plot, which he relates to metonymy, is characterised by the unfolding of meaning through time whereas the latter, which he relates to metaphor, is characterised by similarities between its different elements so that its meanings are present simultaneously. Doherty then applies these different understandings of plot, saying that it is a mistake to claim, as Kermode did, that Lawrence abandoned plot; rather, it is more accurate to say that he abandoned one type of plot, the metonymic for another, the metaphoric. Doherty defines three types of metaphoric plot. The first involves the intrusion of a stranger into a settled community; the second recounts how one person reacts to the stranger, at first blocking his or her advances before surrendering to create a space of retreat. The third plot concerns how the couple emerge from this state having achieved a renewed sense of balance between the 'contradictory' qualities of the world such as identity and difference. Doherty shows how these three plots apply to each of the three couples in *The Rainbow*, pointing out that by the time we get to Anna and Skrebensky plot three is no longer functional. Indeed, their failure to create even a space of retreat results in metaphor, in the form of horses and the rainbow itself, being cut adrift from human relations and being transformed into a form of prophecy that resists subversive readings.

Doherty's article breaks with traditional criticism of Lawrence by its treatment of the novel in linguistic terms. He is not interested in the meaning of Lawrence's symbols but in how metaphor operates in his text, its exchanges, transformations and the resistances it encounters. This is all played out in the interaction of couples in the novel where one is always the literal and the other always the metaphoric term. All references to *The Rainbow* are from the Penguin edition (1978) and are given in parentheses in the text. Eds]

1. Frank Kermode, *Modern Essays* (Suffolk, 1971), pp. 177–81.

2. Ibid., p. 180.

3. Roland Barthes, *Image–Music–Text*, trans. Stephen Heath (Glasgow, 1979), pp. 91–3.

4. David Lodge, *The Modes of Modern Writing: Metaphor, Metonymy, and the Typology of Modern Literature* (London, 1979), pp. 161–3.

5. Patricia Dreshsel Tobin, *Time and the Novel: The Genealogical Imperative* (Princeton, NJ, 1978), p. 101.

6. These various operations of metaphor will be explored in greater depth in the course of the essay.

7. Tzvetan Todorov, for example, distinguishes between plots of causality – metonymic in type – and plots of predestination. These latter turn on the fulfilment of foretold events, and they contain no surprises. They are constituted through the same kind of symmetrical oppositions through which metaphor achieves its effects. See *The Poetics of Prose*, trans. Richard Howard (Oxford, 1977), pp. 64–5.

8. Quoted from Jacques Derrida, *Margins of Philosophy*, trans. Alan Bass (Sussex, 1982), p. 217.

9. Seymour Chatman, *Story and Discourse: Narrative Structure in Fiction and Film* (Ithaca, NY, 1978), p. 88: Todorov, *Poetics* p. 22.

10. Hayden White, *Metahistory: The Historical Imagination* in *Nineteenth-Century Europe* (Baltimore and London, 1973), pp. 45–80; *Tropics of Discourse: Essays in Cultural Criticism* (Baltimore and London, 1985), pp. 197–217, 230–60. See also James M. Mellard, *Doing Tropology: Analysis of Narrative Discourse* (Urbana, IL, 1987), pp. 1–36.

11. Paul de Man, 'The Epistemology of Metaphor', in *On Metaphor*, ed. Sheldon Sacks (Chicago, 1979), pp. 11–28; Derrida, *Margins*, pp. 243, 270.

12. J. Hillis Miller, for example, has shown that the human relations in Goethe's *The Elective Affinities* – a story of marriage and adultery – are dramatisations of those analogies of proportion upon which Aristotle based his theory of metaphor; see 'A "Buchstabliches" Reading of *The Elective Affinities*', *Glyph*, 6 (1979), 1–23. In an essay entitled 'The Secret Plot of Metaphor: Rhetorical Designs in John Fowles's *The French Lieutenant's Woman*', *Paragraph*, 9 (1987), 49–68, I show that the Fowles novel conforms to the same tripartite plot structure as outlined in the present essay.

13. Patricia Parker, 'The Metaphorical Plot', *Metaphor: Problems and Perspectives*, ed. David S. Miall (Sussex, 1982) pp. 133–57.

14. Paul Ricoeur, *'The Rule of Metaphor': Multi-Disciplinary Studies* of *the Creation of Meaning in Language* (London, 1978), p. 21.

15. Paul Ricoeur, 'The Metaphorical Process as Cognition, Imagination, and Feeling', in *On Metaphor*, ed. Sacks, p. 143.

16. Parker, 'The Metaphorical Plot', pp. 137–42.

17. In the Fowles essay, I outline some of these variations, p. 63.

18. Terence Hawkes, *Metaphor* (London, 1972), p. 43.

19. Ricoeur, 'The Metaphorical Process', p. 143.

20. Max Black, *Models and Metaphors: Studies in Language and Philosophy* (Ithaca, NY, 1966), pp. 25,47; 'More about Metaphor', in *Metaphor and Thought*, ed. Andrew Ortony (Cambridge, 1980), pp. 19–43; Monroe C. Beardsley, *Aesthetics* (New York, 1958), pp. 134–47; Nelson Goodman, *Languages of Art: An Approach to a Theory of Symbols* (Indianapolis, 1976), pp. 68–95; I. A. Richards, *The Philosophy of Rhetoric* (New York, 1936), pp. 93–120.

21. Goodman, *Languages*, p. 69.

22. Ricoeur, *Rule*, p. 230.

23. Gerard Genette, *Figures of Literary Discourse*, trans. Alan Sheridan (New York, 1982), p. 49; Ricoeur, 'The Metaphorical Process', p. 145.

24. Ricoeur, *Rule*, p. 247.

25. Northrop Frye, *Anatomy of Criticism: Four Essays* (New York, 1970), p. 124.

26. Frank Kermode, *Lawrence* (Suffolk, 1973), p. 43.

27. Parker, 'The Metaphorical Plot', p. 151.

28. Ricoeur, *Rule*, p. 255.

29. As in plot three of the Will/Anna relationship, these narratives act out the rivalry between literal and figurative interpretations.

30. The term 'vehemence' communicates the power of the metaphorical statement to redescribe the world. Since, however, it is undercut by the presence of the literal 'is not' within the statement, this power is neither simple nor absolute. Metaphorical affirmation thus participates in its opposite, which challenges and qualifies its hegemony.

31. Derrida, *Margins*, p. 243.

32. D. H. Lawrence, *The Rainbow* (Harmondsworth, 1978).

33. Kermode, *Lawrence*, p. 43.

34. Michael L. Ross, ' "More or Less a Sequel": Continuity and Discontinuity in Lawrence's Brangwensaga', *The D. H. Lawrence Review*, 14 (1971), 269.

35. Ricoeur, 'The Metaphorical Process', p. 151.

36. Robert Langbaum, *The Mysteries of Identity* (New York, 1977), p. 310.

37. Derrida, *Margins*, XIX–XX.

38. Jeffrey Meyers, '*The Rainbow* and Fra Angelico', *The D. H. Lawrence Review*, 7 (1974), 142–3.

39. Frank Kermode, *The Sense of an Ending: Studies in the Theory of Fiction* (London, 1977), pp. 39–40.

40. Derrida, *Margins*, pp. 241, 270.

41. D. H. Lawrence, *Phoenix: The Posthumous Papers of D. H. Lawrence*, ed. Edward D. McDonald (Harmondsworth, 1978), p. 454.

42. H. M. Daleski, *The Forked Flame: A Study of D. H. Lawrence* (London, 1967), p. 109.

43. Quoted from Derrida, *Margins* p. 255, where Derrida is summarising Fontanier's analysis of catachresis in his *Supplement to the Theory of Tropes*. Derrida goes on to make the point that in catachresis there is no substitution, 'no transport of proper signs, but rather the irruptive extension of a sign proper to an idea, a meaning, deprived of their signifier' (p. 255).

44. Paul de Man, 'The Epistemology of Metaphor', in *On Metaphor*, ed. Sacks, p. 19.

45. As in the *leg* or *arm* of the chair, where the italicised words have no metaphorical force, but function as commonplace literal terms.

46. Ursula's affair with Winifred Inger offers a rich complication of the three plot structures, which we can briefly outline. Since their relationship is based on a transgression, a deviation from, and disruption of, the sexual 'norm' (p. 170), it conforms closely to the type of plot one. Plot two in turn centres on scenes of rhetorical 'incest', the lovers' homogeneous at-one-ness within the undifferentiated confines of the water – the swimming pool and the lake – where their intimacy is played out, and where they lose their identities and 'fuse into one'. The break-up of their relationship (plot three) turns on a destructive catachresis, but one with a difference. Like Skrebensky, Winifred too is reduced to a cipher, a non-entity, the 'moist clay, that cleaves because it has no life of its own'. Upon this malleable site, however, Ursula refuses to imprint her sign. Instead she hands Winifred over to Tom, so that both may become marked with an identical sign – the 'abstraction' of the 'machine' which brands them both (*R*, pp. 383–400).

3

Strange Bedfellows: D. H. Lawrence and Feminist Psychoanalytic Theory in *The Rainbow*

JORGETTE MAUZERALL

Lawrence still has the reputation of being one of the arch male chauvinists of modern literature. This reputation, largely defined and established by Kate Millett in *Sexual Politics*,[1] is not totally undeserved, but I would argue that aspects of what we think of as Lawrence's sexism make him worth our attention, especially when they are examined under the new lens of feminist theory, in general, and feminist psychoanalytic theory in particular. Ironically, certain feminist theorists can find an ally in Lawrence. He represents, in clear terms, problems between the sexes that these theorists believe need addressing, and he emphasises aspects of human psychology neglected by traditional, male-dominated psychoanalytic theory.

My familiarity with this feminist approach to human psychology helped me understand why I, as a reader, was both drawn to and put off by Lawrence. This ambivalence is often shared by new readers of Lawrence, and I am convinced that they, like me, will find reading him a much richer and less frustrating experience if they begin with an understanding of feminist theory, specifically the branch represented by such writers as Dorothy Dinnerstein, Adrienne Rich, and the psychoanalytic theorist Nancy Chodorow.[2] In the following analysis I outline some important and relevant

61

aspects of this line of thinking and then indicate how these can be used to illuminate one of Lawrence's major novels, *The Rainbow* – although the implications of feminist psychoanalytic theory for any student of Lawrence extend far beyond this work.

Throughout Lawrence's work, the new reader encounters what at times seems an oppressive ideology of gender in which male and female are seen as binaries, complementary and polar opposites: the female principle, Lawrence tells us as early as *Study of Thomas Hardy*, represents the body, while the male principle represents spirit – although, as he also makes clear, 'the diversion into male and female is arbitrary, for the purpose of thought'. Since 'every man comprises male and female in his being [and] a woman like-wise consists in male, and female'.[3] In defence of Lawrence, he is only stating forthrightly a belief that saturates the Western cultural tradition: beginning with the Bible's story of Genesis (in which God grants Adam the power of naming but assigns Eve to give birth in pain to new bodies, to perpetuate the cycle of life and death until a male saviour redeems humankind from this organic process), through Aristotle's form-matter paradigm (Aristotle believed that in the process of reproduction: 'woman's part is ... entirely passive, the man's active; and she contributes only the matter, while he contributes the soul and the form'), right up to the recent populari-sation of this same gender binary by Camille Paglia.[4] All these accounts of the distinction between male and female function to keep women tied to the body while men are associated with spirit and the word, with cultural and intellectual pursuits, with that which transcends the body.

Where does this mutually reinforcing cluster of concepts origi-nate? Is there any truth here? Dinnerstein, Chodorow, and Rich, along with many other influential feminist theorists such as Julia Kristeva, Luce Irigaray, and Sherry Ortner, have explored the gendering of the body as female as well as the way that both the body and the female have been set in opposition to culture.[5] These theorists suggest that we can learn much about gender constructs by seeking their origins in the mother–child bond and the way that bond shapes our conceptions about women, men, and culture. As Dinnerstein points out, '[u]nder the arrangements that now prevail, a woman ... is the parental person ... who exists for the infant as the first representative of the flesh.'[6] Because she is the person 'around whom the ... ambiguous human attitude toward the flesh begins to be formed', through her we develop 'what will be a lifelong internal conflict ... between our rootedness in the body's acute, narrow joys and vicissitudes and our commitment to larger-scale human concerns, in other words, to culture'.[7] According to Dinnerstein, this conflict shows up cross-culturally: 'People under the most diverse cultural conditions seem to feel an ... antagonism, between what is humanly noble, durable, strenuous, and the insistent rule of the flesh ... which is going to die.'[8] If one sex can bear the burden of the body – its pleasures and pains – then the other can more easily be thought of as transcending the body.

If we recognise the pervasiveness of this attitude toward culture, of the effort to transcend the (female) body through (male) cultural achievement, then Lawrence's theories about male and female can be seen as a reflection of larger cultural attitudes. Anne Fernihough, in her introduction to the Penguin Cambridge University Press *Rainbow*, observes that many writers of Lawrence's time saw 'the educated "new Woman" [as] a symptom of degeneration'.[9] Lawrence and his contemporaries were familiar with theories of cultural decay that saw decadence specifically as the blurring of lines between male and female. According to the theory, a woman who took on ' "masculine" qualities ... by seeking access to higher education and the professions, was taken to be a sign of reversion to degeneracy, just as the male who showed signs of "effeminacy" was seen to be regressive'.[10] Lawrence, then, is far from unique in his fascination with and at times anxiety over the move away from life in the body and toward education by 'new women' such as Ursula in *The Rainbow* or even the artist Gudrun in *Women in Love*. *The Rainbow*, therefore, can be seen to illuminate anxieties found in the work of other modern authors and in the culture at large.

Also, with respect to *The Rainbow*, Fernihough cites the theories of Irigaray to account for the gendering that goes on as the novel details the emerging modern individual. According to Irigaray, Fernihough explains, 'the drive towards individual identity entails a repression of the mother ... In order to be a subject, the child must separate from the mother's body and repress all connection with it'; therefore 'the search for perfect, detached selfhood as the goal of evolution is based on an implicit erasure of the female body', and this search can be found 'implicit' in 'the evolutionary theories of the late nineteenth and twentieth centuries'.[11] As Fernihough also observes, the 'apparent paradox, whereby women signify both development and decline, is responsible for many of the interpretative difficulties posed by *The Rainbow*'.[12] Lawrence here set out to write a book based on his lived experience with Frieda Lawrence, her sister Else Jaffe, and other women he knew. The novel was to be about 'woman becoming individual. Self-responsible, taking her own initiative'[13] and Lawrence's sense of the state of women he knew was so strong and sympathetic, his own talent for observation and depiction so brilliant that he created female characters, such as Ursula and Gudrun, who compel our identification and sympathy. The narratives in which these characters move, however, show the women at times as threatening – both to the men in their lives and to the culture at large.

Feminist psychoanalytic theory also helps account for another aspect of Lawrence's work that often baffles readers new to Lawrence: the deeply irrational and powerful emotions felt by both female and male characters in the novels. Traditional psychoanalytic theory is based on a concept of evolving subjectivity in which the individual moves from oneness with the maternal toward greater rationality, distinction, and autonomy. The connection with the original caregiver is seen as something to escape and to leave behind, unexamined. As Coppélia Kahn has said of Freud, his 'matrophobia takes the form of a nearly lifelong reluctance to confront the child's, especially the male child's, early and close relationship to his mother'.[14] For Freud, she argues, 'identification with the mother' is ' "the unknown" ... not because it is unknowable but because he is a man, because manhood as patriarchal culture creates it depends on denying ... the powerful ambivalence that the mother inspires'.[15]

In Lawrence's work, however, we find a deep and penetrating exploration of this ambivalence. Feminist psychoanalytic theory again helps here as a way of illuminating Lawrence's vision of the relationship between men and women. Jessica Benjamin says, for instance, that thanks to Freud we now know 'that the foundation of erotic life lies in infancy'; that is, 'adult sexual love is not only shaped by the events dating from that period of intense intimacy and dependency, it is also an opportunity to re-enact and work out the conflicts that began there'.[16] We need to recognise that '[w]here the site of control and abandon is the body, the demands of the infant self are most visible'.[17] Moreover, this body and the conflicts it arouses are specifically associated with the female because, as Kahn explains, 'a woman is the first significant other through whom both girls and boys realise [their own] subjectivity'.[18] At the same time, though, 'women in general become charged with the ambivalence of fear and desire' because, in the early stage of development, the infant does not 'recognise that the mother exists or has interests apart from it'.[19] All that she provides or facilitates is perceived as an extension of its will; all that she denies is seen as incomprehensible betrayal. Therefore, according to this theory, 'the mother, and all women perceived in her shadow, are tainted with the grandiose expectations and bitter disappointments of a necessarily alienated subjectivity'.[20]

Dinnerstein elaborates on the causes of the infant's extreme emotional response to its initial caregiver: 'because it is immobile longer and at the same time very much brighter, [the child] has a capacity for feeling powerless unlike that of any other baby animal'.[21] Therefore, for this vulnerable infant, especially one raised in the tight nuclear family of Western cultures, the mother represents 'the centre of everything the infant wants ..., fears losing and feels threatened by'.[22] Or, as Nancy Chodorow puts it, since 'mothers have exclusive responsibility for infants who are totally dependent, then to the infant they are the source of all good and evil'.[23]

With this picture of the deepest level of the psyche, we may begin to appreciate why Lawrence's work disturbs readers so much: it deals with what I would suggest is a culturally constructed yet psychologically real fantasy of 'Woman'. Lawrence reminds us of the body and its power over our emotions and taps precisely those repressed, deeply irrational fears and desires that adult readers have spent a lifetime trying to overcome and to forget. Yet it seems clear that adulthood will remain driven by the irrational as long as we refuse to grasp the nature and persistent power of irrational impulses – those that (because of traditional child-rearing practices) stem from early experiences with the maternal body. It is, then, in his focus on gender, the body, and emotion that Lawrence can offer such profound and useful insights.

In *The Rainbow* Lawrence consciously tried to get at the 'carbon' – to reach the depths of the psyche.[24] The character of Tom Brangwen deserves our special attention because of his unique status in the novel. He is depicted in mythical terms – as larger than life, a being of the past linked to the unconscious, to deep psychic levels. Tom also stands out in *The Rainbow* and in the Lawrence canon as, I would argue, the most positive major male character the author ever created. The others, from Rupert Birkin, of *Women in Love*, to Lady Chatterley's gamekeeper, Mellors, are men of the present, the walking wounded, who reflect the damage that Lawrence believed the twentieth century had inflicted on men. Tom, in contrast, is one of the imagined men of the past, before the sexual fall that Lawrence maintained had occurred in modern life. But the portrait of this most 'healthy' and whole of men, Lawrence's prelapsarian Adam, reveals some disturbing cracks. Cursed with a sort of original sin, Tom contains inner psychological fissures that will widen in later generations of men in this novel, in *Women in Love*, and in the works that follow. Since Tom represents the past on which Lawrence quite consciously built the present time of his future novels, we can better understand all of Lawrence's male characters when we carefully analyse this patriarch's inner emotional stresses. I contend that what I call the labour scene throws most light on these stresses. Here Lawrence demonstrates the awesome power of the *magna mater* – both its threat and its attraction – its hold on both Tom and his stepdaughter, Anna. Focusing on this scene effectively can help us see the profound psychological insights found in much of Lawrence's work.

The labour scene has typically been called the barn scene. Critics have tended to linger in the barn – the place where Tom Brangwen moves toward a secure assumption of fatherly authority – but a focus on the barn ignores the crucial relation between what happens there and the events that both precede and follow, thus stressing the man's success at becoming a father rather than the striking resemblance of his state to the child's. A better understanding can be gained of Lawrence's psychological insights, particularly in *The Rainbow* and in *Women in Love*, by attending to the equivalence of man and girl, rather than to his achievement of a state beyond hers.

During the course of his marriage, Tom is disturbed by the frequent crying of Anna at her mother's absences. He thinks, 'There was something heartrending about Anna's crying, her childish anguish seemed so utter and so timeless, as if it were a thing of all the ages' (pp. 65–6). The powerful effect on Tom of Anna's weeping seems connected to his own particular torment, his anxious fear that his wife might leave. 'Was she here for ever?' he asks himself. 'Any moment, she might be gone', he believes: 'he could never quite ... be at peace, because she might go away' (p. 58). There is a childlike simplicity and insecurity in these nagging thoughts. They represent the kinds of fears that plague young children, who are completely dependent on adult support yet without rational understanding of adult life's complexities –

precisely the same kinds of obsessive thoughts that overwhelm Anna in the labour scene.

Lawrence presents in this scene the moment at which the woman is simultaneously mother and antimother – in the process of bearing one child while withdrawing support and recognition from another. In becoming a mother, Lydia becomes unavailable as nurturer to both her husband and her older child as they realise that the support and attention of the woman Tom calls 'the mother' will not always be there. A panic that has been anticipated by Tom's feelings toward the withdrawn, pregnant Lydia overwhelms Anna, who now goes through what resonates as a primal scene: the child's first cataclysmic experience of loss, of helpless abandonment and subsequent violation, of extreme psychic pain. But in Anna's cries for the absent Lydia, her hysterical repetition of 'I want my mother', and her refusal to respond to Tom's voice, Tom recognises the embodiment of his own fears – as well as a symbol of their cause. Having just returned from Lydia, Tom is 'white to the gills' because in her labour pain she can barely recognise him (p. 72). Now Anna, too, denies him recognition – precisely because she shares his state: neither can reach Lydia.

In the image of a tiny girl, then, Tom sees the uncanny reflection of his own deepest anxieties, and, as the ordeal grinds on, the mirror effect persists. Anna cannot stop her nerve-shredding, sobbing chant; and though Tom tries to be rational, to distract her – calmly telling the child to undress for bed – the wailing goes on, and her emotions finally overwhelm his own. 'He crossed over the room, aware only of the maddening sobbing' (p. 73). As Anna stands 'stiff', overpowered, 'violated', Tom forces off her clothing: 'her body catch[es] in a convulsive sob. But he too was blind, and intent, irritated into mechanical action ... unaware of anything but the irritation of her' (ibid.). Reflecting Anna's lack of control, Tom's own mindless, mechanical irritation indicates the deep resonance within him of the child's cries. The image of Anna is more than the man can stand, as she becomes, in a sense, an icon of infant despair, the thing itself:

> The child was now incapable of understanding, she had become a little, mechanical thing of fixed will. She wept, her body convulsed, her voice repeating the same cry ... She stood, with fixed, blind will, resistant, a small, convulsed, unchangeable thing weeping ever and repeating the same phrase ... Unheeding, uncaring ... alone, her

hands shut and half lifted, her face, all tears, raised and blind. And
through the sobbing and choking came the broken:
'I – want – my – mother.'

(pp. 73–4)

It should be that Lawrence does much more here than describe a
childish tantrum. The authorial respect accorded this event is
striking. Rarely does such a scene receive a novelist's attention, let
alone such powerful and emphatic rendering. Earlier Tom called
this 'childish anguish' 'utter' and 'timeless' – 'a thing of all the ages'
(p. 66). Here again Anna is presented as archetypal or iconic – a
'living statue of grief' (p. 74). The words used to describe her insist
that we read Anna's experience, and likewise Tom's response to it,
as deeply symbolic. What begins as a realistic representation of a
childhood tantrum transforms into something far more profound.
As the focus shifts from Tom to Anna, the narrative emphasises her
solitude, her powerfully blind will, the singleness of her wish and
the immutability of her state. In her belief that only one thing can
satisfy her, Anna becomes before our eyes a kind of prisoner in a
world of absolute lack. But, significantly, her feelings are shared
by the adult Tom, produced by the same cause: the woman's
indifference.

In Tom's impulse to take Anna outside through darkness and a
downpour to the barn, Lawrence continues to demonstrate a kind
of intuitive knowledge of ideas now set forth by feminist psychoanalytic theory. After being enclosed within the house, trapped with
the mother in labour, after the monomaniacal shrieks of Anna for
the one answer, the man and girl break out into another world; but
importantly, Anna and Tom do not just undergo separation. A
move toward autonomy, but they also make a comforting movement toward a new kind of union. Both becoming caretakers of the
maternal in themselves, as they symbolically feed cows, animals
that are themselves sources of nourishment. Held by her father in
the rhythm of the feeding pattern, Anna finds an alternative world
of comfort, sustenance, and security. 'Motherness' can be found in
unexpected places. Tom, likewise, recovers the maternal as he
discovers it within himself, caring for both child and animals.

It is significant that 'motherness' here is connected to sensuous
experience, rather than to any words spoken between the two
characters. Tom's verbal, authoritarian efforts to reach Anna fail.
In the house, Anna uses language in a futile attempt to articulate

her lack, but the barn experience – the recovery of the maternal – for man and child is deeply rhythmic and physical, resonating at a level beneath articulation. This sensuously rhythmic experience apparently speaks to some deep need in both of them, replaces what they lacked, what they have left behind in the house. Lawrence's depiction of the barn experience, I would suggest, corresponds to what Kristeva describes as 'the irruption within language of the anteriority of language'.[25] Because early child-rearing is almost always carried out by a female, usually the mother, the pre-linguistic state is associated with her. In this scene, although ostensibly the mother has been left behind, Tom and Anna appear to have stumbled into what Kristeva calls the 'archaic, instinctual, and maternal territory'.[26] Significantly, Lawrence does not present this experience as regressive. If anything, the man and girl seem to circle back in order to move forward.

Lawrence here may be on to something important. Laurence Lerner has specifically noted the honesty, power, and insight of the labour scene, crediting Lawrence's 'willingness to say only what he knows, rendering the emotion even if the psychology is guess-work'.[27] The guesswork in the scene, in fact, again shares much with current feminist psychoanalytic theory which has in various ways pointed to the original bond with the mother – established before the child's entry into the symbolic system of language – as the irrational, repressed, unexplored, and undervalued substructure of consciousness. In the labour scene, as I have noted, Lawrence grants serious attention both to the mother–child relationship and to the pre-verbal, evoking the power of each as he continues to emphasise the connection between early childhood experience and adult behaviour.

The parallels between the adult Tom and the child Anna continue throughout the scene. They both sink into a comforting state of unconscious union and then return to the house – the girl to be settled into the very bed that belonged to Tom as a child. Then, when he hears his wife in labour, she sounds 'not human, at least to a man.' 'A great, scalding peace went over him' when he looks in on her and is forced to recognise her otherness: 'He had a dread of her as she lay there. What had she to do with him? She was other than himself' (p. 77). Yet Tom still retains the old insecurities, and they will persist throughout his life. Years later, reverberations of the labour scene continue when Tom looks toward the barn through another driving rain to see Anna embracing her future mate. Tom becomes 'blackly and furiously miserable', remembering 'the child he had carried out at night into the barn'. 'She was going away', he thinks, 'to leave an unendurable emptiness in him, a void that he could not bear' (pp. 111–12).We recall his former thoughts about Lydia, his 'never [being] at peace, because she might go away'.

Apparently, though the barn experience powerfully affected Tom, it failed to transform him completely; thus, Lawrence indicates something important about male psychology in particular. In the future, Anna will never again manifest the sort of anxiety she experienced that night; however, in subsequent generations, as women in the novel move toward independence, the men become more and more desperate. Lawrence seemed to understand what feminist theorists maintain: that at the deepest psychological level, men need women more than women need men. In Tom's mirroring of Anna's behaviour, there is the suggestion that the fear of female abandonment may be more persistent in adult males. In fact, although men and women share the experience of initial dependence on the mother, men are pressured earlier and more completely to separate from her and thus may have more repressed anxiety about female abandonment as well as a less rational image of woman's power. For this reason men seek refuge from women in activity separate from them, thus finding a 'sanctuary from the impact of women ... in which they can recuperate from the temptation to give way to ferocious, voracious dependence, and recover their feelings of competence, autonomy, dignity'.[28]

If this theory has validity, then we begin to understand why subsequent generations of male characters in the novel become more and more dependent on women toward whom they feel increasing hostility and fear. In Will Brangwen, the man of the second generation with few meaningful outlets beyond his wife, Anna, we see a maddened version of the elder Tom's dependency. The 'only tangible, secure thing was the woman. He could leave her only for another woman', but '[a]nother woman would be a woman ... *Why* was she the all ... why must he sink if he were detached from her?' (p. 173). Anton Skrebensky, of the third generation, fares worst, and his horrific breakdown in a public place is an excellent scene to contrast with the labour scene. When Ursula says that she will never be his, Anton's reaction uncannily mirrors Anna's in the labour scene. We see the same viscerally physical response, the same blindness and lack of control – all brought on by confrontation with the fact of a woman's unattainability: his 'head made a queer motion, the chin jerked back against the throat, the curious, crowing, hiccupping sound came again, his face twisted like insanity, and he was crying ... blind and twisted as if something were broken which kept him in control.' Like Anna's, Anton's emotions are gut wrenching, welling up apparently from some primal source, beyond his power to stop. And, as in the depiction of Anna, the 'living statue of grief', the rendering here goes beyond the merely realistic and personal, approaching the iconic: he weeps 'uncontrollably, noiselessly, with his face twisted *like a mask*, contorted and the tears running down the amazing grooves in his cheeks'; he goes on '[b]lindly, his face always this horrible working *mask*' (my emphasis). As Tom attempted to comfort Anna, so Ursula in this scene tells Anton, 'It's not necessary.' But, again like Anna, Skrebensky 'could not gain control of his face ... weeping violently, as if automatically. His will, his knowledge had nothing to do with it' (p. 433). Echoes of the labour scene, then, resonate from the beginning to the end of *The Rainbow*. The difference here, however, is that this last man finds no comfort – the growing strength and independence of the woman over the course of three generations, Lawrence implies, leave this modern man totally abandoned and helpless.

To look at *The Rainbow* as I have outlined would avoid much of the confused and troubled response to the novel typical of much Lawrence criticism. A study by David Holbrook, *Where D. H. Lawrence Was Wrong about Woman*, is a case in point. This critic sums up the labour scene as depicting Tom's 'tormented concern for his wife, and his urge to distract the child from her anxious need for her mother'.[29] Such a view, I would suggest, contributes to this critic's final assessment of the marital portrait of Tom and Lydia as 'superb and completely realised' compared with Lawrence's subsequent renderings of relationships that, Holbrook contends, leave the reader 'bewildered'.[30] He suggests, 'To most readers ... the turbulent and seething relationship between Will and Anna comes as a surprise', and admits: 'After many readings, I still find it hard to see what goes wrong between Skrebensky and Ursula'.[31] Of *The Rainbow* Holbrook says that 'some of [its] deepest turbulence ... feels extraneous and seems not, in some way, inevitable to the novel'.[32] And he repeatedly asks such questions as 'What are the sources of such turbulence and dread?'[33]

I would suggest that Lawrence's depiction of the source of male psychic development in the novel, as manifested in the patriarch

Tom and particularly in the labour scene, goes a long way toward answering Holbrook's question. When Lawrence attempts to get at the psychic core, he does not hesitate to look into the infant's heart of darkness, even though what he discovers there certainly challenges the culturally constructed image of powerful male autonomy. The events of *The Rainbow*, as well as those of Lawrence's subsequent novels, affirm that irrational, early childhood experience profoundly affects the responses of adult men to women. The deep psychic layers revealed in the labour scene can help us understand Lawrence's depiction of brooding, defensive men in subsequent novels, men who manifest irrational emotional extremes proclaim their omnipotence and their distinction from the women in their lives.

Lawrence was in many ways wrong about women, but, I would argue, he was usually right about 'Woman' – the powerful psychological construct shaped by early childhood experiences – and particularly about this construct's impact on men. Rich has said of the female's bearing and parenting children: 'We carry the imprint of this experience for life, even into our dying. Yet there has been a strange lack of material to help us understand and use it.'[34] She goes further, contending that we must recognise the initial dependency of the male child on woman and the subsequent results of that dependency. In *The Rainbow* and throughout his work, it would seem Lawrence provides recognition of, as well as profound insight into, this much-neglected and crucial aspect of human life.

From Elizabeth M. Sargent and Garry Watson (eds), *Approaches to Teaching the Works of D. H. Lawrence* (2001), pp. 89–98.

Notes

[Like Elizabeth Fox and Liang-ya Liou, Jorgette Mauzerall also confronts the problem of Lawrence for feminist critics, but she differs from them in seeing him as a possible ally rather than an enemy. Mauzerall's focus is Lawrence's understanding of the relationship between the mother and child which she believes corresponds to a number of feminist views on the subject. This relationship, she says, is the foundation of gender differences which identify males with the mind and females with the body. The child has to separate from its mother in order to become an individual. An essential part of this process is the repression of the mother's body which for males is more complete than for females and hence more traumatic. Mauzerall argues that this repression not only alienates males from their own bodies but it also lays the foundations of a life-long fear that women will abandon them. She applies this analysis to Tom Brangwen's anxiety that Lydia will leave him and compares it to Anna's crying the night her mother goes into labour. The mother's absence, however, draws Tom and Anna together and in the barn, feeding the animals, they become 'caretakers of the maternal'. What is more, they enter, momentarily, that pre-linguistic state that feminists see as characterising the relation to the mother. The fact that Anna later is able to separate herself from her mother stands in direct contrast to Skrebensky's breakdown when Ursula tells him she does not want to marry him. This underlines how men are more dependent on women than women are on men, which in turn accounts for male hostility to female independence in both *The Rainbow* and *Women in Love*.

Mauzerall offers a largely psychoanalytic account of the aversion to female autonomy in both these novels and in doing so recuperates Lawrence for at least one strand of feminist thinking. All references to *The Rainbow* are from the Penguin edition, edited by Mark Kinkead-Weekes, introduction by Anne Fernihough (1995), and are given in parentheses in the text. Eds]

1. Kate Millet, *Sexual Politics* (London, 1977).

2. Dorothy Dinnerstein, *The Mermaid and the Minotaur: Sexual Arrangements and Human Malaise* (New York, 1976); Adrienne Rich, *Of Woman Born: Motherhood as Experience and Institution* (New York, 1977); Nancy Chodorow, *The Reproduction of Mothering: Psychoanalysis and the Sociology of Gender* (Berkeley, CA, 1978), and *Feminism and Psychoanalytic Theory* (New Haven, CT, 1989).

3. D. H. Lawrence, *Study of Thomas Hardy and Other Essays*, ed. Bruce Steele (Cambridge, 1985), pp. 60, 94.

4. Margaret Homans, *Bearing the Word: Language and Female Experience in Nineteenth-Century Women's Writing* (Chicago, 1986), p. 154; Camille Paglia, *Sexual Personae: Art and Decadence from Nefertiti to Emily Dickinson* (New York, 1991).

5. See Chodorow, *Reproduction of Mothering*, also Rich, *Of Woman Born*, Julia Kristeva, *Desire in Language: A Semiotic Approach to Literature and Art*, ed. Leon S. Roudiez, trans. Thomas Gora, Alice Jardine, and Leon S. Roudiez (New York, 1980); Luce Irigaray, *Speculum of the Other Woman*, trans. Gillian C. Gill (Ithaca, NY, 1985); Sherry Ortner, 'Is Female to Male as Nature is to Culture?' in *Woman, Culture, and Society*, ed. Michelle Zimbalist Rosalda and Louise Lamphere (Stanford, CA, 1974) pp. 67–87.

6. Dinnerstein, *The Mermaid and the Minotaur*, p. 35.

7. Ibid., p. 29.

8. Ibid., p. 126.

9. D. H. Lawrence, *The Rainbow*, edited by Mark Kinkead-Weekes and with an introduction and notes by Anne Fernihough (Harmondsworth, 1995), p. xvi.

10. Fernihough, 'Introduction', p. xvii.

11. Ibid., pp. xxv–xxvi.

12. Ibid., p. xvi.

13. D. H. Lawrence, *Letters 2: 1913–16*, ed. George J. Zytaruk and James T. Bolton (Cambridge, 1979–93), p. 165.

14. Coppélia Kahn, 'The Hand That Rocks the Cradle: Recent Gender Theories and Their Implications', in *The (M)other Tongue: Essays in Feminist Psychoanalysis Interpretation*, ed. Shirley Nelson Garner et al. (Ithaca, NY, 1985), pp. 72–88, p. 79.

15. Ibid., p. 88.

16. Jessica Benjamin, *The Bonds of Love: Psychoanalysis, Feminism, and the Problem of Domination* (New York, 1988), p. 51.

17. Ibid.

18. Kahn, 'The Hand That Rocks the Cradle', p. 73.

19. Ibid.

20. Ibid., pp. 73–4.

21. Dinnerstein, *The Mermaid and the Minotaur*, p. 33.

22. Ibid., p. 93.

23. Chodorow, *Feminism and Psychoanalytic Theory*, p. 90.

24. Lawrence, *Letters 2*, p. 184.

25. Kristeva, *Desire in Language*, p. 32.

26. Ibid., p. 136.

27. Laurence Lerner, *The Truthtellers: Jane Austen, George Eliot and D. H. Lawrence* (New York, 1967), pp. 78–9.

28. Dinnerstein, *The Mermaid and the Minotaur*, pp. 66–7.

29. David Holbrook, *Where D. H. Lawrence Was Wrong about Woman* (Cranbury, NJ, 1992), p. 137.

30. Ibid., p. 138.

31. Ibid., p. 162.

32. Ibid., p. 137.

33. Ibid., p. 140.

34. Rich, *Of Woman Born*, p. xiii.

4

Closure and Foreclosure in *The Rainbow*

ELIZABETH FOX

Introduction

In the final chapter of *The Rainbow*, Ursula Brangwen's decision to become Anton Skrebensky's wife thwarts her earlier quest for what Lawrence elsewhere calls 'pure independent being'.[1] The resolution to 'ask no more than to rest in [his] shelter all [her] life' (p. 449), as she puts it in a letter to Anton, forecloses the attempt to take responsibility for her own life and her own desires that makes her such a compelling protagonist. In this everyday sense of foreclosure, the decision to marry Anton precludes Ursula's goals for herself and, it is worth noting, Lawrence's goal of showing woman becoming 'individual, self-responsible, taking her own initiative'.[2] While Ursula reneges on the specific marriage to Anton, the chapter confronts her with a compelling crescendo of external forces that makes her strenuously reject any extramarital initiative; further, she celebrates the repudiation. Entitled 'The Rainbow', this chapter builds through an intense sequence of events, carefully examining Ursula's responses, towards the climactic vision of the eponymous rainbow. This 'New Covenant' strives to unite the book's 'theology of marriage', its biblical language, and a poetic and analytic style that attempts to go 'a sub-stratum deeper than ... anybody has ever gone'.[3] Ursula's wish that 'vision translate itself into week-day terms' (p. 264) continues her parents' and grandparents' search for connection with the 'infinite world' (p. 77) and the Absolute (her father's and grandfather's experience, respectively). As she stipulates, 'that which one cannot experience in daily life is not true for oneself' (p. 263). The recuperation of 'the Sunday world' of religion (seen earlier as 'a tale, a myth, an illusion' (p. 263) in the final vision of a rainbow attempts to resolve thematic as well as characterological and technical issues all at once; yet it eclipses the plot of taking 'responsibility of one's own life' (p. 263). The ending fails, then, to pursue the New Woman plot that most of the novel anticipates or develops; moreover, the crisis triggered in closure reveals a psychotic textual process present in a number of Lawrence's works. The psychoanalytic sense of foreclosure provides an explanation of the shutting down of alternate possibilities and, indeed, of the ability to symbolise.

The dramatic sequence of events, the biblical references, and Ursula's embrace of a new reality resemble a religious conversion experience. However, the procreative catalyst for the conversion, along with a preliminary vegetative vision, the sexual as well as psycho-social valences of what seems at stake, plus Ursula's kaleidoscopic responses to her visionary experience, fit a pattern that puts into question the soundness of a religious interpretation. The last chapter starts with Ursula's return home after rejecting Anton, her shocked suspicion of her pregnancy, her conversion to belief in the rightness of marriage and motherhood, and an apologetic letter proposing that she and Anton marry, all on two pages (pp. 448–9). Waiting for his reply, one stormy afternoon she experiences a stampede of horses as a persecutory attack that puts her into a trance (p. 453). The dramatic sequence of events that follows includes her collapsing in a ditch; dragging herself home in a 'profound' and 'cold nausea' that 'plumb[s] the bottom' of her soul (p. 454); and succumbing to a delirium that produces both 'a sense of permanency' (p. 455) and a catechism of alienation. This epiphanic sequence culminates in the image of a germinating acorn, a vision that brings 'a new reality' and the sense that a 'new day had come on the earth' (p. 457). In another rapid series of events, her realisation that 'there would be no child' (p. 457) and Skrebensky's telegram, saying that he is married, trigger a repudiation of him and of 'her own desire' (p. 457). Picking up religious themes from her adolescent struggle with her 'passionate confusion between the vision world and the week-day world' (p. 266), these events leave a much-subdued Ursula awaiting marriage to a man 'from the Infinite' (p. 457), a description reminiscent of the earlier, biblical phrase, 'Son of God', that distinguishes Anton from a 'servile' 'son of Adam' (p. 271). Ultimately, Ursula bears witness to a rainbow that she interprets as connecting creeping, 'hard-scaled' man with a heavenly divinity (p. 458). The independent New Woman whom Ursula had shown such promise of becoming, fades to the point of disappearance: she devolves instead into being a Handmaiden of the Lord as an androcentric religious vision derails her and the book's pursuit of independence and self-responsibility. More than religious faith changes in this closure: the character loses her momentum toward independence; the text, its goal of showing her 'taking her own initiative'.[4]

Many critics have noted the gap between the optimism of the final paragraphs and the lack of support for it in events that precede it in the chapter.[5] For example, in *Time and the Novel*, Patricia Tobin argues the 'aesthetic unwisdom' of this combination of a female quest with a genealogical and patriarchal structure (p. 105).[6] In a recent introduction to the novel, Anne Fernihough uses post-Lacanian feminist theories to explain the double movement in the novel both toward independent identity and back toward a maternal-feminine.[7] Lacanian theory offers a fruitful explanation of the ending's 'grafted' feel, as well. In particular, Lacan's work on psychosis provides a way to read the dramatic events of the last chapter as evidence not only of Ursula's conversion or breakdown but also of a textual psychotic structure and of a psychotic episode triggered by pregnancy and associated questions of paternity. Lacan's notions of the specific mechanism of psychosis and of the psychotic's failure to gain secure entry to the Symbolic Order account for the text's displacement of its material from Ursula's consciousness to externalised visions and for the quick succession of these events; his analysis of pre-psychotic phenomena explains how pregnancy and issues of paternity trigger them. Both the elements and the sequence of this visionary ending fit the psychoanalytic definition of 'foreclosure', a repudiation of reality, and constitute a textual process of psychosis that accounts for the controversial gap. While character and novel exhibit moments of psychotic process, I take the text as a more valid object of analysis, because of its inclusiveness and ability to chart a character's departure from expectations. To avoid analysing the author (who is unavailable for such work) or merely the character, I use Peter Brooks' sense in *Reading for the Plot* of the text as autonomous psychic structure and system of energies, desires, and conflicts.[8] In this approach, analysis of generic conventions and inconsistencies in the plot reveals psychic structures.[9]

Delusion as a patch

Freud's work provides a foundation for Lacan's *Seminar III: The Psychoses (1955–56)*.[10] In 'The Ego and The Id' (1924), Freud describes delusion as being 'found applied like a patch over the place where originally a rent had appeared in the ego's relation to the external world'.[11] Whether as (non-Lacanian) symbolic vision, hallucinated wish-fulfilment, or psychotic delusion, the final rainbow similarly bridges the gap between the life Ursula finds around her and the promise of 'the earth's new architecture ... the world built up in a living fabric of Truth, fitting to the over-arching heaven' (p. 459). The rainbow omits her from this fabric – she remains at best a sibyl gifted with prophetic vision of men's future, at worst a vehicle excluded from this androcentric vision of connection with divine Truth. With its accelerated and implausible move from a focus on Ursula as protagonist to its conversion of her to sibyl or mere textual register, this closure all too visibly joins the edges of a New Woman plot to a traditional marriage plot and a patriarchal genealogy. To wit, the New Woman relinquishes her pursuit of independence and her own desire and returns to an acceptance of the limitations of traditional marriage and a strikingly submissive role. Most significantly, the understanding of Ursula's subjectivity, developed from the middle of the novel, suddenly is occluded in ways that render her remarkably like a 'barren form of bygone living' (p. 458), a phrase describing the old world. As such, she is capable of neither visionary creation, non-consuming procreation, nor eloquent testimony, but only of passive witness to new, male-valenced 'germination' (p. 459). (The image alone speaks an unusual sense of procreation.)

Psychosis

In 'The Neuro-Psychoses of Defence' (1894) and 'Further Remarks on the Neuro-Psychoses of Defence' (1895), Freud argues that 'in the case of hallucinatory confusion' a defensive conflict against sexuality triggers a 'rejection (*verwerfen*) of an idea from consciousness'.[12] The stampede of horses, the delirious vision of a sprouting acorn, the pre-vision of the Sons of God, and the vision of the rainbow all resemble this hallucinatory confusion and spring from Ursula's belief that she is pregnant. In the case of 'The Psychotic Dr. Schreber' (1911), Freud finds the withdrawal of libidinal cathexes by the ego to be crucial, as he does in 'On Narcissism' (1914).[13] Such withdrawal of cathexis appears when Ursula says that she does not value love; her reiterated claim of not caring whether she either loves or not or has love or not (p. 440) also suggests libidinal withdrawal. In the second topographical (or structural) model, Freud sees psychosis as a rupture between ego and reality, with the id first triumphing over reality and then, in a second phase, directing the ego's reconstruction of a new reality. In effect, the id takes the reins, displacing the ego as rider. In similar fashion, Ursula first succumbs to fevered delirium; then, after she deplores the colliers' dead eyes and horny scales, Ursula's envisioning of a new religious order and an earth that fits heaven fulfils her wishes but departs from reality. (Here it is important to stress that the id directing this vision 'belongs' to the text, not to a character [Ursula has never before evidenced enthusiasm for such a submissive, mainly procreative role]; author [who is neither fully represented by the text nor available]; or reader. In fact, Ursula seems at this point to be psychically lobotomised, at least as a New Woman.)

In *The Psychoses*, Lacan elaborates upon Freud's idea of foreclosure as the mechanism specific to delusion and links it to the failure of a subject to symbolise the Mother's lack, the step in which the paternal metaphor replaces the Mother with words. Resorting to language inscribes the subject in the Symbolic Order and brings the unconscious to life. The usefulness of this theory lies in its account of a crucial relation to a paternal metaphor – a Name-of-the-Father that secures an individual's place in language, family, and society – and in its attention to linguistic phenomena. Lacan also describes the flow and arrest of signifiers triggered by a failure to symbolise paternity.

The Rainbow as cascade

As she reconsiders her decision not to marry Anton, Ursula speaks of the moon, elsewhere in Lawrence a symbol of the Magna Mater.[14] Using the moon to represent self-sufficiency or union with the Mother, Ursula recants her wish to have 'the moon in [her] keeping' (p. 449): 'She had been wrong, she had been arrogant and wicked, wanting that other thing, that fantastic freedom, that illusory, conceited fulfilment' (p. 448). Here the moon, the 'other thing', 'fantastic freedom', and 'illusory conceited fulfilment' parallel the denial of castration; as Lacan views it, castration is no literal or concrete event, but a fundamental condition, a 'lack of being'. To deny castration, then, is to cling to the illusion of oneness with the mother, of being the fulfilment of her desire, and hence to avoid the separation, splitting, and constitution as a subject in language that come with recognition of one's failure to satisfy the mother's (or any other's) desire. In a surprising move (given her earlier repudiation of Anna and her 'limited life of herded domesticity' [p. 329]), Ursula turns to her mother as a model. First, she chides herself for her earlier ambitions for independence: 'Who was she to be wanting some fantastic fulfilment in her life? Was it not enough that she had her man, her children, her place of shelter under the sun? Was it not enough, as it had been enough for her mother? She would marry and love her husband and fill her place simply. That was the ideal. ... Her mother was right, profoundly right' (pp. 448–9).

Pledging to be a 'dutiful wife, and to serve [Anton] in all things' (p. 449), Ursula embraces the necessity to submit and considers her letter to him a 'document' worth presenting 'at the Judgment Day' (p. 449), as if it not only recommends but also vindicates her. Her letter (or the mood that produces it) has the additional immediate effect of transforming her (and the text's) sense of herself, as she adopts a self-abnegating definition of womanhood: 'For what had a woman but to submit? What was her flesh but for childbearing, her strength for her children and her husband, the giver of life? At last she was a woman' (p. 450). This passage of interior monologue can be read in terms of the concerns of the character, the implied author, and the text as a psychic system. Taken as Ursula's voice alone, this passage marks her submission to patriarchal and religious orders in which marriage and maternity are destiny. Read as a comment by the implied author, the lines resign her to Milton's depiction of Eve, a vine wound around the stronger, tree-like Adam. As a fulfilment of a textual quest for New Womanhood (or ungendered self-responsible initiative), however, the lines reveal a seriously miscarried independence. This woman is not yet a subject, but still an object. Given the language of her vow and the difficulties with Anton, the relief we feel when the marriage she envisions proves impossible is justified. At first, her escape seems to be a revision of the heterosexual marriage plot like those Rachel Blau Du Plessis identifies in *Writing Beyond the Ending*.[15] Instead of completing the plot of female quest, however, the attempt of the textual psychotic structure to install her in ordered systems (here marriage and religion) gathers momentum.

The obstacle for the text's championing of Ursula's independence is her and the text's synchronised belief that she is pregnant, which she envisions as martyrdom and violation: she imagines being tied to the stake, swooning. The shock also sets off a series of questions in the text that echo the concerns that Lacan identifies in the pre-psychotic phase. Lacan defines pre-psychosis as 'the feeling that one has come to the edge of a hole. ... the question comes ... from where there is no signifier, when it's a hole, a lack, that makes itself felt as such'.[16] Ursula wonders, 'What was she doing? Was she bearing a child? Bearing a child? To what?' (p. 448). While Ursula questions what kind of world she might bear the child into, she also asks who (or worse, what) fathered the child. Like a hinge, this question serves to join the concerns of character and text. While 'the heaviness of her heart pressed and pressed into [Ursula's] consciousness' (p. 448), the weight of these questions pushes to the surface some of the text's concerns, too, to reveal the psychic structure of a textual 'puppeteer' (to anthropomorphise the textual system of energies, conflicts, and desires) manipulating Ursula. The shock of pregnancy makes Ursula stumble in her search for self-responsibility; the resulting questions ventriloquise a textual concern different from (perhaps deeper than) the pursuit of female independence; having travelled to the vertiginous edge of Ursula's ability to signify, character and text detour from female quest and into psychosis.

The possible pregnancy unleashes both questions about paternity and identity and events of persecution, illness, and vision in what Lacan beautifully calls a psychotic 'cascade'.[17] The term echoes Freud's use of fluid dynamics: 'It is the lack of the Name-of-the-Father in that place which, by the hole that it opens up in the signified, sets off the cascade of reshapings of the signifier from which the increasing disaster of the imaginary proceeds, to the point at which the level is reached at which signifier and signified are stabilised in the delusional metaphor.'[18] This use of the term 'cascade' proves an especially apt and elegant term, one that captures the rush of images in the penultimate and last chapters. As channel for textual energies, desire, and conflicts – and therefore as medium – Ursula 'bears' this slippage of signifiers as she might a pregnancy. The passage also proposes a 'disaster point' at which a delusional metaphor stabilises the flow of reshaped signifiers.

The pattern of approach to an edge, followed by a cascade and then stabilisation, fits the closure of *The Rainbow*. Ursula's pregnancy and the underlying question of paternity and relation to a Name-of-the-Father (mediating agent between an infant or subject and its mother)[19] trigger a 'cascade' of reshapings of the signifier at several points; yet at key moments in the last chapter delusional metaphors of germination temporarily 'stabilise' signifier and signified. Lacan says that without a way to symbolise castration (or deracination) as both the prohibition on possessing the mother and the recognition of lack, 'an original and chronic state of self-insufficiency',[20] the individual risks a psychotic episode. Such an episode is 'a mode of delirious experience of reality, a reality devoid of any truly symbolic dimension'.[21] The horses that stampede Ursula, for instance, can suggest general or male aggression but lack specific meaning; so does her consciousness of being a stone. The plot of female quest stalls when the text is content to leave Ursula an object instead of a subject of desire and responsibility. The text converts her into a Handmaiden, a final passive position of witnessing and waiting, receptive and subject *to* a future mate, not subject *of* her own. Ursula's failure to incorporate the notion of fatherhood, is an inability to fully transform her(self) into a questing subject. In *The Psychoses*, Lacan proposes that the lack of a certain number of *points de capiton*, or attachment points, between signified and signifier to secure the subject (if only by illusion) from the constant slippage of language, produces psychosis (pp. 268–9).[22] Further, as the epitome of such an anchoring or quilting point, the paternal metaphor, substitution of the Name of the Father for the desire of the Mother or a redress of losses, is a fundamental metaphor; its incorporation requires the subject to relinquish the fantasy of sufficiency for the mother and to acknowledge that she desires more than her child. The absence of the paternal metaphor and of the very process of metaphoric substitution through language can produce psychosis.[23] The question becomes, then, what phenomena distinguish this failure of subjectivisation.

The re-emergence of signifiers in hallucination

For Lacan, foreclosure is a 'specific mechanism ... [of] expulsion of a fundamental "signifier" ... from the subject's symbolic universe'.[24] Two features distinguish foreclosure from repression: a failure to integrate foreclosed signifiers into the unconscious; and instead of a return from the inside, a 're-emerge[nce], rather, in "the Real", particularly through the phenomenon of hallucination'.[25] Ursula's and the text's stagings (in hallucinatory images) of father-hood as a threat to self-sufficiency reveal the failed integration behind the re-emergence of these signifiers. While these hallucina-tions might be read as representing Ursula's breakdown alone, the overall departure of the ending from conventions of female quest and the resort to a visionary and patriarchal solution constitute evidence of a wider textual breakdown.

The theme of limited agency unifies a series of hallucinatory moments in Ursula's and the text's delirium. The persecutory stampede of the horses restages the submission described in the letter at another level without resolving the conflict; instead, the incident pushes Ursula into a 'trance' (p. 453) accompanied by 'a bluish, iridescent flash surrounding a hollow of darkness. ... large as a halo of lightning' (p. 452). Ursula feels 'seized by lightning' (p. 452), 'thundered upon', and 'conquered' (p. 453) as if subject to an eroticised divine power. She escapes this scene but does so without interpreting it, and (more importantly) without narration that does, and falls 'like a stone, unconscious, unchanging, unchangeable, ... *and passive*' (my italics, p. 454). When she revives during two weeks of delirium, she wonders, 'Could she not have a child of herself? ... Why must she be bound, aching and cramped with the bondage, to Skrebensky and Skrebensky's world?' (p. 455). In answer, the narration offers as her limitation the 'compression [of] Anton and Anton's world' (p. 456). In Lacanian terms, the limitation of sexual difference, of psychic castration or lack, radically prevents a subject from ever being able to satisfy the (m)other and, hence, the self. To apply Lacan's idea of castration to the question of Ursula's 'bondage', Anton's role as paternal agent constrains the illusion of self-sufficiency.

Nothing less than her identity weighs in the balance during this fevered soul-sickness. Ursula complains that she has and wants no place in society: 'I have no father nor mother nor lover, I have no allocated place in the world of things, I do not belong to Beldover nor to Nottingham nor to England nor to this world, they none of them exist, I am trammelled and entangled in them, but they are all unreal. I must break out of it, like a nut from its shell which is an unreality' (p. 456). Like Schreber's fantasy of transformation into a woman, Ursula's sense of being a germinating nut captures her wish that the pregnancy were her own and not circumscribed by the 'unreal shell' of sexual, social and psychic limitation. Although Schreber's fantasy takes him explicitly across sexual and gender borders, Ursula's fantasy (and that of the textual system that animates her) implicitly forecloses the question of a paternal function as it bursts her image into 'the Real'. Both fail to symbolise their relation to the Name of the Father, although hallucinations show their attempted rewritings of this relation. Through foreclosure, a signifier appears externally, as a vision in 'the Real', when it is excluded from incorporation into the Symbolic Order of language.

In Ursula's case, the reshaped signifier stabilises the disorder precipitated by pregnancy. The image that soothes her feverish chant of dispossession and alienation – 'no father nor mother nor lover, ... no allocated place in the world' (p. 456) – is that of a 'naked clear kernel thrusting forth the clear, powerful shoot' (p. 456). Both shoot and kernel suggest the phallus, in Lacan's sense of a delusory signifier for satisfying the desire of the Other. (The kernel also suggests pregnancy, and the two together, a phallic mother.) Founding her future on the stability of this metaphor, Ursula falls into sleep. The hallucinated phallic power 'resolves' her pregnancy, having foreclosed into the external world the pregnancy that often triggers psychotic episodes. If the resulting miscarriage resolves Ursula's pregnancy (thereby evading her questions about paternity), the text fails to resolve female quest.

The 'cascade' of images, the multiplicity of signifiers for the signifieds of castration, pregnancy, and phallic maternity, signifies a failure of symbolisation in the necessity for repeated versions of mediating images. Here Ursula and the text remain in the Lacanian Imaginary (versus the Symbolic, the realm of culture, the unconscious, and language; or the Real, that which is impossible for the subject to symbolise), when she interprets the rainbow multiply. She sees it as not only a meterological effect of light on water droplets but as a covenant with heaven and a germination in the blood of the 'hard-scaled' people on the earth. For Ursula to know so much upon seeing the rainbow is either prophetic, psychotic, or – why not? – both. The multiplication of signifiers for a single signified fits Lemaire's use of Serge Leclaire's distinction 'between the delirious subject (paranoiac) and the schizophrenic'.[26] For a schizophrenic, 'all signifiers can be made to designate a single concept or signified'; the signified is not 'bound to any one signifier in a stable manner'.[27] In this situation, *all* signifiers (A, B, C, etc.) could designate a persecutor and the signified is not stably bound. In contrast, in delirious paranoia, 'a single signifier may designate any signified' and 'is not bound to one definite concept'.[28] Here, the persecutors could be interchangeable, or the rainbow could designate any, even mutually exclusive, meanings (a persecutor, an egg, redemption, etc.). Whether the signified or the signifier is not stably bound, confusion results.

Exemplifying delirious paranoia, Ursula 'knows' too much when she sees the rainbow (because she sees too many things in it): 'that sordid people who crept hard-scaled ... were living still, that the rainbow was in their blood and would quiver to life in their spirit, that they would cast off their horny covering of disintegration, that new, clean bodies would issue to a new germination, to a new growth' (pp. 458–9). Here the rainbow signifies several, not necessarily connected, claims: that reptilian people exist, that they carry internal promise, that such promise will lead to moulting of their hard-scaled exteriors, and that purified bodies will replace the scaly ones. Not only the strangeness of this interpretation but its movement through physical barriers and times to multiple meanings stamp this moment as delirious. The proliferation of readings of the rainbow, the fact that it can represent a new covenant, a woman's legs as she gives birth (as Tony Pinkney suggests[29]), an image of castration, marriage between Tom and Lydia or Anna and Will, or the final version of the arches and doorways that are important to all three generations of Brangwens, attests to the psychotic nature of narrative desire in the chapter.

Lacan traces the stages from initial appearance of pre-psychotic phenomena to a final state that situates Schreber as 'completely feminised' (*III*, p. 63).[30] In respect to *The Rainbow* it is *à propos* to ask Lacan's question about foreclosure, 'what has been rejected from within that appears without?'[31] The answer would be, a coerced submission conveys a deracination and a loss of quest that amount to an unsymbolised castration. Whereas Schreber imagines how nice it would be to be a woman, the text sacrifices Ursula's former active pursuit of agency and substitutes for it a Handmaiden passively awaiting a Son of God; an icon of traditional feminine, wifely, and Christian submission for a feisty New Woman protagonist, this constitutes a 'feminisation' equivalent to Schreber's fantasy of gender transformation, or castration. However, the masculinist vocabulary renders this parallel submission more confusing than it needs to be. We can correct for Freud's arbitrary alliance of active with masculine and passive with feminine by attending more to agency than sex or gender. What is removed is agency, not virility.

As Lacan states in discussing the failure to symbolise the paternal function, where it is impossible for the subject to assume 'the realisation of the signifier father at the symbolic level, he is left with the image the paternal function is reduced to'.[32] The image of the rainbow, and indeed the earlier cascade of hallucinatory images of the stampede of horses, the delirium, and the kernel serve as those images to which the paternal function is reduced. Sometimes, as with the rainbow, the image does more: '[it] initially adopts the sexualised function, without any need of any intermediary, an identification with the mother, or with anything else. The subject then adopts this intimidated position that we can observe in the fish or the lizard.'[33] The subject who cannot symbolise castration must, in Lacan's words, 'adopt compensation for it, at length, through a series of purely conformist identifications with characters who will give the feeling ... [of] what one has to do to be a man'.[34] In fact, Lawrence's works were increasingly to show this concern with masculinity.[35]

The rainbow culminates in a series of just such compensatory hallucinatory, delirious, and visionary experiences that Ursula takes as revelations. The insistent and concerted effort to gain meaning from these experiences, as well as their being addressed to Ursula, reveal a concern to patch over the problem of 'female quest'. Underneath this lies a more androcentric concern, one that emerges in the privileging of the male as life-giving Son of God, as the one to forge a relation with the divine. That Ursula's role is secondary and a placeholder for androcentric textual concerns explains some of the grafted feel of closure. Instead of the fulfilment of female quest, the ending offers a relinquishment of it and an abandonment of Ursula as desiring subject and protagonist. In effect, the text aborts the female initiative it and Ursula earlier pursue. This dehumanisation of the closure, a deracination of the protagonist's quest, signals the move into psychotic process. The text tries to separate itself from Ursula's breakdown, mainly by scapegoating her as too ambitious in attempting to usurp male prerogatives, but it cannot; Ursula functions as a fantasy of the text, a wish it attempts to fulfil. Her failure to realise independent subjectivity serves as an index for the text's failure to symbolise paternity. While the text recognises, to some extent, the problem of achieving subjectivity, it depicts the problem as Ursula's: if she would serve her role, the plot suggests, all would be well. The plot successfully presents the lives of the previous two generations, but it does so using couples. The plot breaks down when an individual, in particular a woman, aims at parenthood.

When is a rainbow just a rainbow?

At the end of The Psychoses, Lacan speaks of a rainbow of his own, representative of a meteor or any atmospheric event, as being 'the most inconsistent of that which can present itself to man'.[36] A rainbow is a fleeting concurrence of atmospheric phenomena but something we conjure by naming, something real and illusory, like the imaginary dialectic or mirror 'stage'. It exists, Lacan says, as an appearance yet is also our name and category for the appearance of iridised water. That is, what makes the rainbow exist for us is our naming it, our designating it a rainbow, an identifiable appearance with nothing 'hidden behind it'.[37]

In order for a primordial signifier (phallus) to be other than a meteor or atmospheric phenomenon, what must exist in the imaginary dialectic is a father, or metaphor for one, a representation or vehicle of the phallus. The paternal metaphor requires the substitution of the signifier Name-of-the-Father for another, the desire of the mother, and the disruption of the illusion of mother–child sufficiency; the paternal function, then, is fundamentally the process of substitution and metaphor (symbolisation and the entry into the Symbolic). Lacan calls his rainbow 'a spherical belt, able to be unfolded and refolded', like the imaginary dialectic in psychoanalysis: the mirror stage can and must occur repeatedly, an illusion of completion and constitution. Rainbow and mirroring are of the same kind, Lacan states: they are things that do not speak, that one does not speak to, that are only appearances, and are insubstantial, before the move into language and symbolisation. Lacan takes the rainbow and the meteor as exemplary of the signifying value that permits 'the most elementary utterance – That's it'[38] because the rainbow is illusory *and* real, somewhere and nowhere, something we locate by saying, 'that's it'. So, too, is the phallus an illusion of completion and constitution; something we locate by naming, not having or being. We may try to have or be it, but it evanesces.

The rainbow exists entirely in its appearance, like the imaginary relation between mother and child, with nothing behind it. As a third element, a father converts the meteor into the phallus by being a vehicle for the phallus, otherwise a 'wanderer' that is elsewhere than with the mother or the child. The father's function is to represent the vehicle of the phallus; the rainbow in the novel, similarly, reconstitutes and stabilises the inassimilable signifier of paternity that is otherwise foreclosed from the text. This visionary closure also excludes Ursula's New Womanhood. As Lemaire points out, 'the discourse of the delirious subject does not belong to his subjectivity, and the ego he describes does not coincide with it; it is other, an object'.[39] When Lacan states that the father 'is that which in the imaginary dialectic must exist in order for the phallus to be something other than a meteor',[40] he gestures toward a stabilising function absent from *The Rainbow*. This lack leaves its final vision elusive and makes the chapter's cascade of images a serial disintegration, a 'removal of the woof from the tapestry, which is known as a delusion'.[41]

From *D. H. Lawrence Review*, 27: 2–3 (1997–8), 197–215.

Notes

[Elizabeth Fox's essay is an example of psychoanalytic criticism. She focuses on the ending of *The Rainbow* which many critics have found unsatisfactory. Fox argues that Ursula's vision of the rainbow is a compensation for her failure to realise herself as an independent woman. Using the language of psychoanalysis, she describes it as a 'patch' that covers the rent between Ursula's ego and the world. She also compares it with Lacan's account of psychosis. This states that when a person suffers a severe psychic trauma their sense of identity is thrown into crisis and they are overwhelmed by a rush of ideas and images, what Lacan calls a 'cascade', which is finally stabilised by a 'delusional' metaphor which restores their sense of self. Fox maps this process onto the last pages of *The Rainbow*. Ursula's pregnancy compels her to question her identity, she feels threatened by horses and imagines herself a stone, but staves off this self-fragmentation not just by her vision of the rainbow but also by seeing herself as a nut in a shell. This last image introduces another dimension to Fox's interpretation of *The Rainbow*. Again drawing on Lacan, she argues that the metaphor of the kernel, with its 'powerful shoot', represents Ursula's desire to engender herself, to be her own father, and as such, it is a rejection of the system of patriarchy. However, we cannot read this in any radical way partly because Ursula ceases her quest for autonomy, settling instead for being a 'Handmaiden passively awaiting a Son of God'. The main reason why this image is not radical, though, is because it is a fusion of male and female elements; it therefore belongs to the imaginary rather than the symbolic realm. The imaginary is a state of plenitude where the child cannot differentiate between its own body and that of its mother's, where its own satisfactions are the mother's too. But the child must learn that it is a separate being and that it cannot satisfy the mother. The intervention of the father, whose law forbids such union with the mother, precipitates the child's entry into the symbolic, basically the system of language, where it learns that it is different from others and that its desires cannot ultimately be satisfied. However, it is only by entry into the symbolic that a child can gain a sense of self. Fox claims that Ursula's desire to be both male and female as evidenced by the image of the nut, and her identification with her mother after her affair with Anton ends, points to her regression to the imaginary, which seriously impedes her efforts to realise her female subjectivity. All references to *The Rainbow* are from the Penguin edition of the novel, edited by Mark Kinkead-Weekes, introduction by Anne Fernihough (1995) and are given in parentheses in the text. Eds]

1. D. H. Lawrence, *Fantasia of the Unconscious and Psychoanalysis and the Unconscious* (New York, 1977), p. 32.

2. D. H. Lawrence, *The Letters of D. H. Lawrence* (Gen. ed. James T. Boulton), 8 vols (New York, 1981), Vol. 2, p. 273.

3. In 'The Marble and the Statue', Mark Kinkead-Weekes calls the novel Lawrence's 'Bible', the place in which his 'theology of marriage ... is embodied, tested, and further explored imaginatively.' Lawrence's comment on what became 'The Insurrection of Miss Houghton' appears in the *Letters I*, 526. Mark Kinkead-Weekes, 'The Marble and the Statue', in *Twentieth-Century Interpretation of The Rainbow: A Collection of Critical Essays*, ed. Mark Kinkead-Weekes (Englewood Cliffs, NJ, 1971), p. 100.

4. Lawrence, *Letters 2*, p. 273.

5. Dennis Jackson, and Fleda Brown Jackson (eds), *Critical Essays on D. H. Lawrence* (Boston, 1988), name other problems addressed in criticism of *The Rainbow*: the scene with the horses, the method of characterisation, the techniques for expressing emotion, and the sexual politics of the novel.

6. Patricia Drechsler Tobin, *Time and the Novel: The Genealogical Imperative* (Princeton, NJ, 1978), p. 105.

7. *The Rainbow*, ed. Mark Kinkead-Weekes, intro. Anne Fernihough (New York, 1995), p. xxv.

8. Peter Brooks, *Reading for the Plot: Design and Intention in Narrative* (New York, 1985). Brooks sees a text as 'a system of internal energies and tensions, compulsions, resistances, and desires', p. xiv. I treat the finally published text, without analysing textual history.

9. D. A. Miller uses a similar strategy in *Narrative and Its Discontents*, a study of the conflict in the novels of Jane Austen, George Eliot, and Stendhal 'between the principles of production and the claims of closure to a resolved meaning' (p. xi). He argues that works of these three authors 'typify … the normal, the neurotic, and the perverse' and accounts for the absence of psychotic desire and other possibilities from this scheme by noting their absence from the traditional novel (p. 268).

10. Jacques Lacan, *The Seminars of Jacques Lacan: Book III The Psychoses 1955–56*, ed. Jacques-Alain Miller, trans. Russell Grigg (New York, 1993; Paris, 1981).

11. Sigmund Freud, 'The Ego and the Id', in Angela Richards (ed.), *On Metapsychology: The Theory of Psychoanalysis*, trans James Strachey (Harmondsworth, 1984), p. 365.

12. J. Laplanche and J. B. Pontalis, *The Language of Psycho-Analysis*, trans. Donald Nicholson-Smith (New York, 1973), p. 371.

13. Sigmund Freud, *Case Histories 2: 'Rat Man', Schreber, 'Wolf Man' 'Female Homosesexuality'*, ed. Angela Richards, trans James Strachey (Harmondsworth, 1979) and Freud, 'On Narcissim', in *On Metapsychology*.

14. In the chapter titled 'Man to Man' in *Women in Love*, for example, Birkin expresses aversion for the Magna Mater, p. 270. Most notably, in the 'Moony' chapter of the same novel, he curses Syria Dea, Asiatic Mother of the Gods, as he throws the dead 'husks of the flowers' and then stones at the image of the moon rippling on the water (p. 323).

15. Rachel Blau Du Plessis, *Writing Beyond the Ending: Narrative Strategies of Twentieth-Century Women Writers* (Bloomington, IN, 1985). Du Plessis analyses the ideology expressed and constructed in the conventions of romance, especially the limit to experience that marriage constitutes: 'the contradiction between love and quest in plots dealing with women … [and] an ending in which one part of that contradiction, usually quest or *Bildung*, is set aside or repressed, whether by marriage or by death' (pp. 3–4).

16. Lacan, *The Psychoses*, p. 202. In psychosis, Lacan states, 'the subject places outside what may stir up inside him the instinctual drive that he has to confront' (ibid., pp. 202–3).

17. Jacques Lacan, *Ecrits: A Selection*, trans. Alan Sheridan (New York, 1977), p. 217; (Paris, 1966), p. 202.

18. Ibid.

19. To accede to the Symbolic, to enter the Symbolic Order, requires recognising the Name of the Father, Lacan's concept for the importance or authority of the Other the mother desires, the third term that breaks the mirroring between subject and mother and alerts the child to something that s/he cannot be for the mother. This paternal metaphor is a function, not necessarily a real father, but a limit on the subject's ability to satisfy the mother.

20. Anika Lemaire, *Jacques Lacan*, trans. David Macey (Boston, 1977), p. 59.

21. Ibid., p. 245.

22. A *point de capiton* literally means an upholstery button, a device that secures a layer of fabric and a shifting mass of stuffing to a firm backing.

23. See Dylan Evans, *An Introductory Dictionary of Lacanian Psychoanalysis* (New York, 1996), for more details on *point de capiton*, paternal metaphor, and psychosis.

24. Laplanche and Pontlais, *Language of Psycho-Analysis*, p. 166.

25. Ibid.

26. Lemaire, *Lacan*, p. 236.

27. Ibid.

28. Ibid.

29. Tony Pinkney, *D. H. Lawrence and Modernism* (Iowa, 1990).

30. Lacan, *The Psychoses*, p. 63.

31. Ibid., p. 87.

32. Ibid., p. 204.

33. Ibid., p. 205.

34. Ibid.

35. Judith Ruderman, *D. H. Lawrence and the Devouring Mother: The Search for a Patriarchal Ideal of Leadership* (Durham, NC, 1984).

36. Lacan, *The Psychoses*, p. 317.

37. Ibid., p. 318.

38. Ibid.

39. Lemaire, *Lacan*, p. 237.

40. Lacan, *The Psychoses*, p. 319.

41. Ibid., p. 88.

5

The Discursive Formations of History in D. H. Lawrence's *The Rainbow*

ROBERT BURDEN

Introduction

History plays a major role in the critical reception of *The Rainbow* (1915). History as subject of the novel, the history of its reception, and more recently the history of its composition and genesis.[1] It is also much clearer now how important the life and ideas of Lawrence are to the meaning and significance of the fiction.[2] Biographical criticism has always played an important and controversial role in Lawrence studies; only now it no longer simply belongs to the biographism of an older literary criticism, despite the long after-life of such a practice in its more popular marketable forms.

The compositional history of *The Rainbow* – which as the introduction to the annotated Cambridge edition explains, now affects our reading of the novel – is the story of two novels. It includes what was to become *Women in Love*, but it also includes the writing of the 'Study of Thomas Hardy' where Lawrence attempts to clarify his religious ontology; plans for an alternative pacifist journal, *The Signature,* with Middleton Murry and Katherine

Mansfield; and a whole series of letters connecting *The Sisters I* and *II* (earlier versions of the two novels), the 'Hardy' study and the final version of *The Rainbow*, with his new life and the question of marriage to Frieda Weekley.

A history of *The Rainbow's* reception begins with its prosecution and suppression for alleged 'obscenity' on 13 November 1915 at Bow Street Magistrates' Court, London.[3] Publication by Methuen, 30 September 1915, was followed by certain reviews that were damning enough to alert the authorities by early November.[4] The novel was withdrawn from circulation, extant copies destroyed, and it only appeared again in a limited edition in 1920, with the American edition in 1924, and finally with the Secker edition in England in 1926 – eleven years after it was first published.[5] For a major new novel which was supposed to speak for the spiritual renewal of industrial England during the Great War, and for the onus of change to be firmly placed on the shoulders of the New Woman, its contemporary impact was for all the wrong reasons. By the time it was more widely available its *raison d'être* had largely been overtaken by history, and by Lawrence's own profound change of heart. In the 1920s he was no longer supporting the Women's Movement but instead stridently opposing it. *The Rainbow* would have to wait until the 1950s before the general revival of interest in Lawrence, twenty years after his death, would lead to a more serious appraisal of its significance, and a more fitting analysis and interpretation as literary criticism became less anecdotal and more formalist.

But it is history as the subject of the novel which will be our main concern in what follows. *The Rainbow* clearly marks its historical intention by a set of dates and references to the period from 1840 to 1905. It covers the coming of the industrial revolution to the Midlands, and the gradual erosion of rural England, represented by the constructions of the canal, the railway, and the coal mine; the changes in education, and the greater opportunities for women; the imperial history, with references to Khartoum, the Boer War, and the British rule in India. The novel also presents that history in its relation to the personal lives of the three generations of Brangwens. To a contemporary of Galsworthy whose *Forsyte Saga* promoted a popular genre, it is a family chronicle of a familiar kind.

The real historical reference and the family history are, however, complicated by their framing in the archetypal or mythic history of the Brangwens established in the opening pages. This complication led to the two dominant but opposed critical positions in the post-1945 reception of Lawrence. First, Leavis's 'essential English history', a forceful reading of English civilisation in 'spiritual' terms that is a cultural-ideological, mythic version of England's past, and one that is not unlike Lawrence's.[6] Second, history as apocalypse, a doom-laden vision of spiritual degeneration and the self-destruction of mankind prefigured in the real catastrophe of the First World War, yet supposedly leading to regeneration. This apocalyptic reading with its emphasis on the biblical reference in Lawrence was first proposed, *contra* Leavis's culturalist reading, by Kermode and revived by Fjagesund.[7]

In order to enable a constructive mediation between these different theories of history as the subject of the novel, we shall, in this paper, draw on the work of Michel Foucault.

Foucault, history and discourse

Instead of discussing the novel and history as discrete entities with history serving as background, context, or influence, as much of the critical reception has it, Foucault will enable us to problematise such static distinctions by turning the discussion towards discourse, thus keeping us close enough to the texts of fiction and history while seeing the traces of history in the discursive practices represented in the novel.

Not that there is a ready-made Foucauldian theory which can simply be applied to literature. He himself insisted, as Macey points out, 'that his texts were a toolkit to be used or discarded by anyone and not a catalogue of theoretical ideas implying some conceptual unity'.[8] In this spirit, we shall make use of Foucault's texts selectively and strategically as toolkits for radical re-readings of the relationship of *The Rainbow* to history.

The various readings in the reception of the novel have in their different ways argued for a relationship between the novel and history. What difference does Foucault make when he assumes that all texts represent history in their letter because they are constructed from the multiplicity of discourses in circulation? A 'discourse' in Foucault's sense is 'a set of rules about what you can and cannot say. It insists on the connections between language, politics, and social practice'.[9] If history is only accessible in textual form, Lawrence's novel, like any writing, is bounded by the discourses contemporary with them, including what counted as history.

Foucault has been appropriately described as a postmodern historian.[10] History consists of a series of practices, deriving from discourses which the historian analyses in the available texts of a period. Thus the dominant way of seeing and understanding defines what is taken as a given or a priori in the knowledges and the practices of a given historical period. This includes the subject. Subjects are produced by discourses: the hysteric and the hypochondriac are subject-positions in the psychiatric discourse of the nineteenth century; the primitive savage and the enlightened humanist are subject-positions in the discourse of western imperialism in the late nineteenth century.

Foucault researches the 'archive', and aims to make explicit the set of rules which define:

1. what has been designated as discourse and thus constitutes the limits of what can be said;
2. what discourses or statements were put into circulation, and what was repressed or censored;
3. what counted as memory – how the past was being understood;
4. what discourses from the past, or from other cultures are retained or imported or reconstituted;
5. what classes, groups, or individuals have access to discourses, which ones are institutionalised, and which have been appropriated by force.[11]

Foucault's historicity, as we can see from these principles of historical analysis, prioritises discourse, because history consists of the reading of texts.

What are the discourses which make up the historical archive of Lawrence's text? We shall claim, in what follows, that *The Rainbow* consists of a plurality of discourses, none of which are original, but some of which exist in contradictory tension at different levels, thus characterising modernist writing as unstable.

The plurality of discourses in *The Rainbow*

The myth of origins

The opening pages of *The Rainbow* are a classic instance of the myth of an origin which then represents both a genealogy and the formation of a discourse. The genealogy is that of the Brangwens;

the discourse, a complex redeployment of the Old Testament Genesis story, and a Georgic pastoral poem to represent an image of Lawrence's ideal of a pre-industrial Golden Age when man was at one with the natural world. The writing has a 'genuine archaic and ritualistic force',[12] because it is 'saturated in scripture'.[13] The style represents the rhythm of the seasons, the work of the men on the land and the succession of the generations, in its paratactic structure, reinforcing an iterative truth that will reappear at key moments in the novel, either thematically or figuratively. The ancient narrative that opens the modern novel insists on the recurrent patterns of nature and the generations of Brangwens. It also presents a much older, cyclical theory of history whose conservative force will be used to counter that other, modern theory of history as linear, teleological, and progressive. However, the two histories will be linked causally by a third history, and one derived from the Old Testament discourse in these opening pages, namely: apocalyptic history. Once the traditional life is destroyed by the process of industrialisation, old values and simple faiths are thrown into doubt, a spiritual degeneration sets in, and the world will have its Flood before the rainbow can stand again on the cleansed earth.

Traditionally, the pastoral idyll – strictly a Georgic because it extols the virtues of nature and the rural life –[14] argues for an ideal state of harmony in a form that is 'mythopoetic'.[15] In *The Rainbow*, the mythic will clash with real history, and the poetic will become a more complex expression, so that the simple ideal itself will be put under severe strain on a number of levels as the novel turns modernist. It is the women who will instigate the process of modernity, as they begin to question the settled life of their men. A gendered opposition, deriving from Lawrence's 'Hardy' study, will take on the force of an archetypal structure: the women will look for change, the men will resist. In the beginning of the novel the women already face outwards to the world beyond their narrow confines. But it is a magic land shaped by literature and focused on the squire's lady who is characterised as the living epic that 'inspired their lives ... they had their own Odyssey ...' (*R*, p. 11; CUP, p. 12). Although this pattern of opposition between the women and the men has rather shaky foundations for a historical argument because it derives from opposing literary fictions: the female epic or Odyssey opposes the male Georgic, Lawrence, in a neat reversal of the history of classical literature, has the women preparing to go on the spiritual journey while the men stay at home. As the modern world encroaches progressively more on the lives of the Brangwens, this feminist gambit of giving the women the role of keepers of the soul of mankind will take on paradigmatic status.

'Real' history begins in the second part of chapter one: 'Around 1840 ...' when the first coal mine opens, and the Industrial Revolution finally reaches the rural heart of England. But Lawrence will keep it on the other side of the canal for most of the book, at a safe distance, only to be observed from the outside on occasional visits, like when Ursula goes to Wiggiston colliery in Yorkshire to pour out all Lawrence's anti-industrial invective at what she sees there. The Brangwen farmers, however, through generations of hard toil, have achieved a certain measure of financial independence. They, like Lawrence, can also remain on the other side of the canal, apart from the modern industrial world. The next three generations, whose growth and maturity and sexual history make up the substance of the novel, will evolve their increasing senses of identity at a tangent to the larger changes of a modernising world. However, when the railway comes to their valley 'the invasion' is complete (R, p. 12; CUP, p. 13). The town grows, the Brangwens get richer as tradesmen, but Marsh farm, that ideological centre for the rural myth, maintains its original remoteness, 'beyond all the dim, smoking hill of the town ... just on the safe side of civilisation' (R, p. 12; CUP, p. 14). Working in the fields, they now hear the new rhythm of 'the winding engines' on the other side of the embankment. There are colliers and the 'sulphurous smell' on the west wind which make the farmers conscious of 'other activity going on beyond them'.

At the beginning of his novel, Lawrence is clearly establishing more than a perspective. History, although amply referenced to real changes in the lives of the people and the topology of the land, is closer to mythology and parable. The myth of origin defines both an attitude to history and the discourse in which it will be represented. Evidently, Lawrence's history of England will be nothing more or less than ideological, a chronology and a chronicle of the three generations of Brangwens which will enable him to illustrate his anti-industrial thesis.

But the historical archive, properly understood in Foucault's terms, should be sedimented in the discourses that make up the substance of the novel. It is to this more implicit level that we now turn. For it is in the use of certain 'operative metaphors' [the term is Foucault's][16] that we see the discursive formation of history in the novel.

The evolutionist discourse

Darwin's theory of evolution had, by the late nineteenth and early twentieth century, established itself in the popular imagination. The general effect had not always been positive. The fact that human beings were not God-given but descended from monkeys had shaken the faith of our Victorian ancestors. Worse, natural selection had led to eugenics. For if the highest form of human development was determined by the imperial powers in the late nineteenth century, then primitivism and savagery are objects of the official history. The 'civilising mission' to the Dark Continent was legitimised by the Church and by Darwin's science.

The evolutionist discourse appears in *The Rainbow* in two forms. First, references to the British Imperial Rule in Africa and India are represented in the latter part of the novel by Skrebensky. Second, as a model or pervasive metaphor for the structure and significance of the narrative: Lawrence's attitude is clearly marked by his Brangwen genealogy, an ambivalent evolution at best, which serves to raise serious doubts about the stage of civilisation reached at the end, on one level, while not neglecting to acknowledge, implicitly, the gains afforded by modern life, on another level. Not that the levels are unconnected. Indeed, they enable the contradictions in the discursive practices ensuing from the metaphor to play an important role in the novel.

The first colonial reference occurs during Ursula's first affair with the young Skrebensky. She starts to question his belief in his military duties, and in the point of wars. He is blindly idealistic; she adopts a thoroughly materialistic attitude: there is no transcendent point to it, you kill, get killed, and so on. He maintains that you do your job, and there is the point: 'it matters whether we settle the Mhadi or not' (*R*, p. 310; CUP, p. 288). The passage contains four key words that carry the full weight of the historical reference: 'working like a *nigger*'; 'the *Mhadi*'; '*Khartoum*'; and 'the desert of the *Sahara*'. The year is precise: 1885; the event: the death of General Gordon at Khartoum. Skrebensky is the voice of the official history. The second reference occurs when Will Brangwen is described as being 'in a private retreat of his own', oblivious 'about the war'. Ursula, though, is very concerned, because Skrebensky – the object of her romantic discourse – is out there in 'South Africa' (*R*, p. 356; CUP, p. 331). Here, the precise historical reference is to the Boer War (1899–1902).

The third, and principal reference, is during Ursula's last year at college, when she receives Skrebensky's letter from Africa after not hearing from him for two years, and not having seen him for six. As a young woman she has become the focus for Lawrence's rampant iconoclasm. Skrebensky is now a first lieutenant in the Royal Engineers. She has continued to imagine him in romantic terms in order to brighten the 'blank grey ashiness of later daytime', still seeing him as the 'doorway' to 'self-realization and delight for ever' (R, p. 438f.; CUP, p. 406). His bright-red officer's tunic will not be enough to meet the expectations of her fantasy version of him. Her profound disappointment will fuel her anger. This, then, is the narrative context in which Lawrence places his anti-British Imperialist tirade.[17] Ursula imagines Skrebensky in India, 'one of the governing class, superimposed upon an old civilization, lord and master of a clumsier civilization than his own' (R, p. 443; CUP, p. 411). However, this view is complicated by the fact that she also represents Lawrence's anti-democratic beliefs. The British ruling class, at its best, would provide 'the better idea of the State'. And India did need 'the civilization which he himself represented: it did need his roads and bridges, and the enlightenment of which he was a part' (R, p. 444; CUP, p. 411).

Thoughts of leaving England, though, offer Lawrence the opportunity to bring together, in Ursula, the colonial-racist and the anti-democratic discourses in one outburst: 'I shall be glad to leave England. Everything is so meagre and paltry, it is so unspiritual – I hate democracy ... . Only degenerate races are democratic' (R, p. 461; CUP, p. 427). Only a 'spiritual aristocracy' could lead the way.[18] The key words here are 'unspiritual' and 'degenerate races'. They bring together, towards the end of the novel, the colonialist appropriation of the evolutionist discourse, and Lawrence's critique of modern western civilisation in 1915 as a spiritual descent of man.

Now, in order to make the link with the second, and more general use of the evolutionist discourse, we should notice the reference to 'darkness' and its figurative thematic associations: Africa, the 'dark continent', blacks, and the hot sensual – references that belong to the historical archive and the motif-structure of the novel at one and the same time. The 'darkness' is a discourse in Foucault's sense, always already a representation of the real in literature (in boys' magazines, popular stories, and 'serious' literature),[19] a well-established colonialist fiction about the white man in Africa. The key passage in *The Rainbow* is pages 446–52 (CUP, p. 413–18) where Lawrence rewrites Conrad's *Heart of Darkness* (1900). Skrebensky represents the white man just returned to civilisation after a tour of the dark continent. Most of what he tells his intended, Ursula, is filtered through her reception of it. She reacts exclusively from her romantic side, and is 'thrilled' by the quality of his voice (like Marlow is of Kurtz's voice), 'a voice out of the darkness', as he conveys 'something strange and sensual to her'. Moreover, what he tells her is exactly what the white woman back in England has been waiting to hear. They, the blacks, 'worship ... the darkness ... the fear – something sensual'. Here, the historical archive needs no comment today. Its use, however, does. The colonialist-racist (and sexist) fiction of the sensual negro to the homegrown white woman transfers – the psychoanalytic term is meant – to Skrebensky and is a symptom of her deep sexual desire, as in 'the hot, fecund darkness ... possessed his blood', and 'they walked the darkness beside the massive river', as if the darkness has now taken on a palpable existence of its own, expanding beyond its status as object of a discourse into the realm of a pervasive symbolism. The sexual potential, though, belongs to the wider implications of the discourse. 'African desire' is strange, powerful and 'fecund': 'he seemed like the living darkness upon her, she was in the embrace of the strong darkness.' And it is at this point that Conrad's darkness elides into a neo-Romanticism of the Dionysian kind first described by Clarke,[20] symbolised in the paradoxial process of creation-dissolution, and here in Lawrence taking on a primary ontological function. The whole passage is framed by this multi-functional context – at once colonialist, sexual, and ontological – and represented in a poetic discourse of a familiar romanticism: 'Dark water flowing in the silence through the big, restless night made her feel wild' (*R*, p. 445; CUP, p. 412). Lawrence manages to keep both the Conrad and the Romantic poetry reference in play. Sex brings Ursula and Skrebensky together 'as one stream'. The images of flowing and darkness bear the full weight of the ontological significance, so that 'the light of consciousness gone, then the darkness reigned, and the unutterable satisfaction' (*R*, p. 447, CUP, p. 414). The darkness is unspeakable in Conrad; and sexual satisfaction is beyond consciousness and rational discourse in Lawrence, and only expressible by the narrator in aesthetic form. The two figures, like the two selves, become one in 'the fluid darkness', as in a canonical Lawrentian moment 'their blood ran together as one stream'.

When she returns to rational consciousness, Ursula reacts like Conrad's Marlow back in the 'Sepulchral City': 'The stupid, artificial, exaggerated town', where life is 'nothing, just nothing' (*R*, p. 447; CUP, p. 414–15), and the people 'only dummies exposed' (*R*, p. 448; CUP, p. 415). This is no longer that sensual darkness of a sexualised colonialist discourse, but Conrad's hollowness at the heart of western civilisation itself. To reinforce the point, Ursula is reminded of 'the Invisible Man, who was a piece of darkness made visible only by his clothes' (*R*, p. 448; CUP, p. 415). The reference to the popular H. G. Wells novel (1897) would no more have been lost on Lawrence's contemporaries than the Conrad references. Moreover, the two kinds of darkness – the sensual-creative and the nihilistic – both serve the purpose of a profound social critique prefigured in the statement: 'primeval darkness falsified to a social mechanism' (*R*, p. 448; CUP, p. 415). As Ursula has now experienced the primeval darkness, her newly sensualised self is so 'real' to her that all else is 'pretence', and, echoing Conrad once more, the real 'jungle darkness' is to be found in the modern, urban English world.

The Conradian discourse will reappear on two more occasions. On returning from a trip to Rouen, France, Skrebensky feels that London is like the 'Sephulchral City': everything is grey, dead, and full of 'spectre-like people' (*R*, p. 457; CUP, p. 423). This profoundly affects him. His life seems 'spectral', foreshadowing the imminent demise of their love. For without her 'the horror of not being possessed him' (*R*, p. 458; CUP, p. 424). In the context of Lawrence's sexual ontology, his newly acquired fullness of being will be destroyed. But we should not overlook the Conradian 'horror' as the key word that enables the colonialist fiction to continue to reverberate at various levels in the novel. Skrebensky returns to it a last time when he marries 'the Colonel's daughter' within four days of Ursula leaving him, and embarks for India; he thinks of her (Ursula) in terms that bring Lawrence and Conrad together: 'She was the darkness, the challenge, the horror' (*R*, p. 483; CUP, p. 447). It is the middle term which belongs firmly to Lawrence, because the highest achievement of fullness of being in 'consummate marriage' is the challenge that Ursula represents for him, and it is one he is not able to meet.

It is always difficult in such a structurally complex novel to hold together in the criticism all the contexts and the recurrent motifs that we perceive in the reading. We ought to have noticed, for instance, the extent to which the evolutionist discourse comments implicitly on the colonialist archive. They reach the same conclusion, necessarily, in a profound critique of the state of western civilisation, a critique derived at least in part from Conrad, but here in Lawrence given a more spiritual-religious emphasis. The myth of origins established at the beginning of the novel, and the narrative logic and its thematic support which it entails, form the basis of that broader critique of the modern, industrial world. In this critique, the evolutionist discourse functions as an 'operative metaphor'.

Darwinian evolution is meant to account for the higher state of civilisation that mankind has reached. It is a paradigmatic story of the ascent of man from primitive tribal existence to the more complex states of being and patterns of social relations pertaining in the modern world. Being the product of a specific epoch, it does not evade its 'archaeological' analysis, which would place it firmly in its nineteenth-century formation. What uses has Lawrence made of it as a model for a historico-narrative pattern that will enable him to give thematic resonance to a genealogical structure?

Prefigured in the metaphor of the widening circle (used twice as chapter headings), it is as if the process of evolution is unstoppable – or even a natural instinct, too. The mothers wish to urge the children towards the 'higher form of being' that education would enable (R, p. 10; CUP, p. 12). And, 'the Brangwen wife of the Marsh aspired beyond herself, towards the further life of the finer woman, towards the extended being she revealed, as a traveller in his self-contained manner reveals far-off countries present in himself' (R, p. 11; CUP, pp. 12f.). This metaphor of the traveller after extended being will finally be reinscribed in Ursula. It will be Tom Brangwen, her grandfather, however, who like Lawrence will first go to the Grammar School in Nottingham. Although the evolution of his being will only reach a certain stage, it will be significant enough: he will bring foreign (Polish) blood into the Brangwen stock, undermining any myth of racial purity, and bringing the foreign world to the Marsh farm before anyone there takes steps to travel, literally and metaphorically. The narrow existence given credence at the beginning for the spiritual integrity it gives to the self in its 'mindless', instinctive relation to the world, will be characterised from now on as a severe restriction on the extension of being; while the price to be paid will be spiritual degeneration. At the very point of its highest stage of evolution, humankind will have discovered its heart of darkness. The greatest achievement of Natural Selection, and the process of civilisation is the Great War. This is not an original critique of modernity, but it is one to which Lawrence gave his specifically religious-theological slant.

The organic discourse

In *The Order of Things* (1966), Foucault described a significant change in natural history in the late eighteenth century which would precipitate the emergence of the biology of the nineteenth century and, subsequently, the life sciences. For instead of the principle of external observation that dominated the classical period, the description of internal structure became the aim of taxonomy. Henceforth, beings had an 'organic structure', and the characters and functions of plants could be classified by their organic structural differences. Foucault quotes Cuvier from the period: 'It is in this way that the method will be natural, since it takes into account the importance of the organs.'[21] It is therefore understandable, writes Foucault, 'how the notion of life could become indispensable to the ordering of natural beings'.[22] The natural sciences will now look for the deeper underlying causes to explain the surface mutations in organisms. Lamarck further assists the emergence of the era of biology by making the principle of internal organic structure 'function for the first time as a method of characterisation. ... Organic structure intervenes between the articulating structures and the designating characters – creating between them a profound, interior, and essential space.'[23] Not, though, that vitalism now simply triumphs over mechanism. Rather, in attempts to define the specificity of living beings, the organic structure is prioritised. The dimensions of this discontinuity were explained by Jameson: 'Such was indeed the history of the organic model, that concept of the organism as a prototype which with a single spark touched off Romantic philosophy and nineteenth-century scientific thinking.'[24]

The primacy of the organic self, and the recurrence of natural figures as ontological guarantee, in works like *The Rainbow,* has not gone unnoticed in Lawrence criticism. Lawrence's relationship to the English Romantic poets is precisely through organicism, described by Clarke as 'the vitalistic virtues – spontaneity, untamed energy, intensity of being, power'.[25] Moreover, the metaphor of growth informs the generational structure of the novel, and especially where the three generations of women are concerned.[26] Schwarz has discussed Lawrence's uses of nature imagery to characterise the sex act as a natural act, placing the characters' 'urgent sexuality in the context of nature's rhythms'.[27] Black writes about the symbolic plant analogies representing 'the growing-point of experience'.[28] Fjagesund points to the organic model as the basis for a cyclical view of history deriving from Romanticism, mythology and ethnology: the generations and the seasons of man are inextricably bound together through the eternally recurrent, key oppositions of birth/death, growth/decay, light/darkness, and so on.[29]

The metaphors of nature go much further than their ostensible function as indirect descriptions of sex. They have profound implications in the ontological scheme that they formally represent. One ought to suspect that such pervasive imagery betokens the reappropriation of a Romantic philosophy and its aesthetic. Even while Lawrence's use of nature verges on pantheism, it also provides the metaphor for the structure of the novel: the organic structure. Furthermore, the novel is encircled by nature, so to speak: it opens with the image of man in harmony with the natural world, and closes with the woman's vision of the 'new germination'. The structure of being – to extend the analogy – grows in complexity in response to the demands of the changing environment. Nature opposes society, the agrarian opposes the industrial, in their vitalist and mechanistic character respectively. The natural goal of life is to be vitally connected, man to woman, the self to its nature. Nature and ontology are bound together. The Lawrentian injunction is: 'Be thyself!'

The organic self always precedes self-consciousness. The sexual ontology is represented by the organic, natural figures. Thus it is that the natural instincts of men and women are aestheticised. Flower-pollination imagery becomes a recurrent motif. Passion is a sudden flood, sweeping all before it; or a bursting into flame, a destructive-creative Dionysian moment where the self is lost and found and recreates 'the world afresh' each time (*R*, p. 62; CUP, p. 60).

The very spring of the unconscious life – and one that Lawrence strictly opposes to Freud's 'mental' unconscious – is a fountainhead: 'Out of the rock of his form the very fountainhead of life flowed'

(*R*, p. 130; CUP, p. 121). Anna and Will are described on the morning after their wedding as 'both very glowing, like an open flower ... both very quick and alive' (*R*, p. 149; CUP, p. 139). 'Quick' and 'alive' are key words in the Lawrence lexicon. The former is the most sensitive, inmost part of the sentient being.

Nature also represents a plenitude where the organic self may develop, and where sex usually takes place. Tight, poky, interiors have a negative resonance in Lawrence. Sexually violent states are dramatised expressionistically (*R*, p. 451; CUP, p. 417f.).

The organic discourse is also represented in animal imagery, and in its most mythological form in the 'phoenix'. In the recurrent, proto-sexist animal imagery in the novel, man is the hunter-bird of prey; but woman is the consuming flame. The young male sexual predator is always consumed by the female fire of passion, never to rise again from the ashes as the reborn phoenix. The animal imagery, however, persists, as if to stress the limits of the phallocentric predatory sexuality in the face of the woman's sexuality. Lawrence is fond of describing the sexual tie between men and women in terms of soul-mates. But, finally, it is the woman's sexuality, perceived by the traditional man, which is both bird-like and witch: 'his heart melted in fear from the fierce, beaked, harpy kiss' (*R*, p. 480; CUP, p. 444).

Thus, Lawrence's sexual ontology achieves its figurative and theoretical support from the organic discourse. The limits of what can be said about subjects and subject-positions are, as Foucault argued, defined by discourse.[30]

The metaphor of electro-magnetism

Another set of figures that represent the full power of the living vitalism of sexual desire and passion in *The Rainbow* derives from the discourse of electro-magnetism.

The electric charge, the like and the unlike poles are pervasive scientific metaphors that represent the force of the sexual attraction between man and woman. Passion is 'primitive and electric' (*R*, p. 48; CUP, p. 47). Will Brangwen finds himself 'in an electric state of passion' (*R*, p. 115; CUP, p. 108). When he chats up the young woman in the Nottingham pub, he is a phallic power to her passive vulnerability: 'The man was the centre of positive force' (*R*, p. 229; CUP, p. 212). The scene figuratively represents the woman's tension between attraction and repulsion, but exclusively from the man's phallic, sexist perception: 'his whole body electric with a subtle, powerful, reducing force upon her' (*R*, p. 231; CUP, p. 214). He draws her nearer to him; she relaxes her resistance; then fights him off again: a rhythm of attraction and repulsion which puts to work the connotations of the figures of the electric charge and the electro-magnetic force-field. About Anna and Will we read: 'all was activity and passion, everything moved upon poles of passion' (*R*, p. 254; CUP, p. 236). Once they accept their separateness and their difference, they attract each other all the more passionately. After Ursula's first kiss, 'she went to bed feeling all warm with electric warmth' (*R*, p. 300; CUP, p. 278).

Clearly Lawrence is prepared to make use of scientific metaphors even while rejecting the scientific explanation of life. Ursula speaks for him when she rejects the rational, materialist grounds of modern science, because there the great mysteries of life are reduced to their 'physical and chemical activities' (*R*, p. 440; CUP, p. 408). The scientific view is represented by her lecturer, Dr Frankstone (a woman): 'We don't understand it [life] as we understand electricity, even, but that doesn't warrant our saying it is something special, something different in kind and distinct from everything else in the universe' (*R*, p. 440; CUP, p. 408). For Ursula, as for Lawrence, the essential mysteries were infinite, and the self 'was oneness with the infinite'. So that here, as elsewhere in his work, Lawrence counters the claims of scientific materialism with an idealist assertion deriving from a quasi-religious argument. Ursula does not feel like an impersonal force – like electricity. Yet the phallic power of her desire is described as 'a dark, powerful vibration' (*R*, p. 451; CUP, p. 418), as if it belongs not to her, not to the man, but to the space between them. It is a force-field of electro-magnetic attraction; a physical activity belonging to the natural world, already known in its structure and function to the modern science of Lawrence's day. Later we read that, under the influence of the bright moon, 'she vibrated like a jet of electric' (*R*, p. 477; CUP, p. 442).

Furthermore, when two beings produce the same force or power to dominate the other, they will be forced apart – as the like poles in magnetism. That is, unless the one gives way, and becoming passive is able to submit to the force of the active other. Will and Anna's struggle for supremacy may thus be understood. She wins as he withdraws into a life of passivity. Ursula proves to be too powerful for Skrebensky, and she destroys him. The force-field of magnetic attraction always leads to a short-circuit. For as the static electricity accumulates to different degrees of intensity at each pole, the force that drives the vibrations of the magnetic field starts to become greater at the positive pole, and the weaker force is drawn to the stronger, and destroyed: 'The struggle for consummation was terrible' (*R*, p. 480; CUP, p. 445). The moon that controls the tides, controls the moods of the woman. It is a glaring, white force that empowers her to give full expression to the 'lunacy' of her sexuality, destroying the man who, afterwards, is 'white and obliterated' (*R*, p. 481; CUP, p. 445). She had realised that he was attractive, 'but his soul could not contain her in its waves of strength, nor his breast compel her in burning, salty passion' (*R*, p. 478; CUP, p. 443). Metaphors of electro-magnetism now give way to the power of the waves under the force of the moon. Her 'strong, dominant voice' seems 'metallic' to him (*R*, p. 479; CUP, p. 444). 'Corrosive' is the word Lawrence uses to describe this process of destruction in the very first sexual encounter in the moonlight. She tries to understand the birth of her sexuality: 'Had she been mad: what horrible thing had possessed her? She was filled with that overpowering fear of herself ... that other burning, corrosive self' (*R*, p. 322; CUP, p. 299). And, significantly, it is a scientific metaphor referring to the chemical process of the corrosion of metal. The moon – the woman's totem – can do that to the hardened soul of man. But, as Middleton Murry was the very first critic to point out, 'she is the woman who accepts the man's vision of herself .... She, therefore, becomes a monster ... .'[31]

Tracing metaphors back to their origin in scientific discourses – here, the tropes of passion as force fields – appears, indeed, to establish a non-transparent historical reference. The relationship between text and history is more complex than most of the critical reception of *The Rainbow* allows.

The discourse of the flesh

Lawrence clearly belongs to the formation of the discourse of sexuality. Sexuality is constructed through a set of representations. For Foucault, the formation of this discourse begins with the early sexologists and Freud, and includes Lawrence in its history. *Sons and Lovers* (1913) is credited with the first appearance of 'sex-instinct'. *Lady Chatterley's Lover* (1929) provided us with 'the sex relation', 'the sex warmth', 'the sex glamour'. Around the same period we see the emergence of 'sex-life', and 'sex-appeal' (1919); 'sexological' (1920); 'sexology' (1927); 'sexy' (1928); 'sexologist' (1929).[32]

Sexuality is a modern phenomenon produced in the discourses of psychoanalysis, literature, sexology, sociology, and the woman's question.[33] In this precise sense, sexuality is a construct with an historical formation. Lawrence's persistent 'sex talk' may, though, seem ironic. For he is conventionally understood to be promoting a pre-discursive, intuitive or instinctive level of consciousness, a form of pre-rational primitivism as in the opening pages of *The Rainbow*. This non-self-conscious 'blood-intimacy' appears to be contradicted by Lawrence's excesses of sophisticated writing, represented by a highly conscious narrator, and especially in that first scene.[34] When the narrative shifts between the consciousnesses of the main characters, and although they are credited with degrees of intellectual skill that give a plausibility to their represented thoughts, some of their pre-conscious, half-formed thoughts or feelings, especially about sexuality, are represented by the highly conscious narrator through the studied artifices of modern aesthetic form. In this very specific sense, Lawrence also puts sexuality into discourse even while proposing, at least in theory, an ideal of pre-conscious living, spontaneity, and the instinctive sexual relation.

Important to Lawrence's post-Romantic, vitalist notion of sexuality is his quarrel with Christianity. Ironically the one book of Foucault's that would have been most useful here – (*HS IV:*) *The Confessions of the Flesh* – has never been published. (Traces of its argument, though, exist in the other volumes; indeed, they form an integral part of them.) Lawrence's quarrel with Christianity is outlined in the 'Hardy' study, and plays a significant role in *The Rainbow*.

Lawrence rejects the Christian love-ideal of *caritas*, the doctrine of pure altruism. Once subsumed under the moralist discourse of the Victorian church, the deeper mystical sources of life gave way to hypocrisy and cant. Modern love, in its forms of emancipation, is only a function of the will, a kind of automatism, proving that love is cut off from its natural, carnal roots. For Ursula, once again representing Lawrence's view, the quest for a new spirituality has become urgent in view of the new modern sterility. Later, Lawrence would insist on male leadership to fill the spiritual vacuum left by the failure of Christian love; and at the end of his life he will once more attempt to counter the Christian depreciation of sexuality through church morality by placing a high value on sensuality and tenderness in the conjugal relation between man and woman, in *Lady Chatterley*. In *The Rainbow*, as we have already noted, there is a return to the old nature mysteries of death and rebirth, here given a new spiritual-sensual form that has to fill that empty space created by the instrumentalities of modern life. Hough explained Lawrence's quarrel with Christianity as follows:

> Catholicism had even preserved some of the old earthly pagan consciousness, and through the cycle of the liturgical year had kept in touch with the rhythm of the seasons, the essential rhythm of man's life on earth. ... However he [Lawrence] may use the Christian language, he uses it for a different end. For Christianity the life of the flesh receives its sanction and purpose from the life of the spirit which is eternal and transcendent. For Lawrence the life of the spirit has its justification in enriching and glorifying the life of the flesh of which it is in any case an epiphenomenon.[35]

For Clarke it is difficult to disentangle Lawrence's debt to Christianity from his debt to English Romanticism. The demonic and Dionysian elements in Lawrence bring him closest to Dostoievsky.[36]

The biblical discourse, in fact, dominates the language of *The Rainbow*. Plausibly so, as Lawrence is true to the place the Bible occupies in the lives of the characters (just as it did in his); and especially in the small, semi-isolated world they inhabit in Victorian England. Towards the end of the novel, this discourse is less prominent, because the narrating consciousness is that of the New Woman, and she has clearly rejected her Christian upbringing in favour of a new, broader spiritual rebirth, that takes us back beyond Christianity and forward to a new future.

The characters try to make sense of their lives in the terms available to them. Their world is indeed limited to their language: 'As he [Tom] walked alone on the land ... and she would be his life' (*R*, p. 40; CUP, p. 39). Later, 'She was with child' (*R*, p. 63; CUP, p. 61), and just before the birth, Lydia only 'knew him as the man ... who begot the child in her' (*R*, p. 81; CUP, p. 77). Further on we read, 'and the Lord took up his abode. And they were glad'; or: 'Her [Anna's] father and her mother now met to the span of the heavens, and she, the child, was free to play in the space beneath, between' (*R*, pp. 96–7; CUP, p. 91). It now becomes increasingly more difficult to distinguish the biblical quotation from characters' discourse. Will Brangwen as a young man in the second generation provides another dominant voice of the Scriptures: '[He] worked on his wood-carving ... . Verily the passion of his heart lifted the fine bite of steel. He was carving, as he always wanted, the Creation of Eve' (*R*, p. 120; CUP, p. 112). Additionally, he represents the Christian occupation *par excellence* – carpentry. The beginning of the chapter, 'Anna Victrix' is characterised by his mind-style so that the parable-form ensues from the statement: 'And he was troubled' (*R*, p. 144; CUP, p. 134). However, it is Anna who first sees the rainbow spanning the day, 'and she saw the hope and the promise' (*R*, pp. 195–6; CUP, p. 181). Christian symbolism reinforces the discourse. There is the Flood and the rainbow; and the two Anthonys, although only the one (Maggie Schofield's brother) represents the real Saint, while the second (Skrebensky) turns out to be a false Saint (St Anthony being the founder of Christian monasticism). St Ursula founded the Ursuline teaching Order. Despite the disillusion of her teaching experience, Ursula's idealism towards the end of the novel is expressed through the Old Testament discourse of apocalypticism and the evangelistic 'fire and brimstone': 'Yea, and no man dared even throw a firebrand into the darkness ... .' (*R*, p. 438; CUP, p. 406). And in the end, 'the rainbow stood on the earth' (*R*, p. 495; CUP, p. 458), and the parable has come full circle, only the parataxis has given way to the complex syntax of a poetry deriving from Romanticism.

Through the uses of the biblical discourse Lawrence is also attempting to reconstitute a relationship with Christianity that will be a revitalisation of the spiritual through the sexual. Decisive here is the recurrence of the verb 'to know', and its eliding into the verb 'to be'. The Lawrentian sexualised self is an epistemological and ontological complexity.

The first mention of 'to know' in its biblical sense is when Tom and Lydia first meet. Here, in fact, Lawrence plays on the two meanings of the verb: 'She did not know him', has a double edge reiterated in: 'He was a foreigner, they had nothing to do with each other. *Yet his look disturbed her to knowledge of him*' (*R*, p. 37: CUP, p. 37) [emphasis added]. He senses 'some invisible connection with the strange woman', and that a new other 'centre of consciousness' burned within him connecting them both 'like a secret power' (*R*, p. 39; CUP, p. 38). Knowing the other takes on a double insistence in their courtship. Not only the biblical sense of carnal knowledge, but also the sociocultural: she is literally a stranger, a Polish aristocratic widow. The class difference is more a problem for Lydia. He was not a 'gentleman', yet he insisted on coming into her life, so that 'she would have to begin again ... *to find a new being*' (R, p. 40; CUP, p. 39) [emphasis added]. The sex ontology is predominantly an object of the Christian discourse of the Flesh. Sex is evil and sinful, and it is only sanctioned by Holy Matrimony: 'It meant a great deal of difference to him, marriage ... he knew she was his woman, he knew her essence, that it was his to possess' (R, p. 59; CUP, p. 57 f.). This patriarchy, legitimised by Christianity, will undergo a severe test in this novel where the women are given the upper hand. His 'powerful religious impulses' need to come to terms with the torment of his sex desire and the 'carnal contact with woman' which he first discovered as a young man (R, p. 20; CUP, p. 21).

Sexuality and religion are brought together in Lawrence in the biblical discourse of the Flesh. However, the language of the Scriptures meets that of Romantic or Expressionist poetry precisely at the moment when sex is represented figuratively. In writing about sex in *The Rainbow* Lawrence refuses the direct naming of the parts (an explicitness so central to the meaning and controversy of *Lady Chatterley's Lover*). Feelings, passion, and the sex act are displaced onto the biblical reference or the aesthetic figure – (aesthetic figure): 'the shocks rode erect; the rest was open and prostrate' (R, p. 121; CUP, p. 113), or: (biblical) 'In himself, he knew her' (R, p. 130; CUP, p. 121). Here, sexual awareness of the other is intuitive. Further on, in the early phase of Anna and Will's marriage, we read: 'Always, her husband was to her the unknown to which she was delivered up. She was a flower that has been tempted forth into blossom, and has no retreat. He has her nakedness in his power ... he appeared to her as the dread flame of power ... like the Annunciation to her ... . She was subject to him as to the Angel of Presence. She waited upon him and heard his will, and trembled in his service' (R, p. 169f.; CUP, p. 157f.). And we should add that Anna will soon reject his patriarchal stance, in the fight for supremacy which she will win.

Here, in one instance, we see the full force of Lawrence's representation of sexuality. He brings three discourses together: first, the Christian, whereby sex is both a temptation of the devil, and a carnal knowledge of the other (Woman is the devil-temptress, of course). Second, the aesthetic enfiguration of nature, both a formal source of imagery and the insistence that sex is natural. Third, sex as power, or the will-to-power. Thus in the representation of sexuality Lawrence tries to match quite contradictory discourses in his tendency towards sexual essentialism. Yet the sexualities on display in *The Rainbow* are the objects of a mixture of discursive formations, ancient and modern. Moreover, the complex psychology of sexual relationships, on the one hand, and the psychoanalytics of desire, on the other, result in a profound representation of power.

Foucault's power/knowledge thesis is even more obviously appropriate for reading Lawrence's critique of education in *The Rainbow*.

The discourse of education

Lawrence's trenchant critique of State education is concentrated in chapter XIII of *The Rainbow*, with its ironic title: 'The Man's World' – for it also addresses the issue of patriarchy. We will use Foucault's *Discipline and Punish* (1975) for this section of the paper.

Foucault's comments on education belong to his general thesis about the power of the modern State apparatus to enforce the process of normalisation through the means of surveillance and discipline, themselves more subtle ways of power than outright coercion. The school, like the monastery, the barracks, or the prison, has developed regimes of discipline designed to exercise power over the body itself. The institution of the school is an apparatus of the State, which, like any such institution, has an immediate hold over the body. Such power relations, 'invest it, mark it, train it, torture it, force it to carry out tasks, to perform ceremonies, to emit signs'.[37] The pupils are subjected to the system by turning them into objects of pedagogic knowledge dictated from above. Supervising, punishing and constraining children to prepare them for citizenship in the disciplinary society is reinforced by the family. These mechanics of power produce docile bodies, useful to the economy and obedient to the political State.[38] The pupils in the Brinsley Street Elementary School where Ursula works are being prepared for the colliery or the factory. The content of their learning is not important, it is the discipline that counts.

The school becomes a mechanism of learning, a precise instrumentality of power, and especially the primary school because it has the task of disciplining the pupils at an early age by teaching absolute obedience to the authority of the teacher. This is precisely Mr Harby's pedagogy in *The Rainbow*, and one that Ursula will have to learn, against her better judgement, if she is to survive.

Discipline 'presupposes a mechanism that coerces by means of observation'.[39] The school building, like its prototype, the *école militaire*, should be designed to function as the perfect disciplinary apparatus by enabling constant surveillance which is then 'integrated into the teaching relationship'.[40] In *The Rainbow*, the surveillance mechanism is both visual and audible: the small building with its over-full (60 pupils), cramped teaching rooms, separated by glass partitions, allows any noisy class to be visibly and audibly 'observed' – noise being the principal symptom of lack of discipline, as any school teacher knows, so that any deviation from teacher-centred rote learning, like group work, more pupil participation, as Ursula discovers to her cost, is simply a provocation to be branded a poor teacher. Moreover, admonishing the class or punishing a pupil in front of the class (corporal punishment in Mr Harby's school) will be heard throughout the building, putting fear into the rest of the kids. Conformity is thus enforced: 'The normal is established as a principle of coercion in teaching with the introduction of standardized education ...'[41]and further supported by the mechanism of the examination which reinforces the formation of a certain type of knowledge bound to 'a certain form of the exercise of power'.[42] The power invested in education 'produces domains of objects and rituals of truth'.[43]

The school itself symbolises the system: 'The whole place seemed to have a threatening expression, imitating the church's architecture, for the purpose of domineering, like a gesture of vulgar authority ... like an empty prison waiting the return of tramping feet' (*R*, p. 369; CUP, p. 343). The metaphors of prison are reiterated several times, until we get the impression of a familiar Victorian representation of a Dickensian type: 'The prison was round her now!' (*R*, p. 372; CUP, p. 346). Or: 'The prison of the school was reality' (*R*, p. 373; CUP, p. 347). She is imprisoned by this microcosm of the man's world with its patriarchal relations. The school is an alien reality to which 'she must apply herself' (*R*, p. 373; CUP, p. 347).

It is soon evident that the pupils are subjected to a military discipline, too: marching, standing in line, sitting silently in rows. Mr Harby: 'Thrashed and bullied ... like some invincible source of the mechanism he kept all power to himself. And the class owned his power. And in school it was power, and power alone that mattered' (*R*, p. 377; CUP, pp. 350–1).

If the elementary school is understood as the barracks or prison, the college to which Ursula now returns is the convent: 'There was

in it a reminiscence of the wondrous, cloistral origin of education'
(*R*, p. 430; CUP, p. 399). She is momentarily in her medieval won-
derland of Gothic architecture where 'the monks of God held the
learning of men and imparted it within the shadow of religion' (*R*,
p. 430; CUP, p. 399). The professors are the 'priests of knowledge',
a fantasy which sustains her during the first year of study, implicitly
reminding us of her namesake, St Ursula. On her return for the
second year, however, the illusion has gone, and the religious
retreat has become, 'a little apprentice-shop where one was further
equipped for making money' (*R*, p. 435; CUP, p. 403). Her deep
desire for the essential mystery of knowledge is significantly undermined when she admits to the essential materialism of education.

The levels of incarceration or imprisonment, described by
Foucault in *Discipline and Punish*, go beyond the institutions of education to infuse other parts of the modern existence that Lawrence
is diagnosing through the character of Ursula. Her family imprisons
her in its madhouse of children running riot, so that there is no
escape (except on Sundays) to a quieter privacy where she can
study. The freeing of the children to give vent to their energies
reduces Ursula's existence to a greater unfreedom. She is also
captive of her father's authority, a social relation of power in a
patriarchal society that extends itself to the school, college, and the
prospect of marriage to the army officer. At a general, symbolic
level the thematic and structural opposition of closure and plenitude is prefigured in the poky, dingy interiors where families live,
and the open spaces of nature where sex takes place, respectively.
For Ursula, any code or convention is a form of imprisonment, and
when she envisages 'the new germination' at the end of the novel, it
is a necessary, new life-force because 'they were all in prison, they
were all going mad' (*R*, p. 495; CUP, p. 458). Moreover, Lawrence
describes and dramatises modern society's rationalisations as forms
of madness and imprisonment. The natural, instinctive self is
trapped in the codes, conventions, and apparatus of its own
collective invention.

Conclusion

Reading Lawrence's novel through Foucault has sought to bring out
the relation of the text to history at the level of discourse. This
proves to be a non-transparent and uneven relationship, as the

pervasiveness of the tropes sometimes undoes the force of the propositions. We have not, though, described that text, as an older stylistics would have done, so as to underline the coherence of the Lawrentian style. If the writing is characterised by a complex unevenness, it is because of a mixture of discourses working at different, and sometimes contradictory, levels. We have concentrated on the discourses of history and science. But we could have discussed more thoroughly the aesthetic discourses. For the uses of Romanticism and Expressionism are noticeable in the description of emotional states, just as Lawrence's idea of the novel is implicit in his organicism. Because it is also there, in that implicit aesthetic and poetics, that we find the historical archive, in Foucault's sense. But that is the subject of another paper.

From *Anglia: Zeitschrift für Englische Philogie,* 115: 31 (1997), 323–51.

Notes

[Robert Burden's essay is an example of new historicist criticism. This takes its inspiration from Michel Foucault's theory of discourse. Discourse is a form of power to the extent that it determines a particular concept of reality and regulates our behaviour in respect of it. The medical profession is one example of discourse. Its specialist terminology conditions how we perceive a disease and we accept the authority of the doctor regarding the best way to treat it. The key element in Foucault's account of discourse is that it is a set of rules for the representation of reality; it is not a means of describing it. It therefore always invites the question of who has the power to make those rules and who has not. This is not a question that Burden asks in his analysis of *The Rainbow.* Instead he challenges the conventional distinction between a text and its context. Foucault's theory of discourse means we cannot make this distinction as easily as it may have been made in the past. Burden cites F. R. Leavis and Frank Kermode as two critics who have made such a distinction. Leavis saw *The Rainbow* as a spiritual account of England's past while Kermode saw *Women in Love* as a comment on the self-destructiveness of man though one which did not altogether exclude the possibility of regeneration. In both cases, the novels are seen as interpretations of history rather than as instances of historical discourses themselves. Burden identifies a number of these historical discourses in *The Rainbow* and how they relate to each other. These include colonialism, evolution, organicism, sexology, electromagnetism and Christianity. The relation of these discourses with one another is uneven and contradictory, which militates against any coherent reading of the novel. Burden's essay shows the novel less as a comment on history than as a collection of discourses that reveal a particular moment, just prior to the First World War, in all its complexity. All references to *The Rainbow* are from the Penguin edition (Harmondsworth, 1949) and from the Cambridge edition edited by Mark Kinkead-Weekes (Cambridge, 1989); they are cited respectively as (*R*; CUP) in the text. Eds]

1. Mark Kinkead-Weekes, 'The Marble and the Statue: the Exploratory Imagination of D. H. Lawrence', *Imagined Worlds: Essays on Some English Novels and Novelists in Honour of John Butt*, ed. Maynard Mack and Jan Gregory (London, 1968), pp. 371–418. Revised for *D. H. Lawrence: Critical Assessments Vol II*, ed. David Ellis and Ornella De Zordo (Mountfield, 1992), pp. 179–213.

2. Corroborated by John Worthen's indispensable biography, *D. H. Lawrence: The Early Years* (Cambridge, 1991), the first of three volumes by different authors. Also crucial are the seven volumes of letters in the Cambridge edition.

3. Introduction, CUP pp. xlv–li.

4. Robert Lynd (5 October), James Douglas (22 October), and Clement Shorter (23 October), in particular. Reprinted in R. P. Draper (ed.), *D. H. Lawrence: The Critical Heritage* (London, 1970).

5. Source of information: CUP, introduction.

6. F. R. Leavis: *Novelist* (London, 1955). For a critique, see G. M. Hyde, *D. H. Lawrence* (London, 1990), ch. 3.

7. F. Kermode, *Lawrence* (Glasgow, 1973); P. Fjagesund, *The Apocalyptic World of D. H. Lawrence* (Oxford, 1991).

8. David Macey, *The Lives of Michel Foucault* (London, 1994), p. xx.

9. Michele Barrett, 'Discoursing with Intent', *THES*, 12 May 1995.

10. T. Flynn, 'Foucault's Mapping of History', *The Cambridge Companion to Foucault*, ed Gary Gutting (Cambridge, 1994), pp. 39–45.

11. Michel Foucault, 'Politics and the Study of Discourse', *Ideology and Consciousness, 3* (1978) (French orig. 'Réponse à une question', in *Esprit* [1968]).

12. Kermode, *Lawrence*, p. 45.

13. Ibid., p. 42.

14. Cf. J. A. Cuddon, *A Dictionary of Literary Terms and Literary Theory* (Oxford, 1991), pp. 366–7.

15. Ibid., pp. 689–90.

16. *Madness and Civilisation* (London, 1992), p. 162 (French orig. *Histoire de la Folie* [1961]).

17. This tirade is now generally believed to have been decisive in the 'obscenity' trial in 1915, as it was 'bad for morale'. Cf. introduction to the CUP edition, pp. xlvi–xlvii. He was also under suspicion for being 'pro-German', of course.

18. Cf. D. H. Lawrence, 'Democracy', *Selected Essays* (Harmondsworth, 1976).

19. Cf. Robert Burden, *The Critics Debate: Heart of Darkness* (London, 1991), pp. 8–11.

20. Colin Clarke, *River of Dissolution: D. H. Lawrence and English Romanticism* (London, 1969).

21. Michel Foucault, *The Order of Things: An Archaeology of the Human Sciences* [OT] (London, 1991), p. 228. French orig. *Les Mots et les Choses* (Paris, 1966). Subsequent references in text.

22. Ibid. p. 228.

23. Ibid. p. 231.

24. Fredric Jameson, *The Prison-House of Language* (Princeton, NJ, 1972), p. vi.

25. Clarke, *River of Dissolution*, p. 122.

26. Edward Engelberg (1963), 'Escape from the Circle of Experience: D. H. Lawrence's *The Rainbow* as a Modern Bildungsroman', in *Critical Assessments*, ed. Ellis and De Zordo, p. 167.

27. Daniel Schwarz (1980), 'Lawrence's Quest in *The Rainbow*', in ibid., p. 248.

28. Michael Black, *D. H. Lawrence: The Early Philosophical Works: A Commentary* (London, 1991) p. 114.

29. Fjagesund, *The Apocalyptic World of D. H. Lawrence*, p. 14.

30. For a thorough philosophical, if more transparent reading of the organic and vitalist principles in Lawrence's work, cf. Meinhard Winkens, 'Zivilisationskritik und Lebensaffirmation bei D. H. Lawrence: Der paradigmatische Bildungsweg von Ursula Brangwen in *The Rainbow*', *Literaturwissenschaftliches Jahrbuch*, 27 (1986), pp. 123–40.

31. John Middleton Murry, *Son of Woman: The Story of D. H. Lawrence* (London, 1931), p. 91.

32. Stephen Heath, *The Sexual Fix* (London, 1982), p. 9.

33. Ibid., pp. 10–11.

34. A point initially made by H. O. Brown (1974), 'The Passionate Struggle of Conscious Being: D. H. Lawrence's *The Rainbow*', in *Critical Assessments*, ed. Ellis De Zordo (repr.), p. 216.

35. Graham Hough, *The Dark Sun: A Study of D. H. Lawrence* (London, 1956), pp. 253–4. This section on Lawrence's quarrel with Christianity is essentially a summary of the appendix in Hough's book.

36. Clarke, *River of Dissolution*, p. 14.

37. Michel Foucault, *Discipline and Punish: The Birth of the Prison* [DP] (Harmondsworth, 1986), p. 26; first translated 1977; French orig. *Surveiller et punir: Naissance de la prison* (Paris, 1975). Subsequent quotations in text.

38. Ibid. p. 138.

39. Ibid. p. 170.

40. Ibid., p. 175.

41. Ibid., p. 184.

42. Foucault, *Discipline and Punish*, p. 187.

43. Ibid., p. 194.

6

Death and the Rhetoric of Representation in D. H. Lawrence's *Women in Love*

GERALD DOHERTY

In Roman Jakobson's celebrated essay entitled 'Two Aspects of Language and Two Types of Aphasic Disturbances', the splitting of rhetoric into two major fields – metaphor and metonymy – has perhaps proved most remarkable for the wide range of its applications.[1] Beyond his initial, purely linguistic, definition of the two tropes in terms of the relationship of similarity/contiguity between signs, Jakobson extended their scope to include verbal narrative, painting and film. In the same essay, he goes even further, declaring that a 'competition between both devices ... is manifest in any symbolic process, be it intrapersonal or social'.[2] For Jakobson, metaphor and metonymy function less as individual figures than as large-scale binary systems.

Following Jakobson's own lead, subsequent writers have deployed his rhetoric in a variety of theoretical enterprises. David Lodge has applied it to distinguish between the symbolic and realistic poles in modernist literature;[3] Peter Brooks has employed it in the field of narrative plotting;[4] and Jacques Lacan has integrated it into psychoanalytical theory to define the dynamics of sexual desire.[5] In all of these areas, Jakobson's theories have generated new forms of discourse as well as new insights and understandings.

The present essay extends their application to yet another sphere – the representation of death in narrative fiction – where Jakobson's binary rhetoric produces its own special kind of illumination. In effect, metaphor and metonymy regulate the way death is configured in the English novel. Not only do they determine the specific styles of the representation of death, and the modes in which it is perceived by the spectators; in addition, they project two antagonistic value-systems, each one of which gives the death-event its own characteristic significance. While I shall glance quickly at traditional death-scenes in the nineteenth-century novel, I shall concentrate on the early modernist novel, and especially on *Women in Love*, because it illustrates in quite an exceptional way the role of Jakobson's binary rhetoric in generating different approaches to dying, and different evaluations of death. In *Women in Love*, Lawrence deploys these two systems to articulate the novel's most dynamic antitheses: between dying and rebirth, decadence and renovation, destruction and creation, between a paralysed immobility and renovatory change. As a first move, however, I shall link rhetorical theory to each of these distinctive approaches to death. The first approach conceives of death less as an end in itself than as a *rite du passage*, involving a transformation, and a transfer of relations from one domain to another. Towards some vision of another world the death-event beckons and the dying person aspires. Essentially theological in orientation, this conception posits the existence of an after-life, predicated on a difference from the present earthly existence, to which it nevertheless bears a resemblance. Dying turns on the revelation of new spheres of existence, new forms of consciousness, new configurations at the threshold of their unfolding, which at once continue, and break with, the forms of the old terrestrial ones.

This enactment of transfers and transformations within the sphere of representation has an essentially tropical basis. Taking metaphor as its model, this conception of death is analogous to the metaphorical process itself. Like the death-process which it resembles, metaphor posits as fundamental the crossing from one semantic site to another, which is its resembling (or contrasting) double: in metaphor, 'there are two conceptual domains, and one is understood in terms of the other ... a whole schematic structure ... is mapped onto another whole schematic structure'.[6] Through this transit, the contours of a new, unfamiliar domain are predicated on the basis of an old literal one that it takes as its model. Metaphor tells the story of a crossing, a carry-over of meaning, and of the transformations of meaning that such a crossing entails.

Conceived of as a transference and a transformation, the death-process has the same basic structure as metaphor. Like metaphor, death too enacts a change in the mode of meaning-relations, achieved through transformation of sense, based on similarities and differences between the domains. This inclusion of difference within the sphere of the similar facilitates the perception of death as a radical transfer, a 'trespass into the unknown' (Lawrence's phrase in 'The Crown'[7]). Structured as metaphor, representations of the death-event are powerfully teleological, geared to future disclosures: the unknown mapped in terms of the known, the invisible in terms of the visible. As such, they possess a vivid explanatory force, mediating the present in the light of a future which it resembles and toward which it is oriented. In Jacques Lacan's formulation, it is precisely the metaphorisation of death that permits the individual demise to be mourned and transcended, 'sacrificed to a greater Individual – the collective Order'.[8]

The special concern with transfers and transformations – the rhetorical turning away from the death-scene – motivates a radical veiling, the occlusion from representation of the material essence of death. As object of pathos or horror or melancholy, the dead body is displaced, supplanted by affirmations about its future destination or destiny. In short, the metaphorical conception of death disincarnates. It shifts the focus away from the corpse, as the detritus of life's meanings, toward the kind of transfiguration that amplifies and augments. In setting the corpse within a new frame of reference, the metaphorical conception identifies the dead body with those literal senses that metaphor raises up and fills with fresh spiritual meanings.[9]

This rhetorical turning away is the most characteristic gesture evoked by traditional death-scenes, where the dying body functions as a vehicle for fresh insights and revelations: 'It is a literary convention of the nineteenth century that in their last moments the dying have a vision of the after-life ...'.[10] In order to indicate how metaphorisation dominates the representation of death in the traditional English novel, I shall glance at three exemplary instances. In *Wuthering Heights*, for example, Catherine's dying body represents a means of escape from the shackles of an earthly condition, and an access to a beyond which transfigures old modes of perception. Troped as a 'shattered prison', it is the vehicle for a change in domains – her release into a 'glorious world' which will transform her relations with Heathcliff.[11] In Dickens's *Old Curiosity Shop*, Nell's transit from a material to a spiritual realm turns on the disclosure of a heavenly paradise, a revelation so immediate that it erases the body of death from the narrative: transformed into a celestial body, she appears as a majestic 'angel'.[12] In a parallel gesture, Magwitch's death-drama in *Great Expectations* involves a spontaneous switch of domains: from Pip's derelict contemplation of Magwitch's remains, the scene quickly turns to his confidence in Magwitch's final salvation.[13] In all of these instances, the veiling of death – its material essence – permits a visionary domain beyond death to make itself manifest.

The same metaphorisation of death dominates the modernist novel, though its specifically Christian resonances are muted. The metaphorical habit survives long after its support in a belief-system has weakened. To take three exemplary moments: Mrs Dalloway's recreation (in the midst of her party) of the physical horror of Septimus Smith's suicide ('Up had flashed the ground; through him, blundering, bruising, went the rusty spikes') generates her immediate apprehension of spiritual dimension of death. For Mrs Dalloway, death functions like a metaphor: it involves the 'attempt to communicate' across boundaries, and the 'embrace' which unites the elements that life forces apart.[14] Likewise in *A Passage to India*, the consignment of Mrs Moore's physical remains to the Indian Ocean signals her instant resuscitation as spiritual force: in this spontaneous apotheosis, she takes her place as goddess – 'Esmiss Esmoor' – in the Indian pantheon.[15] Ulysses offers the most remarkable instance of such an impromptu switch of domains: Stephen's evocation of his mother's death-throes (the 'green sluggish bile which she had torn up from her rotting liver by fits of loud groaning vomiting') coincides with her immediate reappearance as revenant: in her 'loose brown graveclothes', she returns from a ghostly domain, reproaching him for his callous behaviour toward her.[16] In these persistent metaphorisations of death, the corpse signifies less an end in itself than the entry into, or return from, some higher state of existence. It thus charges the death-event with a fresh narrative impetus. In none of these configurations is death conceived of as a dead-end, a no-exit occasion, which, in terminating life's expectations, shows up the dead body in all its dejection and pathos.

This conception of death as an end in itself forms the basis for the second approach to death, which perceives the individual demise as the culminating event in the long sequence of life-events that precede it. As such, death is a denouement, the end of a plotted life, the self's own obituary that sums up and completes its history. It marks the end of the time of the body, and the network of plots that enmeshed it: the corpse stands for nothing but itself. In contrast to the dematerialisation which the metaphorical process induces, this mode materialises the body. It focuses on the concrete context of death, detailing the death-event with obsessive attention and with near-photographic exactitude. As an object of fascination or repulsion or horror, the thereness of the corpse is insisted upon, fixed privately as the space of an absence, a mute retreat from purpose and meaning, the fleshly remains of a life now departed.

This mode has its historical roots in the nineteenth century when Western culture 'gave up looking systematically beyond death for religious meaning'.[17] In its place, an asymbolic conception emerges – 'outside of religion, outside of ritual, a kind of abrupt dive into literal Death'.[18] This conception has one of its graphic early realisations in Flaubert's representation of Emma Bovary's protracted death. Not only are all the gruesome stages of Emma's sufferings and their physical manifestations detailed with photographic precision and accuracy; in their lack of efficacy, the final rites performed by the priest stand as an ironic comment on the death-throes that accompany them, and that they fail to alleviate. Emma's own comment crystallises this particular perception of death: 'There's not much in dying,' she thought. 'I shall go to sleep, and it will be all over.'[19]

This type of 'literal Death' has its rhetorical basis in the second major trope of narrative – metonymy. Since the latter is employed primarily for reference, it lends itself to concrete, realistic description: 'Via metonymy, one can refer to one entity in a schema by referring to another entity in the same schema.'[20] In situating death in its individual and social context, in specific settings and situations, it facilitates the accumulation of detail, as well as the focus in close-up that Jakobson associates with metonymy.[21] There is, however, a further important dimension. Because in metonymy, 'mapping occurs within a single domain, not across domains',[22] metonymic descriptions tend to exclude the transcendent dimension. Instead they focus on the non-symbolic aspects of death, the here-and-now of the death-drama, its grim, reductive appearance without a 'behind' or 'beyond'. In Barthes's phrase, they reproduce a kind of 'flat death', whose paradigm is the photographic click, 'separating the initial pose from the final point'.[23] They mark less an opening into the beyond than the finality of absolute closure.

As such, metonymic death forecloses the future, delivering the body over to the fleshly vicissitudes of the death-process itself. Death's crude indifference is thinly veiled by contingent concerns (familial and social disruptions) that cover over an essential absence of meaning with apparently meaningful happenings. The metonymic denouement signals at once death's necessity (all life-histories must come to an end) and the sheer arbitrariness of its occurrence at this particular time, place and circumstance. Ronald Schleifer sums it all up: such a modernist recognition of death 'without transcendental meaning, without signification beyond itself, simply, materially, and unavoidably there ... is a form of radical metonymy'.[24]

Women in Love is an extended consideration of the consequences of conceiving death in the metaphoric mode as set against the metonymic one. Unlike other modernist fictions, however, it keeps these two modes strictly separate, playing them off against each other as a means of heightening the text's antithetical tensions. This contest of figures constitutes the basis for the novel's construction of character, particularly in the contrasts it draws between the major character pairings – between Birkin and Ursula who embody the metaphoric mode of perceiving the death-process, and Gerald and Gudrun who are their metonymic 'opponents'. Across the vast rhetorical abyss that divides them, they conduct their, often mutually antagonistic, relationships. It is the metonymic pole of this opposition, represented by Gerald and Gudrun, that I wish now to examine.

Gerald's relationship to death foregrounds the contingent aspect of the metonymic connection: through a kind of contiguous contact, he attracts death to himself, and communicates its presence to others through the simple fact of his being-on-the-spot wherever it occurs. On the first occasion that death is introduced in *Women in Love*, for example, when Birkin meditates on Gerald's character, he marks him down as a 'Cain' figure, one who killed his own brother, not through deliberate plotting, but through the accidental association with death that dogs Gerald wherever he goes: 'Gerald as a boy had accidentally killed his brother. What then? ... A man can live by accident, and die by accident. Or can he not?' (p. 26). In posing this last question already at this early point in the novel, Birkin stakes out the parameters within which the death-event takes on significance, and around which the major character pairings range themselves.

In Birkin's conception, death is either a random occurrence, the result of 'pure accident', or it possesses a 'universal significance': in drawing together all the life-elements, and attracting them to itself, death makes them 'all hang together in the deepest sense' (p. 26). In the terms I have already defined, for Birkin death has either a metonymic or a metaphoric significance: it is either an asymbolic, non-transcendental event, the last in an arbitrary sequence of events that precedes it, or it is profoundly symbolic, gathering together all the life-events into a single conjunction, and from that totalising perspective, irradiating them with fresh meaning and light (in reject-ing the contingent explanation – 'he did not believe that there was any such thing as accident' – Birkin already locates himself at the metaphoric pole of the opposition).

Similarly, when Ursula and Gudrun scrutinise Gerald's history (in the episode 'Diver'), a parallel conflict of viewpoints emerges: the nature of Gerald's association with death provokes a 'sharp disagreement' between the two sisters. While Gudrun perceives Gerald's killing of his brother entirely in metonymic terms, as a random event, the 'purest form of accident', Ursula, by contrast, reads it metaphorically as a profoundly intentional act, the expres-sion of an 'unconscious will', a 'primitive desire' for, and attraction to, death. From Ursula's perspective, Gerald's 'playing at killing' loads death with a hugely symbolic significance, as part of a univer-sal tragic drama that unites all human beings, as (unwitting) actors and victims (pp. 48–9).

What up to this point has been general speculation about Gerald's (metonymic) association with death is realised as an accidental event in the episode 'Water-Party'. As local magnate and master, Gerald organises the annual public festival for the people of the district, which has the death of his sister as its climax. From the moment the cry about Diana's drowning goes out, Gerald's presence is linked intimately to 'dread and catastrophe' (p. 179). At one level, Gerald's desperate attempts to rescue this sister represent his demonstration that an accidental death cannot occur: at another, the fact that Diana actually drowns, when it seems that Gerald alone could have rescued her, proves that it can. Because Diana's drowning is linked casually to Gerald's unsuccessful efforts to save her, it seems to him that he killed his sister through acciden-tal default: 'I'm sorry. I'm afraid it's my fault. But it can't be

helped' (p. 183). Retrospectively surveying the scene of the drowning, Gerald reproduces the classic articulation of death as
metonymic event – as an end in itself, without exit, without
redemptive or emancipatory overtones: 'if you once die ... then
when it's over, it's finished. Why come to life again?' (p. 184). For
Gerald, death is an asymbolic event, mediated only through the
accidents that surround it, and requiring no explanation beyond
them.

In confronting Gerald with a second death-drama – that of his
father's demise – the 'Threshold' episode foregrounds the power of
metonymic representation to evoke the material essence of death. In
displaying Mr Crich's body in all the stages of its slow disintegration, the episode transforms death into a theatrical spectacle with
Gerald and Gudrun as the front-line spectators. Since they are the
main focalisers of these particular scenes, it appears that this is their
special mode of apprehending the death process. Both of them are
essentially metonymic perceivers: each detail that they observe
evokes the total death-event for which it stands as a substitute. As
Gudrun scrutinises Mr Crich, lying 'propped up in the library', she
registers his dying body as a composite image, the sum-total of its
visual details, focused in close-up and with a metonymic precision
and realism: the 'yellow wax' of the face, the 'sightless eyes', the
black beard that 'seemed to spring out of the waxy flesh of a
corpse' – all of these effects are 'photographed upon [Gudrun's]
soul' in pictorial terms, like a sequence of film-stills that the cine-
matic trope suggests they resemble (p. 281). For Gudrun (as for
Gerald) death is devoid of transcendental significance: each individual death produces a metonymic gap or hole in the world, a
momentary rupture of context, an unexpected break in life's seam-
less narrative, that the events of the world quickly complete and fill
up again: 'But she loathed the death itself. She was glad the everyday world held good, and she need not recognize anything beyond
it' (p. 286).

Gerald's confrontation with his dying father provides the model
for a 'flat Death' – 'visible and audible' demise that, in its voiding of
symbolic import, overwhelms him. Death's manifestation as a
fleshly paroxysm, a painful physical seizure which nothing allevi-
ates, intensifies the effect of pathos and horror. In their unredeemed
corporeality, Mr Crich's death-throes have a kind of convulsive
carnality, a violent orgasmic intensity that brooks no turning away:
no metaphoric gesture of transcendence can raise them up into

significance. 'Transfixed in horror', Gerald watches his father's last 'frenzy of inhuman struggling', hears the 'horrible, choking rattle', contemplates the 'dark blood and mess pumping over the face of the agonized being' (p. 333). The vehemence of this description – its melodramatic insistence – conceals a radical absence of meaning: the reduction of death to a sequence of extreme physical sensations, to the agglomeration of the metonymic details that constitute it. As such the description also has sexual overtones: as a shattering climax to life, death appears as the body's last orgasmic seizure which, instead of restoring it and making it whole, disintegrates and destroys it.

Precisely because Gerald is unable to metaphorise death – to perceive it in terms of transfers and transformations – he is subsequently caught up in a chain of events that extends his father's death-drama by reproducing metonymic substitutes for it. Take, for example, his visit to the churchyard soon after his father's death. Through contiguous associations with the funereal and the macabre, this visit extends the death-drama, evoking through its detailed description the material and sensuous essence of death. As Gerald walks among the tombstones, he reacts with 'revulsion' to the 'heaped pallor of old white flowers ... cold and clammy' to the touch, to the 'raw scent of chrysanthemums and tube-roses', and to the 'cold and sticky' clay of the graves (p. 338). In carrying the clay on his boots into Gudrun's bedroom (where he makes his way immediately after the churchyard visit), Gerald literally carries mortality into his sexual encounter with Gudrun. By bringing eros and death into contiguous contact, he infects one with the other. As he pours 'all his pent-up darkness and corrosive death into her', she, as passive subject, receives him 'as a vessel filled with his bitter potion of death'. They trade death in a kind of metonymic exchange. Since this exchange lacks precisely the transformations associated with metaphoric transfers, it involves only the simple passing of an untransformed essence back and forth from one to the other. As a climax, Gudrun receives the 'terrible frictional violence of death ... in an ecstasy of subjection, in throes of acute, violent sensation' (p. 344). Indeed Gudrun's orgasmic disintegration has its closest counterpart in Mr Crich's deathly paroxysms: both are forms of a metonymic reduction and fragmentation that sunders, isolates and destroys.

The description of Gerald's own death, as he wanders away among the snow-slopes of the Alps, wavers between representing death as the preordained destiny toward which his own momentum compels him ('He wanted so to come to the end – he had had enough'), and as a purely contingent event, the outcome of the randomness of his movements, completely haphazard and out of control ('He drifted, as on a wind, veered, and went drifting away'). Underscoring this tension, the text juxtaposes two antagonistic images at the climax of the death-drama: the 'half-buried crucifix, a little Christ under a little sloping hood, at the top of a pole' – the central Western symbol of metaphoric death, which is geared to sacrificial transcendence (and which functions as an index of what Gerald's end might have been) – and Gerald's fearful apprehension of his own death in terms of a sudden 'murder', the irruption of a casual violence, which fills him with 'dread'. His moment of death is encoded metonymically in the same way as his father's: both are configured as the sudden snapping of the 'knot' that tied the life-elements together, a dive into literal death: 'as he fell something broke in his soul, and immediately he went to sleep' (pp. 472–4).

The final episode ('Exeunt') extends the representation of death as a radical metonymy, resistant to metaphoric transfiguration, to its extreme limit. In these mortuary scenes, Gerald's corpse is displayed – untranslated, unsubsumed – in all its ugly abjection and pathos. It is fixed in its hideous 'thereness', inhuman and sterile. A bleak contrast is established between the Birkin who remembers Gerald with commitment and love – 'He should have loved me ... I offered him' – and the Birkin who reacts with 'disgust', appalled at the sight of 'the inert body lying there ... so coldly dead, a carcase'. Deathly effects proliferate through contiguous association with the corpse that evokes them. Birkin's prolonged contemplation fore-grounds the essential meaninglessness of the corpse – Gerald's 'dead mass of maleness, repugnant', his body, 'like clay, like bluish, corruptible ice', his 'last terrible look of cold, mute Matter' (the substantive now capitalised to evoke Matter's resistance to transfor-mation). While these cumulative details insist on the absolute closure of death, simultaneously they deprive it of an explanation. They suggest that no special meaning inheres in the death-event beyond the metonymic details that go to compose it. There is no going-beyond, no metaphoric transcendence to raise up the corpse into higher significance. Gerald's 'inert mass' resists precisely those transfers and transformations for which Birkin's word 'love' func-tions as catalyst. In Birkin's perception, '[t]hose who die, and dying still can love, still believe, do not die. They live still in the beloved' (pp. 477–80). In rhetorical terms, only a metaphoric reaching out toward a transfiguration ensures a fresh revelation of meaning. It is this alternative representation of death as metaphoric transfiguration that I wish now to consider.

There is an important sense in which all of Birkin's major speculative excursions are motivated by the need to overcome the limitations of the metonymic vision of death. His periodic 'state of the universe' reports, for example, communicated to Ursula, envisage mankind as imprisoned, caught in a trap of its own fabrication. Locked into their social contexts, people lack the insight and energy to liberate themselves and break loose. In one of Birkin's most vivid designations, they are 'balls of bitter dust ... (that] won't fall off the tree when they're ripe. They hang on to their old positions when the position is overpast ...' (p. 126) ('The Crown' is Lawrence's extended meditation on the theme of not letting-go). In the terms that I have defined, they are locked in a metonymic cul-de-sac, repeating the same actions and gestures within the same narrow field of associations. In a major shift of emphasis away from the traditional novel, Birkin now redefines and reinterprets death. No longer entailing an actual demise, death for Birkin is symbolic: it represents a rupture in the continuity of existence that opens up the truth about life. As such, death is an act from which all the other acts in the novel derive their significance. Contrariwise, the refusal of symbolic death is the mark of a radical failure to live – the hoarding of atrophied energies on this side of the life/death divide. One of Birkin's early remarks to Ursula sums it all up: 'There is life which belongs to death, and there is life which isn't death' (p. 186).

Birkin is thus a metaphor-man par excellence, not only in the sense that he thinks in particular metaphors, though of course he does that: more basically, his thought-processes are regulated by the process of metaphor: they turn on transfers and transformations. For Birkin, the fundamental life-force (eros) is metaphoric in structure: it alone possesses the force to transfigure the death-event, and infuse it with revelatory power. At the same time, in Birkin's diagnosis, this force no longer functions to achieve its effect: it too has been stifled. Contemporary civilisation is marked by an arrest of metaphoric power, a frustration of its potential to revolutionise vision, and thus change the world. Birkin employs a variety of local tropes to define this arrest: mankind is a 'bud' that is unable to break into blossom (pp. 125–6), a chrysalis that never turns into a butterfly (p. 128), an infant that refuses to break through 'the walls of the womb' and be born (p. 186). In all of these instances, the death-process, now defined as the crossing from one domain to another, the transit essential for the emergence of new forms of consciousness, is blocked. If Birkin would 'like to be through with the death-process' (p. 186) – the fundamental mode of the crossing – it is so that fresh metaphoric alignments can come into being.

Until the breakthrough in 'Excurse', however, Birkin fails to achieve the crossing that he so ardently promulgates for others. If, for Ursula, Birkin is 'a foul, deathly thing ... so perverse, so death-eating' (she makes this accusation in their violent initiatory quarrel in that same episode [p. 307]), it is because he too, like the rest of mankind, is trapped in a metonymic dead-end, refusing the transit. In one sense, Ursula's strictures against Birkin are justified, since she herself has been 'through with the death-process', and has accomplished the crossing. In rhetorical terms, she has assimilated death to the metaphorical process: through a complex thought-experiment, based on transfers and transformations, she has opened up a transcendent domain beyond death, predicated on comparisons and contrasts with her present life-situation. As an individual, Ursula has overcome death in precisely the way that Birkin suggests mankind in general should overcome it.

Ursula's *rite du passage* is achieved in the episode 'Sunday-Evening' – her extended meditation on dying. Through analogical inference, her meditation builds an elaborate bridge between the now over-familiar state of her present existence and the unfamiliar 'kingdom of death' that she wishes to enter. In this process, the body fades into insignificance: it functions merely as the transparent vehicle by means of which this 'trespass into the unknown' is accomplished. The thought-experiment commences with Ursula at 'the end of [her] line of life ... in a darkness that was the border of death', poised precariously between the visible and the invisible, the known and the unknown. Initially a simple metonym for the absolute end, death is the 'great consummation', the last in the long series of life's continuing crises that precludes the need to look beyond it for explanations: 'What then need we think for further? ... It is enough that death is a great and conclusive experience'. It is precisely this need to look beyond that motivates prolonging the speculation – for envisioning the 'illimitable space' that lies over the borders of death (p. 191). Through a remarkable process of mapping, the features of the 'kingdom of death' come into view. No longer a domain already charted (as in traditional theological discourse), this new 'kingdom' is constructed piecemeal, shaped by the transfers induced by the metaphorical process itself.

Since the post-death condition possesses all of the attributes that the present one lacks, it is not surprising that contrastive effects predominate. If Ursula's present existence is self-enclosed, claustrophobic, geared to the automatic return of the same – the 'barren school-week, mere routine and mechanical activity' – the death-domain, by contrast, is radically open: it discloses a 'pure unknown' that is devoid of routine or repetition. If her present 'mechanized' life is 'sordid and shameful', the life beyond death is expansive and free: it is 'much cleaner and more dignified to be dead' (pp. 192–3). In short, what the present abysmally lacks, the future holds out in abundance.

At this point, the identification of death as a window ('The only window was death') facilitates a subtle shift in perception: inferential guesswork about the beyond gives way to direct vision. No longer seen through a glass darkly, the vision takes on a luminous clarity. In an ever-expanding horizon, the 'great dark sky' opens up the 'illimitable kingdom of death' as a new sacral domain that, by implication, restores the hierarchical order and freedom that the present world lacks. In this new kingdom, human modes of perception are transfigured: an 'inhuman otherness' defamiliarises the real, putting the possibility of knowing this new domain into question. 'To know is human, and in death we do not know, we are not human' (p. 194). Rhetorically speaking, if this world is known metonymically in its pure immanence – its familiar shapes, its repetitions, its 'mechanical nullity' (p. 193) – the other world is intuited transcendentally through metaphorical transfigurations. In Ursula's thought-experiment, metaphor functions less to communicate pre-existing ideas than to create new horizons of expectation against which present realities are judged and found wanting.

In the episode 'Excurse', these new horizons are opened up by the transfigurations effected by eros. As agent of eros metaphor transforms death, raising it up, endowing it with a visionary potential. As Birkin and Ursula drive into the countryside in the afternoon, the metamorphosis gets under way. It starts typically with Birkin's metonymic 'diagnosis' of the human condition. Imprisoned, locked in a cul-de-sac, people were 'all enclosed in a definite limitation ... (t)hey acted and re-acted involuntarily according to a few great laws, and once the laws, the great principles, were known, people were no longer mystically interesting' (p. 305). In effect, metaphor will disclose the 'mystical interest' that the empirical 'laws' of metonymy shut out from view.

In the violent quarrel between the pair that immediately follows, Ursula places Birkin in precisely the same relation to death as he has placed others: his connection with Hermione 'stands for ... that old, deathly way of living'. In Ursula's perception, Birkin's sex life is 'foul'; his 'truth' and 'purity' stink: he desires nothing but 'dirt' and 'death' (pp. 306–7). Ursula's excremental vision locates the anus as the site at which potentially productive erotic transactions disintegrate, decompose and reduce to waste matter.

The love rites that subsequently take place at the inn of the Saracen's Head enact the most daring of all the novel's transfigurations. As Ursula traces the 'back of [Birkin's] thighs', she discovers the 'strange mystery of his life-motion, there, at the back of his thighs, down the flanks'. In an astonishing revision, the anus becomes the dynamic source of transcendence. In place of the dying body which, as we saw, in the traditional novel is conventionally the source of an ultimate mystical vision, here a specific site in the body is chosen. Previously represented metonymically through contiguous associations (foulness, dirt, stink, decay), the anus is now metaphorised, charged with a fresh range of associations, which reverse and transcend the old modes of perception. The locus of expulsion, rejection, repudiation becomes the 'darkest, deepest, strangest life-source of the human body'; uniting both of the lovers, it offers them the 'most intolerable accession into being' (pp. 313–14). From being the vehicle of the death-flow – of blockage and a lethal constriction – it becomes the fountain of life, releasing 'floods of ineffable darkness and ineffable riches'; from being the abject site of perversion, it becomes the domain of transcendent death. In these erotic exchanges, the habit of metaphorisation associated with death is put to new and extraordinary uses.

These transformations enact the ultimate triumph of metaphor – its power to subsume death into new configurations of being. After which, the 'perfected relation', achieved by Birkin and Ursula sinks into the background, while the lethal antagonisms between Loerke, Gerald and Gudrun usurp by far the greater space of the text. Their entangled death-dramas lend themselves more effectively to the text's terminal vision, which is metonymic in orientation (Loerke's character, for example, is constructed almost entirely in terms of this vision: represented as the waste anal-source, resistant to transformation, he is 'the rock-bottom of all life', a 'mud-child', a rat that 'ebbs with the stream, the sewer stream' [pp. 427–8]). Only at the end of the novel (and in a profound reaction against its own sustained metonymic vision) is a new metaphoric domain opened up, based on a vast impersonal conception, cosmic in scale and scope. It represents a further daring adaptation of the metaphorics of death – this time to the aims of the evolutionary drive, embracing races and species. The dynamics of this new conception is the final dimension I wish to consider.

Wedged between Birkin's sustained mortuary meditations on Gerald's corpse is another meditation, one which the text tells us Birkin finds 'very consoling'. Still focused on death, it shifts attention away from the individual life-span to the vast evolutionary changes in species and types. In so doing, it posits metaphor as the agent of prediction, expansion and change. If Ursula's earlier thought-experiment was essentially theological (the revelation of a new 'kingdom of death'), Birkin's is ontological, centred on the emergence of new orders of being, the revitalisation of cosmic forces and energies. Whether at the personal or impersonal level, metaphoric transfigurations offer the sole means of escape from the cul-de-sac into which (in Birkin's perception) mankind has run, and 'expended itself' (p. 479).

Through analogical projections, metaphor once again maps the contours of an alternative domain, similar to, yet radically different from, the present world which has reached its dead-end. Just as (in Birkin's prophetic vision) the 'ichthyosauri and the mastodon ... failed creatively to develop' – they died metonymic deaths, absorbed back without trace into the contexts from which they emerged – so too mankind may fail to develop. Its mode of extinction is already predicated on that of the great monsters of the past: it too may perish from inanition. In Birkin's rhetoric of progressive change, metaphor is the agent of discovery and expansion: it predicts the modes of evolution's unfolding, its forging of new connections, its generation of new meaningful structures out of the detritus of the past forms of development. In the same way that metaphor (in Paul Ricoeur's conception) draws 'a new semantic pertinence out of the ruins of the literal meaning', opening up 'new aspects, new dimensions, new horizons of meaning',[25] so too (in Birkin's apocalyptic vision) out of the ruins of the present dispensation, the 'timeless creative mystery' may generate 'new races and new species ... new forms of consciousness, new forms of body, new units of being' (p. 479). Indeed Birkin's 'creative mystery' of being has its rhetorical analogue in the creative 'mystery of metaphor',[26] which also generates fresh patterns and meanings through its transfers and transformations.

This up-beat apocalypse, however, is not quite the last word in the novel. Rather it foretends a reversion, a return to metonymic dead-ends, signified once again by the spectacle of Gerald's frozen corpse laid out in the morgue. His demise represents the novel's terminal instance of uncreative death. In the starkest way possible, it configures the conflict between alternative visions of death, which has been the special concern of this essay – between a metonymic decline into nullity, and a metaphoric impulsion, a thrusting forward toward ever-fresh transfigurations. This clash is the stuff of apocalypse: old forms demolished so that new ones may come into being.

As an early modernist text, *Women in Love* articulates that particular moment in time when these two visions intersect, and when their agonistic stance toward each other assumes apocalyptic proportions. They confront each other starkly at the crossing-point where past and future indices meet. At one level, *Women in Love*'s harsh, unrelenting treatment of Mr Crich's and Gerald's deaths points forward to contemporary configurations which strip death of meaning and explanation. As a radical metonymy, death is a random occurrence, a meaningless act, an essential nonsense. It is shown up in its bleak, material manifestations. At another level, Birkin's and Ursula's 'resurrections' hark back to a traditional metaphorics which recuperates death of transcendence, and which *Women in Love* adapts to its own special purposes. In internalising the death-drama, it transforms death into a symbolic event, hinging less on the mystical access to an after-life than on the penetration to the truth about how the present life should be lived. As such, death also prefigures the future: to die a symbolic death is to participate in evolution's unfolding through a radical reforging of forms that enhance the life-process by charging death with an ultimate meaning.

From *Mosaic: A Journal for the Interdisciplinary Study of Literature*, 27: 1 (March 1994), 55–72.

Notes

[In some respects this essay is quite similar to Gerald Doherty's other essay in this volume, on *The Rainbow* (essay 2). Once again his concern is with the operations of metaphor and metonymy, only here they are related not to plot structures but to different conceptions of death, how it is regulated, perceived and valued. Doherty argues that Lawrence uses these tropes to explore *Women in Love*'s 'most dynamic antitheses: between dying and rebirth, decadence and renovation, destruction and creation, between a paralysed immobility and renovatory change'. The metaphoric conception of death stresses that it is a passage from one state to another, from a barren to a more fulfilled existence while the metonymic conception insists that there is no passage to another state and that death is a physical fact that marks the end of the individual's life. Doherty then applies these different understandings of death, the one largely symbolic, the other factual, to the novel. Birkin represents the metaphorical idea of death as the door to a new beginning while Gerald represents the metonymic idea of death as no more than the cessation of breath. The metonymic idea of death looks forward to a wholly secular world while the metaphoric idea of death looks back to a more religious time when death was the entry to a beyond. Living in the secular world, Lawrence does not see death in these religious terms but more as the precondition for the creation of new forms of life.

In his essay on *The Rainbow*, Doherty saw metaphor partly as an elaboration of an existing state whereas here he sees it as the means by which the existing state is transformed. This essay at once shows up the strengths and weaknesses of the criticism inaugurated by the 'linguistic turn'. Doherty gives an exemplary reading of how tropes condition meaning in *Women in Love* and it would be interesting to see how these meanings could be related to Lawrence's reaction to the First World War. All references to *Women in Love* are from the Cambridge edition of the novel, edited by David Farmer, Lindeth Vasey and John Worthen (Cambridge, 1987), and are given in parentheses in the text. Eds].

1. Roman Jakobson, 'Two Aspects of Language and Two Types of Aphasic Disturbance' in *Language in Literature*, ed. Krystyna Pomorska and Stephen Rudy (Cambridge, MA, 1987), pp. 95–114.

2. Ibid., pp. 109–14.

3. David Lodge, *Modes of Modern Writing: Metaphor, Metonymy, and the Typology of Modern Literature* (London, 1977).

4. Peter Brooks, *Reading for the Plot: Design and Intention in Narrative* (Oxford, 1984).

5. Jacques Lacan, *Ecrits: A Selection*, trans. Alan Sheridan (London, 1977).

6. George Lakoff and Mark Turner, *More than Cool Reason: A Field Guide to Poetic Metaphor* (Chicago, 1989), p. 103.

7. D. H. Lawrence, 'The Crown', in *Reflections on the Death of a Porcupine and Other Essays*, ed. Michael Herbert (Cambridge, 1988), p. 266.

8. Juliet Flower MacCannell, *Figuring Lacan: Criticism and the Cultural Unconscious* (London, 1986), p. 159.

9. Jacques Derrida, *Margins of Philosophy*, trans. Alan Bass (Sussex, 1982), p. 226.

10. Elisabeth Bronfen, *Over Her Dead Body: Death, Femininity and the Aesthetic* (Manchester 1992), p. 77.

11. Emily Brontë, *Wuthering Heights* (Harmondsworth, 1973), p. 196.

12. Charles Dickens, *The Old Curiosity Shop* (Harmondsworth, 1972), pp. 653–4.

13. Charles Dickens, *Great Expectations* (Harmondsworth, 1983), pp. 469–70.

14. Virgina Woolf, *Mrs. Dalloway* (London, 1986), p. 163.

15. E. M. Forster, *A Passage to India* (Harmondsworth, 1977), pp. 249–50.

16. James Joyce, *Ulysses* (Harmondsworth, 1992), p. 4.

17. Garrett Stewart, *Death Sentences: Styles of Dying in British Fiction* (Cambridge, MA, 1984), p. 8.

18. Roland Barthes, *Camera Lucida: Reflections on Photography*, trans. Richard Howard (London, 1982), p. 92.

19. Gustave Flaubert, *Madame Bovary*, trans. Alan Russell (Harmondsworth, 1980), pp. 326–7.

20. Lakoff and Turner, *More than Cool Reason*, p. 103.

21. Jakobson, 'Two Aspects of Language', pp. 111–13.

22. Lakoff and Turner, *More than Cool Reason*, p. 103.

23. Roland Barthes, *Camera Lucida*, p. 92.

24. Ronald Schleifer, *Rhetoric and Death: The Language of Modernism and Postmodern Discourse Theory* (Urbana, IL, 1990), p. 9.

25. Paul Ricoeur, *The Rule of Metaphor: Multi-Disciplinary Studies of the Creation of Meaning in Language*, trans. Robert Czerny, Kathleen McLaughlin, and John Costello (London, 1978), pp. 230, 250.

26. Max Black, 'Metaphor', in *Models and Metaphors: Studies in Language and Philosophy* (New York, 1966), p. 39.

7

Staging the Gaze in D. H. Lawrence's *Women in Love*

EARL INGERSOLL

Lawrence's fifth novel, *Women in Love*, has been almost univer-
sally judged among his finest achievements.[1] As a 'war novel'
coming out of what Paul Delany has termed 'Lawrence's
nightmare',[2] it offers a testament of survival, a heroic response to
his radical isolation on the cliffs of Cornwall where he felt like a
fox run to ground. His letters from the period emphasise his
despairing recklessness in constructing a long work which he knew
in advance stood even less chance of reaching an audience than
The Rainbow had in the fall of 1915 when it was burned by the
public hangman on the streets of London.[3]

It was *The Rainbow* that made his achievement in *Women in Love*
'belated'. As Charles Ross has extensively shown in his study *The
Composition of 'The Rainbow' and 'Women in Love'*[4] Lawrence
began what was to be the celebration of his and Frieda's pursuit of
'true marriage' in one of the early drafts of these 'Brangwen novels'
called 'The Sisters', then turned his attention away from the story of
the characters who would become Ursula Brangwen and Rupert
Birkin when he decided that his heroine needed more 'experience'.
That decision produced *The Rainbow*. When he returned to the man-
uscript of *Women in Love*, he had just finished reading Herman
Melville's *Moby Dick* for the first time, and clearly he found in
Melville a kindred spirit. Like his American counterpart, he was strug-

gling to write what looked to be an unpublishable novel, in part because its desperate pursuit of *Blutbruderschaft*[5] would inevitably be read as homoerotic. Much of *Women in Love*'s power is generated by elements of its narrative structure. The organic time frame of an action beginning close to the vernal equinox and ending near the winter solstice seems a gesture toward one of the classical unities. Similarly, the two-couples structure that he found in Hardy's fiction enhances the novel's impact. One other factor that lends *Women in Love* some of its power is Lawrence's development of his two couples within the framework of references to eyes and seeing. It is a framework based in a traditional notion of 'vision', but it is also one that may be read in light of the contemporary concern with looking at and being looked at, or the gaze.

One aspect of the complex relationship between the two couples – Ursula Brangwen and Rupert Birkin, Gudrun Brangwen and Gerald Crich – is the pronounced contrast in the development of visual exchange between the characters. It might be noted at the outset that a concern with looking at and being looked at in Lawrence's work is not unique to *Women in Love*. In *The Rainbow*, for example, Tom Brangwen looks at Lydia Lensky passing him on the road and 'involuntarily' blurts out, 'That's her', and later the young Ursula begins to read her own beauty and desirability in the impassioned gaze of her future lover Anton Skrebensky.[6] These more conventional expressions of visual exchange offer a good starting point since they persist in *Women in Love*. They are increasingly displaced, however, by more intricate expressions of looking.

The contrast between conventional and more complicated expressions of visual exchange is evident in *Women in Love* from the beginning in the descriptions of the two couples' developing relationships. Birkin first becomes significantly aware of Ursula during Hermione's theatricalising of the Ruth story in her drawing room at Breadalby. What he sees is an Ursula who is 'like a strange unconscious bud of powerful womanhood. He was unconsciously drawn to her. She was his future' (p. 92). Birkin's looking at Ursula here and recognising in an instant that she represents 'his future' repeats the healthier consequences of visual exchange in Tom's recognition of Lydia as his future wife. Unlike the Gudrun–Gerald relationship, the growing love of Ursula and Birkin is noticeably lacking in looking and being looked at, with one notable exception. The exception occurs in the 'Moony' chapter in which Ursula comes upon Birkin stoning the moon's reflection. Before she is aware of his presence, however, Ursula suddenly senses the moon 'watching her', and we are told that 'she suffered being exposed to it' (p. 245). Her reaction against the moon's reflection on Willey Water seems to generate the presence of another watcher, whom she immediately knows must be Birkin. Because for a long time she does not betray her presence as a watcher, Ursula becomes a voyeur. Why else is she uncomfortable that he might do 'something he would not wish to be seen doing' (p. 246)? When he becomes aware of her presence while he stones the moon's reflection upon the water, it is clear that his intent gaze upon the moon's reflection has been 'reading', or calling up in his unconscious, an aversion that mutely speaks to Ursula's aversion to this light and her unspoken desire for a darkness beyond the darkness of the night.

The promise of that other darkness is offered in the lovemaking in the 'Excurse' chapter. In the parlour where they have had their tea, Ursula and Birkin make love, in a fashion. Visual exchange becomes prominent in the scene, yet it is implicated in a renewal of vision. Here the visual exchange seems to highlight mutuality and a depth of tenderness released by the power of the metaphoric:

> She looked at him ... New eyes were opened in her soul, she saw a strange creature from another world, in him ... She recalled again the old magic of the Book of Genesis, where the Sons of God saw the daughters of men, that they were fair. And he was one of these, one of these strange creatures from the beyond, looking down at her, and seeing she was fair.
>
> (pp. 312–13)

This scene functions as the annunciation of the potential in their relationship. That potential moves toward its realisation in their night of love in Sherwood Forest. Looking at and being looked at are utterly erased as possibilities in 'pure night'. Only darkness and silence reign in this kingdom of tenderness and touch, 'never to be seen with the eye' (p. 320).

In these key scenes of Ursula and Birkin's maturing love, visual factors contribute to an enhancement of something approaching the traditional mystic vision. It is the vision of love for which Lawrence borrowed the scriptural language of 'a new heaven and a new earth'. It is not a looking at, but a way of seeing the world anew, with eyes able to 'see' at last. Even then, this seeing is subordinate to the darkness of the 'body of mysterious night', just as 'silence' is privileged over even the most inspired 'speech'. These expressions of a more 'positive' visual exchange are crucial to the narrative's attempt at balancing interest in the two couples. In their own frequently under-acknowledged way, they function as a counterpart to a powerful variant that might be called a perversion of looking.

The 'Coal-Dust' chapter offers a valuable starting point for an exploration of the perversion of looking in the relationship between Gerald and Gudrun. The scene stages the spectacle of Gerald's violent mastery of his horse after it becomes frightened by a railroad train. The term 'spectacle' seems appropriate here, because Gerald is a performer exploiting the theatrical potential of the scene. When he rides up, the crossing gate is down, and instead of moving back from the noise or perhaps even demonstrating the mare's skill by flamboyantly jumping over the gate, he pitilessly reins in and spurs his terrified mare into submission. The theatricality of the scene is vividly realised through the eyes of Ursula and Gudrun, especially the latter: 'he was very picturesque, at least in Gudrun's eyes', and perhaps in his own. 'Gudrun liked to look at him', and 'his blue eyes were full of sharp light, as he watched the distance' (p. 110). Although it would seem at first that Gudrun's eyes are being made to function as a camera to record Gerald's external appearance, the focus on Gerald's eyes and his watching provides yet another indication of the pervasiveness in this text of eyes and the domination of or through looking and its inverse image of being looked at.

In staging this scene for its predictably different effects upon the sisters, Gerald is the master of the show, a kind of exhibitionist self-consciously aware of the fixed gaze of his audience. Before he reins in the mare to wait at the crossing, while he is 'looking down the railway for the approaching train', Gerald 'salutes' Ursula and Gudrun. Thus, he knows that they are witnessing the spectacle he is about to produce for their benefit. As the mare first begins to recoil from the frightening noise of the approaching locomotive, we read that 'a glistening, half-smiling look came into Gerald's face'. That 'half-smiling look' reflects Gudrun's earlier 'ironic smile at his picturesqueness', in spite of which she 'liked to look at him'. When the mare again recoils, the sisters' responses begin their more radical differentiation. Gudrun's response is the more complex, for she is reacting not only to Gerald's cruel restraint but also to Ursula's humane and reasonable question: 'Why doesn't he ride away till it's gone by?' Indeed, Gudrun appears mesmerised, as she watches Gerald 'with black-dilated, spellbound eyes'. As the theatrical scene ends, those responses are underscored when Ursula, 'frantic with opposition and hatred of Gerald', cries out once again. Gudrun watches, still 'spellbound' and silent.

The reactions of the two sisters to whom Gerald has been playing this scene are further distinguished by the effect of Ursula's voice upon Gudrun, and undoubtedly on Gerald as well. When Ursula cries out the first time 'at the top of her voice, completely outside herself', the phrase 'outside herself' seems a clumsy misstatement of 'beside herself'. We are told, however that 'Gudrun hated her bitterly for being outside herself', because her voice 'was so powerful and naked'. Thus, Gudrun's gaze has so immersed her within herself that Ursula's 'powerful and naked' voice is a distracting feature of an 'outside' she rejects. To underscore the mesmerising force of that gaze, the scene is likened to one from a 'disgusting dream that has no end', without identifying the 'dreamer' in whose eyes this unending dream is 'disgusting'. The scene underscores conventional 'disgust' at such premeditated cruelty as well as a perverse attraction to violation. These diametrically opposed reactions are polarised in the sisters, and consequently, in the narrator, perhaps even in the reader. Clearly, Gerald is affected by both sisters, as they are by each other. In fact, Gerald's gratuitous cruelty feeds on the pleasure of violating Ursula's conventional aversion to abusing animals. Similarly, Gudrun is powerfully moved by this spectacle not only because she experiences vicariously what Gerald experiences directly but also because she enjoys his and her own perverse pleasure in violating normal sanctions against cruelty to animals.

The real power of the scene, then, is its theatricalisation by Gudrun's imagination after she apparently loses consciousness momentarily. It has been speculated that Gudrun undergoes an orgasmic experience here in identifying herself with the mare that the wilful Gerald coerces into submission between his powerful thighs, after driving his spurs into her bleeding wounds. However, the narrator indicates 'she turned white', before the 'world reeled and passed into nothingness for Gudrun', a reaction which hardly seems 'orgasmic'. It is only as the action completes itself – signalled by the approach of the guard's van – that the real power of the scene builds within Gudrun, as she reshapes it in her own imagination. The guard himself functions as a surrogate for Gudrun's gaze, since he is 'staring out in his transition on the spectacle in the road. And, through the man in the closed wagon, Gudrun could see the whole scene spectacularly, isolated and momentary, like a vision isolated in eternity' (p. 112). In this way the guard is enlisted as another watcher along with the sisters; unlike them, however, he is watching not only Gerald's performance, but also Gudrun's. This new watcher and the gate-keeper record her reaction against her watcher's role of silent passivity as she becomes an active, screaming participant in the 'spectacle'. Springing past the guard, she flings the gate open for Gerald and the mare, crying 'in a strange, high voice, like a gull, or like a witch screaming out': 'I should think you're proud.' With this maenadic gesture,[7] Gudrun celebrates Gerald's 'mastery' of the show.

As this brief rendition of the scene suggests, the visual exchange between Gudrun and Gerald is diametrically opposed to the benign, if not mystical, ramifications of visual exchange between Ursula and Birkin in Sherwood Forest. The reader cannot help feeling the strong impact of powerful forces in the characters' unconscious released, for good or ill, through the agency of their looking at and being looked at by each other. In both cases, the human eye is much more than a 'camera' passively recording images. Looking at and being looked at are clearly implicated in a complex interchange offering insights into the working of the unconscious.

The visual exchange, I would argue, has such power and intensity in the Gudrun and Gerald relationship because Lawrence understood what Freud explained in 'Instincts and Their Vicissitudes' without ever having read it. It is uncannily appropriate to a discussion of *Women in Love* that the two central 'instincts', or drives, and their 'vicissitudes', or reversals, that Freud discusses one after another, are evident in the scene of Gerald and the mare. The first is probably the more obvious – the sadism explicit in Gerald's abuse of the horse. Freud sees the interrelations of sadism and its 'vicissitude', masochism, in terms of three stages: 1) the instinct begins in an impulse to exercise control or to master another person as an object; 2) the instinct reverses itself in the relinquishing of that other person as 'object' and a turning back upon the subject as passive object; 3) the completion of the three stages occurs in the search for another subject in relation to whom the original subject might become a passive object.[8] The 'instincts and their vicissitudes' may be understood as a continuously shifting pattern of oscillation between opposing positions, on the analogy of an optical illusion, in which one can see, for example, the vase or the two profiles, but not both simultaneously.[9]

It is Freud's discussion of the second major instinct and its vicissitude that is most useful to an understanding of looking at and being looked at in *Women in Love*. Freud sees similar stages in the interrelations of the visual, or 'scopic' instinct and its reversal. What seems a simple act of looking is merely the first of three stages in the visual experience. Like sadism, looking is at first an effort to control another subject as an object. In its second stage, looking turns back upon the subject or some part of the subject as though that part were an object viewed. Finally, another subject is introduced in the third stage as a viewer for whom the first subject can function as object. In this way the watching subject may achieve control over the object only to become the object observed and therefore mastered. To understand either of these positions – looking (the voyeur) or being looked at (the exhibitionist) – one or the other must be 'repressed'. When one position is 'repressed', or erased, there remains a trace of that position as a ghost of that absent, repressed opposite.

Returning to *Women in Love*, we discover the dominance of looking and being looked at from the very beginning. The opening scene ends with the suggestion of Gudrun, the incipient watcher in this text, that they go for a walk: 'Shall we go out and look at that wedding?' (p. 10). The walk to the church becomes painful to Gudrun, 'exposed to every stare', of these 'uneasy, watchful common people'. At the same time, of course, she invites their stares with her brightly-coloured stockings. Her surprisingly violent reaction to one spectator's comment prepares us for her attraction to Gerald: 'A sudden fierce anger swept over the girl, violent and murderous. She would have liked them all to be annihilated, cleared away, so that the world was left clear for her. How she hated walking up the churchyard path ... in their sight' (p. 13). Her revulsion against being looked at by these ghoulish spectators is so great that she almost misses the opportunity to be a spectator herself at the Crich wedding, the first of several close encounters with Gerald Crich.

The wedding party and its spectators provide Gudrun with a diverting spectacle at first. However, it is Gerald upon whom her gaze 'lights', perhaps because he has 'the strange, guarded look, the unconscious glisten', which becomes the signature of his personality. The statement that she 'lighted on him at once' suggests a linkage of staring or gazing with an aggressive, almost predatory assault upon Gerald. In a striking inversion of Tom's instantaneous recognition of Lydia, Gudrun says, 'That's him!' so to speak, an ominous indication of her future role as active pursuer/watcher of Gerald. 'I shall know more of that man', she says, emphasising that seeing is at least a double phenomenon here, for gazing at/familiarising herself with Gerald will be her way of knowing him. In this way, she will 'know' Gerald in a mode traditionally reserved for the male eye for which the love object to be pursued is a complex of surfaces in which the eye becomes ensnared.[10]

Here, however, Gudrun becomes involved in the gaze by training her eyes upon Gerald as an object of desire. Clearly the gaze is 'reading' her voyeurism, implicit in her aversion to being looked at, an aversion which the narrative has foregrounded in her revulsion against being stared at by the 'watchful common people' on the way to the church. She stares at Gerald as though he has mesmerised, or 'magnetised' her. What the gaze is reading in her is Gudrun's 'violent and murderous' impulses, suggested by her recognition of similar impulses in him: 'His totem is the wolf.' Gerald's 'clear northern flesh and his fair hair' are metaphorised as 'cold sunshine refracted through crystals of ice'. In this way, Gerald's 'god' is Apollo, the Greek god of light, order, and knowing through the eye, the same Apollo, whose totem was also the wolf. Gerald is a variety of the earliest graphic evidence of classical Greek civilisation – the kouros, or 'Apollo', the 'beautiful boy', to use Camille Paglia's term, the first sex object of Western desire.

Gudrun's bizarre reaction to knowing Gerald visually, that reaction frequently viewed as 'orgasmic', suggests the power of the gaze in reading the unconscious in her. As she stares at Gerald, who seems at this point not yet aware of the role chosen for him as love object/exhibitionist in this theatre of the gaze, Gudrun is being read as an active, even aggressive, and potentially sadistic watcher:

> She was tortured with desire to see him again, a nostalgia, a necessity to see him again, to make sure it was not all a mistake, that she was not deluding herself, that she really felt this strange and overwhelming sensation on his account, this knowledge of him in her essence, this powerful apprehension of him.
>
> (p. 15)

If her reaction seems 'orgasmic', it is the result of the abruptness of her 'lighting' upon Gerald as her potentially perverse soul-mate in this dramatisation of the 'instincts and their vicissitudes'. It might be noted also that her visual knowledge of him is an 'apprehension', i.e., at one and the same time, a 'perception', a 'conception', an 'arrest', and a 'foreboding'.

In a sense, we are witnessing in this scene the first stage of the instinct of voyeurism and its vicissitude of exhibitionism. Gudrun, in her aversion to being looked at, has discovered, as though for the first time, the power of watching, the knowledge and control which come through the eye. Perhaps because Gudrun understands her 'femininity' as a function of her being a vulnerable, powerless object of male staring and rejects it, she adopts the traditionally 'male' position in the staging of this instinct and its reversal. If her 'orgasmic' experience of knowing Gerald through the eye – that 'paroxysm of violent sensation' – is erotically organised, then it functions as a fitting annunciation of what has seemed for readers of the novel a sadomasochistic relationship that reverses conventional gender identities. From this annunciation scene on, she will come to enjoy the power of controlling/humiliating the increasingly masochistic Gerald.

The next encounter is the 'Diver' scene. As in a dream's ritualistic repetitiveness, the sisters are walking again, this time near Willey Water. Suddenly their casual surveying of the landscape is interrupted by the intrusion of 'a white figure', running from the boathouse and diving into the water. At first the diver is identified only as male. As a man who has taken possession of the watery world, this 'white figure' calls up Gudrun's envy, for he has the privilege of swimming nude in such a public place. As the sisters stand 'watching' the diver, their reactions are radically differentiated, a preparation for the mare and train scene toward which this encounter is inexorably moving. The more visceral Ursula has no envy whatsoever of the 'cold' and 'wet' freedom of the swimming 'white figure'. Gudrun, on the other hand, stands 'watching ... as if fascinated'. Eventually, we are told, the sisters 'could see his ruddy face, and could feel him watching them' (p. 47). At this point, Ursula seems present merely to function as a casual, cheery contrast to the 'fascinated' Gudrun. Ursula's statement of the obvious – 'It is Gerald Crich' – rings like a naïve child's reaction over against Gudrun's 'I know'. As in the earlier wedding scene, Gudrun knows through her eyes.

What follows is an ingeniously staged performance of gazing and being the object of the gaze. Part of what 'fascinates', or even mesmerises Gudrun, is Gerald's absolute self-containment. He is not only content in the isolation of his watery world; he celebrates a kind of narcissistic self-sufficiency, wrapping him in an aura of 'glamour'. Like the 'star' of film or rock music, Gerald has 'charisma', and he grows to relish its effect on others. We see that effect on Gudrun in a passage which demonstrates the operation of the gaze:

> And she stood motionless gazing over the water at the face which washed up and down on the flood, as he swam steadily. From his separate element he saw them, and he exulted to himself because of his own advantage, his possession of a world to himself. He was immune and perfect. He loved his own vigorous, thrusting motion, and the violent impulse of the very cold water against his limbs, buoying him up. He could see the girls watching him a way off, outside, and that pleased him. He lifted his arm from the water, in a sign to them.
>
> (p. 47)

In this way, Gerald's exhibitionist propensities are made clear once again in preparation for the crucial scene with the mare.

Gerald's nakedness here clearly contrasts with the London bohemian scene to follow where his nakedness will be a source of embarrassed self-consciousness. Among the sexually ambivalent bohemians, nudity is a kind of 'statement', and, perhaps more menacing, an inducement to expose himself for their voyeuristic purposes. In the nude wrestling scene, although Birkin also strips off his clothes, it is Gerald's nakedness on which the narrative focuses, almost as though he is a classical Greek statue in motion. In 'Diver', although Gerald's nakedness is veiled from the view of the sisters once they have identified him, he finds an autoerotic pleasure in exercising his male privilege of swimming nude, a privilege that 'ladies' of this time would be reluctant even to acknowledge as a desire. But it is his complete nudity as maximum exposure to the external world that is essential here. The complete enclosure of his body in cold wetness defines the contours of his form as a sculptor shapes the surface of a statue. And Gerald thrills to this radical self-containment, as though he were an objet d'art self-consciously enjoying the knowledge that the watching sisters are aware of his hard separateness.

Once again, the reactions of the sisters are crucially differentiated. Ursula continues to be the casual, sociable onlooker, laughing at her own cleverness in comparing Gerald to a Nibelung. Indeed, she almost seems to be enjoying the ironic appropriateness of this comparison of Gerald to a figure in the Nibelungenlied, where Gudrun's Teutonic namesake plays a crucial and destructive role. Gudrun, in contrast, is even further implicated in the gaze. Her silence and immobility, set off by Ursula's bubbly talk and Gerald's mobility, underscore the power of the gaze. By watching Gerald's exhibitionist activity, as though he were an object generated by her watching, Gudrun is being read by the Other, by the unconscious, as it works through Gerald, as object and as other. And he too is being read by her gaze, as it becomes clear in the statement: 'They watched him. He waved again, with a strange movement of recognition across the difference' (p. 47). The word 'difference' seems at first a lapse for 'distance'; however, it is ironically apt here, since the 'difference' between Gudrun as gazing watcher and Gerald as self-conscious exhibitionist collapses upon itself as both are implicated by the gaze.

That subversion of 'difference' by possibilities of similarity helps to prepare for the clearly sadomasochistic overtones of the later scene of Gerald and the mare. As a narcissist with exhibitionist tendencies, Gerald, like Gudrun his soul-mate, is a complex mixture of conventionally 'masculine' and 'feminine' characteristics. He 'exults' in the masculine freedom and mobility which he is exhibitionistically displaying, the metaphoric 'thrusting with his legs and all his body, without bond or connection', yet as exhibitionist, as object of the watcher's gaze, he is positioning himself in a passive and thus 'feminine' position of vulnerability or susceptibility to Gudrun's active, assertive, and eventually sadistic control. In her gaze he reads a celebration of his own 'masculinity' and yet he needs a confirmation of his mastery in the slavishly devoted and envious eyes of the other to whom he gives up power. Thus, he can know power only by sadistically exulting in the knowledge of his own male freedom and mobility by displaying himself to the oppressed female's eyes. Perhaps, even he senses the perverse potential in his relationship with the slavish Pussum, whose self-humiliation foretells his own in the last stage of his affair with Gudrun, who flaunts the power that has devolved upon her through Gerald's admission of a 'feminine' dependence on her.

It is interesting too that this scene is connected with the Water-Party episode in which the sisters have their turn to enjoy the 'male' freedom of swimming nude. The scene is another theatricalisation of the gaze from the very arrival of the Brangwens and Gudrun's recounting of the 'vile experience' of watching impoverished boys diving into the muddy Thames for coins tossed to them by passengers on a steamer. We are told that Gerald 'watched her all the time she spoke, his eyes glittering with faint rousedness' (p. 161), in part because of her cruel disdain for the poor. Like him, she is a hierarchist, who privileges his diving over the loathsome grubbing for money of poor boys in the mud. As the sisters row away, Gerald becomes the watcher:

> [Gudrun's] voice was shrill and strange [like her voice as she throws open the gate for him and his mare], calling from the distance. He watched her paddle away. There was something child-like about her, trustful and deferential, like a child. He watched her all the while, as she rowed. And to Gudrun it was a real delight, in make-belief, to be the child-like woman to the man.
>
> (p. 164)

The scene of Gudrun's becoming aware of the cattle as 'watchers' of her dancing underscores the theme of hypnotised staring in this text. Clearly, the cattle are a projection of her preoccupation with evading the stares of ogling men, since these cattle are not milch cows but 'bullocks', or steers being raised for meat. Her sadistic display, generated through her implication in the gaze as she watches these castrated males, suggests that she is being read by the Other as a complex mixture of scopophilia-exhibitionism and sadomasochism. Obviously enough, she enjoys the 'helpless fear and fascination' of the cattle, 'breathing heavily' with a quasi-sexual arousal. Appropriately, her exhibitionism with his cattle, positioning Gerald as voyeuristic watcher, confers a power upon him which she deeply resents: 'She was watching him all the time with her dark, dilated, inchoate eyes. She leaned forward and swung round her arm, catching him a light blow on the face with the back of her hand ... And she felt in her soul an unconquerable desire for deep violence against him' (p. 170). He recoils in surprise from what is a mere gesture of violence, 'and a dangerous flame darkened his eyes'. Like Gudrun, 'fascinated' by his exhibitionism with the mare, Gerald is rendered speechless: 'For some seconds he could not speak, his lungs were so suffused with blood, his heart stretched almost to bursting with a great gush of ungovernable emotion. It was as if some reservoir of black emotion had burst within him, and swamped him' (pp. 170–1). If Gudrun's reaction to his cruel mastery of the mare was an 'orgasm', surely this is Gerald's.

It takes some time for Gudrun to recover from the effects of her implication by the gaze. As a watcher who resents the 'feminizing' position of being stared at by men – even Gerald – she attempts to escape from the mastering of his eyes: 'She stood negligently, staring away from him, into the distance' all the time he is 'watching her closely. His eyes were lit up with intent light, absorbed and gleaming' (p. 171). When she attempts to avoid his gaze by moving away, Gerald pursues her, admitting that he loves her, once she has played her 'feminine' role as object of that pursuit and asked him not to be angry with her. In this sadomasochistic arena of struggle for power, he shows himself up, to her at least, as one of his steers by 'swooning' in response to her mocking tolerance of his overture. The conclusion of this episode reconfirms the interrelation of the scopophiliac-exhibitionist and sadomasochistic drives in a chilling passage foretelling the cataclysmic relationship to come for the two:

> 'It's all right, then, is it?' he said, holding her arrested.
> She looked at the face with the fixed eyes, set before her, and her blood ran cold.
> 'Yes, it's all right', she said softly, as if drugged, her voice crooning and witch-like.
>
> (p. 172)

If such scenes as these have mysterious power over even the most sophisticated readers, that power inheres in part at least in the intensity of our gaze as we watch these visually realised, theatrical episodes in which the gaze is reading our unconscious. For the male reader at least, Gudrun is a variety of Medusa, that dread image of the powerful female, fascinating, bewitching, and petrifying Gerald and those of us gazing on her along with him.

The 'Coal-Dust' scene, with which we began, provides a link in the chain of psychic encounters between Gerald and Gudrun in which variety of the gaze is operating, if the gaze can encompass the oscillation between looking at and being looked at. This gaze is not quite the Lacanian 'regard', or Gaze, whose full rehearsal would take us beyond the limited range of this brief exploration. Even so, it is possible to see in these powerful scenes Lawrence exploiting the theatrical possibilities of looking in his characters. Clearly, he is staging scenes with which conventional New Critical notions of eyes and seeing imagery cannot satisfactorily cope. At the same time, Lawrence's staging of the gaze offers us the opportunity for what might be termed a New Psychoanalytic Criticism – one less concerned with demonstrating that characters are suffering from Oedipus complexes and more interested in exploring ways in which psychoanalytic insights can provide the means of opening texts for a fuller understanding of textual desire and the energies compelling the reader's attention. Without his having read Freud's 'Instincts and Their Vicissitudes', *Women in Love* demonstrates that Lawrence had independently developed insights into the complexities of visual exchange.

From *Studies in the Novel*, 26: 3 (Fall, 1994), 268–80.

Notes

[Earl Ingersoll's psychoanalytic reading of *Women in Love* suggests that women can objectify men as much as men can objectify women and this questions one of the orthodoxies of feminist criticism, namely that the gaze is solely a function of patriarchy. Ingersoll begins his essay by noting the parallel between Tom Brangwen's first glimpse of Lydia in *The Rainbow* and Birkin's of Ursula in *Women in Love*. He shows that, in general, the relationship between Birkin and Ursula is largely free of 'looking' and this contrasts with Gudrun and Gerald where it is an important element of their relationship. Ingersoll grounds his discussion of the gaze in Freud's essay 'The Instincts and their Vicissitudes' which is a bold move given Lawrence's scepticism of psychoanalysis. Freud finds a correspondence between sadism and masochism and voyeurism and exhibitionism. He argues that just as sadistic instinct undergoes a series of changes culminating in a reversal to masochism, so, too, does the scopophilic instinct, or instinct to look, gradually transform into the instinct to be looked at. The basic pattern is that just as the sadist/voyeur turns someone into an object by looking at them, so the sadist/voyeur then turns this look back on him or herself before seeking another person who can look at him or her as an object, thereby turning him or her from a sadist/voyeur into a masochist/exhibitionist. Ingersoll maps this pattern onto the relation between Gudrun and Gerald. She changes from an embryonic exhibitionist with her coloured stockings to a voyeur who increasingly dominates Gerald, while his early sadism with the mare at the railway crossing gradually modulates into a form of masochism.

Ingersoll's article is of interest not just because it engages, if only implicitly, with one of the central tenants of feminism, but also because it seeks to move beyond the conventional psychoanalytic interpretation of literature as so many manifestations of the Oedipus complex. Indeed, this is a characteristic of poststructuralist psychoanalysis generally, but what makes Ingersoll's approach different is that he uses Freud instead of Lacan to understand 'textual desire and the energies compelling the reader's attention'. All references to *Women in Love* are from the Cambridge edition of the novel, edited by David Farmer, Lindeth Vasey and John Worthen (Cambridge 1987), and are given in parentheses in the text. Eds]

1. H. M. Daleski, for example, in *The Forked Flame: A Study of D. H. Lawrence* (Evanston, IL, 1965), asserts: 'I think that most critics today would agree that *The Rainbow* and *Women in Love* ... are his greatest achievement' (p. 14).

2. From the title of Delany's book, *D. H. Lawrence's Nightmare: The Writer and His Circle in the Years of the Great War* (New York, 1978).

3. In a letter to Barbara Low, 1 May 1916, he speaks of his work *Women in Love*: 'I have begun the second half of *The Rainbow*. But already it is beyond all hope of ever being published, because of the things it says.' See *The Letters of D. H. Lawrence*, volume II, ed. George Zytaruk and James T. Boulton (Cambridge, 1981), p. 602. To his agent J. B. Pinker, he says: 'It is a terrible and horrible and wonderful novel. You will hate it and nobody will publish it.' See *Letters* II, p. 669.

4. Charles L. Ross, *The Composition of 'The Rainbow' and 'Women in Love': A History* (Charlottesville, VA, 1979).

5. See my 'The Failure of Bloodbrotherhood in Melville's *Moby Dick* and Lawrence's *Women in Love*', *The Midwest Quarterly*, 30.4 (1989), 458–77.

6. '[Ursula] was thrilled with a new life. For the first time, she was in love with a vision of herself: she saw as it were a fine little reflection of herself in [Skrebensky's] eyes. And she must act up to this: she must be beautiful.' See *The Rainbow* (Cambridge, 1989), p. 272.

7. Charles L. Ross, 'D. H. Lawrence's Use of Greek Tragedy: Euripedes and Ritual', *D. H. Lawrence Review*, 10.1 (1977), 15–16.

8. Sigmund Freud, 'Instincts and their Vicissitudes', in Freud, *On Metapyschology: The Theory of Psychoanalysis*, trans. James Strachey, ed. Angela Richards (Harmondsworth, 1984), pp. 113–37.

9. I am indebted to Robert Con Davis – see 'Lacan, Poe, and Narrative Repression', *Lacan and Narration: The Psychoanalytic Difference in Narrative Theory* (Baltimore and London, 1983), pp. 983–1005 – for his assistance in reading Freud's 'Instincts and Their Vicissitudes'. Davis argues for 'Instincts and Their Vicissitudes' – see *The Standard Edition of the Complete Psychological Works of Sigmund Freud*, vol. 14, trans. James Strachey (London, 1957), pp. 17–40 – as the basis for Lacan's Gaze; however, he provides little evidence for the connection, other than Lacan's reference to Freud's 'Instincts'. Furthermore, as Ragland-Sullivan reminds us – see Ellie Ragland-

Sullivan, *Jacques Lacan and the Philosophy of Psychoanalysis* (Urbana and Chicago, 1986), p. 94 – Lacan himself emphatically distinguishes his Gaze from literal looking at and being looked at (p. 84). Lacan acknowledges a debt to Jean-Paul Sartre's notion of the gaze, or 'le regard'. See *Being and Nothingness: An Essay on Phenomenological Ontology*, trans. Hazel E. Barnes (New York, 1956) – and to the phenomenonologist Maurice Merleau-Ponty's insights into perception; see *Phenomenology of Perception*, trans. Colin Smith (London, 1962). Part of his 'return to Freud' was Lacan's attempt to stress the early Freud's concern with the unconscious, and it is clearly the unconscious that is energising the shifting positions of looking at and being looked at.

10. I owe a debt to Camille Paglia's controversial and provocative reading of gender in *Sexual Personae: Art and Decadence from Nefertiti to Emily Dickinson* (London and New Haven, 1990). She argues that from its origins in Egyptian civilisation Western art has fed the male eye in its pursuit of beauty in an object caught in its dominating gaze.

8

The Discourse of Knowledge: Historical Change in *Women in Love*

JAMES F. KNAPP

I

Critical work, artistic work, and the work of material production all involve particular appropriations of language. These special uses of language within society are not isolated from one another but rather are mutually implicated. In their continuing, necessary transactions, they inscribe a discourse which continues to act – from factory floor to university classroom – to shape the working lives of men and women. In attempting to understand the enormous complexity of the discursive pattern which came to dominance in the early decades of this century, no example is more challenging than that of D. H. Lawrence. Lawrence was at once the most explicit of the modernists, portraying and denouncing the contemporary transformations of work, knowledge, and subjectivity, and a powerful exemplar of the very discourse which was bringing about those changes. With regard to the specific ways in which this general discourse was deployed, the situation becomes still more complex.

In his preface to *Women in Love*, D. H. Lawrence says that 'we are now in a period of crisis', that 'the people that can bring forth the new passion, the new idea, this people will endure. Those

153

others, that fix themselves in the old idea, will perish with the new life strangled unborn within them' (p. viii). Lawrence's prophetic tone is not accompanied by any concrete definition of what the 'new' might be, as he remains within a rhetoric based upon organic metaphors: 'New unfoldings struggle up in torment in him, as buds struggle forth from the midst of a plant.' He speaks of the First World War's bitterness as a part of his novel's atmosphere, but the war is only a recent, terrible sign for deeper transformations of the social order. The deadly struggle between an 'old', outworn culture – Victorian in its morality, capitalist in its economic relations – and a 'new', somehow more natural society is Lawrence's true subject, and he suspends his characters in a space between two worlds, where they suffer the constraints of the outworn order as well as the uncertainty of social experiment. Although much of the struggle takes place at the level of personality, *Women in Love* is most fundamentally a novel of social crisis rather than one of individual self-definition. In varying ways, all the important characters are made to feel that their personal agonies somehow originate in a historical moment of disorder and change.

If the novel's characters experience their world as broken, discontinuous with the past, however, Lawrence supplies an interpretive frame for their story which is very coherent indeed. Specifically, they are shown as responding to a complex of changes entailed by the movement of industrial capitalism into a new stage of technological and managerial efficiency. The chapter entitled 'The Industrial Magnate', which tells the story of that change, thus occupies a special place within the novel. As a narrative within a narrative, 'The Industrial Magnate' assumes a privileged role within the text as a tale of origins, a governing fiction by means of which we might interpret the historical crisis which is the torment of these characters. At this thematic level of knowledge, the characters' experience of discontinuity is thus shown to be only apparent, as it is recontained by the familiar shape of narrative history. And in formal terms as well, the openness of much of the novel would seem to be contradicted – or resolved – by the closure of this traditional chapter.

To argue that a chapter may be seen to occupy a privileged position such as this, of course, is not to suggest that Lawrence has provided a key to his novel's meaning. The interpretive clarity which this wonderfully coherent narrative of historical change seems to offer the reader is contradicted by nearly everything else in this novel

about the terrible difficulty of even understanding, much less accommodating to, this very process of transformation. Lawrence himself,
of course, often warned against the dangers of a naïve reading which
fails to acknowledge the indirections of literary artifice: 'The artist
usually sets out – or used to – to point a moral and adorn a tale. The
tale, however, points the other way, as a rule. Two blankly opposing
morals, the artist's and the tale's. Never trust the artist. Trust the
tale. The proper function of a critic is to save the tale from the artist
who created it.'[1] Lawrence is quite firm in his contention that good
art 'will tell you the truth' of the artist's day, and yet the language of
art is dense, shifting, always on the verge of fossilising into nontruth,
always ready to mislead or mystify. The notion is an important one
for understanding Lawrence's demanding and suspicious use of
language, and critics have come increasingly to see its power. Frank
Kermode, for example, speaks of Lawrence's art as 'palimpsest-like',
as characterised by a kind of 'overpainting' which enhances the
generally 'indeterminate nature of narrative' and so permits 'an
indefinite range of interpretation'.[2] More recently, Michael Ragussis
has examined some of the ways in which Lawrence's readers are
enlisted in the task of delineating truth and lies in works which
share the equivocity of meaning of most kinds of discourse.[3]
Acknowledging Lawrence's own 'self-critical gesture', Ragussis sees
both artist and reader as engaged in saving the text whenever it
threatens to escape into a realm of specious Truth, unconstrained
by contextuality, which is the contingent but vital ground of any
meaningful statement. Lawrence's language is the central focus here,
as his struggle with 'the subterfuge of art' becomes a test of whether
or not he can succeed in continually renewing his vocabulary and his
syntax.

Lawrence was certainly engaged in a struggle to prevent any
absolute language pointing to its origin in the Word from trapping
the vital substance of his own words, and this need to write beyond
the fossil forms of Truth determines one pole of the reader's
dilemma in confronting works of great interpretive difficulty. But
the difficulties of inventing a language of renewal were set against
Lawrence's equal difficulty in telling the truth of his times by
constructing a story made out of history. Part of the problematic
quality of *Women in Love* lies in the fact that its historical thesis is
made so explicit in a subnarrative which at the same time opens
history to serious question. In addition to the indeterminacy of
language in the novel there is what might be termed an indetermi-

nacy of history, if history is regarded as existing in the space between social event and storytelling.

This problem of how historical narratives function within the context of social change is not unique to Lawrence's fiction. Victor Turner, for example, has studied similar problems of social representation in other cultures, and some of his terms may be helpful in this instance. Turner argues that the genealogy of literary narrative begins in what he calls 'social dramas', public breaches of social norms or rules of morality which are understood to express deeper divisions within a society and which must issue in some redress or reordering of the 'components of a social field'. Several important conditions exist in these social dramas, and they remain embedded in the later forms (such as the juridical procedures and literary narrative) which derive from them. First, liminality is always present: we are witnessing a breach between conflicting interests and forms of social order, and whatever the resolution, 'a momentous juncture or turning point' in the life of the society will have been passed. The process is characterised by an essential indeterminacy, however, because 'indeterminacy is, so to speak, in the subjunctive mood, since it is that which is not yet settled, concluded, and known. It is all that may be, might be, could be, perhaps even should be.'[4]

Thus we are dealing with a passage from one social order to another, a process of social change which is indeterminate insofar as it has not yet been determined and so may be characterised by its openness, its potentiality. Another kind of openness enters when social drama is re-enacted as ritual or narrative. As performance within history, this reinscribing is subject to new conflict and need, and so may itself change, generating 'precedents' which are in fact unprecedented. This second openness, which in literary terms is the indeterminacy of rewriting, is central to an aspect of narrative which demands particular care on the part of critics. A narrative may, on the one hand, inscribe a social passage as paradigmatic, or normative: in Turner's terms, it may serve as a 'model of', validating and reinforcing a particular social condition. But it may equally well serve as 'model for', initiating change in the order of society rather than reproducing the forms of the past.

I have described Turner's argument at some length because I believe that it generates precisely the kinds of questions which need to be asked about the use of history in fiction, such as Lawrence's, which situates itself so explicitly within a process of social conflict and transformation. If we are dealing with a narrative which treats some crucial juncture within history, we may ask what specific structure and meaning the passage from one social state to another is made to assume in its narrative form. What kind of resolution is enabled? Would an archaeology of a text such as *Women in Love* reveal that a social process which is characterised by indeterminacy and potentiality at some points has been made to appear closed and natural at others? To what extent is the reader to assume that any narrative is a 'model' of history, recounting a reality which must be accepted because 'true'? When is it, in part at least, a 'model for', a rewriting of history which is itself an intervention in the continuous play of social power? The rhetoric of Lawrence's fiction claims to practise both kinds of narrative, and while I would argue that both are in fact bound up with social meaning and power, it is useful to distinguish between Lawrence the analyst of present-day social reality and Lawrence the prophet of a future which has not yet come to pass. As Christopher Caudwell pointed out many years ago, one of the great problems of Lawrence's writing is that the prophet largely ignores the insights of the social critic.[5]

II

Women in Love places its characters in the bewildering space of a radically changing world. 'The Industrial Magnate' tells the story of how that change came about through the succession of generations, a story which has at its centre the social drama of Gerald Crich and his father. There is a long-standing, unspoken enmity between these two men, and when power is finally handed on and Thomas Crich accepts his retirement, both father and son understand that the transition over which they preside is not simply a personal one. The older man had lived his life in accordance with the dominant nineteenth-century pattern of social and economic order. A patriarch in industrial and domestic settings alike, he imagined there to be no great distance between himself and his workers, largely trusting their skill and experience to extract the resources which would provide a more abundant life for all. His own role was that of benevolent overseer, guided by Christian charity, assuring the well-being of those men and women whose subservient position made them his responsibility. The order which Gerald initiates is very different indeed. Following the notion that business should concern itself with profile, and not charity, he installs what Lawrence terms 'the great reform':

> Expert engineers were introduced in every department. An enormous electric plant was installed, both for lighting and for haulage underground, and for power. The electricity was carried into every mine. New machinery was brought from America, such as the miners had never seen before, great iron men, as the cutting machines were called, and unusual appliances. The working of the pits was thoroughly changed, all the control was taken out of the hands of the miners, the butty system was abolished. Everything was run on the most accurate and delicate scientific method, educated and expert men were in control everywhere, the miners were reduced to mere mechanical instruments. They had to work hard, much harder than before, the work was terrible and heart-breaking in its mechanicalness.
>
> (p. 223)

Although this is an account for the reorganisation of work within a single industry, its features are representative of the general movement in early twentieth-century society. To be sure, the Taylorism which had been at the forefront of the movement to rationalise the workplace in the United States (and in the other industrialised nations of Western Europe, as well as the Soviet Union) was more bitterly resisted by British labour than by American, and management too was wary of this new instance of Americanisation. Nevertheless, such resistance did not mean that England was a place apart from the larger discursive transformations, with all their attendant social consequences, which Taylor had begun to regularise, publicise, and apply to specific industrial situations.[6]

Several details in the account of Gerald's new programme are particularly significant. First of all, though the introduction of powerful new machinery is hardly surprising, this development is linked with several others. Expert engineers are introduced, and while their apparent function is to oversee the new technology, they enable another development far more crucial to the new organisation of production: the withdrawal of control over their work from the men in the pits. The 'butty system', for example, was a kind of subcontracting in which experienced miners were responsible for hiring and paying their own immediate workmates.[7] In the account of his earlier experiments in the systematic study of management, Frederick Taylor explicitly argued that nineteenth-century management could not increase its power as long as it allowed workers to retain control over the knowledge upon which industrial processes depend. By appropriating knowledge as its own exclusive function, distinct from and superior to practical execution, management could assume an entirely new level of effective control.[8]

Lawrence seems to be as fully aware as any contemporary student of Taylor's scientific management that a fundamental shift of power was occurring, and that its necessary agents were the educated and expert men who 'were in control everywhere'. The 'most accurate and delicate scientific method' was the final arbiter, not only authorising the power of a new class of managers, but effecting a radical division of work itself into that of mind and that of hand.[9] The further degradation of industrial labour which Lawrence describes was one consequence of the split, but he also notes that 'a highly educated man costs very little more than a workman', and that as the men become mere instruments even Gerald the owner finds himself reduced to a 'supreme instrument of control'. In concluding that 'the mines were nothing but the clumsy efforts of impure minds' (p. 215) and that mankind was 'pure instrumentality', Gerald embraces a 'systems approach' entirely congruent with the 'information society' and its search for artificial intelligence which characterises late twentieth-century society. Although he retains the considerable material benefits of ownership, Gerald experiences a loss of autonomy like that of the men, as an apparently objective logic of systems, rather than individual will, comes to govern the processes of production.

The patterns I have pointed out in Lawrence's description may be found in any standard account of early twentieth-century industrial change. His critique of the process he has described in these straightforward terms is also well known. It turns most fundamentally on the opposition, organic/mechanical: 'It was the first great step in undoing, the first great phase of chaos, the substitution of the mechanical principle for the organic, the destruction of the organic purpose, the organic unity, and the subordination of every organic unit to the great mechanical purpose. It was pure organic disintegration and pure mechanical organisation. This is the first and finest state of chaos' (p. 223). Gerald and his men, though embracing mechanism in very different ways, are all implicated in the loss of living, purposeful order. That vital order is set over against a mechanical organisation which is, paradoxically, not order at all, but chaos, because it flattens individuality in its relentless structure of equality and repetition. This critique runs throughout the novel, as, for example, in the scene in which Birkin and Ursula buy and then give away an old chair. Birkin's contention that the chair still expresses thought, in contrast to the 'foul mechanicalness' of present-day production, is consistent with the view of Gerald's new order as dependent on a radical separation and hierarchisation of hand and mind.

In denouncing the reduction of men and women to the status of cogs in a machine, however, Lawrence does not simply romanticise the past. If the workers were less constrained before Gerald's 'reforms', they were nevertheless subject to a system of control which is unmasked only when the lock-out forces a confrontation between master and men. Coming hat in hand to receive old Mr Crich's charity, the workers were playing their part in an economy governed by the image of Christ humbling himself in the service of mankind. Believing 'that in Christ he was one with his workmen', Mr Crich is actually shown (through the eyes of his wife) to be indulging in a necessarily hierarchical relation of master and servant, 'as if her husband were some subtle funeral bird, feeding on the miseries of the people'. This dark side of charity is eliminated by Gerald when he rejects the provision of widow's coal, a practice based on the illusion (vital to his father) that the family firm is indeed an institution of charity. In rejecting his father's desire to be one in Christ with his men, however, Gerald yearns for a divine presence which is equally destructive in Lawrence's eyes: 'the desire to translate the Godhead into pure mechanism' (pp. 209, 221). Gerald's merger with the God in the machine stands in Lawrence's critique as the final, fraudulent authorisation of mechanism's triumph over the vital ineffability of true divinity.

III

Lawrence's novel presents itself to the reader as the exploration of a discourse of opposition, the difficult struggle to forge a language of life rather than mechanical death. History is essential to this stance because it constitutes the supposed ground of reality which justifies the author's prophetic voice as well as the urgency of his characters' struggles. But though Lawrence's presentation and critique of the direction of contemporary social change seems familiar enough, even 'natural' at this point, some of its key terms are highly problematic. If the succession of Gerald Crich to his father's power figures most concretely the larger transformation of society which is the novel's subject, this interrelation of father and son is part of a still more inclusive concern of Lawrence's with old and new.

The American struggle to forge an identity apart from its European origins offered an example of great historical importance for Lawrence, who read in it a pattern very similar to the one which he created for the Crich family. In *Studies in Classic American Literature*, he identifies America's failure to break free with its preeminence as a technological power: 'All this Americanizing and mechanizing has been for the purpose of overthrowing the past. And now look at America, tangled in her own barbed wire, and mastered by her own machines. Absolutely got down by her own barbed wire of shalt-nots, and shut up fast in her own "productive" machines like millions of squirrels running in millions of cages.'[10] Lawrence characterises the American response as a 'rebellion against the old parenthood of Europe', and this generational figure for social change (as in the instance of Gerald and his father) operates within a metaphor which runs through much of Lawrence's writing during these years. His metaphor of the tree, and more specifically of the tree's 'leading-shoot', as a figure for human life, in 'The Study of Thomas Hardy', is particularly revealing:

> It seems to me as if a man, in his normal state, were like a palpitating leading-shoot of life, where the unknown, all unresolved, beats and pulses, containing the quick of all experiences, as yet unrevealed, not singled out. But when he thinks, when he moves, he is retracing some proved experience. He is as the leading-shoot which, for the moment, remembers only that which is behind, the fixed wood, the cells conducting toward their undifferentiated tissue of life. He moves as it were in the trunk of the tree, in the channels long since built, where the sap must flow as in a canal. He takes knowledge of all this past experience upon which the new tip rides quivering, he becomes again the old life, which has built itself out in the fixed tissue, he lies in line with the old movement, unconscious of where it breaks, at the growing plasm, into something new, unknown.[11]

Here the contrast between new and old becomes one of living shoot set against the fixed matter of previously defined cells. Only the undifferentiated tip is acknowledged to possess life, while the trunk out of which it grows is 'fixed wood', a 'canal', little more than old lumber. To think is always a 'retracing', a turning back from life, which is essentially unconscious. Knowledge is therefore limited to the rigid structures of the past, and can play no part in the mysterious being of life.

Throughout *Women in Love* this knowledge which turns away from life is a key site of struggle for all the lovers. Hermione and Ursula repeatedly seek to 'know' Birkin, and he resists with a kind of vague horror that his vitality would be threatened by their knowledge. Gudrun is 'like Eve reaching to the apples on the tree of knowledge' as she kisses Gerald. Her desire to 'touch him, till she had him all in her hands, till she had strained him into her knowledge' (p. 324) brings death with it as surely as Eve's mythic apples. As a medium through which the interpersonal struggles of these characters are played out, knowledge represents the acceptance of fixed, imprisoning structures of personality, in contrast to the dangerous, unknowable vitality of true self-definition. The notion that reason is a threat to vitality and spontaneity remains a powerful one, as the pop psychology of any grocery store magazine rack will quickly testify. But while this struggle for personal salvation may be viewed as a psychological and metaphysical conflict, it remains rooted in a crisis of social change, both in the novel's narrative frame and in the details of its metaphoric patterns.

In elaborating his figure of the tree, Lawrence describes the man who turns away from the living tip as 'happy' where 'all is known, all is finite, all is established, and knowledge can be perfect here in the trunk of the tree, which life built up and climbed beyond'. But consider the statement which follows these words: 'such is a man at work'. In Lawrence's formulation, the fixed cells and rigid channels of the tree trunk are equated with the mechanistic quality of modern work. If the cells of old wood signify nothing more than the retracing of past movements, man working is equally the image of fruitless repetition: 'A man who can repeat certain movements accurately is an expert, if his movements are those which produce the required result. And these movements are the calculative or scientific movements of a machine. When a man is working perfectly, he is the perfect machine.' When Gerald experiences his vision of what he might accomplish with his newly gained control of the firm, his terms are precisely the same: 'And for this fight with matter one must have perfect instruments in perfect organisation, a mechanism so subtle and harmonious in its workings that it represents the single mind of man, and by its relentless repetition of given movement, will accomplish a purpose irresistibly, inhumanly.'[12] Thus, in social terms, the mechanistic repetition of modern work replicates the fixed sameness of cells which no longer contain life.

At the heart of Lawrence's social critique there is the metaphor of the organism: 'the destruction of the organic purpose, the organic unity, and the subordination of every organic unit to the great mechanical purpose.'[13] But Lawrence's recurring figure requires us to accept a rather troubling paradox. The vital tip of emergent life is set against its contrary, the fixed channels (mechanism) of the dead trunk. And yet trunk and tip are one organism, the living shoot depending absolutely on the branch which supports it. Whether explicit or submerged, these contradictory implications of the organic metaphor are widespread in Lawrence's writing. Consider, for example, Birkin's revulsion against speech, which would trap him in the fixed cells of the already-said. He seeks a language beyond the imprisoning old forms, and yet, even the most exploratory act of language, like a 'leading-shoot', is inseparable from the fixed structures, the grammar, of past utterance.

What are the consequences of this figure which is so pervasive, and so contradictory, in Lawrence's thought? This is Birkin, struggling to find his new language: 'There was always confusion in speech. Yet it must be spoken. Whichever way one moved, if one were to move forwards, one must break a way through. And to know, to give utterance, was to break a way through the walls of the prison as the infant in labour strives through the walls of the womb.' Prison or no, the womb of old speech must be acknowledged as an unavoidable necessity. Nor is our physical survival any less dependent on work, however mechanistic and life-denying. This is how Lawrence puts it in 'The Study of Thomas Hardy': 'Work is, simply, the activity necessary for the production of a sufficient supply of food and shelter: nothing more holy than that. It is the producing of the means of self-preservation. Therefore it is obvious that it is not the be-all and the end-all of existence. We work to provide means of subsistence, and when we have made subsistence, we proceed to live.'[14]

What is most revealing about Lawrence's equations of tree with mechanism, and womb with prison, is the way these images allow him to distance the realm of fixed cell/mechanism/dead speech. Since the presentation of this realm is governed by the various forms of the organic metaphor, it appears to be natural and thus inevitable, and as a consequence the mechanical seems to exist in a kind of isolated state prior to any meaningful contention within society. Thus Lawrence can argue, with all the zeal of Frederick Taylor himself, that a man's movements in work (whether he be doctor, lawyer, or mechanic) should approximate 'the calculative or scientific movements of a machine'. It follows then that whatever new techniques are capable of increasing industrial productivity should be employed, because work falls entirely within the sphere of practical necessity and has little or nothing to do with the real struggle for human salvation. By taking this view of work, Lawrence the vitalist ends up in agreement with his mechanistic enemies.

Thus Birkin, in his quarrelling with Gerald over the value of material production, shows no interest in what Gerald actually does to increase that production. He focuses instead only on the 'higher' questions which can be asked after the coal has been dug and the rabbits stewed. Insofar as Birkin is a mouthpiece for Lawrence's critique of recent social change, however, his message is largely consistent with the traditional assumptions of British management. For the most part, managers in Britain were not expected to interest themselves in engineering issues, but rather to practise a style of management which Judith A. Merkle has characterised as 'moral leadership and technical ignorance'.[15] This style of management was rooted in a complex system of social class traditions, particularly the long-standing hostility on the part of British aristocracy toward those engaged in business and industry, and the corresponding desire of the rising industrialists to share in the cultural prestige of the aristocrat. The cultural assumptions of this system of social hierarchy made British managers fearful of being identified as technocrats, with the result that scientific management had more difficulty in being openly accepted in Britain than elsewhere in Europe and North America.

In Lawrence's novel, Gerald does apply many of Taylor's basic principles to the workings of his mines, and his identity (social as well as personal) seems to be fatally undermined as a result of this embrace of mechanistic thought. It is for Birkin, in his affirmation of 'higher matters', to reflect not only the more typical attitude of British managers, but an important contradiction in Lawrence's own position. In basing his critique of Gerald's innovations on a hierarchy subordinating work to consciousness, Birkin was unwittingly repeating a strategy crucial to the programme of scientific management. If work were to be rationalised as Taylor hoped, then a radical division between mind and hand would first have to be instituted, with knowledge withdrawn from the shop floor and installed in a separate, and superior, realm of management expertise. Furthermore, knowledge itself would have to be redefined along strictly instrumental lines.

With regard to the status of knowledge, Lawrence's metaphor of the growing tip of the tree branch as mystery and the unspoken, in contradistinction to knowing, which he associates with dead wood and mechanistic repetition, is particularly important. Like work, Lawrence consigns knowledge to the realm of the merely instrumental.[16] This instrumentalisation of knowledge was essential to the reorganisation of work in Europe and America which was taking place during the first two decades of the twentieth century, and it is in fact described by Lawrence as central to Gerald's reordering of the mines. The 'experts' who have placed knowledge at Gerald's disposal as a powerful new agency of industrial control have at the same time effectively withdrawn knowledge from the workers, who may henceforth function mechanically according to procedures worked out elsewhere. By ceding knowledge to the sphere of the mechanistic and the pragmatic, Lawrence has powerfully reinforced the very movement within society which, at the same time, he denounces as destructive of 'organic unity'. Thus there is a counterargument within Lawrence's writing at this time which is surprisingly congruent with contemporary traditions of genteel management, and which precisely contradicts 'The Industrial Magnate's' overt narrative of a world made less and less receptive to genuine life by the growing power of mechanistic thought.

IV

In the account of Gerald's great transformation of the mines, the response of the men themselves poses a number of questions. After describing their new work as 'terrible and heart-breaking in its mechanicalness', Lawrence writes, 'But they submitted to it all. The joy went out of their lives, the hope seemed to perish as they became more and more mechanised. And yet they accepted the new conditions. They even got a further satisfaction out of them' (p. 223). In his description of the worker's perception of these new ways of organising work, Lawrence echoes what was in fact the overwhelming response of the British unions, which (like the traditional management class, though for different reasons) were unvarying in their hostility to anything remotely suggestive of Taylorism.[17] And yet in spite of their perception of the changes as overwhelmingly negative, Lawrence's narrative portrays the men as actually accepting these new conditions which are so oppressive, which at first had even led them to consider murdering Gerald. The suggestion seems to be that it is somehow in the nature of the workers to accept, that the mechanicalness of their work meets a need which is deep within them: 'But as time went on, they accepted everything with fatal satisfaction. Gerald was their high priest, he represented the religion they really felt. His father was forgotten already. There was a new world, a new order, strict, terrible, inhuman, but satisfying in its very destructiveness. The men were satisfied to belong to the great and wonderful machine, even whilst it destroyed them' (p. 223).

If it could be argued that there is something in the nature of these men which Gerald's new order touches, it is nevertheless the case that under Gerald's father they felt themselves to be very different. In the older man's world of Christ made flesh, the miners had come to regard themselves as equal in the sight of God, and they eventually used that belief to challenge the great disparity between their earthly state and that of the owners. When Gerald takes control of the firm, the men learn to regard themselves in a way which is not simply new, but which has the effect of accommodating them to the changed conditions of their work. One explanation for this new attitude among the men is that their instincts have become perverted as a result of Gerald's corruption, that they are enacting Nietzsche's vision of cultural decadence.[18] However, the fact that the men have assumed two very different ways of acting and understanding their actions, writing the space of a brief narrative, suggests rather that their identities have been redefined by powerful forces within their society.

Under the rubric of 'socialisation', such forces have been studied by social scientists for many years, of course, though in ways which tend to accept the social norms and concern themselves only with how those norms are inculcated and enforced. 'Ideology' would be more likely to suggest the political nature of the process by which men and women are shaped by their society, but regardless of the terminology, the point is that individuals need not be forced to accept dominant social values and patterns of behaviour. The assent of the miners to Gerald's new order illustrates what Foucault means by a 'disciplinary' society, in which institutional practices, rather than public spectacles such as floggings or hangings, regulate behaviour. And contrary to commonly held belief that labour generally opposed the scientific rationalisation of industry, Lawrence's depiction of the miners' assent is historically accurate. According to David F. Nobel, the 'widespread notion' of labour opposition 'is fundamentally mistaken ... so far as twentieth-century workers are concerned. For, like those in management and academia, labour has swallowed whole and internalised the liberal ideology of progress.'[19]

As a novel about historical change, *Women in Love* identifies the social crisis which its characters are experiencing with a movement of industrial capitalism to new levels of complexity in this management practice, its increasing dependence on science, and its manner of employing labour. Lawrence in no way presents Gerald as the author of his innovations, but only as the agent of their introduction, as he imports machines from America and hires the expertise of engineers. Though Lawrence never obscures the fact that Gerald gains materially from the changes he initiates, he depicts Gerald as ultimately possessed and destroyed by them. We might well include the master in the question I have posed with regard to the men: Why do they assent?

The answer is that the society shown in Lawrence's narrative is not a society in decadence, but rather a society being taken over by a powerful new version of technological discourse, a version powerful enough to bind individuals at all levels of society. The men are happy to be part of a 'great and wonderful machine' which represents 'the highest that man has produced'. It is perceived as 'perfect system' based on 'pure mathematical principles'. Gerald's terms are essentially the same: 'a great and perfect machine, a system', the search for 'perfect co-ordination', the translation of 'the mystic word harmony into the practical word organisation' (pp. 223, 220). This is the discourse of instrumental knowledge, and it structures itself around several key points: an evolutionary metaphor of ever 'higher' levels of invention; the elevation of mathematics to a normative role in the judgement of social organisation; a validation of the 'systems approach' to knowledge as well as practice. The continuing power of this discourse for the twentieth century is suggested by a proposal by Herbert A. Simon (one of the fathers of artificial intelligence, and a theoretician of 'management science') to displace humanistic study as the centre of liberal education. He wrote, in 1969: 'The proper study of mankind has been said to be man. But I have argued that man – or at least the intellective component of man – may be relatively simple; that most of the complexity of his behaviour may be drawn from his environment, from his search for good designs. If I have made my case, then we can conclude that, in large part, the proper study of mankind is the science of design, not only as the professional component of a technical education but as a core discipline for every liberally educated man.'[20]

To install the science of design at the centre of liberal education would simply be to complete the institutionalisation of a process which Lawrence saw beginning fifty years earlier. *Women in Love*, like much of his writing, is about men and women who, confronted by this turn in history, succumb to it or seek to resist its power. Lawrence creates men and women who rail against the inroads of the mechanistic, and he locates his fiction within the frame of a coherent historical narrative which seems to be offered as a 'model of' that reality against which his characters struggle. But Lawrence's narrative is not a simple representation of history. It is rather an enactment of history which moves in fundamental ways against its own overt message. If the miners assent to become interchangeable parts in a machine, they do so not because Gerald has the power to force them to, but because they, and he, have been constituted by a discourse which makes their assent natural and meaningful. And Lawrence's text is a part of that discourse, reproducing it while at the same time groping for some way to counter it.

For Lawrence's discourse of organicism takes place within, not outside, the discourse of modern mechanisation – or rather, both discourses are part of an interrelated complex, not opposites as we tend to think of them. Like the earlier generations of Romantics, Lawrence denounced the machine and used organic metaphor to celebrate life. In doing so, however, he disabled his own counterdiscourse. Against a discursive sphere in which 'organisation' is a term yielding power, while 'harmony' is a concept that can only serve to disqualify and subjugate, Lawrence consigns himself to silence by surrendering knowledge to the realm of the instrumental. In doing so he participates in what Gerald Graff has called the 'scepticism toward reason' which has been so prominent a response to industrialisation.[21] Birkin may struggle to articulate a new being capable of defying the mechanistic world which surrounds him, but he dooms his project to the status of an irrelevant and outworn humanism by accepting the most crucial terms of Gerald's new order.

But even Gerald is expendable in that order, which defines its power through the very gesture that Lawrence himself makes in dividing the vital and the material, the leading-shoot from the solid wood which supports it. For Lawrence, inchoate life, in all its promise and vitality, is set against the fixity of mechanical production. But for all too many of his contemporaries, that dichotomy has already received a new and unquestionable meaning: trivial mysticism exists on sufferance at the hands of the only meaningful kind of knowledge, knowledge as power. And it is that premise, defining knowledge as instrumental power, which founds the social and economic order of advanced industrial societies in the twentieth century.

From James F. Knapp, *Literary Modernism and the Transformation of Work* (Evanston, IL, 1988), pp. 59–73.

Notes

[The subject of *Women in Love*, declares James Knapp, is the struggle between the 'old culture of Victorian morality and capitalist economic relations and a new, somehow more natural society'. This struggle is reflected in the opposition between a mechanical language that belongs to the old order and an organic one which belongs to the new. However, this apparently clear-cut difference is complicated by Lawrence's own metaphor of the tree, found in his *Study of Thomas Hardy*. The wood of the tree is the old life and the bud is the new, and because these contraries can be contained in one image we cannot finally distinguish between organic and mechanical language. The discourse of scientific management, which Knapp sees as the chief form of mechanical language in *Women in Love*, also blurs the boundary between these two ostensibly opposing idioms. Birkin resembles the figure of the manager in that both are distinguished by their moral leadership rather than their knowledge. Birkin spends much of the novel criticising characters like Hermione who want to 'know' and, in his metaphor of the tree, Lawrence devalues knowledge by associating it with the past. The social ambitions of the scientific manager, at least in Britain, meant that he did not want to be identified with the realm of work but with the realm of culture. Lawrence shared this rather disdainful view of labour which he saw as a 'practical necessity' that had nothing to do 'with the real struggle for human salvation'. Knapp concludes by arguing that because Lawrence devalued work and knowledge, he weakened the attempt to articulate a new order of being. A language bereft of experience and tradition in all its forms cannot contribute effectively to that 'struggle for human salvation'.

Knapp's essay is similar to Burden's (essay 5) in that both look at the discursive context of Lawrence's work. Knapp also uses Foucault to account for why the miners accept the changes that Gerald imposes on them; they 'have been constituted by a discourse which makes their assent natural and meaningful'. All references to *Women in Love* are from the Viking edition (New York, 1960) and are given in parentheses in the text. Eds]

1. D. H. Lawrence, *Studies in Classic American Literature* (New York, 1964), p. 2.

2. Frank Kermode, *D. H. Lawrence* (New York, 1973), p. 14.

3. Michael Ragussis, *The Subterfuge of Art: Language and the Romantic Tradition* (Baltimore, MD, 1978), p. 176f.

4. Victor Turner, 'Social Dramas and Stories about Them', in *On Narrative*, ed. W. J. T. Mitchell (Chicago, 1981), pp. 146,153.

5. Christopher Caudwell, *Studies in a Dying Culture* (London, 1938), p. 58ff.

6. Hubert Zapf, 'Taylorism in D. H. Lawrence's *Women in Love*', *D. H. Lawrence Review*, 15:1–2 (Spring–Summer 1982), 129–39, has pointed out parallels between Taylor's scientific management and *Women in Love*, though he takes Lawrence's narrative as a realistic and radical social critique, in contrast to my view that the discursive context of Lawrence's novel makes its social stance more complex and problematic.

7. E. P. Thompson, *The Making of the English Working Class* (New York, 1966), p. 243.

8. Frederick Winslow Taylor, *The Principles of Scientific Management* (1911; rpt., New York, 1967), pp. 36–8, 53ff. For a discussion of the origins of scientific management in British industry, including practices which, as early as 1890, had anticipated Taylor's theories, see E. J. Hobsbawm, *Labouring Men: Studies in the History of Labour* (London, 1964), pp. 355–62. Also, Sidney Pollard, *The Genesis of Modern Management: A Study of the Industrial Revolution in Great Britain* (Cambridge, MA, 1965) pp. 250–9.

9. Taylor, *Principles*, p. 38; David F. Noble, *America by Design* (Oxford, 1977), pp. 3–49; Harry Braverman, *Labor and Monopoly Capital* (New York, 1974), pp. 124–37.

10. Lawrence, *Studies in Classic American Literature*, p. 21.

11. D. H. Lawrence, 'Study of Thomas Hardy', in *Phoenix*, ed. Edward D. McDonald (New York, 1936), p. 424.

12. Lawrence, *Phoenix*, pp. 424, 423, 220.

13. Ibid., p. 223.

14. Ibid., pp. 178,423.

15. Judith A. Merkle, *Management and Ideology: The Legacy of the International Scientific Management Movement* (Berkeley, CA, 1980), p. 224.

16. Geoffrey H. Hartman has noted the modern tendency to restrict the 'work' of understanding to 'productive' activities, but he regards this vital change as the result of curiously ahistorical 'attitudes'. See *Criticism in the Wilderness* (New Haven, CT, 1980), p. 166.

17. Merkle, *Management and Ideology*, p. 224ff.

18. Aidan Burns, *Nature and Culture in D. H. Lawrence* (Totowa, NJ, 1980), p. 80.

19. David F. Noble, *Forces of Production: A Social History of Industrial Automation* (New York, 1984) p. 248.

20. Herbert A. Simon, *The Sciences of the Artificial* (Cambridge, MA, 1969), p. 83.

21. Graff argues that 'industrialism intensified the separation of fact and value by institutionalising objective thought in the form of technology, commerce, and, later, bureaucracy, administration, and social engineering. "Reason" thus became equated with amoral mechanism, with the commercial calculus of profit and the *laissez-faire* economy, with means and instrumental efficiency over ends, with a regimented, over-organised society which destroys ritual, folk customs, and the heroic dimension of life.' See *Literature Against Itself* (Chicago, 1979), p. 41.

9

The Politics of Sexual Liberation: D. H. Lawrence's *The Rainbow* and *Women in Love*

LIANG-YA LIOU

D. H. Lawrence is concerned with representations of female sexuality in *The Rainbow* (1915) and *Women in Love* (1920). Originally conceived as *The Sisters* in early 1913, the book became two novels in a sequence, although there is some discontinuity in the characterisation of Ursula Brangwen.[1] Lawrence's overt eroticism and attention to the physiological details of sexual acts distinguish him from many of his contemporary writers. Moreover, while *The Rainbow* highlights female desire, *Women in Love* explores sexual deviations in both men and women. *The Rainbow* was denounced and tried for obscenity due to its sexual explicitness, particularly its representation of lesbianism,[2] while *Women in Love* underwent bowdlerisation in passages concerning male homosexuality.[3] In his explicit eroticism and fascination with deviant sexualities, Lawrence thus departs from nineteenth-century domestic fiction, where heterosexuality is taken for granted and where emotion rather than lust is the marked term.

Nevertheless, Lawrence's break with literary tradition is more ostensible than substantial, since he adheres to previous ideologies. He perpetuates the bourgeoisie's heterosexism and regulation of

172

female sexuality by viewing lesbianism and undomesticated female desire as perverted. He condemns male homosexuality, though he is deeply fascinated with certain forms of it. Like his nineteenth-century predecessors, Lawrence celebrates heterosexual love and marriage. One great difference is that he is equipped with a new language drawn from late-nineteenth-century and early-twentieth-century sexology and, most importantly, from Freud's theory. H. M. Daleski's succinct explanation of Lawrence's sexual theory reveals the latter's middle-class underpinnings:

> the sex act is a tangible manifestation of the Holy Ghost; that is to say, in the act man and woman are brought more closely than in any other way into a pure relation, both spiritual and physical, and are transcended in a consummation which, uniting both male and female, is greater than either and provides the stimulus for creative self-fulfilment.[4]

F. R. Leavis and his followers canonised Lawrence in the fifties, praising his 'healthy, normative spirit'. Leavis even contrasts Lawrence's 'moral seriousness' with Oscar Wilde's 'cruel levity' to make his point.[5]

Lawrence voices a strand of contemporary thinking that locates the ills of Victorianism in sexual repression, particularly the repression of female sexuality. He connects the construction of chastity and spirituality with the sexual anxieties of both men and women. Consequently, he sees sexual liberation as more important than suffrage for women. His critique of the women's suffrage movement is valuable in pointing out the movement's general neglect of the issue of female sexual freedom. On the other hand, he is reluctant to grant sexual autonomy to women. His denigration of lesbianism and of female extra-marital affairs is no less harsh than his diatribe against frigidity. He retains the virgin/prostitute dichotomy and rails against the New Women who move away from the traditional erotic terrain assigned to them. Simone de Beauvoir rightly criticises him for promulgating bourgeois, masculinist conceptions of femininity and dubs his novels 'guidebooks for women'.[6] In his eagerness to prescribe female sexuality, his priggishness and phallocentrism contrast with the views of sexual radicals such as Emma Goldman and Margaret Sanger, who led the birth control movement in the United States from 1914 to 1917, about the same time when *The Rainbow* and *Women in Love* were being written. While both Goldman and Sanger put into practice notions of free love implicit in the works of Freud and Havelock Ellis, Lawrence, influenced by the same works, reinforced the bourgeois normative standard for women.

Lawrence's conservatism is further revealed in his hostility to professional women who seek economic and political independence. Like Freud and Ellis, he fails to critique bourgeois notions of femininity and feels threatened by feminist revolt. He conflates feminism, penis envy, and lesbianism or frigidity. His ideal New Woman, Ursula Brangwen, flirts with the idea of sexual experimentation and having a career in *The Rainbow*, and yet happily adopts the traditional role of wife and mother[7] in *Women in Love*.

To his credit, Lawrence sanctifies heterosexual monogamy in both its physical and emotional aspects with an intensity that had rarely been achieved in nineteenth-century domestic fiction. Unlike his predecessors, who seem prudishly reticent, he stresses the value and importance of sex in individuals' lives and the pleasure that can be got from it. He shows how people attain self-understanding and self-fulfilment through sexual relations. At the same time, however, he is horrified by deviant sexualities such as promiscuity, lesbianism, and some forms of male homosexuality. *The Rainbow*, which chronicles three generations of love relationships that span the sixty-five years from around 1840, contrasts the traditional middle-class couples' physical and spiritual intimacy with the difficulties of relations between modern men and women. *Women in Love* is permeated with an apocalyptic sense of cultural degeneration which recalls Richard von Krafft-Ebing's denunciations of sexual perversions in *Psychopathia Sexualis*. For Lawrence, as well as for Krafft-Ebing, deviant sexuality is dangerous and detrimental to civilisation. The Lawrentian hero Rupert Birkin's misanthropy and utopianism about the survival of the Elect resembles the eugenicist rhetoric which, according to Jeffrey Weeks, 'became pervasive in the decade before the First World War, covering a political range from far right to far left'.[8] Ironically, Rupert/Lawrence[9] is 'contaminated' by 'degrading' sexuality as well. The anal intercourse between Rupert and Ursula in *Women in Love* and between Anna and Will in *The Rainbow* disrupts the distinction between normal/deviant sexuality. Lawrence's attitudes toward male homosexuality are far from clear and 'straight'.

One cardinal attribute of Lawrence's fiction is that sexual relations become the domain where social relations are played out. In sexualising and personalising social relations, he frequently equates deviant sexualities with flawed personalities and whatever social evils he finds in modern society. A salient example is his equation of Loerke's homosexuality with his decadent character and his 'degrading' art. Thus, he stresses the normal/deviant divide as a sharp distinction between pure/corrupt and between healthy/unwholesome. Although his fascination with the second term of each binarism indicates the falsity of the distinctions, his insistence on discrimination suggests how sexual identities define social and gender identities for him.

Lawrence, however, does not feel comfortable with androgyny or homosexuality. He portrays characters such as Rupert and Hermione Roddice as craving heterosexual monogamy with a view to acquiring a secure sense of masculinity and femininity. This sexual awareness and anxiety are tied to dominant ideological constructions, particularly in sexological discourse. It is peculiar to Lawrence that he condemns the manly woman for her sexual deficiency in order to deflect the anxieties of the effeminate man. Nevertheless, Rupert's explicit homosexual desire in the discarded 'Prologue' to *Women in Love* makes it plain that he should be just as responsible for the failure of love between him and Hermione. His yearning for a spiritual male lover in the published text demonstrates the homosocial/homophobic double bind which Oscar Wilde delineates so well in Basil Hallward.[10]

Paradoxically, Lawrence affirms the effeminate man for his moral sensitivity and tenderness of feelings. This shows the influence of the homosexual socialist Edward Carpenter, who befriended Lawrence's friends and was active in Lawrence's home county of Nottingham in positing the existence of an 'intermediate sex' and championing private relationship and traditional 'feminine' qualities. Like Carpenter, Lawrence conjoins his 'feminised' sexual politics with social criticism. Lawrence's privileging of 'blood consciousness' over 'mental consciousness'[11] extends to his sweeping attacks on industry, technology, and war and people who are engaged in these 'male' domains.[12] Of special importance is his critique of the Victorian construction of manhood in his portrayal of the aggressive, virile Gerald Crich. However, Lawrence eventually departs from Carpenter. Just as he condemns male homosexuality despite his interest in certain forms of it, so does he undercut his critique of 'masculinity' by reasserting the primacy of the phallus. In his resolution of Gerald's relationship with Gudrun Brangwen, he reinstates bourgeois notions of gender and perpetuates the misogyny intrinsic to patriarchy.

The problematics of Lawrence's politics of sexual liberation vis-à-vis suffrage for women

Lawrence presents quite a few New Women in *The Rainbow* and *Women in Love*: Ursula, Winifred Inger, Dorothy Russell, Maggie Schofield, Gudrun, and Hermione. All of them, at least at first, rebel against playing 'the angel in the house' and seek to become professional women. Moreover, the first four participate in the suffragist movement, and the last one is active in the 'man's' world. However, Lawrence's interest in the 'manly' women is political: he intends to co-opt them into patriarchy. Just like many of his contemporaries, he views women's moving toward political and economic independence as a threat. In addition, he is aware that along with this new independence comes greater sexual freedom than is allowed in heterosexual monogamy. In 'The Study of Thomas Hardy' (1914), he disparages supporters of the women's suffrage movement and, in the same breath, insinuates their 'sex-perversions'.[13] In his portrayal of Winifred, Dorothy, and Hermione, Lawrence not only deplores the new aggressiveness in women, but he interprets it as a sign of masculinity that leads to either lesbianism, asexuality, or frigidity. This indicates his indebtedness to late-nineteenth-century and early-twentieth-century sexology, especially Freud's theory. Whereas both Oscar Wilde in *The Picture of Dorian Gray* and Radclyffe Hall in *The Well of Loneliness* praise androgynous beauty in women, Lawrence treats any deviance from 'femininity' as a disease. Lawrence's conservatism also distinguishes him from Virginia Woolf. Woolf deals with heterosexual love and marriage as well, but, unlike him, she critiques notions of femininity and domesticity. Furthermore, while Lawrence stresses that love and sex are of greater importance than the suffrage in *The Rainbow*, he comes to link women's aggressiveness or 'masculinity' to promiscuity in *Women in Love*, blaming it for the strained love relationship between men and women. His agenda of sexual liberation for women is therefore problematic.

Lawrence took a stand against the women's movement. The target of his attack was the Women's Social and Political Union (WSPU), whose militant activity culminated from 1903 to 1914 and earned its participants the name of 'suffragettes' in distinction from constitutional suffragists.[14] The suffragettes' militancy was manifest in their employment of such tactics as arson, window-breaking, confrontation with the police, interrupting male politician's speeches, and hunger strike during imprisonment, which drew national attention. As Jane Marcus points out, in demolishing British culture's equation of female virtue with politeness and giving women a political voice, the suffragettes broke out of 'the strait-jacket of the female role'.[15] Lawrence's obsession with female aggressiveness or 'masculinity' seems to be partly a reaction to the suffragettes' transgression of traditional notions of femininity.

On the other hand, Lawrence's criticism of the puritanism of suffrage politics is apt. In her desperate campaign for the vote, the leading suffragette Christabel Pankhurst waged a 'sex war' against men by falling back on the social purity rhetoric of the Victorian women's movement and taking up issues of prostitution and syphilis. Displacing the stigma attached to prostitutes, she asserted that men were the cause of venereal disease and that wives should blame their husbands for giving them gynaecological diseases. Stressing women's chastity and moral superiority over men, she insisted that virgins and spinsters were more fit for the vote. Although, as Jane Marcus argues, Pankhurst's strategy might not represent her personal views on female sexuality,[16] it strengthened the Victorian construction of female chastity and spirituality and showed its indifference or opposition to sex-radicals' call for recognition of female desire. Rebecca West, a loyal suffragette, attacked the hate campaign and the reversion to puritanism.[17]

Lawrence's portrayal of Dorothy as a spiritual woman who manifests signs of sexual 'atrophy' appears to be a caricature of suffragette symbolism. A dedicated suffragette, Dorothy:

> wore a wonderful purple or figured scarf draped over a plain, dark dress. ... She was quiet and intense, with an ivory face and dark hair looped plain over her ears. Ursula was very fond of her, but afraid of her. She seemed so old and so relentless towards herself. Yet she was only twenty-two. Ursula always felt her to be a creature of fate, *like Cassandra*.
>
> (*R*, p. 400, my emphasis)

As Emile Delavenay observes, Lawrence compares the priestess-figure Cassandra to Hermione, Ottoline Morrell (after whom Hermione is modelled), and Thomas Hardy's Sue Bridehead and Tess of the d'Urbervilles, in order to show that these are types of women deficient in femaleness.[18] In 'The Study of Thomas Hardy', Lawrence argues that Sue Bridehead 'belonged, with Tess, to the old woman-type of witch or prophetess, which adhered to the male principle, and destroyed the female'.[19] For Lawrence, the exercise of intellect seems to be incompatible with the development of female sexual instincts. His masculinist view aligns him with contemporary sexologists' conceptions of femininity and female sexuality. And while Dorothy is still likeable despite her austerity, Hermione is depicted as morbid and denigrated relentlessly. As I shall demonstrate below, Lawrence appropriates Freud's theory in describing the complicated relationship between Hermione and Rupert.

In his portrayal of the suffragette Maggie, Lawrence (via Ursula) shows that what she really needs is sexual liberation rather than the suffrage:

> Maggie was a great suffragette, trusting in the vote. To Ursula the vote was never a reality. She had within her the strange, passionate knowledge of religion and living far transcending the limits of the automatic system that contained the vote. ... For her, as for Maggie, the liberty of woman meant something real and deep.
>
> (R, p. 377)

Ursula contrasts her own search for love and sex with Maggie's 'fundamental sadness of enclosure' ensuing from her celibacy (R, p. 382). Thus Lawrence sets up a crude dichotomy between the suffrage and sexual happiness. Although it is a fair critique of the WSPU's social purity rhetoric, it dismisses too facilely the significance of women's political emancipation.[20] As Susan Kingsley Kent notes, the puritanical feminists subverted ideologies of domesticity and femininity by demanding the vote and resisting marriage. Along with political and economic independence, they obtained a certain degree of sexual autonomy by rejecting conventional roles.[21] More important, Lawrence's division fails to take into account women who were both suffragettes and sex radicals. From 1911, dissidents within the WSPU such as Rebecca West and Teresa Billington-Greig grouped around the journal The Freewoman, espousing 'a new feminism' and freely discussing contraception, sexual pleasure, and lesbianism. These feminists campaigned for birth control, abortion, family allowance, and better conditions for maternity in the 1920s. Furthermore, the WSPU was just one organisation among many in the women's suffrage movement, during whose long history since 1860 there had been radicals such as Olive Schreiner who explored the sexual implication of feminism.[22]

Lawrence conceived *The Sisters* with the purpose of educating the New Woman about the sexual gratification of being a domestic woman as opposed to a suffragette. As he wrote to a friend: 'I shall do a novel about Love Triumphant one day. I shall do my work for women, better than the suffrage.'[23] In a letter on 23 April 1913, he highlighted the damage sexual repression caused women and undertook to 'liberate' them: 'I am so sure that only through a readjustment between men and women, and *a making free and healthy of the sex*, will she get out of her present atrophy. ... I do write because I want folk – English folk – to alter, and have more sense.'[24] His letter on 2 May 1913 also underscored that for him *the* problem of his day was 'the establishment of a new relation ... between men and women'.[25] Moreover, in a letter on 5 June 1914, he declared that he would explore the instinctual, physiological aspect of women: 'I only care about what the woman *is* – what she *is* – inhumanly, physiologically, materially.'[26] All of these letters suggest he intended to deal explicitly with female sexual desire. However, it is noteworthy that his stress on 'free and healthy sex' prescribes that female sexual desire be contained within hetero-sexuality. In addition, his attack on promiscuity and free love in *Women in Love* clearly shows his adherence to cardinal bourgeois values such as monogamy, fidelity, and the nuclear family

Lawrence's sexual politics in relation to contemporary debates on female sexuality

Lawrence's politics of sexual liberation in *The Rainbow* and *Women in Love* is to woo the New Woman back to domesticity by his representation of the sexual delights of heterosexual love and marriage. His discussion of female 'atrophy' not only draws from the suffragettes' social purity rhetoric, but taps into contemporary debate on female sexuality. Victorian conceptions of gender and the Victorian double standard glorified women's chastity and men's virility. The double standard was buttressed by the virgin/harlot dichotomy, which 'outlawed' desire for a decent bourgeois woman. According to Jeffrey Weeks, Victorian ideology contained a host of contradictory definitions of female sexuality. Weeks argues that notions of female asexuality, which are often seen as the most characteristic manifestation of Victorian prudery and hypocrisy, were by no means a majority view in the nineteenth century. On the contrary, older and common-sense views of women as carnal by virtue of their reproductive systems were also prevalent. Nevertheless, there was no concept of female sexuality that was independent of men's. Whereas male sexuality was defined as instrumental, direct, and forceful, female sexuality was seen as expressive and responsive, and shaped within the context of female emotionality.[27]

Since female sexuality was defined as inseparable from motherhood and maternal emotions, the expression of female desire was limited by women's conventional role. Thus female sexuality was lost sight of in the cultural construction of femininity. Moreover, while nineteenth-century advances in gynaecology such as the discovery of the place of ovulation in the menstrual cycle might have helped develop notions of autonomous female sexuality, they were instead used by professional doctors to validate the belief that women were dominated by their reproductive systems. Indeed, Victorian doctors stressed that biology incapacitated women physically and intellectually. These conceptions naturalised woman's biological and social role as mother and limited female self-determination. To further regulate female sexuality, cultural myths associated sex with danger by depicting the male sex drive as uncontrollable and easily aroused by any show of female desire. Victorian feminists who campaigned for social purity advocated female 'passionlessness' as a counterattack on men, yet they simultaneously proliferated such myths and thus denigrated 'deviant' female sexuality. The social purity movement began as an effort to abolish prostitution and exercise control over sexual politics, but ended up allowing the patriarchal terms of discourse to dictate norms. Female desire was defined by sexual ignorance as well as by women's conventional role, ineffective contraception, and fear of venereal disease.

Freud and Havelock Ellis separated female sexuality from procreation to a certain degree. Both took issue with constructions of female asexuality and attacked the Victorian sexual inhibitions that made frigidity a prevalent phenomenon among women, but their view of Victorian female sexuality is a distortion fostered by taking a few pathological cases for the norm. Both recognised the existence of female masturbation and stressed the importance of foreplay to women. Moreover, both discussed lesbianism and acknowledged the occurrence of 'perversions' such as sado-masochism in normal behaviour. Thus both intimated that female sexuality could be dissociated from the genital act that leads to reproduction. Ellis's theory of companionate marriage loosened women from the constraints of traditional monogamy, lending support to sexual radicals like Olive Schreiner, Emma Goldman, and Margaret Sanger in their campaign for birth control. Freud's hypothesis of bisexuality and exploration of the 'masculine' clitoris and the 'feminine' vagina stirred women's interest in sexual experimentation.

Nevertheless, Freud and Ellis remained conservative. Both failed to critique Victorian constructions of femininity and masculinity, and would only assign to women passive or reactive sexuality. Ellis shared in nineteenth-century assumptions about the biological imperative of motherhood and the debilitating effects of menstruation, claiming that 'in a certain sense, [women's] brains are in their wombs'.[28] He believed that female sexuality was more diffuse and soulful than male sexuality, and that consequently 'modesty' was a characteristic part of femininity. He endorsed the ideology of separate spheres and perpetuated notions of femininity that confine women to their conventional role.[29] Freud, too, portrayed female sexuality as different from male sexuality, suggesting that girls were more susceptible to 'the wave of repression' and that the abandonment of the 'masculine' clitoris as the leading erotogenic zone was essential to femininity.[30] He opposed lifting social bans on unrestricted masturbation in female puberty.[31] Although Freud's theory is implicitly radical and theories of autonomous female sexuality may rely on revisionist readings of it, Freud himself did not countenance female sexual aggressiveness.

Thus regardless of their attack on Victorian prudery, neither Freud nor Ellis broke away from nineteenth-century construction of female sexuality. Small wonder that Lawrence retains Victorian notions of masculinity and femininity. His opposition to intellectual aggressiveness in women aligns him with Ellis and Victorian doctors. His deprecation of sexual aggressiveness in women is shared by Freud, Ellis, and all contemporary and nineteenth-century sexologists. Since his agenda for sexual liberation is to tighten the bonds of heterosexual monogamy rather than the other way around, he moves from attacking the suffragette's intellectuality and spirituality in *The Rainbow* toward condemning female promiscuity in *Women in Love*. Most intriguingly, he associates not only lesbianism but frigidity and sexual aggressiveness with 'masculinity', which indicates his indebtedness to Freud's sophisticated theory of female sexuality.

Lawrence's construction of 'destructive' female sexuality in relation to men's sexual anxieties

Both Freud and Ellis conflated lesbianism, masculinity, and feminism. Lawrence follows suit in his portrayal of Winifred Inger. At first it seems quite a positive representation, as Lawrence depicts Ursula's infatuation with Winifred's androgynous beauty: 'what Ursula adored so much was her fine, upright, athletic bearing and her indomitably proud nature. She was proud and free as a man, yet exquisite as a woman. ... Ah, Miss Inger, how straight and fine was her back, how strong her loins, how clean and free her limbs! ... She wanted to ... touch her, to feel her' (*R*, pp. 312–13). Like Mary and Stephen in *The Well of Loneliness*, Ursula and Winifred develop their lesbian relationship spontaneously, and Winifred appears as an advanced, emancipated suffragist who enlightens Ursula more than anyone else in *The Rainbow*. Yet Winifred is condemned after they are further on in their lesbian relationship. Lawrence connects Winifred's interest in the suffrage with her lesbianism, and then presents the latter as the product of both an insatiable female desire and a bitter contempt for men: '[the men] are all impotent, they can't *take* a woman' (*R*, p. 318). Thus, Lawrence denigrates lesbianism and feminism in one stroke. It seems that, at this juncture, Ursula becomes aware of the stigmatised depiction of lesbians in contemporary sexology. Consequently, she soon feels nauseated by the body she once adored: 'sometimes she thought Winifred was ugly, clayey. Her female hips seemed big and earthy, her ankles and her arms were too thick' (*R*, p. 319). Her homophobia becomes so intense that she decides 'no more to mingle with the perverted life of the elder woman' (*R*, p. 319). She concludes that their affair is 'a sort of secret side-show to her life, never to be opened' (*R*, p. 319, p. 378). The title of the chapter in which their relationship is portrayed, 'Shame', clearly represents Ursula's (and Lawrence's) revulsion against lesbianism, despite the spiritual and physical gratification she got earlier.

Moreover, Lawrence associates Winifred with the machine and marries her off to the equally mechanical Tom Brangwen Jr: 'His real mistress was the machine, and the real mistress of Winifred was the machine' (*R*, p. 325). Whereas Winifred's masculinity may be one reason why Lawrence abruptly links her to the machine, the metaphor also suggests the unnaturalness of homosexuality. And there are strong hints that Tom is homosexual, too. Lawrence vilifies them by presenting them as united in a kinship of 'dark corruption' (*R*, p. 322). Tom marries to propagate himself, and Winifred probably to have a traditional social identity.

In his negative representation of Winifred's lesbianism, Lawrence suggests that her insatiable desire is actually symptomatic of her masculinity. While this is consonant with the contemporary sexological view, it is slightly different in that Lawrence insinuates that Winifred actually has had sexual intercourse with men, and that her masculinity made men impotent – '[the men] are all impotent, they can't take a woman'.[32] This phallocentric distortion of lesbianism indicates Lawrence's paranoia about the danger of the latter. Lesbianism becomes the sexual counterpart of the suffragettes' militancy, which threatens patriarchy.

But Winifred is not the only female character in these two novels who displays 'masculine' sexuality; so do Hermione, Dorothy, Ursula, and Gudrun, in different ways. Ursula 'annihilates' or emasculates Anton Skrebensky, just as Gudrun subjugates Gerald Crich in their battles for power; Hermione embodies frigidity and Dorothy asexuality. As I said earlier, both Havelock Ellis and Freud saw frigidity as a prevalent phenomenon among Victorian middle-class women, but Lawrence is specifically indebted to Freud in associating both frigidity and sexual aggressiveness in women with masculinity.

In 'Three Essays on the Theory of Sexuality' (1905), Freud postulates that the libido is 'invariably and necessarily of a masculine nature', and that little girls, just like little boys, manifest a 'wholly masculine' sexuality in their auto-erotic and masturbatory activities, the clitoris being the female counterpart of the penis.[33] He argues that women's primary erotogenic zone changes from the 'masculine' clitoris to the 'feminine' vagina, and that the change coincides with 'the wave of repression' in female puberty, which mandates the cessation of masturbation. Since the change may not come easily and 'the wave of repression' may have detrimental psychic effects, women tend to develop neurosis and hysteria; yet both transference and repression are most germane to 'the essence of femininity', Freud claims. Freud views frigidity or genital 'anaesthesia' as a special form of hysteria and locates its causes in young women's psychic refusal to abandon clitoral excitability and in prolonged repression.[34] Thus Freud suggests that frigidity is masculine as well as a sign of arrested development. Freud's followers critique his stress on the difference between 'masculine' clitoral sexuality and 'feminine' vaginal sexuality and his belief in the imperative of repression in constituting 'femininity'.[35] But Lawrence obviously embraces Freud's conception of 'masculine' clitoral sexuality. Not only does he agree with Freud that frigidity is 'masculine' but he views female sexual aggressiveness as an assertion of clitoral sexuality. His paranoid presentation of Winifred's ability to emasculate men is just one example. I shall return to this in my discussion of his portrayals of Ursula's subjugation of Skrebensky and Gudrun's of Gerald.

Hermione is the most extreme of Lawrence's caricatures of 'frigid' New Women. Although she is the most remarkable woman in the Midlands by virtue of her baronet-father and her political activism, she is portrayed as having an 'almost drugged' long pale face, 'as if a strange mass of thoughts coiled in the darkness within her' (*W*, p. 15). Since she is 'full of intellectuality, and heavy, nerve-worn with consciousness', she 'always felt vulnerable, vulnerable, there was always a secret chink in her armour. ... It was *a lack of robust self*, she had no natural sufficiency, there was a terrible void ... within her', declares the narrator (*W*, p. 16, my emphasis). The phrase 'lack of robust self' recalls Havelock Ellis's euphemism in his description of the feminine 'invert' as a lesser woman.[36] Thus Lawrence intimates that the New Woman's intellectuality hampers the development of her sexual impulse. Rupert condemns Hermione for her inability to be spontaneous and sensual and Ursula denigrates her as an 'untrue spectre of a woman' who 'betrayed the woman in herself' due to her belief 'only in men's things' (*W*, pp. 40, 42, 297, 295). As if these vilifications of Hermione's frigidity were not enough, Lawrence has her hit Rupert in a fit of hysteria with a ball of lapis lazuli and later has Rupert think that he will never dare to break her morbid will-to-power for fear that he may 'let loose the maelstrom of her subconsciousness, and see her ultimate madness' (*W*, p. 140).

Most intriguingly, Lawrence portrays Hermione as acutely aware of her frigidity and dependent upon Rupert for consolidating her gender identity: 'And she wanted someone to close up this deficiency ... She craved for Rupert Birkin. When he was there, she felt complete, she was sufficient, whole. For the rest of time she was established on the sand' (*W*, pp. 16–17). However, Rupert 'was perverse too. He fought her off, he always fought her off' (*W*, p. 17). In fact, Rupert is also afflicted with anxieties about his sexual and gender identities but, instead of dwelling on this, Rupert displaces his problem onto Hermione. Lawrence shows Rupert's anxieties only obliquely. When Rupert accuses Ursula of an 'assertive will' and 'frightened apprehensive self-insistence', she points out that he is the one who has apprehensions about sex (W, p. 251). Tacitly admitting this, Rupert turns to oppose Ursula's 'Dionysic ecstatic way' (W, p. 251). In a way, Lawrence's treatment of Hermione's and Rupert's neurasthenia resembles Freud's treatment of male impotence and female frigidity. Although Freud was aware of the frequency of both impotence and frigidity under repression, he chose to highlight the latter. In a long meditation, Rupert blames his woman for being 'the Great Mother of everything', seeing himself as bound by both Hermione and Ursula like a son (W, p. 200). This seems to amount to an unwitting recognition of his own unresolved Oedipus complex and his share in his failed relationship with Hermione. Moreover, it is a variation on the triangular relationship in *Sons and Lovers*.

In a letter of 19 November 1912, after a long summary of the destructive Oedipal relationship between Mrs Morel and her sons in *Sons and Lovers*, Lawrence went on: 'It's the tragedy of thousands of young men in England – it may even be Bunny's [i.e., David Garnett's] tragedy. I think it was Ruskin's and men like him.'[37] The mention of Ruskin suggests that Lawrence's appropriation of Freud's theory in *Sons and Lovers* focuses as much on the inhibitions imposed by the mother as on the mother–son incestuous feelings. As his mother's pet, Paul Morel grows up feeling overawed by notions of spirituality and propriety. On the other side are Victorian constructions of virility and manhood, which he is expected to attain. As a result, he expresses both fear of and desire for sex and women. His unsatisfying sex with Miriam indicates how mutual ignorance and shyness create difficulties for consummation. However, he displaces his own sexual anxieties by blaming Miriam's frigidity and his mother's dominance.

Rupert further shows his misogyny in his vision of Hermione as the Mater Dolorosa, who, 'in her subservience [claimed], with horrible, insidious arrogance and female tyranny, her own again, claiming back the man she had borne in suffering' (W, p. 200). Thus Hermione becomes his patient but domineering mother as well as his spurned frigid lover. This view seems to be borne out by Hermione's advice to Ursula about Rupert's needs: 'He is frail in health and body, he needs great, great care. Then he is so changeable and unsure of himself – it requires the greatest patience and understanding to help him' (W, p. 295). However, Hermione's remarks also reveal a Rupert who is immature and effeminate by Victorian standards. As far as the erotic dynamics between Hermione and Rupert go, his precarious sense of masculinity is aggravated by his respect for her spirituality.

Significantly, Lawrence's portrayal of their relationship suggests his awareness of Freud's construction of male inversion, contained in a 1910 footnote to 'Three Essays on the Theory of Sexuality'. In this footnote, Freud described male inverts as identifying themselves with women due to their intense fixation on their mothers in early childhood. At his most normative and heterosexist, Freud went on to connect homosexual desire with narcissism and flight from women.[38] Rupert's accusations about Hermione's morbidity reveal his anxieties about both homosexuality and heterosexuality. His vehemence is an overreactive attempt to justify his flight from Hermione and refute any suspicion of his homosexuality. Not that he 'suffers from a homosexual fear of women' as Eugene Goodheart claims,[39] but he is hypersensitive about such allegations. Even in the discarded 'Prologue', where his homosexual desire is explicit, he has sexual relations with both Hermione and other women. In Rupert the binary opposition between homosexuality and heterosexuality collapses. He exemplifies Freud's revolutionary conception, articulated in 1915, that humans, by virtue of their innate bisexuality, display a continuum of homosexual and heterosexual orientation.[40] Nevertheless, as I shall show later, Rupert retains a deep-seated homophobia, which leads him to relate homosexuality with degeneracy. Consequently, his anxiety about his sexual identity triggers a heterosexual imperative in him. That Lawrence seems to be obsessed with Freud's 1910 footnote to 'Three Essays' is further shown in his letter to Bertrand Russell in 1915, to which I shall return later.

It is noteworthy that Rupert includes Ursula in his attack on the Magna Mater. For Rupert, maternity remains the cardinal quality of femininity. As the novel develops, Rupert shifts from seeing both Hermione and Ursula as mother-figures to viewing only Ursula as maternal: Hermione is 'the perfect Idea ... and Ursula ... the perfect Womb' and Rupert contrasts Ursula's 'emotional and physical intimacy' with Hermione's 'abstract spiritual intimacy' (W, p. 309). Moreover, in the scene in which Ursula tosses off the wedding rings and leaves after a quarrel with Rupert, their reconciliation makes him feel as if he were 'borne out of the cramp of a womb' (W, p. 311).

Despite his tongue-in-cheek berating of the Magna Mater in Ursula, Rupert accepts her on the grounds that she is his ideal heterosexual partner. Their sexual intercourse is, at its best, something like a sexual transfusion that makes a 'pure' man and a 'pure' woman of them: 'passion is the further separating of this mixture, that which is manly being taken into the being of the man, that which is womanly passing to the woman, till the two are clear and whole as angels, the admixture of sex in the highest sense surpassed, leaving two single beings constellated together like two stars' (W, p. 201). He even anticipates a day when

> we are beings each of us, fulfilled in difference. The man is pure man, the woman pure woman, they are perfectly polarised ... There is only the pure duality of polarisation, each one free from any contamination of the other. In each, the individual is primal, sex is subordinate, but perfectly polarised.
>
> (W, p. 201)

What is problematic about his formulation is not so much his ideal of sexual polarity as his insistence on having distinctly 'uncontaminated' gender identities. His yearning to live up to traditional constructions of masculinity intimates his anxieties about heterosexuality and homosexuality. His notion of 'star-equilibrium' implies a new power relationship to balance what he calls 'the horrible, merging, mingling, self-abnegation of love', or the form of love offered by Ursula the Magna Mater. And Ursula rightly points out that what he really wants is a 'satellite' (W, p. 150). Rupert and Ursula enjoy several forms of role-playing; on the other hand, it may not be far-fetched to say that, when Rupert notes that his marriage with Ursula is 'his resurrection and his life', he partly means that she assures his heterosexual identity. Sexually more uninhibited than Hermione, Ursula gives him his sense of manhood.

Lawrence's disparagement of female sexual aggressiveness and his critique of Victorian notions of masculinity

Rupert's allusion to Ursula's 'Dionysic ecstatic way' is a recognition of her desire. For Lawrence, female desire seems no less unnerving to men than frigidity. Lawrence's portrayal of Ursula's subjugation of Anton Skrebensky in *The Rainbow* draws on Freud's notion of clitoral sexuality and shows how sexually aggressive women can emasculate men. In the kiss scene in 'First Love', Ursula's lips substitute for her clitoris to resist penetration and deny Anton orgasm. While Anton's soul groans 'Let me come – let me come', Ursula's kiss 'seized upon him, hard and fierce and burning corrosive as the moonlight' (*R*, pp. 298–9). She soon crushes him: 'she held him there, the victim, consumed, annihilated. She had triumphed: he was not any more' (*R*, p. 299). In 'The Bitterness of Ecstasy', Ursula turns wild and overpowers Anton with her 'fierce, beaked, harpy's kiss' (*R*, p. 444).[41] But here Anton wants to prove his manhood through genital sex: 'He felt as if the ordeal of proof was upon him, for life or death' (*R*, p. 444). Their sexual intercourse turns into a battle in which Ursula seems both to want and to repulse Anton so that his efforts to give Ursula an orgasm do not come off: 'He came direct to her, without preliminaries. She held him pinned down at the chest, awful. The fight, the struggle for consummation was terrible. It lasted till it was agony to his soul, till he succumbed, till he gave way as if dead' (*R*, p. 445). The language here suggests that he attains penetration, but fails to satisfy her. And her tear emasculates him: 'He felt as if the knife were being pushed into his already dead body' (*R*, p. 445).

It is unclear whether Anton is sexually inadequate or intellectually incompatible with Ursula. Lawrence stresses Ursula's antagonism toward him prior to both of his two major bouts of impotence. A soldier who fights in the Boer War, Anton strikes Ursula as conventional and common: 'He was just a brick in the whole great social fabric, the nation, the modern humanity' (*R*, p. 304). Thus, Lawrence's deprecation of Ursula's 'masculine' sexuality is deflected by his criticism of Anton as a hollow man. Contrasted retrospectively with Rupert, Anton does not meet Ursula's expectation of a 'Son of God', whose higher intellect excites her. It is significant that Lawrence has Ursula compare her union with Rupert as 'the daughters of men coming back to the Sons of God, the strange inhuman Sons of God who are in the beginning' (*W*, p. 313). Ursula even physically worships Rupert before their first consummation: 'Kneeling on the hearth-rug before him, she put her arms round his loins, and put her face against his thighs. Riches! Riches!' (*W*, p. 313). Ursula's notions of heterosexual love correspond with the bourgeois idea that men must be intellectually superior to women. And Hermione is right to see in Ursula 'a good deal of powerful female emotion, female attraction, and a fair amount of female understanding, but *no mind*' (W, p. 297, my emphasis). Like traditional women, Ursula sees men as 'naturally' smarter than women. She is only too happy to be guided by a man whom she idolises.

Like Havelock Ellis, Lawrence seems to believe that women's brains are in their wombs. Whereas he portrays Ursula as self-sufficient and spontaneous because she is never really committed to entering 'the man's world' and having a career, he characterises New Women such as Hermione and Gudrun as suffering from nervousness and a sense of deficiency. While he condemns Hermione for her frigidity, he deprecates Gudrun's intellectual aggressiveness, male envy, and denial of maternal instincts. Elevating Ursula's maternal qualities, he implicitly attacks Gudrun for deviating from the paradigm of femininity:

> Ursula saw her men as sons, pitied their yearning and admired their courage, and wondered over them as a mother wonders over her child, with a certain delight in their novelty. But to Gudrun, they were the opposite camp. She feared them and despised them, and respected their activities even overmuch.
>
> (W, p. 262)

Just as Ursula subjugates Anton in *The Rainbow*, so Gudrun breaks Gerald in *Women in Love*, but Lawrence is harsher toward Gudrun than Ursula. Whereas Lawrence sets Ursula's desire against both the intellectual inferiority of Anton and the spirituality of her suffragette-friends, he associates Gudrun's desire with the New Woman's transgression of conventional notions of femininity. Rupert's remark that '[Gudrun] is a born mistress, just as Gerald is a born lover' (W, p. 371) seems to represent Lawrence's final judgement on Gudrun, although she does not actually have love affairs with any man other than Gerald. The disparagement indicates Lawrence's adherence to the conventional virgin/harlot dichotomy. Lawrence depicts Gudrun as desiring 'the abandonments of Roman licence' with Gerald (W, p. 287). And never satisfied, she withholds the love that can save him – the way Ursula's love saves Rupert – and drives him to his death.

In the scene in which Ursula gives her 'beaked, harpy' kiss to Anton, Lawrence describes her as crying to Anton in a 'high, hard voice, like the scream of gulls' (R, p. 424). In *Women in Love*, this peculiar crying becomes Gudrun's trait. But the symbolism takes on a new nuance: it signifies an insatiable desire in Gudrun which is indistinguishable from a sado-masochistic mindset. When Gerald brutally forces his mare to stop, Gudrun cries to him 'in a strange, high voice, like a gull, or like a witch screaming' (W, p. 112). Moreover, identifying herself with the mare, she

> was as if numbed in her mind by the sense of indomitable soft weight of the man, bearing down into the living body of the horse: the strong, indomitable thighs of the blond man clenching the palpitating body of the mare into pure control; a sort of soft white magnetic domination from the loins and thighs and calves, enclosing and encompassing the mare heavily into unutterable subordination.
>
> (W, p. 113)

Likewise, when she dances before a cluster of bullocks in shivers of fear and pleasure, she cries out 'in a high, strident voice, something like the scream of a sea-gull' (W, p. 167), exposing her throat 'as in some voluptuous ecstasy towards them' (W, p. 167). She then drives them down the hills. Not coincidentally, the bullocks turn out to be owned by Gerald; and after an exchange of words, which is virtually a contest of wills, she lightly slaps Gerald on the face and feels 'in her soul an unconquerable desire for deep violence against him' (W, p. 170).

Thus Lawrence portrays Gudrun as both desiring and fearing Gerald. Her identification with the mare intimates her inflated sense of Gerald's virility and physical power, which are dangerously beautiful for her. The scene with the bullocks further shows that she wants at once to dominate, and to be dominated by, Gerald. As she muses to herself in 'Death and Love': 'He was the exquisite adventure, the desirable unknown to her. ... How perfect and foreign he was – ah, how dangerous! ... *He was such an unutterable enemy*' (W, pp. 331–2, my emphasis). While Lawrence obviously deprecates Gudrun in depicting her antagonistic lust, he also unwittingly deconstructs Rupert's sexual theory. He shows that the flip side of Rupert's idealised vision of polarised difference in sexual relationship is destructive conflict. Toward the end of the novel, Lawrence makes Gudrun seem more and more 'unnatural' by depicting her repudiation of love, marriage, and bourgeois notions of femininity. She appears 'like a vivid Medusa' (W, p. 449). Her soul is occupied by 'a pungent atmosphere of corrosion, an inflamed darkness of sensation, and a vivid, subtle, critical consciousness, that saw the world distorted, horrific'; and all that is left in her is 'the subtle thrills of extreme sensation in reduction'

(W, p. 451). In addition, rejecting the role of a nurturing woman, she expresses an infanticidal wish: 'how she hated the infant crying in the night. She would murder it gladly. She would stifle it and bury it, like Hetty Sorrell did' (W, p. 466).

On the other hand, Lawrence also criticises Gerald for failing to live up to Gudrun's idea of a man. Advanced as Gudrun is, she craves a man who is not just virile but chivalrous and protective so she can be a childlike, clinging woman to him. In a scene in 'Water-Party' where Gudrun rows away with Ursula, Gerald sees 'there was something childlike about her, trustful and deferential, like a child. ... And to Gudrun it was a real delight, *in make-belief,* to be the childlike, clinging woman to the man who stood there on the quay, so good-looking and efficient in his white clothes, and moreover the most important man she knew at the moment' (W, p. 164, my emphasis). Nevertheless, with her New Woman's awareness, Gudrun realises the danger of reverting to a beautiful little fool. The stakes of losing her intellectual independence are too high for her to relish the idea beyond her fantasy. Thus only in her sexual life does she wish to fulfil this fantasy. However, Gerald fails to heed her emotional needs. An industrial magnate, Gerald turns out to be 'a pure, inhuman, almost superhuman instrument', insensitive to Gudrun's yearning (W, p. 418).

Through Gerald, Lawrence critiques the Victorian construction of manhood by showing that the underside of aggressive virility and chivalry is infantile self-pity and sentimentality. Despite Gudrun's yearning for a glamorously virile and strong Gerald, their relationship tilts disproportionately to a mother–son attachment. Their sexual relationship is unfortunately determined by their first consummation, in which Gerald seeks maternal solace from Gudrun after his father's death. 'Like a child at the breast, he cleaved intensely to her, and she could not put him away' (W, p. 345). While he falls into 'a sleep of fecundity within the womb', she is left awake, feeling that her passion for him is not satisfied (W, p. 345, p. 348). In the Tyrol, Gudrun ponders over the dichotomy between a promiscuous, virile Gerald in the daytime and a childlike, clinging Gerald in the night:

> Gerald! Could *he* fold her in his arms and sheathe her in sleep? Ha! He needed putting to sleep himself – poor Gerald. ... Perhaps this was what he was always dogging her for, like a child that is famished, crying for the breast. Perhaps this was the secret of his

passion, his forever unquenched desire for her – that he needed her to put him to sleep. ... What then! Was she his mother? ... An infant crying in the night, this Don Juan. ... Ha – the Arthur Donnithornes, the Geralds of this world. So manly by day, yet all the while, such a crying of infants in the night.

(W, pp. 465–6)

On the other hand, when Gerald does come to her as a Don Juan, he tends to be too self-absorbed to attend to her wish. In a rape-like scene in 'Snow', the insensitive Gerald forces himself on Gudrun against her will: 'She moved convulsively, recoiling away from him. His heart went up like a flame of ice, he closed over her like steel. He would destroy her rather than be denied' (W, p. 402). Whereas he overpowers her and finds her 'so sweet', Gudrun 'only lay silent and child-like and remote ... [feeling] lost' (W, p. 402).

Lawrence's portrayal of Gerald is influenced by Edward Carpenter's conception of the 'ungrown man'. In *Love's Coming of Age* (1896), Carpenter criticised the aggressive, virile man typical of the English ruling class as emotionally stunted. Carpenter maintained that men's lack of affection and tender feelings was the chief cause of women's oppression. Therefore, he espoused the rebellion of women.[42] Lawrence toys with similar ideas in depicting Gudrun's defiance, yet he eventually reverts to a patriarchal condemnation of her. Lawrence makes it clear that Gudrun's decision to 'combat' or resist Gerald comes from her realisation that he is 'naturally promiscuous' (W, p. 413). He seems to sympathise with her when he describes her revolt from playing a maternal, sacrificial, magnanimous woman to a promiscuous, insensitive, egotistic man. He depicts delicately Gudrun's struggle to free herself from a sentimental notion of herself bound to Gerald by fate: she 'still had some pity for Gerald, some connection with him. And the most fatal of all, she had the reminiscent sentimental compassion for herself in connection with him. Because of what *had* been, she felt herself held to him by immortal, invisible threads' (W, p. 454). However, once Gudrun severs her ties with Gerald, Lawrence makes her take the blame for Gerald's death and stresses her cold callousness before and after the tragedy.

Since their sexual battle ends in Gerald's victimisation, Gudrun is portrayed as the one responsible for their failure in love. Gudrun's scepticism about their love is presented as resulting from her sexual and intellectual aggressiveness, whereas Gerald's clinging to her is depicted as indicating his moral seriousness. As I have quoted earlier, Gudrun's soul is described as permeated with 'a pungent atmosphere of corrosion, an inflamed darkness of sensation, and a vivid, subtle, critical consciousness' (W, p. 451). Whereas '[Gerald's] nature was too serious, not gay or subtle enough for mocking licentiousness'; 'He was ... subject to his necessity, in the last issue, *for goodness, for righteousness, for oneness with the ultimate purpose*', declares the narrator (W, p. 445, p. 452, my emphasis). Earlier Rupert has dubbed Gerald and Gudrun 'fleurs du mal', alluding to their desire for, and bad faith in, marriage. Here Lawrence affirms Gerald's yearning for marriage, irrespective of his promiscuous disposition, and denigrates Gudrun for her rejection of Gerald.

Lawrence's misogyny undercuts his critique of Victorian notions of masculinity. Blinkered by his entrenched belief in the supremacy of the phallus, he fails to denaturalise conceptions of gender. Lawrence reasserts notions of masculinity and femininity in the resolution of the relationship between Gerald and Gudrun. He intimates Gudrun's immorality by having her challenge the dominance of the phallus and assert her sexual autonomy. As Gudrun ponders over Gerald's virility and promiscuity, she concludes that 'But really, his Don Juan does not interest me. I could play Dona Juanita a million times better than he plays Juan. ... His maleness bores me. *Nothing is so boring as the phallus, so inherently stupid and stupidly conceited*' (W, p. 463, my emphasis). Despite his claim to restore 'free and healthy sex' to frigid modern women, Lawrence abhors female sexual autonomy. Gudrun's assertion echoes Rupert's earlier horror of female sexualities that break free of the constraints of heterosexual monogamy. In a long meditation provoked by seeing African artworks at Halliday's flat, Rupert singles out an African female statuette as the crystallisation of 'mindless progressive knowledge through the senses ... knowledge in disintegration and dissolution, knowledge such as the beetles have ... sensual, mindless, dreadful mysteries, *far beyond the phallic cult*' (W, p. 253, my emphasis). It is noteworthy that Rupert conceives unbound female desire as perverted and dangerous. Paul Delany points out that beetles are symbols of anal intercourse, since they copulate by mounting from behind and collect balls of dung to lay their eggs in, and feed from.[43] Significantly, too, Rupert's repugnance is interwoven with a racist deprecation of the African civilisation as both primitive and corrupt. It evokes Krafft-Ebing's view that heterosexual monogamy represents both the pinnacle and the moral basis of Western civilisation, and that unbridled sexual impulse threatens to bring it back to an earlier, lower stage of evolution or even destroy it altogether. Lawrence's paranoia about the danger of sex seems just as intense as his celebration of the pleasure it offers.

Lawrence's (de)construction of normal/deviant sexualities

At the core of *Women in Love* is Lawrence's horror of deviant sexualities, which makes the book very different in tone from *The Rainbow*.[44] He sees deviant sexualities as perversions and signs of functional, moral, and cultural degeneration. He expresses this horror through Rupert's apocalyptical vision. George Ford rightly observes that 'the Biblical story of Sodom ... provided Lawrence with his principal analogue *for Women in Love*'.[45] In 'In the Train' Rupert compares London to Sodom and wishes for the extinction of degenerate mankind. 'He always felt [a sort of hopelessness], on approaching London. His dislike of mankind, of the mass of mankind, amounted almost to an illness'; and he reflects on what would happen 'if mankind is destroyed, if our race is destroyed like Sodom' (W, p. 61, p. 59). In 'Water-Party' he expounds to Ursula his apocalyptical vision of the 'destructive' sexualities that prevail in their day and find their flowering in people like Gerald and Gudrun:

> The other river, the black river ... is our real reality[,] ... the dark river of dissolution. ... When the stream of synthetic creation lapses, we find ourselves part of the inverse process, the flood of destructive creation. Aphrodite is born in the first spasm of universal dissolution – then the snakes and swans and lotus – marsh-flowers – and Gudrun and Gerald – born in the process of destructive creation.
>
> (W, p. 172)

Rupert not only believes that 'destructive' sexualities will lead to human extermination ('Dissolution rolls on ... and it ends in universal nothing – the end of the world' [W, p. 173]) but he looks forward to 'a new cycle of creation after' (W, p. 173). His speech resembles the rhetoric of social Darwinism and eugenics, which is all the more significant retrospectively as he and Ursula become the only survivors in his moral landscape. On top of that, just like the far Right today, he equates deviant sexualities with the moral perversity of a degenerate race. In his letter to Halliday – which the latter reads at the Pompadour Cafe – he writes, 'There is a phase in every race ... when the desire for destruction overcomes every other desire. In the individual, this desire is ultimately a desire for destruction in the self' (W, p. 383).

Rupert clarifies that he means by 'destructive' sexualities all forms of sexuality that deviate from the middle-class norm of love and marriage. In the same letter, he accuses London Bohemian artists and models of

> reacting in intimacy only for destruction, – using sex as a great re-
> ducing agent, by friction between the two great elements of male and
> female obtaining a frenzy of sensual satisfaction – reducing the old
> ideas, going back to the savages for our sensations, always seeking to
> *lose* ourselves in some ultimate black sensation, mindless and infinite
> – burning only with destructive fires.
>
> (W, p. 384)

Rupert is referring specifically to the Bohemians' practice of male homosexuality and female promiscuity as exemplified by Halliday and his model-mistress the Pussum early in the book. Reiterating his theory of the polarity between the male and female principles in monogamous heterosexual union, he condemns their transgression as unmasculine and unfeminine respectively. Halliday and the Pussum are in a constant struggle for domination/power. But unlike that between Gerald and Gudrun, their fight is intensified by the social and economic disparity between them. Halliday both despises and desperately wants the licentious Pussum. Getting her pregnant and not intending to marry her, he nevertheless sees her as his woman. However, she overturns their master/slave relationship through resorting to violence and prostitution. Rupert condemns the Pussum as 'the harlot, the actual harlot of adultery to [Halliday]' without criticising Halliday's mishandling of the girl (W, p. 95). And Gerald, who has slept with her, concurs by offering a male-centred disgust with the bodily smell of prostitutes (W, p. 95). Thus, just like the writers of nineteenth-century domestic fiction, Lawrence adheres to the Victorian double standard. The African female statuette is also associated with the Pussum. Gerald sees her in a carved African figure in childbirth and Rupert obviously relates Halliday's fascination with obscenity and with 'pure culture in sensation' to his fascination with her. Even more than Gudrun, the Pussum asserts her sexual autonomy. She embodies for Lawrence the most abhorrent example of female desire, second only to Winifred.

If Lawrence stigmatises the Pussum's unbridled desire, he attacks Halliday for his homosexual relations. Described as having a 'degenerate' face and a high-pitched 'squealing' voice, Halliday is seen 'stark naked' with Libidnikov by the fire in his flat. The fact that men at Halliday's flat usually sit around in the nude in the morning suggests that Halliday and his friends take homosexual relations for granted. This is borne out by Gerald's later observation that 'Halliday, Libidnikov, Birkin, the whole Bohemian set ... were only half men' (W, p. 81). Obviously shocked, Gerald reveals his homophobia when staring at the naked Libidnikov: 'He was so healthy and well-made, why did he make one ashamed, why did one feel repelled? Why should Gerald even dislike it, why did it seem to him to detract from his own dignity? Was that all a human being amounted to? So uninspired! thought Gerald' (W, p. 78). The naked Rupert is apparently one of them. Lawrence links these men's homosexuality to Halliday's African fetishes by having the naked Rupert adore the artworks for representing 'really *ultimate* physical consciousness, mindless, utterly sensual' and then having Gerald criticise Rupert for liking 'the wrong things ... things against yourself' (W, p. 79).[46]

Lawrence's homophobic representation of the Bohemians is nothing to compare with his own homosexual panic and hysteria in reaction to seeing the Bloomsbury homosexuals. In a letter to David Garnett on 19 April 1915, he recounted how during a visit to Cambridge he was so wrought up by seeing Keynes in pyjamas that he associated Keynes as well as Duncan Grant and Birrill with corruption:

> Why is there this horrible sense of frowstiness, so repulsive, as if it came from deep inward dirt – a sort of sewer – deep in men like K[eynes] and B[irrell] and D[uncan] G[rant]. It is something almost unbearable to me. And not from any moral disapprobation. I myself never considered Plato very wrong, or Oscar Wilde. I never knew what it meant till I saw K., till I saw him at Cambridge. ... Then suddenly a door opened and K. was there, blinking from sleep, standing in his pyjamas. And as he stood there gradually a knowledge passed into me. ... And it was carried along with the most dreadful sense of repulsiveness – something like carrion. ... Never bring B. to see me any more. There is something nasty about him, like black-beetles. He is horrible and unclean. I feel as if I should go mad, if I think of your set, D. G. and K. and B. It makes me dream of beetles.[47]

The predominantly excremental symbols here show how he inter-
nalises the religious condemnation of sodomy as an abominable,
unutterable sin by linking these men to 'deep inward dirt', sewer,
carrion, and beetles (see my discussion of beetles early on). Both his
abhorrence and his desire to keep himself intact from their contami-
nation suggest his own anxieties about homosexuality. Not surprisingly, in the same letter he justifies his revulsion by echoing
Krafft-Ebing's view that homosexuality represents the decay of
Western civilisation.

In a letter to Bertrand Russell prior to his visit to Cambridge, he
also attacks the Bloomsbury group by insinuating that some of its
members indulge in masturbation and fear the otherness of women:
'The repeating of a known reaction upon myself is sensationalism.
This is what nearly *all* English people now do. When a man takes a
woman, he is *merely* repeating a known reaction upon himself, not
seeking a new reaction, a discovery. ... When this condition arrives,
there is always Sodomy.'[48] Thus, he constructs the 'Bloomsbuggers''
homosexuality as a flight from women, solipsism, de-creation, and
sterility. The underlying assumption is that a sexual relationship
depends for its creative dynamics on the two parties' polarised
difference, which for him means gender difference. What is problematic here is not so much his didactic insistence on polarised difference as his reductive formulation that, as far as a man is
concerned, any woman is necessarily more different than any man.
As I shall show later, he belies this very formulation in the discarded
'Prologue' to *Women in Love*, where he portrays the effeminate
Rupert as treating women as sexually 'the same' and men as 'the
other'. On the other hand, the idea that a man has more in common
with any other man than with any woman also implies a belief that
it is easier for a man to love men than women, which runs counter
to its manifest heterosexism.

Indeed, Lawrence hardly conceals his deep fascination with, and
susceptibility to, homosexual desire. In a letter on 2 December
1913, he writes: 'I should like to know why nearly every man that
approaches greatness tends to homosexuality, whether he admits it
or not: so that he loves the body of a man better than the body of a
woman.'[49] As he rambles on, he shows the comparative easiness of
same-sex love vis-à-vis heterosexual love; and he concludes almost
regretfully: 'one is kept by all tradition and instinct from loving
men, or a man – for it means just extinction of all the purposive
influences'.[50]

If Lawrence's representation of homosexual practices among the London Bohemians is derogatory, his treatment of the homosexual Loerke is vituperative. Lawrence portrays Loerke as a decadent artist who worships the beauty of machines and teenage girls' bodies as well as primitive art, all of which Lawrence finds degrading and obscene. 'He was really like one of the "little people" who have no soul', declares the narrator. Lawrence not only dumps on him all the excremental symbols with which he has associated the Bloomsbury set, but he stresses his 'despicable' diminutiveness and unmanliness. Loerke is called 'a mud-child', 'a little obscene monster of the darkness', 'a rat in the river of corruption', 'the wizard rat that swims ahead [in the sewers]', and 'a noxious insect' (W, pp. 427, 428, 448).[51] That Gudrun abandons Gerald for Loerke is presented by the narrator as signifying that 'there were no more *men*, there were only creatures, little ultimate creatures like Loerke' (W, p. 452). Lawrence depicts Loerke as half seducing Gudrun into obscenely sensual experience and even offending Gudrun slightly by his denial of women and love (W, p. 458). Thus, Lawrence implicitly equates Loerke's homosexuality with his narcissism and sterility as well as his degradation. Moreover, Lawrence's homophobia goes hand in hand with his anti-Semitism, as Rupert tells Gerald about his hatred and repugnance for Loerke: 'I expect he is a Jew – or part Jewish. ... He is a gnawing little negation, gnawing at the roots of life' (W, p. 428).

Rupert's condemnations of both Loerke and the London bohemians cohere into the apocalyptical vision central to the book. Just as Lawrence sets up a purity/degradation distinction between himself and the 'Bloomsbuggers', so Rupert distinguishes himself from the 'degenerate' practitioners of homosexuality. Lawrence celebrates Rupert and Ursula's married love as representing a life-affirming ideal. Paradoxically, the perfect union has a cleft: Rupert needs an intimate same-sex friend. As he tells Ursula near the end of the book, 'You are enough for me, as far as woman is concerned. You are all women to me. But I wanted a man friend, as eternal as you and I are eternal.'

In the discarded 'Prologue' to the book, Rupert explicitly expresses his secret homosexual desire. He realises that he likes the bodies of men better than the bodies of women:

> All the time, he recognised that, although he was always drawn to women, feeling more at home with a woman than with a man, yet it

was for men that he felt the hot, flushing, roused attraction which a man is supposed to feel for the other sex. Although nearly all his living interchange went on with one woman or another, although he was always terribly intimate with at least one woman, and practically never intimate with a man, yet the male physique had a fascination for him, and for the female physique he felt only a fondness, a sort of sacred love, as for a sister.

(W, pp. 501–2)

The effeminate Rupert finds women to be his sisters, and men his object choice. Lawrence goes on to depict Rupert as having 'a small gallery' of desirable men, which fall into two classes: the blond 'northmen' and the 'dark-skinned, supple, night-smelling men' (W, pp. 503–4).

In the published text, Rupert's sexual desire for Gerald is mystified and translated into a desire for a spiritual brother. Nevertheless, the sexual aspect of their friendship looms throughout. In Chapter II Lawrence strongly suggests their homoerotic interest in each other.

... always their talk brought them into a deadly nearness of contact, a strange, perilous intimacy which was either hate or love, or both. They parted with apparent inconcern ... Yet the heart of each burned for the other. They burned with each other, inwardly. This they would never admit. They intended to keep their relationship a casual free-and-easy friendship, they were not going to be so unmanly and unnatural as to allow any heart-burning between them.

(W, p. 33)

One recalls Basil Hallward's intense feelings of love and fear on first seeing Dorian Gray. The same culturally imposed homophobic homosociality prevents Rupert and Gerald from developing their love.

In 'Man to Man', Rupert ponders over 'the problem of love and eternal conjunction between two men' and admits to himself 'Of course he had been loving Gerald all along, and all along denying it' (W, p. 206). He then offers to Gerald 'blood brotherhood', stressing the spiritual nature of such bonds, to which Gerald fails to respond. Even here Birkin contradicts his own offer by noting that what he usually likes so much is 'the physical, animal man ... in Gerald' (W, p. 207). In 'Gladiatorial', the unison they achieve through wrestling leaves them in physical excitement. Rupert expresses his appreciation of Gerald's 'beautiful plastic form', and Gerald concedes that

'I don't believe I've ever felt as much *love* for a woman, as I have for you – not *love*. You understand what I mean?' (*W*, p. 273, p. 275). However, it is Rupert who draws back here as he feels Ursula is gaining ascendance over Gerald in his mind (*W*, p. 274). Despite the apparent change in his sexual orientation, Rupert hardly sublimates his desire for Gerald. As he tells Ursula in 'A Chair': 'It's the problem I can't solve. I *know* I want a perfect and complete relationship with you. ... But beyond that. *Do* I want a real, ultimate relationship with Gerald. Do I want a final, almost extra-human relationship with him – a relationship in the ultimates of me and him – or don't I?' (*W*, p. 363). As we know from the ending, his answers to these questions are affirmative. It is noteworthy that here the phrase 'extra-human' has the Lawrentian connotation of 'physical or sexual'.[52] Thus, Rupert does not stop desiring men and the 'eternal union with a man' for which he yearns does not exclude a sexual possibility.

If Rupert's homosexual desire aligns him with practitioners of homosexuality such as Loerke and the Bohemian set, the sodomy he practises with Ursula further breaks down the purity/degradation distinction which he self-righteously establishes between himself and those men. His heterosexism makes him displace onto them the guilt and shame he feels about his homosexual desire, yet he cannot deny his own propensity for 'perverted' sexuality. Significantly, Lawrence depicts Rupert's anal intercourse with Ursula from her perspective and has her celebrate it:

> How could anything that gave one satisfaction be excluded? What was degrading? – Who cared? Degrading things were real, with a different reality. ... So bestial, they two! – so degraded! She winced. – But after all, why not? She exulted as well. ... How good it was to be really shameful! There would be no shameful thing she had not experienced. – Yet she was unabashed. ... She was free, when she knew everything, and no dark shameful things were denied her.
>
> (*W*, p. 413)

This passage does not simply suggest that Rupert uses Ursula as a 'sexual substitute' for Gerald, as Jeffrey Meyers observes.[53] Moreover, to have Ursula feel liberated by the 'degrading', 'shameful', 'bestial' sex is a political move on Lawrence's part to deflect, and sublimate into heterosexuality, Rupert's homoerotic desire. As Jonathan Dollimore points out, the narrator seems to be 'in the position of the woman being fucked by the other of woman

(man)'.[54] Even more overtly, Lawrence has Ursula idolise and fantasise about Rupert's anal 'riches' in 'Excurse':

> She closed her hands over the full, rounded body of his loins. ... It was a perfect passing away for both of them. ..., the marvellous fulness of immediate gratification, overwhelming, outflooding from the Source of the deepest life-force, the darkest, deepest, strangest life-source of the human body, *at the back and base of the loins*. ... She had thought there was no source *deeper than the phallic source*. And now, behold, from the smitten rock of the man's body, from the strange marvellous flanks and thighs, deeper, further in mystery than the phallic source, came the floods of ineffable darkness and ineffable riches.
>
> (W, p. 314, my emphasis)[55]

Despite his condemnations of sodomy in both *Women in Love* and his letters, Lawrence is helplessly fascinated with it.

Ursula's celebration of sodomy also deconstructs Rupert's denunciations of female sexual 'perversions' with which he charges the African statuette, the Pussum, and Gudrun. Since his love relationship with Ursula is contaminated by, and indeed dependent on, 'perversions', Rupert's moralistic distinctions between normal/deviant, creative/destructive sexualities prove to be lame and hypocritical. He at once asserts the bourgeois mandate of heterosexual monogamy and shows that his fear of sexual deviations is sheer paranoia. It is noteworthy how many Lawrentian heroes and heroines enjoy anal sex. Apart from Rupert and Ursula, practitioners include Anna and Will in *The Rainbow* and Connie and Mellors in *Lady Chatterley's Lover*. In each case the shame of 'perversions' is treated as something which one must overcome in order to achieve a higher, more exhilarating and liberating sensation. Most intriguingly, Will emerges from 'the darkness and death of ... sensual activities' to be a 'real, purposive self' (R, p. 219, p. 221).

Thus Lawrence contradicts his insistence on the normal/perverse division. As he unwittingly shows, neither deviant desire nor deviant sexual acts – so long as they are consensual – are threatening to civilisation. The discrimination he expects us to make in *Women in Love* between what George Ford terms 'sensual experiences enjoyed by a pair of loving men and women (which are regarded by the novelist as innocently enjoyed) ... and degenerate indulgences of a society which has cut all connections with spiritual values' is perplexing and unnecessary.[56] It only reveals the gap between his idealisation and fear of the same things. As I have shown in my discussion, both his homophobia and fear of female desire are culturally imposed. He falls short of a real sexual 'liberation' because he fails to critique heterosexism, misogyny, and the double standard of sexual morality. However, while he perpetuates heterosexual monogamy and condemns the Other as degenerate, he cannot but admit that the Other is also in himself.

From *Studies in Language and Literature*, 7 (August 1996), 57–87.

Notes

[Liang-ya Liou's essay is in some way similar to Robert Burden's but where he largely identifies a number of contemporary discourses in *The Rainbow* without really building them into an argument, Liou, in her discussion of *The Rainbow* and *Women in Love*, makes them part of her analysis of Lawrence's attitude to feminism and sexuality. She makes two main points. The first is that Lawrence's advocacy of female sexuality is at the expense of female politics and the second is that while Lawrence may repudiate homosexual practices, he nevertheless remains fascinated by them. Liou relates Lawrence's views about female sexuality to contemporary ideas, particularly those of Freud, showing that he is only prepared to countenance female pleasure if it is heterosexual and takes place within a monogamous relationship. He was hostile to the suffragettes because he believed they behaved like men and because a section of them promoted chastity. Lawrence felt the repression of 'natural' sexuality resulted in 'perversions' like lesbianism which was yet another instance of masculine behaviour in women. At the same time, Lawrence's presentation of lesbianism was not entirely negative and this ambiguity also surrounds his treatment of homosexuality. At one extreme he is revolted by it, as is clear from his repeated image of beetles to indicate sodomy but, at the other, he not only countenances anal intercourse between men and women but he positively promotes the importance of male relationships. This is most clear in his portrayal of Rupert Birkin whose homosexual desire was evident in the discarded prologue of the book.

Liou's essay is noteworthy for the way it combines psychoanalysis, feminism and politics in its account of *The Rainbow* and *Women in Love*. Liou shows how despite being constrained by binary oppositions that dominated the conceptions of sexuality, Lawrence nevertheless subverted them in ways of which he himself was not aware.

All references to *The Rainbow* are from the Cambridge edition, edited by Mark Kinkead-Weekes (Cambridge, 1989) and to *Women in Love* from the edition edited by David Farmer, Lindeth Vasey, and John Worthen (Cambridge, 1987) and are given in parentheses in the text. Eds]

1. Ursula strikes one as more uninhibited and more of an intellectual in *The Rainbow* than in *Women in Love*. Whereas in The *Rainbow* she sharply disputes Anton Skrebensky's political beliefs, is sexually aggressive, and even proposes to Dorothy Russell the notion that sex is more important than love, in *Women in Love* she is comparatively inarticulate and domesticated. She becomes the disciple of Rupert Birkin and often acts as if she were learning new things from him, although he only reiterates her unconventional views in the previous book.

2. Three hostile reviews in October 1915 contributed to the suppression of the book. Robert Lynd called the book 'a monotonous wilderness of phallicism' (5 October 1915, *Daily News*); quoted in R. P. Draper, *D. H. Lawrence: The Critical Heritage* (New York, 1970), p. 92. James Douglas vehemently condemned its immorality: 'These people are not human beings. They are creatures who are immeasurably lower than the lowest animal in the Zoo.' Obviously alluding to the chapter 'Shame', Douglas savaged Lawrence for using a subtle style to 'express the unspeakable and to hint at the unutterable'. Above all, he hinted strongly that the book should be prosecuted: '[Art] must conform to the ordered laws that govern human society. If it refuses to do so, it must pay the penalty. The sanitary inspector of literature must notify it and call for its isolation. ... A thing like *The Rainbow* has no right to exist in the wind of war. It is a greater menace to our public health than any of the epidemic diseases' (22 October 1915, *Star*; quoted in Draper, *D. H. Lawrence: The Critical Heritage*, pp. 93–4). Clement Shorter also found 'there is no form of viciousness, of suggestiveness, that is not reflected in these pages' and singled out the book's representation of lesbianism as his major objection. More importantly, he, too, seemed to favour censorship in suggesting that the publishers should protect the public from such books and that, after this, no writer who was also an artist would run any risk of prosecution (23 October 1915, *Sphere*; quoted in Draper, *D. H. Lawrence: The Critical Heritage*, pp. 96–7). Significantly, Herbert Muskett, the prosecuting counsel, quoted the reviews by Douglas and Shorter in court. On the other hand, it was also believed that the book was actually prosecuted because of its anti-war sentiment and its criticism of the nation-state. See Alistair Davies, 'Contexts of Reading: the Reception of D. H. Lawrence's *The Rainbow* and *Women in Love*', in *The Theory of Reading*, ed. Frank Gloversmith (Sussex, 1984), pp. 215–16; and Emile Delavenay, *D. H. Lawrence: The Man and His Work: The Formative Years, 1885–1919* (London, 1972), pp. 235–48.

3. According to Charles Ross, at the request of his publisher Martin Secker, Lawrence reduced the explicit references to homosexuality. He robed the men at Halliday's flat and removed the phrase that described the sleeping arrangements of Loerke and his male companion, Leitner, who, 'lived together in the last degree of intimacy'.

Ross points out that the most substantial alteration concerned Rupert Birkin's homosexuality and was probably made by Secker without Lawrence's knowledge. In this excised passage, notes Ross, 'Birkin all but proposes a sexual aspect to *Blutbruderschaft* that would place a homosexual marriage on a basis of equality with heterosexual marriage'. See Charles Ross, *The Composition of 'The Rainbow' and 'Women in Love': A History* (Charlottesville, VA, 1979), pp. 126–8.

4. H. M. Daleski, *The Forked Flame: A Study of D. H. Lawrence* (London, 1975), pp. 38–9.

5. F. R. Leavis, *D. H. Lawrence: Novelist* (New York, 1956), p. xi.

6. Simone De Beauvoir, *The Second Sex*, trans. H. M. Parshley (New York, 1961), p. 209.

7. In *The Rainbow*, Ursula is averse to becoming a baby-producing machine like her mother. In the opening chapter of *Women in Love*, however, she distinguishes herself from Gudrun when the latter expresses her nonchalance toward child-bearing.

8. Jeffrey Weeks, *Against Nature: Essays on History, Sexuality and Identity* (London, 1991), p. 180.

9. I equate Rupert with Lawrence only provisionally. Although by and large he is an authorial surrogate, there are places in *Women in Love* where, instead of him, Ursula or even Gerald speaks for Lawrence.

10. Liang-ya Liou, 'The Politics of a Transgressive Desire: Oscar Wilde's *The Picture of Dorian Gray*', *Studies in Language and Literature*, No. 6 (Oct. 1994), 101–25.

11. D. H. Lawrence, *The Letters of D. H. Lawrence*. Vol. I: *September 1901–May 1913*, ed. James T. Boulton and George J. Zytaruk (New York, 1979), p. 506.

12. Among the characters he denigrates are Anton Skrebensky, Ursula's Uncle Tom, and Gerald Crich. On the other hand, Lawrence also owes his 'feminised' sexual politics to the politics of nineteenth-century domestic fiction, which celebrates the middle-class woman's moral superiority and delicacy. Thus, his emphasis on human nurturing and caring qualities and on organic relationship with an undefiled nature sounds like the rhetoric of mainstream feminism.

13. D. H. Lawrence, *Phoenix: The Posthumous Papers of D. H. Lawrence*, ed. Edward McDonald (New York, 1936), pp. 405–6.

14. Lisa Tickner, *The Spectacle of Women: Imagery of the Suffrage Campaign 1907–14* (Chicago, 1988), p. 8. See also Hilary Simpson, *D. H. Lawrence and Feminism* (De Kalb, IL, 1966), for her discussion of Lawrence's relationship with the women's suffrage movement.

15. Jane Marcus, 'Introduction: Re-reading the Pankhursts and Women's Suffrage', in *Suffrage and the Pankhursts*, ed. Jane Marcus (London, 1987), p. 9.

16. See ibid., p. 14.

17. See ibid., p. 15.

18. Emile Delavenay, *D. H. Lawrence and Edward Carpenter: A Study in Edwardian Transition* (London, 1971), pp. 212–13.

19. See Lawrence, *Phoenix*, p. 496.

20. Lawrence is more sympathetic to the women's movement in his earlier novel *Sons and Lovers*. He presents Gertrude Morel as participating in the activities of the Co-operative Women's Guild and deeply respected by her children when she writes essays for it. He portrays Clara Dawes as an active and sexually unconventional suffragette, although he eventually diminishes her by having Paul Morel 'return' her to her bitterly estranged husband.

21. Susan Kingsley Kent, *Sex and Suffrage in Britain, 1860–1914* (Princeton, NJ, 1987), pp. 3–23.

22. Active in the 1880s and 1890s, Olive Schreiner was unconventional in acknowledging women's strong sexual drives. Arguing that economic dependence on men reduced all women to prostitutes, she maintained that the women's movement would free women from the position of sexual serfdom. See Kent, *Sex and Suffrage in Britain*, pp. 145–7.

23. See *The Letters of D. H. Lawrence*, Vol. I (23 December 1912), p. 490.

24. See ibid., p. 544, my emphasis.

25. See ibid., Vol. I, p. 546. For many Lawrence scholars, Lawrence re-envisions the relations between men and women by stressing sex and linking it to mystical life forces. I contend that what Lawrence presents is nothing more than mystified heterosexual monogamy. He never departs from the bourgeois ideal of love and marriage. Rupert Birkin, his best spokesman, despises the word 'love' but would not have sex with Ursula until they have commitment. As he tells Gerald Crich, he wants an 'absolute marriage' with a woman.

26. See *The Letters of D. H. Lawrence*, Vol. II: *June 1913–Oct. 1916*, ed. James T. Boulton and George J. Zytaruk (New York, 1981), p. 183.

27. Jeffrey Weeks, *Sex, Politics and Society: The Regulation of Sexuality Since 1800* (London, 1981), pp. 40–3.

28. See Havelock Ellis, 'Sex in Relation to Society', in *Studies in the Psychology of Sex*, Vol. II, Part III (New York, 1905), p. 68, p. 415,

and 'The Sexual Impulse in Women', in *Studies in the Psychology of Sex*, Vol. I, Part II (New York, 1905), p. 253.

29. As Jeffrey Weeks puts it, for Ellis, fundamental 'feminine' characteristics included 'not only modesty, but affectability, sympathy, maternal instincts, devotion, emotional receptivity'. See Jeffrey Weeks, 'Havelock Ellis and the Politics of Sex Reform', in *Socialism and the New Life: The Personal and Sexual Politics of Edward Carpenter and Havelock Ellis*, ed. Sheila Rowbotham and Jeffrey Weeks (London, 1977), pp. 170–1.

30. Sigmund Freud, *The Standard Edition of the Complete Psychological Works of Sigmund Freud*, trans. James Strachey (London, 1957), Vol. VII, p. 221.

31. In ' "Civilized" Sexual Morality and Modern Nervous Illness' (1908), Freud claimed that women who have preserved their virginity by resorting to 'perverse' practices and masturbation 'show themselves anaesthetic to normal intercourse in marriage'. See Freud, *The Standard Edition*, Vol. IX, p. 201.

32. In *Lady Chatterley's Lover*, Mellors condemns his ex-wife and women who take an active role during sexual intercourse for the same reason, claiming that 'they're nearly all Lesbian'. See D. H. Lawrence, *Lady Chatterley's Lover*, intro. Richard Hoggart (Harmondsworth, 1960), p. 212.

33. See Freud, *The Standard Edition*, Vol. VII, p. 219.

34. See ibid., p. 221.

35. In a footnote added in 1915, Freud intimates that he uses the conventional concepts of 'masculine' and 'feminine' as substitutes for activity and passivity. See Freud, *The Standard Edition*, Vol. VII, p. 219. Still, this qualification does not amount to a real conceptual breakthrough. It seems that Freud recognised the constructedness of gender, but his patriarchal, sexist prejudice prevented him from investigating it critically.

36. Havelock Ellis and John Addington Symonds, *Sexual Inversion* (London, 1897), p. 87.

37. See *The Letters of D. H. Lawrence*, Vol. I, p. 477.

38. See Freud, *The Standard Edition*, Vol. VII, p. 145.

39. Eugene Goodheart, *The Utopian Vision of D. H. Lawrence* (Chicago, 1963), p. 122.

40. See Freud, *The Standard Edition*, Vol. VII, pp. 145–6. Here Freud was at his most radical. He opposed the separation of homosexuals from the rest of mankind. He argued that heterosexuality, just like homosexuality, shows a limited object choice and needs to be

explained. He maintained that the causes of homosexuality are multiple and stressed that seemingly normal people may also have homosexual desire.

41. Compare these kisses with Mellors's bitter account of his sexual intercourses with women who take an active role: 'Then there's the hard sort, that are the devil to bring off at all, and bring themselves off, like my wife. They want to be the active party. ... Then there's the sort that puts you out before you really "come", and go on writhing their loins till they bring themselves off against your thighs.' See *Lady Chatterley's Lover*, p. 212.

42. Edward Carpenter, *Love's Coming of Age* (New York, 1927), pp. 29–37, p. 62.

43. See Paul Delany, *D. H. Lawrence's Nightmare: The Writer and his Circle in the Years of the Great War* (New York, 1978), pp. 88–9.

44. Despite its denigration of lesbianism and deprecation of Ursula's willed sensuality, *The Rainbow* strikes one as by and large a celebration of sex, albeit sex within or leading up to marriage.

45. George Ford, *Double Measure: A Study of the Novels and Stories of D. H. Lawrence* (New York, 1965), p. 168.

46. For Lawrence's views on homosexuality see *The Letters of D. H. Lawrence*. For example, in *Letters* II he writes, 'I should like to know why nearly every man that approaches greatness tends to homosexuality, whether he admits it or not: so that he loves the body of a man better than the body of a woman', p. 115.

47. See *The Letters of D. H. Lawrence*, Vol. II, pp. 320–1.

48. See ibid., p. 285, 12 February 1915.

49. See ibid., p. 115.

50. See ibid.

51. I pointed out earlier that beetles symbolise anal intercourse. 'A noxious insect' is a variation on beetles. As Lawrence discussed his phobia of anality in a letter to Ottoline Morrell on 30 April 1915: 'I like sensual lust – but insectwise, no – it is obscene. I like men to be beasts – but insects – one insect mounted on another – oh God!' See *Letters* II, p. 331.

52. Compare Lawrence's statements about his conception of *The Rainbow* and *Women in Love* in one of the letters quoted above: 'I only care about what the woman is – what she is – *inhumanly*, physiologically, materially' (my emphasis).

53. Jeffrey Meyers, *Homosexuality and Literature 1890–1930* (Montreal, 1977), p. 149.

54. Jonathan Dollimore, *Sexual Dissidence: Augustine to Wilde, Freud to Foucault* (Oxford, 1990), p. 275.

55. This passage has been hotly debated. Some scholars interpret it as Ursula's discovery of mystical life forces in Rupert's body, but I agree with Jeffrey Meyers that 'at the back and base of the loins' and 'deeper than the phallic source' suggest the anus. See Jeffrey Meyers, *Homosexuality and Literature*, p. 148.

56. Ford, *Double Measure*, p. 205.

10

Into the Ideological Unknown: *Women in Love*

DAVID PARKER

I

Recent poststructuralist theory has rejected the notion of a literary canon, largely on the now-familiar grounds that the canonical works univocally speak the ideology of a hegemonic class, thus marginalising such groups as blacks, women and the working class.

Of particular concern to the poststructuralists is the pretension of these texts to ethical authority. As Frederic Jameson has said: 'it is ethics itself which is the ideological vehicle and legitimation of concrete structures of power and domination'.[1] He goes on to outline his (sub-Nietzschean) idea of ethics as a system of binary oppositions, of good versus evil, where 'evil' inevitably denotes imagined characteristics of those who are other to the hegemonic class. For this reason ethical criticism, which – hoodwinked by these texts' strategies of containment – confines itself to 'surface' exposition of them, is worse than useless because it perpetuates the work of legitimation, giving it added institutional authority. Nor does the newer psychological criticism fare much better in Jameson's book, for this is merely a sub-genre of the ethical, replacing 'myths of the re-unification of the psyche' for the 'older themes of moral sensibility and ethical awareness'.[2]

The canonical texts are said to repress their ideological function, consigning it to their unconscious where it can only be retrieved by political analysis. To this extent they are mad texts, dangerously so, because, unless we are capable of analysing them politically, they can only offer, as Lennard J. Davis says, to reinforce in us 'those collective and personal defences' which are our 'neurotic' constructs of the world.[3] Using Freud's famous essay, 'Remembering, Repeating and Working Through', Davis argues that in reading novels we merely 'repeat' repressed narratives which in the long run impair our capacity to know 'what really is'.[4]

Just why it should be supposed that political analysis alone can confront us with non-ideological reality is rarely made clear in the criticism I've been citing. The question that is so often asked remains unanswered: what privileges Marxist history? Or why should it be true to say, as Jameson does, that 'everything is "in the last analysis" political' and not equally true that, according to a different sort of analysis, everything is ethical? Or psychological? What these questions reveal in such theory is a not very thinly disguised will-to-*uber*narrative that mirrors closely its own account of the hegemonic narrative it wants to supplant. If, for a moment, we entertain the neurotic fantasy that everything is in some sense psycho-ethical, we might say that this usurpation of the old authority looks like an Oedipal reaction. The point of making this observation is that almost everywhere this new discourse finds its identity, not by coming to terms inclusively and dialectically with humanist criticism and the texts it helped to canonise, but by attempting to marginalise all of them. This comes out plainly in the apparent disinclination or inability of many theorists to look with care and disinterest at the works they are adducing; instead they offer straw-man accounts of them that often grossly underestimate their complexity and intelligence.

Not all such recent theory wants to suppress the canon though. According to Jonathan Culler, de Manian deconstruction provides at least one justification for canonical texts – that they are often 'the most powerful demystifiers of the ideologies they have been said to promote'.[5] This at least gestures in the direction of noting the true complexity of such works, though this would hardly have been news to the authors themselves. Lawrence makes the point almost identically in his *Study of Thomas Hardy*:

> Yet every work of art adheres to some system of morality. But if it be really a work of art, it must contain the essential criticism on the morality to which it adheres. And hence the antinomy, hence the

conflict necessary to every tragic conception. The degree to which the system of morality, or the metaphysic, of any work of art is submitted to criticism within the work of art makes the lasting value and satisfaction of that work.

A few pages later, Lawrence expands on the same point:

> It is the novelists and dramatists who have the hardest task in reconciling their metaphysic, their theory of being and knowing, with their living sense of being. Because a novel is a microcosm, and because man in viewing the universe must view it in the light of a theory, therefore every novel must have the background or structural skeleton of some theory of being, some metaphysic. But the metaphysic must always subserve the artistic purpose beyond the artist's conscious aim. Otherwise the novel becomes a treatise.[6]

All too often ideological analysis produces straw-man readings precisely by taking works of art as univocal treatises, seeing only 'the conscious aim' and not the 'artistic purpose' – its sources in part unconscious – that transcends the intentional 'system of morality' or 'theory of being' of the author. What this involves is reading not simply for static hermeneutic structures or systems of signification but also for *process*, for art as discovery, exploration. Whatever static binary oppositions an author may start out with, one test of the true classic is the degree to which the work either clings to them or entertains doubts, uncertainties, dialogic 'criticisms', which allow these terms to interact, become unstable, fluid, even altogether to change places. *Women in Love* is interesting and important as a work of art not because it expresses a Romantic ideology of 'innocence' versus 'social being', or opposes preconceived 'good' human possibilities to 'evil' ones, but because it explores these things in their dynamic interrelatedness.

Women in Love especially foregrounds, in the lives it represents, the ways in which fixed ideas, modes of what it calls 'knowing' that is, consciously constructing – the world, are actually a defence against repressed feelings and realisations. The novel's searching, in fact, is a good deal directed towards understanding the conditions under which such defences can be dropped and one can move into what it terms 'the unknown'. It is a novel very much *about* transformation, selves in process, about both reinforcing psychic resistances and 'working through' them. At the same time, in a process analogous to and reflecting the represented ones, the novel's ultimate 'artistic purpose' can be seen as a 'working through' of that over-insistent will-to-vision which keeps threatening Lawrence's art from *The Rainbow* on.

II

Most accounts of *Women in Love*, such as the one in Dan Jacobson's recent book,[7] stress the polarisation between two sets of characters, one struggling through to freedom and life, the other going down the slope, with the rest of the race, to various forms of death. This view of the novel has of course a lot to be said for it. The opening dialogue, for instance, immediately presents a distinction between two ways of thinking about something – which turn out to be, more importantly, two ways of being.

On the one hand, there is Ursula, 'calm and considerate', deciding that she doesn't know whether she *really wants* to get married; for her, it will depend on what sort of man turns up, which can't be known in advance. Her calm already hints at a fundamental trust, or underlying ease, in face of this unknown future. The prose is soon to suggest the shaping underlife from which these thoughts and words come. Though she feels curiously 'suspended', we're told, Ursula accedes to what she senses darkly at centre: a new potential life like an infant in the womb, held in by 'integuments' but pressing for birth. Leaving aside for the moment the ideological question of the sort of transformation-narrative this image might seem to imply, it's clear after a few pages that Ursula's capacity to be at ease with uncertainty is connected with a strong potentiality for growth. In this first page, her 'I don't know' and 'I'm not sure' are the first hints of that, and it's important to note that they indicate an openness, not least of *mind*.

Gudrun by contrast wants to be 'quite definite'; for her it seems possible that 'in the abstract' one might need the *experience* of having been married. The dramatic imagining also suggests that, despite this drive for definiteness, Gudrun isn't, as Ursula is, really 'considering' possible consequences of marrying for the experience. When Ursula points to the most likely consequence, that it will be the end of experience, Gudrun 'attends' to the question as if for the first time. Two things then happen; the conversation comes temporarily 'to a close', and Gudrun, almost angrily, rubs out part of her drawing in a way that indicates suppressed emotion. These little closures keep occurring, and always they're brought about by Gudrun. A bit later, Ursula questions her about her magnificently stated motive for coming back home – *'reculer pour mieux sauter'*:

> 'But where can one jump *to?*'
> 'Oh, it doesn't matter,' said Gudrun, somewhat superbly. 'If one jumps over the edge, one is bound to land somewhere.'
> 'But isn't it very risky?' asked Ursula.
> A slow, mocking smile dawned on Gudrun's face.
> 'Ah!' she said, laughing. 'What is it all but words!'
> And so again she closed the conversation. But Ursula was still brooding.
> 'And how do you find home, now you have come back to it?' she asked.
> Gudrun paused for some moments, coldly, before answering. Then, in a cold, truthful voice, she said:
> 'I find myself completely out of it.'
> 'And father?'
> Gudrun looked at Ursula, almost with resentment, as if brought to bay.
> 'I haven't thought about him: I've refrained', she said coldly.
> 'Yes', wavered Ursula; and the conversation was really at an end. The sisters found themselves confronted by a void, a terrifying chasm, as if they had looked over the edge.
> They worked on in silence for some time. Gudrun's cheek was flushed with repressed emotion. She resented its having been called into being.
>
> (p. 10)

Gudrun's conversational closures show a way of talking and thinking – or rather, *not*-thinking – that's at least as interested in the impression it's making on others as it is in getting at the truth of something. As the fashionable cynicism of 'What is it all but words!' reminds us, this is the sociolect of glittering Chelsea bohemia. It is what poststructuralism would call a 'discourse': the cynical 'words' to some extent speak Gudrun. It's a discourse, above all, of power, which is exercised precisely in clipping off whatever subject might reveal one, give one away, show a chink in the armour. The chilly formality of 'I've refrained' does this to Ursula, who until then wants to go on thinking about the matter of their father, to think it through, not least for her own sake. Like everything else, the words add to Gudrun's impressiveness, but they also instantly resist any possibility either of closer contact with Ursula or, more significantly, of getting at the blocked feelings that are obviously calling out for expression within herself. For Lawrence's imagining insists that the expressed 'words' of any individual or group, their sociolect or discourse, can't really be understood as such without reference to the whole state of being they involve. Gudrun in a sense *is* in a prison house of language ('what is it *all* but words'), but that's only intelligible in terms of the underlying 'repressed emotion' her particular language both manifests and helps to contain. It's a language of repression, of resistance, in other words, designed, like her stockings, to cover up magnificently. And already, the novel is suggesting the price to be paid for this magnificence – thwarted energy, the feeling of everything withering in the bud.

In Hermione Roddice we see a similar thing in a more extreme case. As she walks into the church she shows the continuities between the drive for definiteness, the need to 'know', and the need to cover up vulnerabilities. The repeated 'knew' in she 'knew herself to be, well-dressed ... knew herself the social equal ... knew she was accepted' dramatise an inner texture of thoughts which cloak sublinguistic states that the novel quickly puts before us. Hers is assuredly, if you like, a neurotic text in that the story it has to keep repeating about her and about the world is always going to be containment, rationalisation, compensation, projection, and so on, of what lies beneath. And it's worth pointing out that the novel puts clearly before the reader in her the ways in which 'aesthetic knowledge, and culture, and world-visions, and disinterestedness' (p. 17) – in short, the impulses to theorise, to ideologise – can all be 'defences', ways precisely of blocking and resisting insight. *Women in Love* is a good deal about theories and 'world visions' as false consciousness, symptoms of resistances that need to be worked through.

At the same time, the novel's own impulse isn't to 'know' with this sort of drive for finalising definiteness. The central figures certainly aren't, as most of the wedding guests are for Gudrun, 'sealed and stamped and finished with' (p. 14). What the usual thematising readings fail to see is the whole process of signification by which the novel questions its leading intuitions as it registers them. No sooner do we think we have a settled sense of the contrasts being drawn between Ursula and Gudrun than the novel turns about and re*minds* us of what has also been implied in the imagining of them: that they are, as the chapter-heading says, sisters. Another characteristic of these little scene-closures is the way they serve to defeat ideological closure in our reading of them – construing the issues simply as 'innocence' versus 'social being' – by pointing to what the women have in common: 'The sisters found themselves confronted by a void, a terrifying chasm, as if they had looked over the edge'. A little earlier: 'They both laughed, looking at each other. In their hearts they were frightened. … The sisters were women. … But both had the remote, virgin look of modern girls …' (p. 8).

What these sentences illustrate in miniature is that dialectical interplay between difference and similarity which is another aspect of the 'frictional to-and-fro' characteristic at every level of Lawrence's thinking at its best. It's above all a *movement* of dramatic exploration and signification that never lets differences harden into structures of static opposition but keeps turning back on them, threatening to dislodge them. One moment we find Gudrun wanting to be quite definite, the next we find her *not* wanting to be (p. 9) – and Ursula afraid of the depth of feeling within her (p. 11) or saying to herself, in a way that faintly echoes Hermione's intensely apprehensive projections about Birkin in the Church: 'The wedding must not be a fiasco, it must not' (p. 18). This conventionality in Ursula, which Birkin will spend a lot of energy trying to dislodge, is in part the self-protective 'integument' preventing her at moments from peering over the edge into that 'void' or 'terrifying chasm' of the unknown faced by 'both' sisters. It too manifests itself as self-concealing discourse – Ursula's being of the less sophisticated 'things are just dandy' kind – especially when the vertiginous chasm gets too close. 'I know!' she cries in response to Gudrun's *reculer pour mieux sauter* – 'looking slightly dazzled and falsified, and as if she did *not* know'. This tendency of Ursula's to lie to herself comes out as *looking* false because of that vigorous life coming into being within her, which simply *won't* be falsified. Gudrun is in better control of herself than that, except at those moments when she darkens and the held-in life appears on her cheek as a resented 'flush'. At such moments she and Ursula show themselves to be sisters in a full sense.

It's important to reflect on what this sisterhood means. Nearly all accounts of the novel, including Leavis's pioneering one, either overlook or understate the degree to which, at least in all four major figures, the novel keeps sight of that core of 'innocent' life in them which remains as a *permanent possibility*. This is why it is seriously reductive to say, as Dan Jacobson does, that the 'others' – that is, other than Birkin and Ursula, whom he calls the 'good' characters – 'can barely say or do anything – make love, give to charity, paint, teach, talk – without revealing or being said to reveal how advanced, how gangrenous, their condition really is'.[8] What this ignores is that these figures can barely do these things or reveal their 'dissolution' without, at the same time, also revealing the thwarted or twisted *life* in them which continues to express itself in their deathward disintegration, in a sense as its very motive-force. Lawrence describes the process in a contemporary essay, 'The Crown' (1915):

> Still the false I, the ego, held down the real, unborn I, which is a blossom with all a blossom's fragility. Yet constantly the rising flower pushed and thrust at the belly and heart of us, thrashed and beat relentlessly. If it could not beat its way through into being, it must thrash us hollow.[9]

What this underlines is the profound interrelatedness established at the beginning of *Women in Love* between Ursula's 'unborn I' and that bud – 'Everything withers in the bud' – which is the image of the same undeveloped possibility in Gudrun, a blossom very much 'held down', suppressed, by her Chelsea-nurtured 'ego'. What beats its way through into being in Ursula and Birkin is the same life-source that thrashes Gudrun and Gerald hollow.

In part this inter-relatedness makes itself felt metaphorically: there's a far-reaching suggestive continuity between the flowers, say, that Ursula gives Birkin – in place of those rings – in 'Excurse', and the 'open flower' of Gerald's love in 'Snowed Up'. In each case, the implication is precisely the same: to be given over to the other is to be open both to the possibilities of transformation and of annihilation. Which way the process goes is seen to depend on a complex interactive enablement or disablement between the lovers, where each of these courses continues to be imagined in terms of the opposite possibility. The destruction of Gerald is so final precisely because, to the extent of his capacity for it, he is so open to Gudrun; his love-wound and his death-wound are one and the same thing: 'This wound, this strange, infinitely-sensitive opening of his soul, where he was exposed, like an open flower, to all the universe, and in which he was given to his complement, the other, the unknown, this wound, this disclosure, this unfolding of his own covering, leaving him incomplete, limited, unfinished, like an open flower under the sky, this was his cruellest joy' (p. 446). For Gudrun, being the object of Gerald's 'cruellest joy' feels like being torn open, a feeling that underlines the incapacities of both; yet with her too the imagery also hints at what might otherwise have been realised: 'She felt, with horror, as if he tore at the bud of her heart, tore it open, like an irreverent, persistent being. Like a boy who pulls off a fly's wings, or tears open a bud to see what is in flower, he tore at her privacy, at her very life, he would destroy her as an immature bud, torn open, is destroyed' (p. 446).

This sort of writing, far from dismissing Gerald and Gudrun as 'gangrenous', presents their inter-destruction as a tragic inevitability involving all that they are, including their most valuable possibilities. Gerald dies because he can't be, as Loerke is and Gudrun becomes, merely 'indifferent'; his nature is, as we're told, 'too serious' (p. 445). At the same time, Gudrun seems to bury with Loerke a longing for belief in something more than her modish ironies will ordinarily allow. At unguarded moments, such as when – significantly – Gerald is asleep in bed beside her, she works through to a realisation of what, at centre, she longs for:

> Her heart was breaking with pity and grief for him. And at the same moment, a grimace came over her mouth, of mocking irony at her own unspoken tirade. Ah, what a farce it was! She thought of Parnell and Katherine O'Shea. Parnell! After all, who can take the nationalisation of Ireland seriously? After all, who can take political Ireland really seriously, whatever it does? And who can take political England seriously? Who can? Who can care a straw, really, how the old, patched-up Constitution is tinkered at any more? Who cares a button for our national ideals, any more than for our national bowler hat? Aha, it is all old hat, it is all old bowler hat?
>
> That's all it is, Gerald, my young hero. At any rate we'll spare ourselves the nausea of stirring the old broth any more. You be beautiful, my Gerald, and reckless. There *are* perfect moments, oh convince me, I need it.
>
> He opened his eyes, and looked at her. She greeted him with a mocking, enigmatic smile in which was a poignant gaiety. Over his face went the reflection of the smile, he smiled too, purely unconsciously.
>
> That filled her with extraordinary delight, to see the smile cross his face, reflected from her face. She remembered, that was how a baby smiled. It filled her with extraordinary radiant delight.
>
> 'You've done it,' she said.
>
> 'What?' he asked, dazed.
>
> 'Convinced me.'

> And she bent down, kissing him passionately, passionately, so that he was bewildered. He did not ask of what he had convinced her, though he meant to. He was glad she was kissing him. She seemed to be feeling for his heart, to touch the quick of him. And he wanted her to touch the quick of his being, he wanted that most of all.
>
> (p. 419).

Here Gudrun is as given over to Gerald as she will ever be, and while the scene dramatises what *is* alive between them – it almost is a perfect moment – the imagining never loses touch with what must thwart that life. On the one hand, there's Gerald's regressive 'wanting' – the baby-smile hinting at the way in which, for him, the world is an udder to feed his supreme self. Before long, he will be exultant; she will feel used. At the same time, Gudrun's characteristic defences have only been able to fall because she is alone. In fact her thinking here has an exploratory freedom that it never seems to have in conversation; others, even her sister and her lover – perhaps especially these – always inhibit the open expression and so the true discovery of the fundamental needs we see displayed here. Afraid above all of giving herself away, she can only fully be herself by herself. And the clear price to be paid for being like that, for remaining enclosed in a defensive sheath of cynicism, is to remain an immature bud.

And yet – as Lawrence would put it, using his most significant connective – the imagining here is so inward as to present a problem with even that formulation. The problem is that Gudrun's defensive cynicism here is so close to the novel's own attitude to these political and social questions. Or, to put the point in a more pointed way, we wouldn't be surprised to hear *Birkin* saying all that about political England and Ireland. At moments he says things that are even more extremely disillusioned. At the beginning of 'Excurse', for instance, he thinks thoughts that show his kinship with the nihilism of Loerke:

> His life now seemed so reduced, that he hardly cared any more. At moments it seemed to him he did not care a straw whether Ursula or Hermione or anybody else existed or did not exist. Why bother! Why strive for a coherent, satisfied life? Why not drift on in a series of accidents – like a picaresque novel? Why not? Why bother about human relationships? Why take them seriously – male or female? Why form any serious connections at all? Why not be casual, drifting along, taking all for what it was worth?
>
> (p. 302)

This couldn't be Loerke, of course, partly because for him these wouldn't have been questions but settled convictions. Yet there is something in what Leo Bersani says about the novel when he talks of Lawrence playing 'dangerously with similarities; we are always being asked to make crucial but almost imperceptible distinctions'.[10] This is over-stated, as the present case illustrates: neither Loerke nor Gudrun would have gone on to reflect, as Birkin does, that they were 'damned and doomed to the old effort at serious living'. And yet there can be no doubt that Lawrence does endow many of the characters, including those who are usually thought of as objects of his critique, with his own characteristic thoughts. Bersani goes on to make a similar point when he says that 'Lawrence nonchalantly exposes what the realistic novelist seems anxious to disguise: the derivation of his work from a single creative imagination'.[11] There's nothing 'nonchalant' or merely modernist in this, however. What it shows, in fact, is the strenuous innerness of Lawrence's dramatic thinking about the various life-possibilities his work is exploring: very little is merely external or notational in this novel, or left as unrealised 'metaphysic'.

Which is to say, above all, that there's very little in the novel that remains merely Other to the novel's thinking and feeling. One good reason for thinking of this as a canonical text is that, like *Middlemarch* and – supremely – *Anna Karenina, Women in Love* is for the most part both supple-minded and imaginatively generous enough *not* to fall into the repressive ethical oppositions which, according to Jameson, are supposed to characterise such books. In these books the over-defended 'social beings' ever retain a core of innocence, a mostly unrealised capacity, and unconscious longing, for change and growth; while the 'innocents' must always struggle against defensive integuments in themselves if they are to *beat their way through* into being. The necessity for permanent struggle in these figures precludes the simple idealisation of them that George Eliot falls into with Dorothea towards the end of *Middlemarch*, for instance, or our thinking of them as 'good' characters. This is why it's a notable strength in *Women in Love* that Birkin, even as late as 'Excurse', is still tempted to chuck in the whole thing with Ursula and retire back into his shell, for the moment a Loerke look-alike.

Right from the beginning, Birkin has been saying other characters' lines in a way that reveals the repressed 'social being' in him.

One extremely telling moment is at the wedding at Shortlands when Mrs Crich hints that she'd like him to be Gerald's friend:

> Birkin looked down into her eyes, which were blue, and watching heavily. He could not understand them. 'Am I my brother's keeper?' he said to himself, almost flippantly.
>
> Then he remembered with a slight shock, that that was Cain's cry. And Gerald was Cain, if anybody. Not that he was Cain, either, although he had slain his brother. There was such a thing as pure accident. ... Or is this not true, is there no such thing as pure accident? Has *everything* that happens a universal significance? Has it? Birkin pondering as he stood there, had forgotten Mrs Crich, as she had forgotten him.
>
> He did not believe that there was any such thing as accident. It all hung together, in the deepest sense.
>
> (p. 26)

Assuming that Birkin is right and there's no such thing as pure accident, then what are we to make of Birkin 'accidentally' uttering Cain's cry, and then when he remembers whose cry it is instantly associating it with Gerald? What it all suggests is something that Freud, who didn't believe in accidents either, would have seen as a significant slip, a revelation 'in the deepest sense' of an aspect of Birkin that he didn't want to know about – namely the Cain in himself. One way in which Birkin is Cain isn't hard to see; after all, he is a mass brother-murderer in his often-expressed wish that the rest of mankind would simply disappear. He has just said so to Mrs Crich: 'Not many people amount to anything at all', he answered, forced to go much deeper than he wanted to. 'They jingle and giggle. It would be much better if they were just wiped out. Essentially, they don't exist, they aren't there' (p. 24).

Saying this kind of thing is obviously much more disturbing to Birkin than he can allow himself to know, which is one reason for resisting Dan Jacobson's assertion that Birkin is allowed by the novel to get away with this sort of sentiment 'without being accused by the narrative voice or the other characters of manifesting a murderously diseased will'.[12] What this overlooks is a much more subtle form of placing: Birkin's annihilating wishes and Gerald's brother-killing as a ruthless mine owner – thus annihilating his father's sort of troubled brotherhood – are being unmistakably linked.

In this and in other ways Birkin and Gerald are seen to be brothers in spirit if not in blood long before explicit *Blutbruderschaft* comes into question. As with the sisterhood of Ursula and Gudrun, this is so even when the imagining of them draws strong attention to difference. The dialogue that concludes 'Shortlands' for instance has Birkin analysing Gerald's conventionality and opposing it to true spontaneity, when suddenly the focus shifts to what connects them:

> There was a pause of strange enmity between the two men, that was very near to love. It was always the same between them; always their talk brought them into a deadly nearness of contact, a strange, perilous intimacy which was either hate or love, or both. They parted with apparent unconcern, as if their going apart were a trivial occurrence. And they really kept it to the level of trivial occurrence. Yet the heart of each burned from the other. They burned with each other, inwardly. This they would never admit. They intended to keep their relationship a casual free-and-easy friendship, they were not going to be so unmanly and unnatural as to allow any heart-burning between them. They had not the faintest belief in deep relationship between man and man, and their disbelief prevented any development of their powerful but suppressed friendliness.
>
> (pp. 33–4)

Here it is *Birkin*, as much as Gerald, who's showing that, as Birkin himself has just said, 'It's the hardest thing in the world to act spontaneously on one's impulses ...' (p. 32). This is only remarkable because in context it was a dictum directed at *Gerald's* supposedly Cain-like suppressed desire/fear of having his gizzard slit. What Birkin's whole argument suppresses in fact is his own suppressed feeling for Gerald, which has a good deal to do with why it *is* such a provocatively cutting sort of argument. In yet another Cain-like way then, Birkin is denying that in himself which is common to both men; and he has the analytical knife out for Gerald precisely because, at some level, that brotherhood itself is deeply 'perilous' to him.

Brotherhood, commonality, movements of responsibility or pity for others, notably Hermione, are ever the threatening Other in Birkin's psyche. His conscious ethic is that of Nietzschean single-ness and self-responsibility. The sentence on spontaneity continues: '... and it's the only really gentlemanly thing to do – *provided you're fit to do it*' (my italics). The problem is that most of mankind are evidently not fit. As he said to Mrs Crich, they 'just jingle and giggle. It would be much better if they were just wiped out'. But fortunately it doesn't have to come to that because, as he says, 'Essentially they don't exist, they aren't there.' Which isn't simply saying all over again that they don't really *live*, spontaneously and with *ubermensch* singleness. It's saying rather that one doesn't have to take them into account. They don't matter; one can forget them. And Birkin does that, very largely, for he seems to know, in advance, that any larger political responsibility or social consciousness is a form of false consciousness – a strategy for avoiding the responsibility of looking closely into oneself.

Granting Birkin's point, that social consciousness can be a form of false consciousness, or unconsciousness, his own refusal to know about the jinglers and gigglers surely involves another form of false consciousness, what Trigant Burrow in the book that Lawrence himself praised called 'the social unconscious'. This is the 'fallacy of implied subjective differentiation', which is for Burrow 'the whole meaning of unconsciousness and the basis of all delusion'.[13] It's the thank-God-I-am-not-as-other-men attitude that George Eliot has in her sights in the figures of Bulstrode and Lydgate, when the whole burden of her imagining is to underline the realities of mutual interdependence and Burrovian 'subjective continuity' – whereby we only begin to know others by looking into the depths of ourselves. Where Eliot's emphasis runs the risk of sentimentality, Birkin's 'disquality', in emphasising discontinuity – the other side of the truth about others – is always in danger of the sort of delusive belief in his own superiority and uniqueness that George Eliot called 'egoism' and Burrow the 'social unconscious'.

It's here that *Women in Love* itself is most open to criticism because there are strong grounds for thinking that Lawrence largely backs Birkin in his thoughts about 'disquality'. Indeed, one might say that his text fulfils Birkin's murderous wishes by hardly allowing these jinglers and gigglers to exist in it. Only a superior class of people *does* exist in *Women in Love*. Most of them, of course, belong to the artistic and intellectual *avant-garde*, but at centre-stage are those potentially able to beat their way through to new life. The novel leaves us in no doubt that is a very tiny elite indeed, surrounded by a great mass – typified by Palmer the electrician, the middle-aged Will Brangwen, and the couple who take the Birkins' chair – about whom there is nothing interesting, and certainly nothing hopeful, to be said. The rest presumably belong to meaningless mediocrity or to the great industrial machine. It's usual to say at this point that Lawrence himself, surrounded by the originals of most of these characters, had lost any touch he once had with the world in which such ordinary people lived. This doesn't quite go far enough, because after all he was the author of one of the most compelling novels about English working class and provincial life ever written – and (what partly accounts for this triumph) one written *from within*. That the Midlands colliers of *Women in Love* are caricatured as sexually potent underworld automata, imagined in the mass rather than as individual Walter Morels, needs another explanation: Lawrence was denying his social roots, suppressing many things he knew – in the service of an ethic of individual self-transcendence.

Marxists have already had their say about this, and I don't think there's any point in denying the force of the case here. *Women in Love* does have a political unconscious; to this extent it is ideology-bound, symptom of a particular historical process. But this can only be the final word about the novel if one is prepared to grant, as I am certainly not, some sort of trans-historical privilege to Marxism that guarantees it against counter-deconstruction. In the absence of this, one can only say that there are various different stories about what is real and important – and about transformation. All, as Lawrence freely admitted, have in them the bones of an ideology. What matters for art is the extent to which that is criticised from within, subjected to a dialectical pressure that will bring to light its characteristic suppressions – in this way 'working through' them into what I can only provisionally call an 'ideological unknown'.

III

[*Women in Love* differs from *The Rainbow* in its attitude to knowing. In *The Rainbow* Tom intuits a connection between himself and Lydia] but the importance given to blood-knowing in some ways imposes an element of ideological closure in *The Rainbow* or, to revert to Lawrence's own terms, the presented world of the novel in some respects lacks that implied internal 'criticism' of its 'metaphysic' which 'makes for the lasting value and satisfaction of that work'. 'Knowing' in *Women in Love* mostly means something very different: it's usually a form of *false* consciousness clung to in order to suppress subconscious realisations. At the same time, without rejecting the essential intuitions or formal discoveries of *The Rainbow*, the later novel goes back to a realistic surface of things that includes, crucially, an interest in what the person 'feels', as distinct from what she or he is 'known' to 'be'. Indeed one of the primary nodes of interest in *Women in Love* is often the gap between what is intuitively – that is, projectively – 'known' about one character by another and what is in other ways revealed.

We see this in a particularly telling way in Gudrun's attempts to come to terms with Gerald. By the chapter 'Death and Love' it begins to become clear that her intense desire to 'know' him – led on by all that seemed desirably unknown about him – is actually a subtle form of resistance to his otherness. Right from the beginning, her response to him has been passionately visionary, alive with an imaginative energy that, for her, seems to be indistinguishable from sexual desire. She's momentarily taken out of her self-consciousness by what she sees as his arctic dangerousness, his wolf-like single-ness, a conception which both genuinely lights him up for us and yet makes him curiously difficult to square with, for instance, the man Birkin loves. In short, there's an element of abstraction in Gudrun's Gerald, of assimilative vision, that's related to her own modernist carvings and beyond them to Loerke's futuristic friezes in *Women in Love*, the stylisations of modernism are now themselves problematic – and deeply implicated in the mechanical reductions of the modern world.

As we see when Gudrun and Gerald kiss under the railway bridge – and she yields passionately to an *idea* of Gerald as the powerful 'master' of all the colliers – Gudrun's sexuality is bound up with imaginative appropriation, this being an ultimate sort of light-in-the-darkness, a form of control that can never lapse finally in surrender to *him*. She in fact seems partly to recognise this:

> She reached up, like Eve reaching to the apples on the tree of knowl-edge, and she kissed him, though her passion was a transcendent fear of the thing he was, touching his face with infinitely delicate, encroaching, wondering fingers. Her fingers went over the mould of his face, over his features. How perfect and foreign he was – ah how dangerous! her soul thrilled with complete knowledge!
>
> (pp. 331–2)

The thrill of Gudrun's exploratory way to trying to 'know' Gerald's face – we never forget that she is a sculptor – is itself rendered exploratorily, in prose that focuses the limits of her knowledge. To put it simply, Lawrence's imagining of her experience, unlike her sense of Gerald, is sympathetically inward.

In fact Gudrun's fear of knowing Gerald in *that* way, of under-standing 'the thing he was' (as the flow of Lawrence's sympathetic consciousness has given him to us), is linked with those conversational closures of hers in the conversation with Ursula at the very beginning of the novel. There we see that, for all her apparently dazzling originality, Gudrun is very much bound by the language of the society that she affects to despise. Unlike Birkin and Ursula, Gerald and Gudrun mostly talk in conventionalities, even at their most intense moments, which is associated with their inability either to push through or to lapse into new understanding:

> 'Why don't I love you?' he asked, as if admitting the truth of her accusation, yet hating her for it.
> 'I don't know why you don't – I've been good to you. You were in a *fearful* state, when you came to me.'
> Her heart was beating to suffocate her, yet she was stony and unrelenting.
> 'When was I in a fearful state?' he asked.
> 'When you first came to me. I *had* to take pity on you – but it was never love.'
> It was the statement 'It was never love', which sounded in his ears with madness.
> 'Why must you repeat it so often, that there is no love?' he said in a voice strangled with rage.
> 'Well you don't *think* you love me, do you?' she asked.
> He was silent with cold passion of anger.
> 'You don't think you *can* love me, do you?' she repeated, almost with a sneer.
> 'No,' he said.
>
> (p. 442)

The novel suggests that the conventional terms in which Gudrun and Gerald mostly talk to each other are partly a sign of the blockage from which they can provide no release: whatever the lovers may think they want from each other, they can only 'repeat' the same limited set of sentiments over and over again. The present is hostage to the past. In Freudian terms, Gudrun and Gerald seem merely able to 'repeat' the past to each other symbolically rather than 'work through' their mutual resistances to an understanding of the other's separate being.

In the case of Gerald, the Freudian terms are especially relevant because part of our sense of 'the thing he was' is provided by the story of childhood trauma that hovers over all accounts of him like a suggestive pathogenesis. It's merely suggestive because the novel reaches for no definite explanation about its importance in Gerald's life, but rather questions the various versions that enter the characters' heads. In Birkin's meditation on Gerald's shooting of his brother, two possible ways of regarding this episode are raised. At first, Birkin thinks of the shooting as an 'accident' that has 'drawn a curse across the life that had caused the accident'. But he quickly moves away from this more ordinary 'surface' explanation to ponder another one – that there is 'no such thing as pure accident', that '*everything* that happens [has] a universal significance', such that 'it all [hangs] together in the deepest sense'. These are obscure reflections, of course, and we can only make sense of them cumulatively as the novel goes on pondering them. From the hints that emerge, we see that this 'deepest sense' of all human actions is that they are obscurely *willed*, as in the extreme case Birkin envisages, of murderer and murderee in which even the victim desires his execution. This is of course about as close *ad absurdum* as any *reductio* can be allowed to go, and it keeps us wondering about the state of the man putting it forward.

The novel by no means simply backs the idea that everything that happens is in some ultimate sense willed, though it by no means rejects it either: time and again events are shaped so as to disclose the 'deepest' will in them. And yet, as is already evident, the drive for single coherent vision, the drive to see things *simply* 'in the deepest sense' as opposed to a more ordinary, commonsense, 'surface' way of seeing them, is something about which the novel is properly sceptical. In fact, it is constantly opening a space to see some things as accidental, including Gerald's childhood trauma, which is much more generous to him than Gudrun or Birkin sometimes are.

More specifically, Birkin's drive for coherence at the 'deepest' level of vision is seen as partly a variant of Gudrun's will to 'know' things, a will that obscurely resists entertaining their otherness. Especially at the beginning of Birkin and Ursula's various lovescenes, we see his sort of drive to 'know' partly as an elaborate *defence* against her, a way of fending her off. They are unable to connect; she slips into an embarrassed conventionality, he, into a brutal intellectualising directness:

> 'How nice the fuchsias are!' she said, to break the silence.
> 'Aren't they! – Did you think I had forgotten what I said?'
> A swoon went over Ursula's mind.
> 'I don't want you to remember it – if you don't want to', she struggled to say, through the dark mist that covered her.

There was silence for some moments.

'No,' he said. 'It isn't that. Only – if we are going to know each other, we must pledge ourselves for ever. If we are going to make a relationship, even of friendship, there must be something final and infallible about it.'

There was a clang of mistrust and almost anger in his voice. She did not answer. Her heart was much too contracted. She could not have spoken.

Seeing she was not going to reply, he continued almost bitterly, giving himself away:

'I can't say it is love I have to offer – and it isn't love I want. It is something much more impersonal and harder, – and rarer.'

There was a silence, out of which she said:

'You mean you don't love me.' She suffered furiously saying that.

'Yes, if you like to put it like that. ...'

(p. 145)

This is characteristic of Birkin: even as he talks of final pledges and being 'without reserves and defences, stripped entirely into the unknown' (p. 147), he is bristling with them, untrustingly throwing the theory in her face precisely as a way of holding off those things in her. This 'abstract earnestness' is exactly what wouldn't enable Ursula to be stripped entirely, as Birkin, beside himself with deep fears, obscurely knows.

At the same time, Birkin's drive to theorise about this 'something more impersonal' has an importance that can't simply be psychologised away. As he realised himself: 'There was always confusion in speech. Yet it must be spoken. Whichever way one moved, if one were to move forwards, one must break a way through the walls of the prison, as the infant in labour strives through the walls of the womb' (p. 186). This reminds us why clinging to the conventional language of love – as Gudrun and Gerald do, and Ursula wants to – doesn't get anywhere. As we've seen, it is indeed a 'prison'; it's a repressed and ultimately repressive language that obscures the often ambiguous underlife of sexuality. For Birkin, to move forward to new life is partly to *force* one's way through into expression, to break through the current limits of thought and language to new vision, however crude or violent or confused or abstract the first attempts might be. *This* sort of breaking through – as opposed to the flow of *sympathetic* consciousness – applies in one way to the novel as a whole, of course, but it applies in a particular way to Birkin, who clearly dramatises a similar impulse in Lawrence himself. He embodies Lawrence's own insurgent will-to-vision, the discursive or ideologising drive of the essays and pamphlets that gets all too much free rein in the later novels.

It's revealing that Lawrence in the famous letter to Garnett sounds rather like Birkin when he's trying to explain something to Ursula and ends up sounding, as she would say, too 'cocksure'. Indeed, in 'Mino' his terms are strikingly similar to those in the letter:

> 'I want to find you, where you don't know your own existence, the you that your common self denies utterly. But I don't want your good looks, and I don't want your womanly feelings, and I don't want your thoughts nor opinions nor your ideas – they are all bagatelles to me.'
>
> 'You are very conceited, Monsieur', she mocked. 'How do you know what my womanly feelings are, or my thoughts or my ideas? You don't even know what I think of you now.'
>
> 'Nor do I care in the slightest.'

> (p. 147)

The crucial difference, of course, between the letter and the novel is that in *Women in Love* woman is there to talk back and to insist on the importance of those womanly feelings that Birkin says he doesn't care about. In doing so, she also insists on the importance of a more ordinary sense of 'knowing' – not blood-knowing, but mere acquaintance with facts, such as what she actually *does* think, as opposed to what he 'knows' her to be thinking, or not thinking.

The importance of Ursula to the imaginative process and power of *Women in Love* can hardly be overestimated. It's usual to say that the strength of Birkin as a creation – as opposed, say, to Mellors – is that he's constantly being revealed and illuminated, his views being tested, refined and contradicted, by the drama of which he's part. And Ursula provides much of the internal 'criticism that makes the lasting value and satisfaction of [the] work of art'. Yet her part in the novel is very much more important than this. Not only is she Birkin's complement, his other, the one in whom he finds what he is after; she is the one in whose realised resistant spirit Lawrence's own will to 'utterance' finds its complement and other too.

We can see this at the end of 'Mino', where Birkin and Ursula are in contact in a new way:

> 'Proud and subservient, proud and subservient, I know you', he retorted dryly, 'proud and subserved, then subservient to the proud – I know you and your love. It is a tick-tack, tick-tack, a dance of opposites.'

'Are you so sure?' she mocked wickedly, 'what my love is?' 'Yes I am', he retorted.

'So cocksure!' she said. 'How can anybody ever be right, who is so cocksure? It shows you are wrong.'

He was silent in chagrin.

They had talked and struggled till they were both wearied out.

'Tell me about yourself and your people', he said.

And she told him about the Brangwens, and about her mother, and about Skrebensky, her first love, and about her later experiences. He sat very still, watching her as she talked. And he seemed to listen with reverence. Her face was beautiful and full of baffled light as she told him all the things that had hurt her or perplexed her so deeply. He seemed to warm and comfort his soul at the beautiful light of her nature.

'If she *really* could pledge herself,' he thought to himself, with passionate insistence but hardly any hope. Yet a curious little irresponsible laughter appeared at his heart.

(p. 153)

The 'curious little irresponsible laughter' that comes to Birkin here is a hint that something like the star-equilibrium he's been talking about is beginning to take place between himself and Ursula. It's important to note that, although it might signal the beginning of what he's after, it doesn't come simply *because* he's been after it. In that important sense it comes from beyond his conscious aim, from the 'unknown' to which at last he seems to be open.

Birkin is slowly transformed in these love-scenes. Ursula's unfearful loving mockery sets in train something like a Freudian 'working through' of his defences, his tendency to neurotic repetition, such that he comes slowly to understand that she is not like the Hermione he 'knows' and fears she is. The key sign of this is that his ideas fall away and are reborn as experience – experience all the more remarkable for being, at the same time, so ordinary. When Birkin can be quiet enough to allow it to happen, their relations take on a simplicity and an ordinariness that is itself extraordinary in the world of this novel: Ursula tells him about her past; they have tea; they joke with each other, tease each other.

It's important to see that this remarkable ordinariness – which is so valuable because it lies, so to speak, on the other side of the prison walls from which all of the characters long to be released – reveals a good deal about the art that embodies it. The transformation of Birkin in these love-scenes recursively mirrors the novel's own creative transformation of the psycho-ethical thinking from which it partly springs into an art that goes 'beyond the artist's

conscious aim'. Ursula's loving subversion of the preacher in him
reflects the novel's 'working through' of the sort of prophetic will
that came to express itself more and more in the latter half of *The
Rainbow* as over-certain knowledge of what the world is like.

The world of *Women in Love* is much more mind-resistant than
the one that keeps disclosing its meanings to the student Ursula in
the earlier novel. Which is partly to say that the later novel's 'theory
of being', like Birkin's is constantly being met dialectically by a
'living sense of being' that refuses simply to be badgered into
passive agreement with it. The cats in 'Mino', for instance,
altogether shrug off not only the sort of anthropomorphising
signification that both Birkin *and* Ursula try (half-seriously) to force
upon them – and which readers commonly try to read into them –
but they lie altogether beyond human ken. Their apparent handi-
ness to the characters', and what is often taken to be Lawrence's,
argument, dissolves when the focus comes back to the 'uncanny
fires' of the cats' eyes that are constantly looking beyond or through
the human beings into a landscape that is utterly 'unknown'.

The cats' final unknowableness means that, so far as the human
drama is concerned, they aren't part of that remorseless coherence
'in the deepest sense' which is often supposed to characterise
Women in Love. Their most important role in fact is that they
tempt the characters (and us) to read them as symbolic, and then
run off, fundamentally unread and unsymbolised. To that extent
they remain *accidental* to the thrust of the drama, part of what
might be called, not a realistic surface, but a realistic depth, of
things that keeps impinging on events in ways that are utterly unexpected. Just at the point at which the quarrel between Birkin and
Ursula is about to flare up again, Mrs Daykin comes in with a tray:

> '*You prevaricator!*' she cried, in real indignation.
> 'Tea is ready, sir', said the landlady from the doorway.
> They both looked at her, very much as the cats had looked at them, a
> little while before.
> 'Thank you, Mrs Daykin.'
> An interrupted silence fell over the two of them, a moment of breach.
> 'Come and have tea', he said.
> 'Yes, I should love it', she replied, gathering herself together.
> (p. 151)

The essential action here is what it always is for Lawrence, the ebb
and flow of vital feeling within and between the two lovers. By this

point in their quarrel, we sense that Ursula's 'real indignation' is on the point of playing itself out and metamorphosing into something quieter and more responsive to Birkin. Yet Mrs Daykin really does impinge on this process, enforcing on both of them (and us) a vital sense of relativity: compared to someone really on the outside of their little world, they are, for all their momentary antagonisms, in profound connection with each other. And that implied realisation helps to precipitate the shift of feeling that is already coming into being between them.

It's one sign of what's so deeply convincing about *Women in Love* that its 'living sense of being' includes realistic rhythms of episode and accident as subtly reshaping cross-currents to the master-rhythms of love and withdrawal between the lovers. Here mutual defences fall away partly because the lovers are distracted by tea or because they get simply 'wearied out' – too fatigued to argue any longer. The transformed, 'worked through' quality of these moments is extremely important: Lawrence is defining an ordinariness that is significantly different from the mere conventionality of Gerald and Gudrun. At a given moment, tea with beautiful china can revive closeness for Ursula and Birkin as easily as the great living continuum of the fields can for Anna Brangwen. In *Women in Love*, realistic episode and detail aren't simply subsumed and effaced as they are in the most modernist sections of *The Rainbow*, with its rather fixed pattern of variation within endless repetition. The imagining in the later novel is able to embrace much more of a world that, like Mrs Daykin and the cats, quite cuts across the rhythms of the lovers' connection.

The importance that small accidents and unexpected events have in *Women in Love* draws attention to the importance of the 'unknown' in the imaginative process that produced them. Lawrence is constantly working on an edge where precise ends aren't pre-known – in such a way that decisive moments can spring into being (in the novel's own phrase) 'accidentally on purpose', out of the suggestive interstices of surface happenings. In fact, Birkin downing his champagne accidentally on purpose before giving the wedding-speech nicely illustrates the combination of willed ends yet unwilled means that characterises the artistic process of this novel. The 'ordinary' moments between Ursula and Birkin are, from their point of view, so poised and free and, in a certain sense, blessed, precisely because they seem to happen so spontaneously: one minute Ursula is attacking Birkin as a prevaricator, the next she is drinking tea and telling him about her people. At the same time, the art that embodies this moment is only 'right' because it too comes into being in an utterly unsignalled way that simultaneously takes up and clinches the deeper purposes that have been latent in the imagining of the whole scene and indeed the whole novel. The story Ursula tells of her mother and of Skrebensky shows the necessary connection here between the represented life and the art itself: in remembering them she is dramatising the return to conscious expression of latent purposes that go right back into the prehistory of *Women in Love* – to a time when this novel and *The Rainbow* were one story.

Looked at from this larger perspective, the will for the lovers to connect in some such way has of course been there all along (in both their minds and their creator's), and has been expressing itself even in their quarrelling. Indeed it is expressed *especially* in their quarrelling: though they aren't conscious of it, their arguing, unlike that of Gerald and Gudrun, is itself part of the process of 'working through' their resistances to each other. And just as it's impossible for them to plan consciously the overcoming of these defences, so it's impossible for Lawrence to plan consciously the precise realisation of these unplanned moments that are at the same time a consummation of all that he's been 'in the deepest sense' striving to realise. In a real sense, such moments come out of an 'unknown' that keeps transcending, even as it completes, the artist's will-to-meaning.

The notion that art can in a certain sense transcend its so-called ideological underpinnings isn't one that would be necessarily persuasive or even intelligible to someone committed to seeing *any* representation of personal transformation as 'neo-Freudian nostalgia for some ultimate moment of *cure*'.[14] Nor would pointing out that, in this novel, there is no 'ultimate moment', only continuing process. There is in short no answer here to those who insist ideologically that there can be nothing in a work of art but enfleshed ideology. Yet clearly *Women in Love* demonstrates that, to conceive, as some do, of embodied morality in a novel as a static system of binary oppositions is to miss the *dynamic* nature of intentionality as a restless process of undermining, interrogating and repositioning the work's key terms. And to insist, as others do, that novels can only reinforce our resistances to non-ideological reality, is to miss the fact that some significant ones actually represent such resistances and are centrally concerned with the possibility of 'working through' them. Not only this, but as *Women in Love* also demonstrates, the dynamic intentionality of some novels is an embodiment of the 'working through' process itself, whereby ideological purpose issues in represented meanings that were unplanned and, in a relevant sense, 'unknown'.

From *Critical Review*, 30 (1990), 3–24. (A version also appears in David Parker, *Ethics, Theory and the Novel* [Cambridge, 1994].)

Notes

[David Parker's essay represents a new direction for criticism after the waning of poststructuralism. It is therefore no surprise that he begins by drawing attention to what he considers to be the limitations of that approach. Parker believes that poststructuralist critics view canonical literature as the site of empty ethical debates which serve no purpose other than to uphold the existing order. Parker argues that this account represents a failure to engage with canonical works which, if studied closely, do not function in the way poststructuralists say they do. On the contrary, a novel like *Women in Love* is not a static encounter between ethical opposites but an exploration of the 'dynamic interrelatedness' between different and apparently conflicting viewpoints. Hence we cannot distinguish so readily between Ursula and Gudrun or Birkin and Gerald. A character's beliefs about the world, Parker continues, are forms of defence which have to be worked through if they are going to change. Parker contrasts *Women in Love* with *The Rainbow*, claiming that in the earlier novel characters knew things intuitively and this meant they did not progress whereas in the later novel their ideas about the world tend to be 'forms of false consciousness' which can be corrected by an attention to others and the 'surface' of reality. Here Parker draws another contrast with *The Rainbow*. In that novel, Lawrence is more interested in the vision of things whereas in *Women in Love* he is more concerned with their actual nature. And it is by attending to that rather to any apparent epiphany that the individual has a chance of transforming his or herself.

Parker's basic argument, that great novels put binary oppositions into 'dialectical interplay', reasserts the priority of art over criticism. Poststructuralists, Parker claims, are merely pointing out what great novels already do and that is why they are canonical. Ultimately, then, Parker's view of criticism is conservative since it returns us to the idea of a canon of works. But it does so by seeing those works precisely in the terms valued by poststructuralism, that is difference and multiplicity. All references to *Women in Love* are from the Cambridge edition, edited by D. Farmer, L.

Vasey and J. Worthen (Cambridge, 1987), and are given in parentheses in the text. Eds]

1. *The Political Unconscious: Narrative as a Socially Symbolic Act* (London, 1981), p. 114.

2. Ibid. p. 60.

3. Lennard J. Davis, *Resisting Novels: Ideology and Fiction* (London, 1987), p. 15.

4. Ibid. p. 24.

5. Jonathan Culler, *Framing the Sign: Criticism and its Institutions* (Oxford, 1988), p. 52.

6. *Study of Thomas Hardy*, ed. E. McDonald (New York, 1936), pp. 476, 479.

7. Dan Jacobson, '*Women in Love* and the Death of the Will', in *Adult Pleasures* (London, 1988).

8. Ibid., p. 96.

9. 'The Crown', in *Phoenix II: Uncollected, Unpublished and Other Prose Works by D. H. Lawrence*, ed. W. Roberts and H. T. Moore (London, 1968), p. 388.

10. Leo Bersani, *A Future for Astyanax: Character and Desire in Literature* (London, 1978), p. 176.

11. Ibid., p. 178

12. Jacobson, *Adult Pleasures*, p. 96.

13. Trigant Burrow, *The Social Basis of Consciousness: A Study in Organic Psychology Based upon a Synthetic and Societal Concept of the Neuroses* (London, 1927), p. 125.

14. Jameson, *The Political Unconscious*, p. 283.

Further Reading

Criticism specific to *Women in Love* and *The Rainbow*

Adelman, Gary, *Snow of Fire: Symbolic Meaning in 'The Rainbow' and 'Women in Love'* (New York: Garland Publishing, 1991).
Bloom, Harold (ed.), *D. H. Lawrence's Women in Love* (New York: Chelsea House, 1988).
Edwards, Duane, *The Rainbow: A Search for New Life* (New York, Twayne Publishers, 1990).
Kinkead-Weekes, Mark (ed.), *Twentieth-century Interpretations of The Rainbow* (Englewood Cliffs, NJ: Prentice-Hall, 1971).
Miko, Stephen J., *Toward Women in Love: The Emergence of a Lawrentian Aesthetic* (New Haven and London: Yale University Press, 1971).
Ross, Charles L., *Women in Love: A Novel of Mythic Realism* (New York, Twayne Publishers, 1992).
Worthen, John and Lindeth Vasey (eds), *The First 'Women in Love'* (New York: Cambridge University Press, 1998).

Criticism of Lawrence fiction in general, with some reference to *Women in Love* and *The Rainbow*

Black, Michael, *D. H. Lawrence: The Early Fiction* (New York: Cambridge University Press, 1986).
Black, Michael, *D. H. Lawrence: The Early Philosophical Works* (New York: Cambridge University Press, 1992).
Daleski, H. M., *The Forked Flame: A Study of D. H. Lawrence* (Madison: University of Wisconsin Press, 1987).
Holderness, Graham, *D. H. Lawrence: History, Ideology and Fiction* (Dublin: Gill and Macmillan, 1982).
Humma, John B., *Metaphor and Meaning in D. H. Lawrence's Later Novels* (Columbia: University of Missouri Press, 1990).
Kearney, Martin F., *Major Short Stories of D. H. Lawrence: A Handbook* (New York: Garland, 1996).
Marsh, Nicholas, *D. H. Lawrence: The Novels* (New York: St. Martin's Press, 2000).
Poplawski, Paul, *D. H. Lawrence: A Reference Companion* (Westport, CT: Greenwood Press, 1996).

Preston, Peter, *A D. H. Lawrence Chronology* (New York: St. Martin's Press, 1994).

Scheckner, Peter, *Class, Politics, and the Individual: A Study of the Major Works of D. H. Lawrence* (Rutherford, NJ: Fairleigh Dickinson University Press, 1985).

Worthen, John, *D. H. Lawrence: The Early Years, 1885–1912* (New York: Cambridge University Press, 1991).

Language

Bell, Michael, *D. H. Lawrence: Language and Being* (New York: Cambridge University Press, 1991).

Bonds, Diane S., *Language and the Self in D. H. Lawrence* (Ann Arbor, MI: University of Michigan Research Press, 1987).

Ingram, Alan, *The Language of D. H. Lawrence* (Macmillan – now Palgrave Macmillan, Basingstoke, 1990).

Desire and sexuality

Balbert, Peter, *D. H. Lawrence and the Phallic Imagination: Essays on Sexual Identity and Feminist Misreading* (New York: St. Martin's Press, 1989).

Dorbad, Leo J., *Sexually Balanced Relationships in the Novels of D. H. Lawrence* (New York: Peter Lang, 1991).

Ingersoll, Earl, *D. H. Lawrence, Desire, and Narrative* (Gainesville, FL: University Press of Florida, 2001).

Kelsey, Nigel, *D. H. Lawrence: Sexual Crisis* (Macmillan – now Palgrave Macmillan – Studies in Twentieth-Century Literature, Basingstoke, 1991).

Poplawski, Paul, *Promptings of Desire: Creativity and the Religious Impulse in the Works of D. H. Lawrence* (Westport, CT: Greenwood Press, 1993).

Williams, Linda Ruth, *Sex in the Head: Visions of Femininity and Film in D. H. Lawrence* (Detroit: Wayne State University Press, 1993).

Feminist criticism

Feinstein, Elaine, *Lawrence and the Women: The Intimate Life of D. H. Lawrence* (New York: Harper Collins, 1993).

Holbrook, David, *Where D. H. Lawrence Was Wrong about Women* (Lewisburg: Bucknell University Press; London and Toronto: Associated University Presses, 1992).

Lewiecki-Wilson, Cynthia, *Writing Against the Family: Gender in Lawrence and Joyce* (Carbondale: Southern Illinois University Press, 1994).

Nixon, Cornelia, *Lawrence's Leadership Politics and the Turn Against Women* (Berkeley: University of California Press, 1986).

Siegel, Carol, *Lawrence Among the Women: Wavering Boundaries in Women's Literary Traditions* (Charlottesville: University of Virginia Press, 1991).

Simpson, Hilary, *D. H. Lawrence and Feminism* (DeKalb: Northern Illinois University Press, 1982).
Storch, Margaret, *Sons and Adversaries: Women in William Blake and D. H. Lawrence* (Knoxville: University of Tennessee Press, 1990).

Lawrence: biographies

Maddox, Brenda, *D. H. Lawrence: The Story of a Marriage* (New York: Simon & Schuster, 1994).
Montgomery, Robert E., *The Visionary D. H. Lawrence: Beyond Philosophy and Art* (New York: Cambridge University Press, 1994).
Schneider, Daniel J., *The Consciousness of D. H. Lawrence: An Intellectual Biography* (Lawrence: University Press of Kansas, 1986).

Letters

Boulton, James T. (ed.), *The Selected Letters of D. H. Lawrence* (New York: Cambridge University Press, 1997).
Healey, E. Claire and Keith Cushman (eds), *The Letters of D. H. Lawrence and Amy Lowell, 1914–1925* (Santa Barbara, CA: Black Sparrow Press, 1985).

Lawrence and modernism

Crumpton, Philip (ed.), *Lawrence, D. H. Movements in European History* (New York: Cambridge University Press, 1989).
Meyers, Jeffrey (ed.), *D. H. Lawrence and Tradition* (Amherst: University of Massachusetts Press, 1985).
Pinkney, Tony, *D. H. Lawrence and Modernism* (Iowa City: University of Iowa Press, 1990).
Preston, Peter, and Peter Hoare (eds), *D. H. Lawrence in the Modern World* (New York: Cambridge University Press, 1989).
Ross, Charles L. and Dennis Jackson (eds), *Editing D. H. Lawrence: New Versions of a Modern Author* (Ann Arbor: University of Michigan Press, 1995).

Further criticism

Brown, Keith (ed.), *Rethinking Lawrence* (Philadelphia: Open University Press, 1990).
Cowan, James C., *D. H. Lawrence and the Trembling Balance* (University Park: Pennsylvania State University Press, 1990).
Cushman, Keith and Dennis Jackson (eds), *D. H. Lawrence's Literary Inheritors* (New York: St. Martin's Press, 1991).
Draper, R. P. (ed.), *D. H. Lawrence: The Critical Heritage* (London and New York: Routledge & Kegan Paul, 1986).
Fernihough, Anne (ed.), *Cambridge Companion to D. H. Lawrence* (Cambridge, Cambridge University Press, 2001).
Hoffman, Frederick J. and Harry T. Moore (eds), *The Achievement of D. H. Lawrence* (Oklahoma, University of Oklahoma Press, 1953).

Jackson, Dennis and Fleda Brown Jackson (eds), *Critical Essays on D. H. Lawrence* (Boston: G. K. Hall, 1988).

Meyers, Jeffrey (ed.), *The Legacy of D. H. Lawrence* (New York: St. Martin's Press, 1987).

Scherr, Barry J., *D. H. Lawrence's Response to Plato: A Bloomian Interpretation* (New York: Peter Lang, 1996).

Squires, Michael and Keith Cushman, *The Challenge of D. H. Lawrence* (Madison: University of Wisconsin Press, 1990).

Worthen, John, David Ellis, and Mark Kinkead-Weekes (eds), *Cambridge Biography of D. H. Lawrence* (Cambridge, Cambridge University Press, 1998).

Miscellaneous

Ebbatson, Roger, *The Evolutionary Self: Hardy, Forster, Lawrence* (Sussex: Heritage Press; Totowa: Barnes and Noble, 1983).

Ellis, David, and Howard Mills, *D. H. Lawrence's Non-Fiction: Art, Thought and Genre* (New York: Cambridge University Press, 1988).

Roberts, Warren and Paul Poplawski. *A Bibliography of D. H. Lawrence*. Third edition (New York: Cambridge University Press, 2001).

Sklenicka, Carol, *D. H. Lawrence and the Child* (Columbia: University of Missouri Press, 1991).

Stewart, Jack, *The Vital Art of D. H. Lawrence: Vision and Expression* (Carbondale: Southern Illinois University Press, 1999).

Notes on Contributors

Robert Burden is Reader in English Studies in the School of Arts and Media at the University of Teesside, Middlesbrough. He teaches modern literature, drama and critical and cultural theory. He is currently working on a major study of the uses of psychoanalytic concepts in cultural theory, literature, and criticism. He is is the author of *Radicalizing Lawrence: Critical Interventions in the Reading and Reception of D. H. Lawrence's Narrative Fiction* (2000).

Gerald Doherty taught Renaissance literature at University College, London (1969–72), and then literary theory at the University of Turku, Finland, until his retirement in 1995. His books include *Theorizing Lawrence: Nine Meditations on Tropological Themes* (1999), *Oriental Lawrence: The Quest for the Secrets of Sex* (2001) and *Dubliners' Dozen: The Games Narrators Play* (2003). His essays on Lawrence have appeared in *PMLA*, *Modern Fiction Studies*, *Style*, *Mosaic*, *Criticism*, *The D. H. Lawrence Review*, and many other journals and collections.

Roger Ebbatson is now Visiting Professor at Loughborough University, having previously taught at University College Worcester and the University of Sokoto, Nigeria. His publications include *Lawrence and the Nature Tradition* (1980), *The Evolutionary Self* (1982), and *Hardy: Margin of the Unexpressed* (1993). He is currently completing a study of literary Englishness.

Elizabeth Fox is a Lecturer and Instructor in the Program in Writing and Humanistic Studies at MIT. She has published on Lawrence, modernism, and psychoanalytic theory. She served as secretary of the D. H. Lawrence Society of North America from 1995 to 2002, and co-edited a Special Issue of the *D. H. Lawrence Review* on Lawrence and the Psychoanalytic.

Earl G. Ingersoll is Distinguished Teaching Professor and Distinguished Professor of English, Emeritus, at the State University of New York College at Brockport. He is a former president of the D. H. Lawrence Society of North America and the author of *D. H. Lawrence, Desire, and Narrative* (2001).

James F. Knapp teaches and writes on literary history, including Anglo-Irish literature, and Modernism. He is the author of *Literary Modernism and the Transformation of Work*, and *Ezra Pound*, and most recently he has edited *The Norton Poetry Workshop*, a multi-media CD-ROM introduction to poetry. His articles have dealt with such topics as primitivism in modern art, nationalism, work, modern poetry, and the culture of modernity. He is Professor of English and Associate Dean for Faculty Affairs in the Faculty and College of Arts and Sciences at the University of Pittsburgh.

Liang-ya Liou is a Professor of English at the Department of Foreign Languages and Literatures, National Taiwan University. Her main publications are *Engendering Dissident Desires: The Politics and Aesthetics of Erotic Fictions* (1998), *Race, Gender, and Representation: Toni Morrison's 'The Bluest Eye', 'Sula', 'Song of Solomon', and 'Beloved'* (2000), and *Gender, Sexuality, and the Fin de Siècle: Studies in Erotic Fictions* (2001).

Jorgette Mauzerall is an Associate Professor of English at Fort Valley State University. The article 'Strange Bedfellows' grew out of her doctoral dissertation at the University of Virginia: 'The Body of Culture: Decadence and Gender in the Novels of D. H. Lawrence'. She contributed to the Modern Language Association's *Approaches to Teaching the Works of D. H. Lawrence*. She has also published in the *ADE Bulletin* and the *D. H. Lawrence Review*.

David Parker is Professor and Chair of English at the Chinese University of Hong Kong. He has written fiction as well as literary criticism. His books include *Building on Sand* (novel), *The Mighty World of Eye* (stories), *Ethics, Theory and the Novel*, *Shame and the Modern Self* and *Renegotiating Ethics*. He is currently working on identity and the good in autobiography.

Index